Clift H. Young

Merry Xmas.
From
Mabel E. Parker

1926

TEEFTALLOW

Books By
T. S. STRIBLING

BIRTHRIGHT
CRUISE OF THE DRY DOCK
FOMBOMBO
RED SAND
TEEFTALLOW

TEEFTALLOW

BY
T. S. STRIBLING

GARDEN CITY　　　　NEW YORK
DOUBLEDAY, PAGE & COMPANY

1926

TO
THE HILL PEOPLE
THE LAST THEOCRACY

CONTENTS

BOOK I

NESSIE . . . . PAGE 1

BOOK II

ADELAIDE 255

BOOK I. NESSIE

TEEFTALLOW

CHAPTER I

MR. JAMES SANDAGE, overseer of the county poor farm, jolted monotonously against his steering wheel, against the standards of his car top, against the youth in the seat beside him as he ground along in low gear over the stony rut-lined trail which represented a public road in Lane County, Tennessee, in summer weather. Now while Mr. Sandage's thoughts were not actually occupied with this road, still as he jolted onward he held a subconscious sense of easy travel and vehicular comfort. He could not help feeling how much better the roads were in high summer than in the spring or winter. The whole countryside agreed that the roads were "always good this time o' the year" and that a man "*could* git over 'em"; an hypothesis dubiously demonstrated by Mr. Sandage's roaring plunging forward movement.

But all this was merely in the fringe of Mr. Sandage's mind. In reality he was thinking neither of his car nor the exceptionally fine condition of the thoroughfare. His actual ponderings flowed in two entirely separate streams, and his attention whipsawed from one to the other and back again, over and over, without the overseer being conscious of these restless shifts.

One of Mr. Sandage's mental alternatives concerned the survey of a railroad which was about to be built through Lane County. This cocked up Mr. Sandage's spirits mightily. He thought to himself, "Just another stride forward in our county's progress. Ever'thing's getting better. That railroad will give an outlet for our products; bring trade and travel our way. Old Lane's comin' to the front shore!"

He knew the man back of this big heartsome new enterprise; a particular friend of his; in fact, more than a friend, a kind of political guide and philosopher who had engineered Mr. Sandage into the office of poor-farm overseer, and now Mr. Sandage hoped and believed that his friend Railroad Jones would engineer him out of his present predicament into another and a higher office. . . .

At this point the change had been made. Mr. Sandage's antiphonal theme now filled him with anxiety. He glanced around dubiously at the boy who jounced in the seat beside him. This boy, in a way, was a kind of son of his . . . raised him from a shaver until he was now blamed near as big as he was . . . now to get into trouble over a kind act, a charitable act. . . .

"Abner," inquired Mr. Sandage out of these anxieties, "jest exactly what did that fool Professor Overall say to you and B'atrice Belle, anyway?"

The youth, Abner, a large black-haired, brown-eyed boy, came out of some reverie of his own, and stated the situation lucidly enough but in drawling hill accent,

"Soon as he found out you was a-runnin' for county trustee, too, he said he'd shore bill you for not sendin' me to school none."

Mr. Sandage shook his head, "I—be—derned" —he spaced his ejaculation with renewed scorn of such baseness. "Makin' political capital out of a thing like that! You know, Abner, if he wasn't running for the same office, he never would have mentioned my breakin' the compulsory edjercation law!"

"Why, of course not!"

"But that won't be no excuse now that he's mentioned it."

"Ort to be."

"'Twon't be, though. What ort to be an' what will be ain't on speakin' terms before a court of law, Abner."

The two hillmen sat silent, filled with the chronic hill distrust in all legal proceedings whatsoever. Mr. Sandage continued pondering in an undertone, searching for some more feasible, if less candid, defence.

"I could say nobody was direckly responsible for ye— daddy dead these years; mammy went crazy and died in the poorhouse—nobody left to send you to school—you're the last of the Teeftallers. . . ."

At this point Mr. Sandage's whole attention became occupied by a dangerous descent in the trail. It fell away from the high bleak ridge down a steep stony hill into a blue undulating valley where lay the hamlet of Lanesburg, county seat of Lane County. Mr. Sandage clamped on both his brakes and shifted to low gear. He stared fixedly ahead as he ground and bounced down the breakneck descent. The ramshackle motor hooted through an outlying fringe of dilapidated Negro shacks, roared across three wooden culverts where a brook crossed and recrossed the trail; it honked desperately at one or two farm wagons which were rattling more leisurely into the village; cut out of the road, missed the wagons by a palm's breadth, cut in again; and presently clashed into Court House Square, which was the centre of Lanesburg and the political heart of the county.

Mr. Sandage shook off his anxieties as he drove into the crowded square and began shouting at this and that man with tremendous gusto. He parked his machine along with scores of other ramshackle automobiles in the hot sunshine to the south of the courthouse yard. He climbed out and went about shaking hands with everybody with a politician's ubiquity. He used both hands, extending right and left to anybody in his reach, as he had seen the greater political lights do—such as state representatives or an occasional candidate for Congress.

"Hey oh, Bill! Hey oh, Milo! How je leave yo folks, Sam?" Here Mr. Sandage became portentously serious. "Boys," he would begin his set electioneering speech, "I'm sailin' out ag'in on the sea of the people's favour. On election day I want to come home a conqueror. I don't want to git conquered, boys. Remember me on election day. I'm runnin' for the trustee's office."

The men were impressed by these serious and slightly oratorical phrases. "We're fer ye, Jim; we put you to overseein' the pore farm, didn't we? We're all true-blue Republicans, Jim."

Mr. Sandage's gravity dropped from him like a cloak. He slapped the nearest backs. "Much obliged, boys. I won't fergit the favour. By the way, have you seen Railroad Jones anywhere around here to-day?"

"He's nursin' that bond issue in the County Court," said one of the hillmen.

"I saw him goin' acrost to his office a little while ago," directed another. "I think he's gittin' ready fer a suit in the Circuit Court."

"Well, I got to look him up. What's the Gran' Jury doin'?"

"That Shelton murder case is comin' up ag'in. They're gittin' a lot of pistol-totin' bills; an' gamblin'. I understan' they've billed Tim Fraley an' Zed Parrum."

"That so? Somebody ort to tell the boys an' let 'em skip out before the sheriff gits 'em."

"That's a fact."

"Well, come uhlong, Abner, we got to be movin'."

The youth moved forward mechanically and the two started across the sun-smitten square toward a small yellow office on the west side. On the way over, the poorhouse overseer paused to electioneer half-a-dozen groups, repeated his brief speech a number of times, and some hour later reached the little yellow building on the side of the hill.

The back part of Railroad Jones's office was fitted into an excavation in the earth while the front part was underpinned with timbers. To enter, the two callers were forced to climb a flight of stairs, and as Sandage went up, he stamped his feet and cleared his throat because he was not quite certain what were the formalities of entering an office; whether one shouted hello from the front, as if it were a residence, or simply entered without warning, as if it were a store. Not knowing, Mr. Sandage always compromised on a certain amount of stamping and hawking, and in this he was abetted by Abner Teeftallow, who also had a feeling for the proprieties.

The doors and windows of Mr. Jones's office were open, and when the eyes of the two companions rose above the top steps, they could see the railroad builder bending over a large box, groping in it with his arms.

"Lost somethin', Mr. Jones?" called Sandage.

At the first sound the fat man lifted his head quickly and stared at his visitors over the rim of the box. He had a vast head topped with a black mane and set with small puffy black eyes. At this moment his face was duskily red from stooping. Against this complexion a purple birthmark showed just in front of Railroad Jones's left ear and ran halfway down his heavy jowl. The birthmark had a narrow yellowish margin, and this cleared for a stubble of black beard which swung under the sag of his chin and up the other side of his face.

Abner had seen Jones a few times in his life, and this birthmark always made a strong and somehow a favourable impression on the boy. It seemed the sort of marking a wealthy man would possess.

Mr. Jones stared at his two visitors, said, "Damn the thing, I can't find it," then broke off to bob down into the box again and continue pawing among his papers. From this uncomfortable position he wheezed.

"I put a contrack—in this box—on yaller blue-lined paper—a page tore out of a ole cash book." He swung his arms amid the jumble of papers with the desperation of a fat man already overheated.

"When ju put it in there, Mr. Jones?" asked Jim.

"Bout ten year' ago."

The poorhouse keeper was thunderstruck. "Ten year' ago! Think o' that, Abner!"

"Yeh," panted Mr. Jones, "and now the damn comp'ny's suin' me on it!"

"They is always some comp'ny or somethin' suin' you, ain't they?" asked Sandage cheerfully, coming up and peering down into the box. The receptacle was a large dry-goods carton lined with tin to make it mouse proof. It was three quarters full of a most hopeless jumble of papers.

"Yeh, fellers sue me because they ain't got no reason about 'em. They sue me because I out-trade 'em and they git riled. A man who sues because he's mad is jest a plain fool—— Well, thank Gawd!"

He heaved himself up with a single leaf of some old book, and continued his philosophy of lawsuits:

"You've got to have justice and the law on yore side—more specially the law."

"What's you got there?" asked Jim, who was not a philosopher.

"The contrack Buckin'ham Sharp wanted to see, I reckon it's that. . . ." Mr. Jones opened the paper and perused it all over, the back as intently as the front; finally he handed it to Mr. Sandage. "Don't that say somethin' about stoves, Jim?" he asked.

Sandage took the paper with a certain air of importance, cleared his throat, and began reading in the long whine which the hill folk reserve for such tasks. Some of the words he spelled in a whisper before attempting to pronounce.

"The Cin, c-i-n cin, n-a-t nat, 't-i, Cincinnati Stove Comp'ny h-e-r-e-b-y hereby agrees . . ."

"That's it," interrupted the fat man, taking the paper from his companion. Mr. Jones required only four words to identify an instrument he had dropped into the box ten years before. He folded the contract and put it into his pocket.

"Now, what can I do for you, Jim?" inquired the magnate in his affable buzz.

Sandage scratched his head. "Is Perfessor Overall in town to-day?"

"Believe I seen him at the courthouse. I understan' he's

going to make a speech up there this evenin'" (meaning "this afternoon").

"I bet he is," agreed Sandage gloomily. "It's about this boy here."

Jones looked at Abner.

"I don't guess you know him," said Sandage, "but you did know his daddy. It's Abner Teeftaller, Linsey Teeftaller's boy."

Mr. Jones appraised the well-set-up lad. "Yes, I ricollect Linsey; I—er—got him out of a little trouble oncet or twicet. In fact, he sent the sheriff to me to bail him out the last time he was in jail, and I've allus felt kinder bad fer not doin' it. If I'd uh knowed he was as sick as he was, I'd uh seen to it."

Here the big man aroused himself from his memories to say briskly, "Well, I'm not surprised that his boy is in trouble—the Gran' Jury's settin' now—what's he done?"

"Tain't so much him as me," admitted Sandage ruefully.

"You! A politician, Jim, I'm surprised!"

"That's the reason," explained Sandage. "Lem Overall is a-goin' to prosecute me under the compulsory edjercation law fer not sendin' this boy to school. Of course, it's because me an' him air runnin' fer the same office."

Railroad Jones waxed sarcastic. "Lem Overall prosecutin' a boy fer not goin' to school when edjercation has made a complete fool out of him! Why, Jim, you done exactly right. Don't you never teach that boy to read nor write. Readin' an' writin' 'll ruin anybody's ricollection. Why, it jest makes a plum blank out of a man!"

"That's the truth," agreed Sandage earnestly.

The magnate was mounted on his hobby now. "When I see these edjercated fellows goin' aroun' puttin' things they want to ricolleck down in a little book, I think, 'You pore addle-headed fools, when you lose yore little book, what'll you do? Why don't you put it up here where you kain't lose it?'" He lifted his arm with a massive gesture and tapped his great head. "An' yet," he added justly, "if I'd ever a-learnt to read an' write I might be jest as bad as them."

"I reckon everybody'll agree you've got the beatenest ricollection in this whole county," acknowledged Sandage.

"Well, don't you worry no more about it," advised Jones. "I'll come down to the county court an' fix it up for ye." He waved a pudgy hand at the overseer. "Jest you lay low."

"I'll be much obliged," said Sandage, greatly relieved.

The three men walked out of the office and climbed down the steps into the intense sunshine again. As they moved toward the courthouse a dribble of hillmen came up to the magnate to ask directions about his farms, about his saw mills, about his cattle. Mr. Jones gave precise directions to one and all. He knew instantly the whole situation and the solution necessary. He was like one of those expert chess players who sit blindfolded and play a half-dozen games simultaneously. And as he performed this mental feat he waddled along as if he really had his mind on something else. Finally he asked:

"Teeftaller—Teeftaller——   Didn't Linsey Teeftaller marry a Coltrane, Jim?"

"Yeh," nodded the politician, surprised at this turn.

"An' didn't she die crazy on the pore farm, or something of the sort?"

"Yeh."

"Uh-huh . . ." Mr. Jones nodded his massive head and played with a small gold nugget, a watch charm on a gold chain which swung around his abdomen. "Yeh, ol' Judge Coltrane's daughter, she married when she was jest a gal, didn't she—run away and married and then went crazy?"

"I reckon you ricolleck ever'thing!"

"Oh"— the fat man spread his hands—"I jest happened to . . ." He pulled thoughtfully at his chin and glanced out of the corner of his black eyes at Abner.

At that moment the raucous voice of the bailiff boomed

from the second-story window of the court building: "Oh yes, David Jones come into court! Oh yes, David Jones come into court! Oh yes!"

The fat man nodded. "They're callin' up my case. . . ." He felt in his pocket to assure himself that the contract was still there, then could not resist giving the youth a parting shaft of advice, "Young man, I ricolleck when yore grandfather, Jefferson Coltrane, uster be circuit jedge here. Ole Jefferson Coltrane would uh had a great head on him if he hadn't been spiled by edjercation. I hope you do take after him one way and don't t'other. Well, see you later, Jim," and the great man took himself up the gravelled path and into the courthouse.

Abner stood looking after him shadowed by the vague melancholy which any mention of his unfortunate mother always aroused in his heart.

CHAPTER II

WHEN Railroad Jones had disappeared in the court-house, Mr. Sandage said he had some electioneering to do, and that Abner might fool around and watch the crowd or do whatsoever he wished. According to the sardonic hill view of life, simple human leisure was a fooling around, a futility.

Abner's fooling consisted in leaning against the bole of one of the live oaks in the courtyard and watching the play of the square under his eyes. He stood as still almost as the trunk of the tree itself, for he was only a generation removed from Indian fighters and wild-game hunters, and the woods-man's manner of observing still clung to him.

Numberless things entertained Abner's simple eyes: the horses and mules strung along the courthouse fence; the hogs of the townspeople which ran at large in the streets and rooted in the droppings of the livestock; country dogs beneath their masters' wagons growling at the town dogs on the outside, for the antipathy between country and village extended down to the very dogs themselves.

On the inside of the courtyard groups of men stood about talking loudly or shouting from one group to another. Women and girls were seated or stood on the grass in the peculiar silence of hill women in public places. Where two or three acquaintances sat together they occasionally would lean over and whisper a remark and then relapse into their motionless watching. One or two held babies in their arms. If one of these infants whimpered, the mother would loosen her bodice, lift out one of her breasts, and suckle the child as unself-consciously as a cow her calf, and continue her silent gazing at the scene.

One girl especially attracted Abner. She was a tall, rather bony girl with a milky face and hair the colour of corn silk. Her eyes were a lake-blue against her pale complexion. She, too, was standing watching the crowd, and her only movement was an occasional shifting of her weight from one foot to the other; and alternately throwing her right and left hip into a little undue prominence after the listless fashion of the hills.

Out of perhaps a score of women on the grass this girl alone drew Abner's eyes even for a return glance. The others appeared to be just people; strangers whom he had never seen before and with whom he had nothing in common; but something in this girl's face established in Abner some vague understanding of her or sympathy for her. The boy gazed at her fixedly, with an odd impression that he knew her, that somewhere he had seen her before. But with the exact placement of the hill folk for faces, he knew he never had, and this puzzled him and now he stared at her, trying to solve this faint mystery.

Presently, as if she felt his prolonged scrutiny, the girl looked around at him. The youth withdrew his eyes with a faint sense of embarrassment. But although he looked at the lively scene in front of him he did not see it any longer. He continued his speculations about the girl: who she was, what was her name, where she lived. He fancied she must be rich; something about her hat, which was not quite countryfied, suggested it. From this stepping stone he proceeded to the time-honoured hill-country deduction that she was "stuck up" and thought herself too good to speak to him. But when he glanced at her again something in the gentleness and wistfulness of her face denied this defamation. She was not "stuck up"; she was sweet and pensive, and, it seemed, a little sad. Well . . . Abner didn't know who she was; he never would know who she was. He wished he could know her; just as boys see and sigh for attractive faces every day and babies reach out for the moon; but that was impossible. Any plan to meet her and speak to her was completely outside of Abner's social resources. As far as Abner knew, men met only those women who lived on neighbouring farms. A certain inarticulate criticism of such narrow intercourse was beginning to arise in the youth when a voice beside him said, "Hello, Abner, you up to court—what they got *you* up about?"

Abner took his eyes from the girl with a little start and was forced to stare for a second or two before he recognized the rough-cut face of Zed Parrum. Zed was grinning at the poorhouse youth with a kind of odious admiration on his face that Abner should have so asserted his manhood on the poor farm as to get into trouble before the Grand Jury.

"Nothing brought me up here," denied Abner. "I jest come."

"Uh," Zed nodded and removed his grin. The fellow's eyes were a little brightened with whisky, but he was sober. He looked around and then said, "That ain't a bad-lookin' gal you was kinder noticin' when I come up."

"Nope," agreed Abner woodenly, but his face warmed and he wished Zed would go on away.

"Know who she is?"

"Nope."

"Want to know her?"

"Nope."

"Well," opined Zed, "I guess you ralely air too young to begin sparkin' yet, but that shore is a purty gal. She'll make a high-steppin' woman when she gits broke to harness."

Abner replied nothing at all to this.

Zed was not discouraged by taciturnity; it was usual among the hill folk. He struck off on another tack,

"I hear the Gran' Jury got a true bill agin Solon Askew fer public drunkenness and disturbin' public worship." He paused a moment and then added, "Solon shore raised hell at Big Bethel over on Moccasin. I was with him—tryin' to ca'm him."

This was interesting; there was a certain glow of adventure

about rousing a churchful of people which would appeal to any hill youth. "Is that so?" said Abner.

"Yep, a juryman told me confidenshul so's I could git the boys out of harm's way before the officer reached 'em. This same feller told me also that the Gran' Jury had billed me agin for totin' concealed weepins an' disturbin' public worship." Zed gave a disgusted snort. "That comes of tryin' to ca'm some fool who ralely is disturbin' public worship; and as fer totin' concealed weepins, how'd anybody know I had a gun if it was concealed? That's one kind of bill that don't make no sense, Abner."

Zed drew out a red handkerchief and mopped his face, which was wet from summer heat and the rising flush of whisky. He wadded the sour handkerchief back into his hip pocket and ruminated, "Well, I dunno whether to skip the country and go to Texas fer awhile, or hire a lawyer and beat my case, or walk up an' pay my fine, or jess plead guilty and lay her out in jail. . . ." Zed sucked his teeth calmly to salvage the shreds of an orange as he pondered these four possibilities. The prospect of spending a period of time in jail did not even break the sequence of his customary movements to cleanse his teeth. He opened the blade of his jackknife to a right angle with the handle, and with this instrument got at some of the more inaccessible teeth very handily.

Now Abner was not attending Zed's account of the jury's findings; he was still thinking about Mr. Parrum's question, "Do you want to know her?" As a matter of fact, Abner did very earnestly want to know her, and now he wondered why Zed had asked such a question. The fact that Zed had not called her name told Abner Zed himself did not know the girl, so why should Zed ask, "Do you want to know her?" That sounded as if by some hook or crook Zed knew some way of crossing the conventional abyss which separated Abner from the girl and bringing them together. The boy wondered curiously and with a faint rising excitement how this could possibly be. At last he interrupted a continued account of the doings of the Grand Jury to ask, "Uh—Zed —you know, talkin' about that gal—you astin' me did I want to know her—well, how could I git to know her?"

Mr. Parrum halted amid a decameron of rustic misdemeanours.

"So you'd kinder like to set up to her after all?"

"No, I wouldn't," drawled Abner in irritation. "But I'd luff to know how I could!"

"Easy enough," declared Zed, coming back to the idea with the enthusiasm of a touch of alcohol. "All you got to do is jess walk over an' stan' 'in ten or twelve feet of her; jess keep stan'in' there, don't pay no mortal attention to her, an' purty soon I'll come by an' make you acquainted with her."

Abner nerved himself. "Well, I don't know anything about gittin' acquainted with nobody, but, dad burn my riggin', I'll do anything oncet."

"Well, she kain't eat you alive," observed Mr. Parrum cheerfully, "an' if she does she kain't swaller you whole. All right now, here we go!"

With this cheerful prophecy that Mr. Teeftallow would have to be masticated before being swallowed, Zed took himself off and out of the gate and, after a few moments, lost himself completely in the crowd.

Upon the withdrawal of Zed's moral support Abner's courage waned, but pride forced his legs to move slowly, with a fine imitation of inattention, in the direction of the girl. The thought that he was really about to get to speak to the girl with the corn-silk hair set up a queer tremulousness inside of him. He wondered how in the world Zed would ever bring it about. When he reached the spot where he should stop, his courage quite deserted him and he was tempted to continue walking. He felt uncomfortable from heel to scalp. Finally he did pause with an elaborate pretence of inspecting a mule hitched to the fence. He moved his head this way and that as if he were tremendously curious about the opposite side of the mule, but as if unfortunately his legs had halted and left him marooned on the spot with a burning but unsatisfied curiosity concerning the colour, shape, and general condition of the other side of the mule. So all he could do was to stare fixedly at the mule's available side and speculate on the animal's entirety as astronomers speculate on the farther side of the moon.

It was hardly a convincing pose. It seemed to Abner that the girl saw through him, had become angry at him, and was wishing for him to go away. He could feel her pushing at his back with invisible arms, shoving him away from her.

The girl herself had become absolutely motionless, as a squirrel "freezes" to a tree when in danger. The utter novelty and uncertainty of the enterprise jangled at the boy's nerves. He was within the specified distance of the girl and now waited tensely for Zed to come and introduce him, yet he dreaded the ordeal tremendously.

Just as a hope began to dawn that Zed had forgotten this social engagement, he saw his friend and two other rustics enter the courthouse gate together. A lump arose in Abner's throat; he cursed himself for not having fled minutes ago.

The three young men entering the gate were in a gale of spirits. All were slightly drunk. One gave the other a hard but playful blow, then started to run. The second thrust out his foot and with a trip sent the first forward in a stumbling fall. Zed headed into the two, and so the three came ricochetting across the grass in this rough horse-play until with a whirl and a shove Zed sent one of the youths flying sidewise at the boy. The next moment Abner was catapulted squarely into the flaxen-haired girl behind him.

Teeftallow tried desperately hard to miss her, but Zed was as good as his word in bringing the two together. Abner struck her in the chest with his shoulder, but succeeded in keeping his feet and even prevented her from falling.

"Lord-a-mercy!" gasped the hill boy in the utmost confusion, "please excuse me; them blasted fellers bumped into me . . ." He got her balanced on her feet.

The helpful Zed and his two assistants in the receiving line had careered on around the courthouse and were now out of sight.

The girl looked at Abner, her delicate complexion a high pink.

"They're drunk!" she trembled in a furious voice.

"Yeh. . . ." Regard for the truth made Abner add, "I reckon."

"I think it's uh shame—bumpin' into nice folks. They ort to get a bill against 'em!"

Abner pondered what to say and finally volunteered, "One of em's name is Zed Parrum."

"Oh, well," the girl tossed her head, "I don't want to git it. A girl wouldn't go before the Gran' Jury."

"No-o," admitted Abner emptily, "a girl wouldn't . . .'"

Here his small talk ran out and left him pondering something else to say. To gain time he repeated, rather ineffectively, "No, she shore wouldn't . . ." and then for several moments his mind was completely blank. The silence between him and the girl widened and deepened until it impinged upon the very confusion of the crowd in the square. It seemed to Abner that everyone in sight must observe that he had ceased talking. He stood groping tensely for words; finally moistened his lips and said in a rush, "Zed told me they was a-gittin' a lot of true bills this court. . . ."

"Don't git any more than they ort," declared the girl bitterly.

Abner looked helplessly at her delicate complexion, her blue eyes and fair hair.

"I never was here before on court day. . . . I live on the pore farm."

At this the unknown opened her eyes wide with the first interest she had exhibited since Abner had made his introductory assault.

"Do you live on the pore farm?"

"Yeh. Mr. Sandage brought me up here to-day. He got into trouble on account of not sendin' me to school."

This was still more astounding information. "Why, ain't you never been to school none?"

"Not much."

"Why, when I was a-lookin' at you I thought you must be a awful smart boy and had been to school a lot."

The admission that she had been looking at him and thinking about him struck the first chord of pleasure in Abner's bosom during this interview.

"Well, I ain't. . . ." He was sorry to admit it, although, undoubtedly, to stay away from school was the helpful course to pursue.

"How come you not to?" she asked curiously.

"Well, ralely, there wasn't nobody to send me. My mammy died in the porehouse when I wuz jest a baby."

"O-oh!" breathed the girl, and the high pink of her face faded.

"She didn't haff to go to the porehouse for bein' pore," explained Abner quickly; "she went crazy and they wa'n't no place for her at the asylum in Nashville."

"Jess think!" cried the girl, deeply moved, staring spellbound at Abner. "Why, that's jest like a novel!" Wonder was in her blue eyes, reminiscent of the wonders she had found in novels. "I bet you are smart," she added with conviction, "even if you ain't been to school, especially with your mammy goin' crazy."

For the first time in his life Abner was openly admired by a girl, and this one delicately fair.

"I dunno about that," he said, sticking to his modesty even in the face of such flattery. "I know I'd hate to go to school and git to be a edjercated fool like Lem Overall."

"You wouldn't be like him, you'd be some great somebody if you was educated, a big lawyer or something, and you would come back home and marry your old sweetheart."

The girl was now following the outlines of her hill-country fiction reading.

"Marry my sweetheart—why, I ain't got none!"

"You will have one by the time you are a great lawyer!"

"My granddaddy was a judge," recalled Abner.

"What did I tell you!" cried the romantic one. She smiled at this corroboration, and it seemed to Abner she had the most charming smile he had ever seen.

In the midst of this absorbing prophecy of Abner's future, a stream of cachinnating and guffawing men came pouring out of the courthouse door. In the centre of this hilarious press flowed the large form, ponderous head, and black mane of Railroad Jones. The magnate was grinning amid the mirthful throng, and everyone appeared trying to clap his broad back. A confusion of voices shouted, "Ain't he a sight!" "Ain't he the beatenest man in town!" "Brainiest man in Lane County to-day, countin' in jedge and law-yers. . . ."

It was evident that Railroad Jones had made another great coup in court. It was the sort of thing that would go down in the folk stories of the hill people and would circulate for years after Railroad Jones was dead and gone. The drama, the bigness of the situation rushed on Abner. Without a thought he deserted the girl and went running toward the crowd. He seized the arm of a man whom he did not know,

"What's he done? What's Railroad Jones done now?" shouted Abner in the uproar.

The man slapped Abner's shoulder and guffawed to the skies.

"By gum. There's a man here tryin' to c'lect a bill fer some stoves Railroad bought ten years ago, but Jones showed a contrack with the comp'ny agreein' not tuh c'lect tull Railroad had sold all the stoves. Now R-R-Rail-road won't sell the l-last un!" The farmer crimped over, roaring with laughter. "He's holdin' it f-f-fer enough money tuh-tuh pay fer all the rest put together. . . ."

More guffawing, the man wiped his eyes. "By gosh, braini-est man in Tennessee to-day. . . ." He drifted away from Abner in the hilarious crowd.

Abner himself was tremendously moved and elated over this piece of successful chicanery. Like all public heroes Railroad Jones was pervasive. His feats became every-body's feats. When he escaped payment for a shipment of stoves, everybody escaped paying for stoves.

"Why, gosh all hemlock!" reflected Abner excitedly, "anybody could uh thought of that! I could uh done that, myself!"

Like all great masterpieces, it presented a deceptive sim-plicity.

The poorhouse boy was drawn into the crowd by emotional suction and followed in its wake toward the magnate's office. He forgot all about the girl, who, perhaps, was waiting to hear the cause of the uproar. Or, since she was a hill girl, perhaps she was not waiting; perhaps she did not expect her chance acquaintance to come back to her any more. . . .

CHAPTER III

THE admiring procession followed Mr. Jones through the July sunshine to his office. The fat man mounted his high porch and announced that the county court had voted the railroad bonds, and now he wanted labourers at Irontown to begin work on the following Monday morning. The pay, the financier announced, would be two and a quarter a day for a man, and four a day for a man and his span of mules; feed and stable furnished.

Apart from the consideration of these high wages, every man within the sound of Mr. Jones's buzzing voice already was predisposed to work for the magnate because of his victory over the Cincinnati Stove Company. That was a salutary turning of the tables on the city smart-alecks. It satisfied a vague animosity which every hillman felt toward the great world beyond the hills, with its opulence and social classes. Which, in brief, the hill people feel toward the American nation which has usurped the rôle of oppressor, tax gatherer, and maker of grinding laws; a rôle once occupied, centuries ago, by the British Government toward the forbears of these same hill folk. Now for Railroad Jones to beat the law with a legal contract was certainly a very turning on the enemy of his own cannon.

A number of men came up and enlisted as labourers in Railroad Jones's enterprise, and still others, who eventually would hire, put off their decision a few days or a few weeks to think the matter over.

When the hiring was finished, Abner saw Mr. Sandage beckoning to him, and a few minutes later the boy and the poor-farm keeper rejoined the railroad builder and set out once more for the courthouse to settle Abner's little case, as the magnate put it.

As they walked back Mr. Jones rehearsed his non-educational theories very earnestly, after the manner of a man priming himself for a forensic effort.

Abner listened with conviction to the fat man's diatribe against the weakening influence of literacy on the mentality, but on his way through the courthouse yard a recollection of the girl with the corn-silk hair and the lake-blue eyes brushed away the great man's homily. Abner searched the grounds for her with his glances, but she was gone. He scrutinized the groups of women who were still on the lawn, but she was not among them. Her absence gave him a queer tightening of the heart. He had a panicky impulse to desert his companions and search for her over the yard, the square, the stores. He felt sure she was just about to start home, and that if he would hurry he could reach her in time for a word. He did not know her name or where she lived; and indeed he did not know what was this last word which he so ardently desired to express.

But naturally he could not desert his companions on the instant. The greater ponderousness of the purposes of age over the whims of youth swept him irrevocably into the courthouse. He entered the door looking back, searching with a kind of inward ache for some glimpse of her, but the walls closed about him, shutting out the lawn and sunshine, shutting in the gloom, and the girl was lost.

Abner had straggled three or four men behind his monitors. He was in a narrow corridor through which struggled the inflow and outflow of the two courtrooms. The two streams of men ground past each other smelling of sweat, horses, leather, whisky, tobacco. An occasional Negro lent his pungent odour to the mélange. Abner tried to catch up with his friends, but a farmer immediately in front of him told him to "take it ca'm."

The reason for this extraordinary packing was that a jury was being empanelled for the Shelton murder trial in the

second story. Abner heard the crowd whispering about this
trial, "Peck Bradley's got Buckingham Sharp for his
lawyer." "The Sheltons have fee'd John A. Stone." A
murder trial is the one event in Lane County where life is
sufficiently concentrated and foreshortened for the hill folk
to feel the grip and drama of its flow. Listening to these
rumours, Abner forgot the girl again and struggled forward
with a desire to get into the Circuit Court and see this legal
battle. Unfortunately, his serious business of avoiding an
education lay in the relative penny show of the county court
on the lower floor. He followed Railroad Jones and Mr.
Sandage through a dirty door into the county courtroom,
which was itself congested. The best the trio could do was
to press themselves around the walls and finally line up
when they came to an open space. Here they stood and
looked over the crowded house. In a little railed-off chancel
sat the justices of the peace of the county who composed the
court. Behind a desk facing the justices lolled a musty old
man who was the county judge, and by virtue of his office,
the chairman of the court. At his side sat the county court
clerk, a rough blond young man with a bored look. An
officer "waited" on the court; this was a constable from an
outlying district. The constable now beckoned a crippled
man inside the chancel before the justices. The county
judge leaned over to expectorate into a private cuspidor beside his chair, then looked appraisingly at the cripple.

"Gentlemen of the court," he mumbled around a quid of
tobacco, "this crippled man wants to peddle goods in Lane
County without a license; you-all see how crippled he is,
are you ready for the question?"

A voice from the justices signified readiness.

"All in favour of lettin' him peddle without a license vote
aye; all opposed, no."

A grunting of ayes filled the courtroom.

"Ayes have it. Mr. Clerk, enter among yore notes that
Tobe Weatherby can peddle goods in Lane County without
a license. What's next on docket?"

The blond clerk said, "Elvis Compton has put in a claim aginst the county fer a cow."

The judge drew a plug of inky tobacco from his hip pocket, set his snaggled teeth in it, and bit off a chew.

"How does the county owe you for a cow, Mr. Compton?" he asked in a muffled tone.

A small dark man stood up in the audience,

"The tick inspector made me dip her and it killed her."

"How's that?" asked the judge with interest.

"Why, we drove her through the vat and a lot of the truck got in her years and dreened into her brain an' killed her."

Astonishment filled the audience at this deadly effect of tick dip on a cow. Just then the tick inspector himself arose.

"Jedge, that's redickerlous," he drawled, "the guv'ment dip kain't dreen through a cow's years into her brains— they ain't nothin' kin do that."

The chairman waved him down.

"That's fer the court to decide. Gentlemen, you hear the question. All who believe the tick dip dreened into the brains of Mr. Compton's cow an' killed her let it be known by votin' aye."

Came a grunting of ayes.

"All who don't believe it vote no."

Came a grunting of noes.

"The clerk will haff to call the roll on that," announced the judge.

The clerk began calling the names of the justices; when he finished the roll stood at fourteen ayes and fifteen noes.

"Mr. Compton," announced the judge in a tone still muffled by his new quid, "the guv'ment dip liked jest one vote dreenin' into yore cow's brains an' killin' her. What's next on docket, Mr. Clerk?"

Laughter filled the courtroom as the clerk drawled out, "Professor Lem Overall and Brother Blackman want to put a proposition before the court."

As he spoke the two men mentioned arose from the crowd and entered the chancel. A trickle of dismay went over Abner

on seeing the stranger with Professor Overall. His black
coat and a certain unsmiling quality about his long sallow
face stamped him for a preacher. Abner's spirits sank and
sank at these elaborate preparations to force him to go to
school and thereby weaken his mind. He began to doubt even
if Railroad Jones could rescue him from such a situation.

Professor Overall took the floor and stood rolling his
prominent eyes about the room for several seconds, after the
approved fashion of Lane County orators, then began with
the utmost solemnity:

"Honourable Judge and justices of the court, Brother
Blackman an' me has come before you to-day to address you
on what I an' all the scholarly world considers to be the most
important base on which our civilization rests, an' that is the
edjercation of the young. Ain't that right, Brother Blackman?"

"Amen, Brother Overall," rumbled the minister in a basso
profundo.

"Brother Blackman, as a great many of you all know, is an
evangelist now holdin' a meetin' at Shady Grove Church on
Big Cyprus, an' from all reports, God shore has been blessin'
him in a wonnerful manner with a great outpourin' of the
spirit." He turned for corroboration to the minister.

"That's right, Brother Overall," assented the divine in
his sepulchral tone, "we shore have got the devil on the run
on Big Cyprus."

"But in his work of savin' souls," continued the pedagogue, "Brother Blackman goes jest a grain furder than
savin' the ol' sheep from destruction; he's after the innocent
lam's, the little childern of this county an' them that's to
come in the fewcher."

A pause here as the room became intensely quiet except
for a whisper somewhere, "edjercated fool, but he shore
han'les a speech. . . ."

"Brother Blackman ast me as a man of science an' as a
representative of the edjercational intrusts of this county to
git up an' tell you-all what I thought of his plan. I want

ter say I'm with him heart an' soul. I want you justices to
hear what he is goin' to ast you to do an' you do it. It'll be a
blessin' to you an' yore childern the longest day you'll live.
Honourable Judge an' justices of the court, lemme interduce
Brother Blackman."

The evangelist stepped forward as the pedagogue retired.

"Gentlemen of the court," began the minister in his profound voice, "Brother Overall says it will be a blessin' to
you as long as you live. I say it will be a blessin' to you
through etarnity. I tell you the angels are leanin' this
minute over the battlements of Heaven, waitin' with hushed
breaths an' beatin' hearts to see what the justices of Lane
County air goin' to do here at this hour an' this minute!"

The minister paused with a certain effect of embodying the
supernatural world, of solidifying it in the air somewhere
above their heads. He proceeded in his ponderous voice, and
inquired slowly and solemnly, "My frien's, do you b'lieve
yore great gran'daddy was a monkey?"

He paused, then with the revivalist's trick, shouted the
same question with a different stress at the top of his lungs,
"Do you *b'lieve* yore great gran'daddy was a monkey?"

This jarred the nerves of his audience. The preacher
brought down his fist on the chancel rail with a sounding
blow, "Is there a *man* in the sound of my voice that *b'lieves*
his great gran'daddy was a monkey?

"Oh, brethren, don't you *know* the Bible says man was
made in the image of *God!* Then how *can* he be made in the
image of a monkey?

"Brothers, judges," gasped the divine, pausing to mop
his dripping face, "you know that our school books air full
of this damnable doctrine. What air ye goin' to *do* about it?
Air ye goin' to let the deceivin' agnostic, hell-bound college
perfessers send our childern to *hell?* Air they goin' to cry fer
bread an' you give 'em a *stone!* It's a sin unto God an' a
cryin' out of unrighteousness from the earth! What air ye
goin' to do—what you goin' to *do?* I'm talkin' to you justices now; what *you* goin' to do?"

Reverend Blackman shook a long forefinger at the justices.

"You know what you can do," he replied to his own question, "tear this infidel doctrine *out* of the school books! Tear it *out!* Give the old devil a thrust in the heart with the sword of truth! Strike a match to his sulfurious fires an' roast him out of the school books our blessed little childern's got to read. *Roast him out!* Ain't I right, Brother Overall?" he bellowed, beet-coloured.

"You're right, Brother Blackman!"

"Then, let's *all* be right!" chanted the preacher. "Now, brothers an' justices of Lane County, when the clerk passes aroun' the petition I have drew up, I want ever' man who believes in God and wants to meet his childern in Heaven—I want him to *sign* it. I want you to tell our legislatur' that we don't want no more infidel doctrines of the Godless Yankees sent down here in our school books, an' we won't *have* it! Let 'em know ol' Lane stan's fer God, an' God stan's fer ol' Lane! An' we do this hopin' our county escapes the destruction that God is shore to send on our Sodom an' Gomorrah nation! Brethren, let us pray!"

The parson lifted his hands and the whole courtroom bowed its head. His prayer was as vehement as his address and covered the same points. When he made an end, he retired, dripping with perspiration, while the blond clerk, rather hastily, passed around a petition which the minister had drawn up asking the Tennessee state legislature to remove all traces of the science of evolution from the school books of the state.

The justices looked at it rather blankly and signed one after another. One of the court hesitated a moment. "Professor Overall," he asked, "does our present school books teach there ain't no God an' our gran'fathers was monkeys?"

Professor Overall rolled his prominent eyes on the questioner reprovingly. "They certainly do, Brother Boggus. You can take my word as a teacher and a scholar."

"I jest wanted to know," said the justice in a chastened tone, and signed his name hurriedly.

There was some slight cheering among the audience when the petition went back to the table. The judge of the court rapped for silence.

"Quiet! Quiet! Now, gentlemen of the court, le's git to work on somethin' we know somethin' about. Mr. Clerk, what's nex' on docket?"

Railroad Jones broke the pause. In his buzzing voice he began explaining that his friend Jim Sandage had raised a boy on the county poor farm until now the boy was seventeen turning eighteen, and he thought the time had come to set him free; and that he, David Jones, was going to ask the court, for Mr. Sandage, to set Mr. Abner Teeftallow free and give him all the contractual rights of a man of twenty-one so he could hire to work and receive pay, sue and be sued, like any other man. The reason of this, Jones explained, was that he wanted to hire Abner to work on his railroad, and that if it met with the court's approval the clerk could draw up a paper to that effect and have it passed.

"It is right and fitting," explained the magnate in conclusion, "that this young man whose grandfather was circuit judge in this county should come out an' help build a railroad as his first lick of work as a man that would help develop the county his grandfather started."

There was some cheering at this which the judge had to rap down.

Abner looked at Railroad Jones in the greatest consternation at this amazing turn of the game. The magnate nodded back encouragingly.

"That's all right. It stops all school action complete. It gits Jim here out of a mean fix, an', young man, it puts you where you can begin to make two dollars an' a half a day an' be your own boss. The fewcher certainly looks bright fer you, my boy; you with a brain unspiled by book learnin', a judge fer a grandfather an' a crazy woman for a mammy."

He reached a puffy hand and clapped Abner warmly on the shoulder.

CHAPTER IV

ABNER TEEFTALLOW had been thrown out upon the world to make his own living in the unforeseeable fashion in which come nearly all the crucial events of life. There was something dismaying in it; this abrupt whirling about of his fortunes and his own utter helplessness to control anything. The boy followed the men to the yellow office with the strangeness of his new position already fallen upon him. The short, powerful Mr. Sandage walking just in front of him was no longer his foster-father but a man with whom he presently would part and go his way alone into the untried experiment of keeping himself alive. This quality of estrangement permeated the way Mr. Sandage walked and extended even to the little blond curls of hair over the top of his blue denim shirt. Abner glanced at his foster-father from time to time with rather a drawn feeling in his face and a lump slowly growing and pressing the back of his throat.

Presently the three climbed the steps into Railroad Jones's office. The magnate had a list of names and Abner was directed to sign this or make his mark as a contract to work in the railroad gang at Irontown.

The fat man watched the boy stoop over the table and begin writing his name in a great unformed hand. As Abner wrote he moved his under jaw in and out with the making of each letter.

"Well," buzzed the magnate, "he can write his name, after all."

"Yes, an' he can read some, too," added Mr. Sandage. "He jest picked it up hisse'f."

"Uh-huh, bad habit," nodded the rich man. "Childern'll

form 'em if you don't watch 'em." Then, suddenly breaking away from his moralizings, "Well, Abner, I've got Square Meredith to carry you over to Arntown with him. He'll be by in a minute. The Square's a good ol' man. He'll look after ye tull ye git a boardin' house an' collect your first week's wages, an' here's a couple o' dollars to run you tull then." The fat man drew two silver dollars from his pocket and handed them casually to the boy. As he did so the noise of a wagon drawing up in front of the office sounded through the door, and looking outside Abner saw a gray-haired teamster sitting on the hounds of his wagon frame driving two roan mules. As he came to a stop he called out in a cracked voice, "Got that there boy in there, Railroad?"

"Yeh, comin' right out," called the fat man, moving himself and his two guests in front of him toward the door. He extended a pudgy hand. "Well, Abner, I wish you well. You're startin' out now in life, an' I hope you'll git on with ever'body an' not have no trouble."

Abner swallowed at the lump pressing in his throat. "No, sir, I'll—try not," he managed to say.

Abner was staring at Mr. Sandage, who looked back at the boy he had reared. Again it did not seem possible to Abner that he really was separating himself finally from Mr. Sandage and Mrs. Sandage and Beatrice Belle. Mr. Sandage held out his hard hand and cleared his throat.

"Well, so long, Abner."

Abner pressed the poorhouse keeper's hand and swallowed. "So long, Mr. Sandage."

"I'll have Mammy send over yore things by partial post, Abner."

"All right, Mr. Sandage."

"I reckon that'll be all right, won't it, Mr. Jones—jest direct it to Arntown?"

"Shore! Shore!" agreed the fat man cheerfully, "Abner Teeftaller, Arntown, Tennessee. In a day or two you can go down to the post office an' call for yore things, Abner."

Abner nodded and said, "yes, sir," in a pinched voice.

Mr. Sandage was resaying, "Well, so long, Abner, an' good luck to ye."

Abner tried to repeat the so longs and good lucks but his throat was aching so dismally as to stop all articulation whatsoever.

Mr. Sandage patted him on the back; they were now marching him out on the porch into the yellow light, down the steps toward the wagon. He stumbled a trifle on the top step, which caused the mules to start. Old Squire Meredith called, "Whoa there, Sam; whoa, Lige!"

Everything was blurred to Abner. He groped his way to a place on the wagon. The old Squire sucked his lips at the mules and Abner saw the blur of them lunge and felt himself jerked forward. The wind struck his face; the wagon set up its rattling, and the boy was off on the unsure adventure of manhood.

Abner eased himself over the bolster on to the backhounds where he could wipe his eyes with his shirt sleeve unobserved. Squire Meredith was too much engrossed in passing the slower-moving wagons and giving the road to automobiles to pay much attention to his guest for a while. The wagon rattled along merrily over stones and ruts, causing the world to dance before Abner's blurred eyes. Presently, when the traffic on the road was strung out and had eased somewhat the strain on the old man's attention, he began drawling, "Well—votin' about them school books—I reckon I done right, but I don't know as it makes much diff'runce one way or t'other, as they'll never be printed noway."

"Won't they?" asked Abner, under the erroneous impression that an old man wanted a young one to answer his monologue.

The Squire drove on silently and presently began on a new tack: "You know, in these murder trials, they could save a lot of time and expense by jest turnin' the man aloose an' lettin' him give the lawyers a mortgage on his farm—come to the same thing."

Abner did not follow this at all.

"Peck Bradley," proceeded the Squire, ruminating on the trial then in progress, "is jest as shore a broke man as he killed old man Shelton.   The Bible says the way of the transgressor is hard, Abner," the old fellow clicked at his mules, shook his reins, and added in melancholy tone, "Ay, Lord— Buckingham Sharp fer his lawyer   .   .   ."

Abner gave his eyes a final rake and sat staring at the passing landscape, which was growing yellow in the last rays of the sun.   As the wagon rattled down some declivity, Abner could feel himself entering a cooler layer of air, and then as the mules climbed the ascent on the other side, the temperature rose again to summer warmth.   This alternation of warmth and coolness, mingled with the wraithlike sweetness of wild cucumber, set up a poignant homesickness in the youth.   It was through just such perfumed strata of warm and cool air that his foster-sister Beatrice Belle was driving home the cow from the pasture at this very moment.

The old Squire broke in upon his mood with unconscious kindness and shattered it by saying, "I seen you sparkin' Nessie Sutton in the court yard to-day."

Abner looked around in amazement.   "Wha-at?"

"Sparkin' Nessie Sutton," repeated the Squire woodenly.

Abner jolted along for upward of half a minute, staring at his host.   Finally he asked with the drawl of his kind, "Who is Nessie Sutton?"

"You nee'n' to deny it," nodded the old man solemnly. "I knowed you-all was sparkin' by the way you stood aroun' not able to say nuthin'."

"Why, I don't even know who Nessie Sutton is," cried Abner.

"Don't know the gal you was a-talkin' to in the courthouse yard 'long about dinner time!" exclaimed the Squire, astonished in his turn.

"Was her name Nessie Sutton?"

"I swan," cried the old fellow, "was you stan'in' there sparkin' a gal you didn't know!"

"Well, I wasn't exactly sparkin'."

"Oh, yes, you wuz."

"Where does she live?"

"In Arntown."

This information picked up Abner's spirits in a most extraordinary manner.

"She does—well, I be blamed!" A sort of warmth came into his face and he beamed on the old Squire. "Now, don't that beat you?"

"Ay, Lord," grunted the Squire misanthropically, turning to his endless gazing at the rumps of his mules. "The gal had to live some'er's."

Abner marvelled that he had got the girl's name after all— "Nessie Sutton" . . . a nice name, a pretty name— "Nessie Sutton." The syllables seemed to fill some empty space in his thoughts, to settle in his head as if they always had belonged there.

The old Squire gave his reins a twitch which did not provoke his mules out of the walk which was in keeping with this hour of the day.

"Ay, Lord," he said, shaking his head. "You young folks of this generation nee'n' be thinkin' about marryin' an' raisin' famblys." Here he reached into a pocket, drew out a disreputable pipe, looked at it, and put it back.

Abner listened to this opinion with a certain curiosity.

"Why hadn't we ought, Mr. Meredith?" he asked at length.

"'Cause you an' that gal ain't got no time to be marryin' in, that's why."

"Ain't got no time?" puzzled Abner. "Ain't we both young?"

"Ay, lad, *you're* young," assented the old man, "but this earth air in her last days, my boy. She ain't goin' to last long enough for no more marryin' an' givin' in marriage."

"Square Meredith, what in the worl' do you mean?" ejaculated Abner, straightening up out of the hump in which all hill folk ride a wagon.

"Why, Abner, I mean the worl's comin' to a end, my boy.

She ain't goin' to last no longer than the sixteenth of next October. Then the heavens is goin' to unroll an' the graves give up their dead, an' the Lamb o' God is goin' to come down an' jedge the wicked an' the righteous; the quick an' the dead."

The roll of the old hillman's rude eloquence moved Abner with a strange emotion. It filled the quiet evening with a sense of queer impermanence.

The sun, a vast ball of fire, was sinking behind a distant fringe of trees. The wagon was now on a hilltop and the valleys were filled with dark blue shadows, while the tops of the hills, rising above them, were emblazoned with the dying day. In the west the sky was an abyss of green light which merged at the zenith into the profound blue of coming night.

The old man went on with his monologue:

"And not them as say 'Lord! Lord!' shall be carried up into Heaven in the arms of the Lamb, but them that doeth the will of the Father."

The far-flung colours of the evening lent a sort of corroboration to the old man's chanting.

"What makes you think it ain't goin' to last but tull next October?" asked Abner in an awed tone.

"Why, that's all in the Bible explained jest as clear as day. Ay, Lord; it's comin' jest as shore as we're drivin' over this hill, Abner. I don't reckon you never read the works of Reverend Solomon Molner? Well, it ort to be taught in ever' school to young an' old. It's called, 'The Word Unveiled.' It comes in 'leven volumes an' it makes it jest as clear as day. It shows you all the signs an' warnin's of the end of time, an' they're happenin' now, Abner, right now! Ay, Lord!" The old man shook his head, fumbled out his pipe, blew through the stem, and put it back into his pocket.

"But next October?" questioned Abner, frightened.

"Well, in the ninth chapter of Revelation, John says, 'Nine hundred an' ninety-nine. Yea, the beast had six horns.' Now the Reverend Solomon Molner shows that each one of them horns was a dispensation, an' five of 'em's gone. The flight of the childern of Egypt, the sack of Jerusalem by the Romans, the reign of the Emperor Napoleon who was the Anti-Christ mentioned in the Book of Revelation. Now, multiplyin' these by nine hunderd an' ninety-nine gives you the limit of Time, an' that ends on the sixteenth of next October. Then Saint John says, 'The heavens shall roll up like a scroll an' pass away; an' there shall be a new heaven an' a new earth. An' Satan shall be chained for a thousan' years, an' after that the Lamb o' God shall come down to——''

In the midst of this dithyramb a shudder ran through Abner, and he pointed, gasping, "Oh, Mr. Meredith, Look! Look!"

The old Squire looked. A meteor had flamed suddenly against the lemon-coloured west. It moved with deliberate brilliance across the sky and faded.

The old mystic looked at the burning sign without an extra heart beat. Christ Himself, walking down the sky along the lanes of light, would not have disturbed the rhythm of his thought, so many times had he imagined exactly such a scene. He turned to the boy.

"That's a sign from God, Abner," he said solemnly. "It's a sign to me an' you who b'lieve in Him and who trust His Holy Word. Jest a few more short months an' all this will pass away."

He made an awkward gesture over the blue-and-orange evening, and then the mules, impelled by the coming night, suddenly trotted down the hill with the wagon and men into the chill and gloom of the valley below them.

CHAPTER V

SQUIRE MEREDITH lived something near a mile west of Irontown in a gray frame house with two enormous stone chimneys buttressing its gables. Across the public road from the house stood the Squire's barn and stable. Abner and the old man arrived at this place late at night, fed the mules, then went in and had their own supper. Immediately after eating, the old justice sat down in the family room and began reading a volume of his beloved Molner.

The Squire's wife, a rather spectral old lady, made shift to keep up a halting conversation, or rather an intermittent monologue with the boy. She reckoned the railroad would mean a lot to Lanesburg; there was a sick man up the road a piece, that they believed was going to die; a neighbour, Mr. Ferns, had been smoking his horse that day for the blind staggers; she herself had a knee that was hurting her, and she had tied red flannel around it which she thought had done it a little good; and so in driblets, on and on and on.

There was a girl in the room, a daughter of the house, who sat as mutely as Abner in the undecided light of the oil lamp. The old Squire read of the coming of the end of time. His book told him signs and portents which marked the end of this dispensation, and then there would be a new people and a new earth; the author unrolled the dramatic prelude to the second coming before the old man's eyes. Of the four persons in the sitting room only one, the old Squire, escaped the pinched and meagre present, liberated through the magic of his prophet. Presently the old woman bestirred herself and advised Abner not to wait up for her husband, as lots of nights he would set there readin' tull nine or ten o'clock, and that ever'body on the place went to bed an' left him.

The youth was glad enough to go. He took the candle the old woman provided and was directed out of the door across a dark hall into the guest room on the other side.

The candle showed dimly the walls of the guest chamber which were plastered and whitewashed. The windows were small and high, which gave the room a certain vague resemblance to a prison. A rude crayon portrait of one of the Meredith ancestors hung on the wall. It was the work of an enlarging house in Chicago and had been sold to Mrs. Meredith by a travelling salesman. Abner's sleeping place was a mighty four-poster in the corner which was surmounted by a feather bed of enormous depth.

Abner took off his shoes and trousers in the utmost depression; he blew out his breath and looked around the melancholy room without finding a point where his eyes could rest. He thrust his toe under the overhang of the feather bed and on top of the rail, leaned down and blew out his candle, and then made a rather desperate lunge upward and over in the darkness and fell into a mass of feathers. The smell of feathers and the mustiness of long-unused sheets filled the air. The youth straightened out and lay staring up into the blackness. The feathers cupped around his body and between his outspread legs and grew warmer and warmer in the warm night. Presently perspiration dampened his shirt and drawers, and he flung about shifting to places which were temporarily cool. He sickened with longing for the poorhouse, for Mrs. Sandage and Colonel Wybe and Beatrice Belle. He remembered the county court had made him a free man, that he was alone in the world, a being without any family connection whatever; no one would ever pay him two thoughts again; desolation seized him. He gave up trying to find a cool place in the bed and so went to sleep.

The worst of nights finally pass and are no more. At length morning came with its coolness and dew and its salvo of light saluting the day. The celebration of chanticleers far and near aroused Abner, who turned out of bed, replaced his trousers and shoes and thereby was "dressed." When he had washed his face in a tin pan and had dried it on a sour towel he undertook the hill guest's obligation to help feed and water the stock. Squire Meredith fed his hogs by whooping them up and throwing corn to them in the middle of the public road between his house and his barn. Just here the road was fairly covered by tramped-under cobs, and this morning he began throwing out more corn on this feeding place. Hogs came running from up and down the road and through by-lanes.

As Abner helped throw out the corn he saw coming down the road a team driven by a man walking behind it. Above the jingle of the harness Abner could hear the fellow whistling a country breakdown at a merry lilt, and occasionally he broke into his own whistling to sing a snatch of the chorus,

"Hum tiddy um tum . . . turkey in the straw,
Tum tiddy um tum . . . turkey in the stra-a-aw . . . ."

When he came closer Abner could see that the troubadour presented a sorry sight. His trousers were torn so that one leg was exposed from the knee down. His shirt was frayed, his hat gone, leaving his shock of disordered greasy black hair glistening in the morning sunshine. When he came still closer Abner saw that one of his eyes was black and there was dried blood on one ear and on his shirt collar below, where the blood had dripped.

Both Squire Meredith and Abner paused in their work to regard this remarkable sight.

The Squire drew a breath and called out in the formula of the hills, "Hey-oh, stranger, air ye travellin' or goin' somewher'?"

"Goin' somewher', by God . . . um tiddy um tum, turkey in the straw. . . . How fur is it to Arntown?"

"You're right in it now," said the Squire.

The stranger glanced about the lonely landscape to verify the Squire's words.

"Lemme see," he said. "What do you call yore name?"

"I don't call it," said the Squire drily, for he had formed a distaste for the teamster. "I don't haff to. I'm genully with myse'f most of the time."

The teamster was not piqued at this answer but burst into loud brief laughter. "Well, I be damned, I see you air a ole man full of ketches." He looked at the old Squire with the crude superiority of youth. "Well, you've had a lot o' time to learn 'em in. We grow wiser an' weaker, as the rabbit said when the dawg chawed him up."

"I don't know whether you air any wiser or not," said the Squire stiffly, "but you certainly look chawed up some yorese'f. Where's yore waggin, an' what happened to ye?"

"Comin' down here to work on the railroad last night an' my team run away an' kinder strung my waggin out over three or four miles of road, an fin'ly wropped what was left aroun' a black jack; I figgered we had gone fur enough fer one night, so I got my mules stopped, cut 'em some grass fer fodder, an' jess laid down an' went to sleep."

"I guess you was pretty well lit up when all that was goin' on, wasn't ye?" asked the Squire with the teetotaller's scorn of the tippler in his voice.

"Wuz when I started," agreed the teamster frankly, "but I was sober as a jedge when I got 'em stopped. I'm like that. Whisky ain't got no holt on me. I sober up the minute anything happens."

This ability to react in crises must have touched even the Squire, for he asked somewhat drily, "Have ye had any breakfast?"

"Nope. I calkerlate to git some cheese an' crackers in Arntown."

"Well, we're jest about to set down," invited the Squire without enthusiasm. "Might come on in an' jine us."

"Don't keer ef I do."

The stranger reined his mules to the side of the road and hitched them to the barn fence, and the three men went into the house. As they walked through the hall into the kitchen the old man called out, "Ma, here's a stranger I'm takin' in. He's purty bad bunged up from a runaway." The phrase "stranger I'm taking in," referred subconsciously to the Biblical injunction for acts of this description, and the wife accepted it in the same spirit. The teamster added, "You'll haff to excuse my looks, ma'am," but he got his bloody face clean and his hair combed before he entered the kitchen.

Squire Meredith's kitchen was dark and heated like an oven. In building the room the Squire apparently had forgotten to put in windows, for there was none; and even with the brightness of a summer morning outside, the women were forced to light an oil lamp on the table. Now this lamp dimly illuminated platters piled high with fried chicken, fried ham, a sorghum stand, plates of string beans, new potatoes, turnip greens, apple pies so old that they had turned bluish. The greater part of these dishes were cold because Mrs. Meredith put on the breakfast table all that she had left over from yesterday's dinner.

The men stood around a little awkwardly until the Squire said, "Well, set down," and they all sat. The stranger made a false move toward his plate just as the Squire bent his head to return thanks for the meal. He corrected his mistake in time to bend his own oily head while the Squire rattled off some unintelligible grace which concluded with "name of our Lord and Saviour, Jesus Christ, Amen . . ." and glided without a break into "What part of the chickun will you have, brother? . . . I fergit yore name."

"Beavers," replied the teamster solidly, "Tug Beavers— an' I fergit yo'rn."

"That's because you never knowed it," said the host.

"Fur the lan's sake, Pa!" cried both women in the back of the kitchen, scandalized. "Why, it's Meredith, Mr. Beavers. I don't know *what's* the matter with Pa. He simply never will tell his name. He makes me so ashamed sometimes."

"That's all right, ma'am," responded Mr. Beavers, broadly generous. "I've seed the time an' place when I didn't want to give my name myse'f, an' I didn't."

"Fuh the lan's sake!" ejaculated the girl in a repressed tone.

Mr. Beavers, who had been doing this talking with strict attention to his eating, now looked up for the first time and attempted to peer through the darkness of the kitchen. There was something primitive in the way he halted his chewing and swallowing to stare through the glow of the lamp at the girl beyond. When he saw he could make out nothing at all he said, "Could you bring me a glass of watter, please, young lady? I'm powerful thirsty."

"I vence you air after yore drunk," said the Squire's wife sympathetically. She evidently looked upon all "drunks' as disasters which overtook young men at more or less untimely intervals. She brought the water herself in a glass tumbler tinted with green.

Mr. Beavers drank thirstily and then finished his high-piled plate. Then after two quarter sections of pie, he tipped his chair back comfortably until his body and legs were in a straight line, resting on the front edge of the seat and the top slat of the back. "Best breakfust I ever et," he said, drawing a long breath and patting his stomach. "Yes, sir, the best one I ever et. Yore gal shore does cook good chicken and make fine pies, Mr. Meredith. She shore is goin' to make some man a fine wife." He sighed with comfort, then leaned forward with a bang and said sharply, "Well, I guess I better be goin'. I signed up fer that railroad job, an' I want to start with the gang this mornin'."

The old woman came forward. "You better eat some more, Mr. Beavers; you ain't et enough to keep a bird alive."

"I think I done purty well," said Mr. Beavers politely, as he glanced over the stripped dishes.

"You must come back some time an' see us, Mr. Beavers, workin' so clost like this."

"Shore will," accepted Mr. Beavers heartily.

"Now, Ma," put in the Squire bluntly, "you know these young folks ain't goin' to have no time fer nothin' like what you've got in yore head when the whole caboodle is goin' to be wiped out an' started over on a diff'runt plan in fourteen months."

"What in the worl' do you mean by that?" asked the teamster in amazement.

The Squire began explaining the end of Time to Mr. Beavers. It was the one topic on which the old hillman was eloquent and convincing. Again as he talked it seemed to Abner that the hot kitchen, the house, the earth, and the very people about him took on a queer insubstantiality. All life became a mere temporary arrangement awaiting the end of Time which was due in a few months. Just what the rearrangement would be, Abner could not imagine; nor did it occur to him to try to imagine. He simply knew that it would be something infinitely better than the world he saw before him.

The teamster was astounded. "Well, I declare, jest think of that! Dividin' the goats frum the sheep . . ." He stood in the door of the kitchen, scratching his greasy head, and presently observed frankly, "Well, that bein' the case, I guess I better tell you folks good-bye, for I guess I shore am bound fer hell an' won't see you no more." He came back holding out his hand with the greatest simplicity.

The implication that the teamster, a soul bound for hell, was bidding good-bye to a family who would be caught up to a happier event held a certain drama.

"I'll pray fer ye, Brother Beavers," said the Squire. The wife promised the same thing, and when the girl put her hand in the mule driver's, she murmured a barely audible, "An' me, too."

Abner, who had no certain destination for his soul, was not told good-bye, but was entirely overlooked. He simply followed Mr. Beavers out of the house and out of the gate.

The teamster unhitched his mules and set out driving them down the road and the boy went by his side.

They had gone hardly two hundred yards when they reached the top of a hill and Irontown lay in their view.

Involuntarily both stopped and stood looking at the goal of their pilgrimage. Mr. Beavers reached very solemnly in his hip pocket and drew out a pint bottle about a fourth full. He removed the cork and held the flask up toward Irontown, and then toward Abner.

"Here's luck," he said.

He drank, then wiped the mouth of the bottle on his dirty sleeve and handed it to the youth.

Abner never before had taken a drink. He looked at the bottle with a queer trembly sensation and asked uneasily, "Will it make me drunk, Mr. Beavers?"

"Why, it never does uffeck me none," stated the rather bunged-up mule driver simply.

Abner suddenly became ashamed of his qualms. He took the bottle and held it up toward the village.

"Here's luck," he repeated; took a mouthful of the fiery liquid, strangled, sputtered, but swallowed it, and then stood blinking at Mr. Beavers with tears in his eyes.

CHAPTER VI

THE two hillmen found Irontown filled with the material and spiritual resonances of the coming railroad. The village merchants were doing a brisk business in work shirts, overalls, and brogan shoes. The price of board had advanced. "Men Wanted" signs decorated the telephone posts. In a little open space between Irontown Bank and Fuller's Drug Store, one of those adventurers who flock in the wake of any industrial development had hung a sign across the pavement:

SILVER MOON QUICK LUNCH

SOFT DRINKS A SPECIALTY

CALY STEGALL, PROP.

From the other side of the street, the town constable scanned Mr. Stegall and the soft drink feature of his sign with an appraising eye.

Beyond the drug store arose the Grand Drygoods Store. And even the Grand was stimulated by the arrival of the railroad. Four new hats appeared in its show windows: two toques, a leghorn, and a sailor with a red feather in its band.

Beyond the Grand was a tiny jeweller's shop with the sign, "A. M. Belshue, Watch and Clock Repairing." Just inside the single dusty window Mr. Belshue always could be dimly discerned bending over his work with one eye exaggerated by a jeweller's glass. When Abner Teeftallow settled in his boarding place, the Scovell House, farther up the street, he had to pass the jewellery shop twice a day. When he first saw this curious elongation in the eye of the man behind the desk he was minded to step into the shop and see what it was, but the project faded from his thoughts, and thereafter the grayish head with the magnifier screwed into its eye became simply a part of the dusty window and held no human interest whatsoever.

The construction which Railroad Jones had set going so prosperously was best displayed at the L. & N. depot, for Irontown already was on a main-line railroad, and the Lane County magnate meant to form a junction with this system as an outlet for his own jerkwater road. At the depot was a confusion of gasoline caterpillars, graders, traction ploughs, rock crushers, dirt scoops, and what not. It was extraordinary how the hillmen laid hold of these huge and unfamiliar machines and, after a brief experimental stage, launched themselves into the task of cutting a level thoroughfare through the full-bosomed hills.

Abner Teeftallow found a job of driving a team of mules hitched to a dirt scoop. He and some thirty or forty other teamsters drove their scoops around and around in a great ellipse, moving ploughed dirt forward down a declivity, emptying it at a designated place and then turning and climbing up the hill to the ploughed ground again. Under the ardour of a July sun this was melting work; the steadying of the scoop handles to dip the loose earth, the heave to upset it and spread it down the declivity, the effort of walking in the soft dirt, and above all the nervousness and irritability of the mules. When one mule danced or kicked in the great ellipse the whole string was disorganized. This caused a continual outpour of profanity and whip-cracking from the teamsters. The bitterest qualifications, the lewdest objurgations were repeated endlessly.

For several days Abner refrained from the use of such language, but after a while, when the afternoons reached their greatest heat, and his mules their worst impishness, it seemed to Abner as if a sort of fury arose up inside of him in response to his bouncing scoop and fighting mules. He lashed his whip, spat out the vilest invectives, and struggled on desperately. Why he should work so fiercely, why objurgate so filthily and indecently, he had not the faintest idea. All the teamsters did the same thing and none of them had the slightest notion why they were so stirred and so bitter.

At one o'clock Saturday afternoon, the construction gang were to be paid off at the Irontown bank. Railroad Jones had arranged for this bank to finance his operations, and the weekly payrolls were to be distributed from the teller's window. So a little past noon on Saturday all the construction gang tramped into the village. They came in groups or pairs with here and there a surly or a meditative fellow walking alone. As the men tramped in they jested among themselves with the peculiar sardonic thrusts of the hill people; each witticism was meant, very cheerfully, to wound its object as much as possible. Some of the boys began annoying others about certain disreputable women of the village. Somebody shouted at Abner in this fashion, and a terrible embarrassment swept over the youth, but to his immense relief the subject was not pressed. The talk of the crowd swung to the pay they were going to receive. Zed Parrum announced in a loud voice that he didn't believe the crowd would get a cent because they stood a lot better chance of drawing a pair of Perry Northcutt's eye teeth than a dollar out of his bank.

Laughter crackled up and down the street at this hit. It inspired other efforts. Such gloomy predictions began to shake Abner's faith in the payroll. He turned to Tug Beavers, with whom he was walking.

"Tug, d'reckon we're goin' to git anything on these?" He shook his pay check.

"Hell, yes," asserted Tug broadly, "it's either the money or a cussin' out with me."

Now Abner had not yet reached that stage of hill culture where a cursing out represented a distinct spiritual asset and could be accepted as *quid pro quo* for other and more material values, so he asked very innocently:

"Tug, what good will it do you to cuss out the bank, if you don't git yore money?"

Mr. Beavers scratched his head. "Well, a cussin' out is a cussin' out, Abner. Nobody likes to take a cussin' out, an' I reckon that's why ever'body likes to give one."

Abner began to perceive dimly Mr. Beavers's point of view, when Tug suddenly bawled out to someone up the street, "Well, for the love of Sukey, look yonder what the dawgs drug home!"

Abner looked and saw a short stocky man with a typical hard hill-country face now set in a grin of pleasure at Mr. Beavers's perfumed greeting. The moment he was espied half-a-dozen voices took up the chorus simultaneously, "Why, hey-oh, Peck Bradley!" "How'd je git out, Peck?" "Air ye out fer good, Peck?"

The man continued his hard-lined grin and explained laconically, "Same as—hung jury."

"But looks like they'd slapped you back in jail?"

"Hab a corpse," elucidated Mr. Bradley briefly.

"Well, I be derned!" cried Tug with genuine admiration in his voice. "You shore are a hellion! Out on hab a corpse—though of course you did."

Here Mr. Bradley's hard face straightened from its smiling into something wooden and somewhat troubled. "Shore! Shore!" he drawled, and evidently would have done with the topic.

Abner was thrilling with curiosity. He clutched Mr. Beavers's arm.

"What do you mean, Tug, out on hab a corpse?"

The hillman frowned on the boy and explained in a hurried undertone, "When you kill a man and can show the corpse, they kain't keep you in jail."

Abner was aghast, "Fuh God's sake—why?"

"Damn it!" whispered Mr. Beavers, thoroughly irritated at such an awkward explanation in the presence of Peck, "because you got the corpse there to show, I reckon. Anyway, yore lawyer gits you out on hab a corpse."

"Did he kill somebody?" whispered Abner in an awed voice.

"Damn it, yes. That's Peck Bradley, the feller that killed ol' man Shelton. You ort to know him, Abner, you wuz up at the murder trile in Lanesburg. Good God, boy, do you set aroun' asleep?" Here Mr. Beavers lifted his whispers to full voice again, and said cordially, "Well, Peck, by God, I didn't hope to see you out so soon."

Mr. Bradley began his hard-lined grinning again and ejaculated the single name, "Buckingham Sharp." "

"A fine lawyer," put in a third voice commendingly.

"That's a fack," nodded Tug, "a feller kain't do nothin' hardly but what Buck Sharp kin git him off scot free. A mighty fine man to have in a community. Well, Peck, what you doin' down here?"

"Work"—from Mr. Bradley.

Half-a-dozen of his admirers gathered around Mr. Bradley, who turned and strolled with the crowd back to the bank.

Abner, following behind, peered through this escort at the man killer and received of him the most unearthly impression: the stocky body, the short, powerful legs, the round head with its rough black hair that might very well have been pig's bristles—this Peck Bradley really had murdered a man; had erased another human being cleanly from the earth. In the crowd were other men much like Peck, but the aura of this murder set him apart from all the other labourers; it cast a strange atmosphere over him. Abner peered at him with fascinated eyes until the crowd reached the bank. The labourers filed in. Peck Bradley walked on up the street with stiff wooden movements through self-consciousness from having a whole streetful watch him. As he went he smoked a cigar, holding it between his thumb and finger, looking at it, giving it his whole attention.

All of the labourers could not enter the lobby of the Iron-town bank at the same time, and some had to wait out on the pavement before the building. Abner and Tug entered with the first draft and stood for their turn before the window.

Just inside the cashier's window was a thin, sandy-haired man, and when the crowd had entered and their little noises had subsided somewhat, he began speaking with a disagreeable crack to his voice:

"Howdy, boys, I'm glad to see you, an' I hope you'll all come out to church to-morrow. You are strangers in our little city, and I extend you this invitation to our religious services. Well, so you've all come to make your deposits? Mighty glad to see that. If you haven't already got an account started here, you certainly can't find a better time than right this minute to start one. You all know what the Bible says about the faithful steward who put his money out at usury and when the Master called for his talents, he had four pieces instead of two. Yes, boys, God wants you to save your money. It's your Christian duty. All right now, you," the cashier pointed a thin possessive finger at the man nearest him, "will you let me have your slip?"

The man pushed through the window his slip which contained his name and the amount due him.

"Do you want to deposit all this, Mr. Fraley?" asked the cashier with a certain disagreeable quality in the solicitous glide of his voice.

"Naw, I don't want to deposit none of it," said Fraley.

"You *don't!*"—with pained astonishment at Fraley's obduracy in the face of a Biblical quotation.

"Naw, I don't."

"What are you going to do with this money, Mr. Fraley?"

"Pay my board," said Fraley, with somewhat shortened temper.

The cashier gave Fraley a pale bloodless smile. "Now, you'll just throw away this money, Fraley, shooting craps, or spend it for moonshine over at Caly Stegall's place. There ain't no use in you fooling away your money like that. Five dollars will pay your board, and you just leave the rest here in the bank so you can get it when you *want* it and *need* it!" The cashier stressed the two words with religious unction as if he and Mr. Fraley were both sure that at present Fraley neither wanted nor needed the money. As he said this he made an entry in a fresh little bank pass book, handed it to Mr. Fraley, then motioned him toward the teller's window with a "Give him five dollars, Chester."

Chester, a washed-out blond youth with eyebrows that seemed pulled up to the middle of his forehead, hurriedly handed a five-dollar bill to the new depositor.

The next man who took Mr. Fraley's place at the window went through the same queries and arguments and came off with seven dollars and a new pass book, and the injunction to keep his money where he could lay hands on it *when he wanted it!*

Not a single workman wanted to make a deposit, but the cashier contrived, nevertheless, to retain about three fourths of their wages and sent them away with a dollar or two and a new pass book.

When Mr. Beavers came to the window and was asked how much he wanted to deposit, Tug stated bluntly that he wanted every damn cent he had in the bank.

Mr. Northcutt smiled bloodlessly and asked him what he wanted with so much money—to buy moonshine with?

Mr. Beavers pushed his face up to the little brass bars of the window and said, "You damn little spindlin' money sucker, I want ever' damn cent I got in this bank, an' I don't haff to tell no damn little white-headed ant what I'm goin' to do with my own money! It's mine! You give it to me an' the quickest way you can reach it out will be too damn slow fer me!"

Without another word or a change of countenance Mr. Northcutt O. K'd Mr. Beavers's slip and waved him to the teller; then as Abner stepped up next in turn, the cashier with his usual etiolated smile glanced at the boy and in his usual disagreeable voice asked, "Well, how much board do you pay, my boy?"

Abner began to speculate uncertainly on how much of his money he could persuade the cashier to pay him when a voice inside the grating said in a low tone, "That's that Teeftallow boy, Perry."

Mr. Northcutt's face instantly took on a different, a more ingratiating, and somehow a more disagreeable expression. He said, "Oh, is it?" and immediately afterward, "Abner, would you mind stepping inside the grating just a moment, please?"

At this elaborate preparation to make him a depositor, all hope of getting any money whatever forsook Abner. He began to defend himself as best he could.

"I don't mind comin' aroun'," he began unhappily, "but I want my money same as Tug Beavers, I want——"

"Oh, that's all right," smoothed the cashier suavely. "Chester, just pay Abner twelve dollars and a half as he goes by your window. We want to see you on quite a different business, Abner, quite a different, and, we hope, a profitable business for you, Abner." Mr. Northcutt fairly purred out these "Abners," to the youth's utter nonplussing; the stripling in the teller's window pushed through two five-dollar bills, one two-dollar bill, and half dollar. Abner wadded these up awkwardly and tremulously and decided on what pocket he could entrust with so much money, as he passed around to the door which admitted him behind the grating of the bank.

Inside the enclosure sat three men, a girl, and a boy working at an adding machine. The youth with the blond hair remained at his window, but Mr. Northcutt, with the indifference characteristic of a banker in a one-bank town, where lack of competition breeds lack of courtesy, turned away from his grating as Abner entered and left the labourers to cool their heels in the lobby.

Mr. Northcutt smiled at Abner, and this drew the skin over his lean jaws and gave his face a queer corpselike appearance.

"You got your money all right, Abner?" he asked affably.

Abner, with a certain suspicion that the cashier might attempt to get it from him, admitted that he had it.

"Very good, Abner, that's very good. I hope you'll use your little nest egg wisely, to the benefit of yourself and the glory of God."

Abner agreed vaguely to this vague suggestion.

The banker rubbed his thin bony hands together. "Your grandfather was old Judge Jefferson Coltrane, was he not, my boy?"

Abner drawled an affirmative, studying the cashier's bony face.

"Old Judge Jefferson Coltrane, he and my father were great friends, Abner, that's one of the reasons I called you around here, my boy; you've come into our midst more or less alone and on account of the friendship of my family for yours"— here Mr. Northcutt glanced at one of the men in the office—"you know we folks here in the South are great sticklers for families, Mr. Ditmas, when a boy like this comes from a good family——" the banker broke off, smiling with bloodless benevolence.

Abner glanced around and was surprised to see a man whom he knew. This Mr. Ditmas was an engineer, and Abner had seen him working on the right-of-way of Railroad Jones's new road near the poorhouse.

"Yes, I'd observed that," returned Ditmas in an agreeable manner. "I think it's a fine old custom."

"Quite so," nodded the banker. "You know, Mr. Ditmas, I think we Southern people—you mustn't take offence——" the cashier smiled placatingly, "but I think we stand just a little closer to God than—er——"

A third gentleman in the room, with a faint smile on his rather round face, put in: "The South has often been called God's country, Perry."

"Why, certainly, Mr. Sharp," agreed the banker in a faintly undecided voice, as if he were not quite sure whether Mr. Sharp was agreeing with him or jibing at him very delicately. He paused a moment, then turned to Abner again.

"Now, to get down to business, Abner—er—I was just wondering whether you don't need a little money, maybe?"

"Money!" repeated Abner, astonished.

"Yes, you might require some money just at this period of your life, say to go to school on."

"No, I don't want to go to school," returned Abner promptly.

"I didn't know. Your grandfather was a very bookish man. Then perhaps you'd like three or four hundred dollars to buy yourself an automobile; most boys want an auto."

An automobile had been, up to that moment, furthest from Abner's thoughts, but now the mere hint that he possibly might get one set up a trembling inside of him.

"I'd shore like that, but how in the worl' kin I git it?"

"As an old friend of your family," smiled the banker, "I might advance you that amount."

"Jest because my gran'daddy knowed yore daddy?"

"Well, yes, and because, too—" here the banker hesitated, placed the tips of his bony fingers delicately together —"because too, Abner, there was a little cloud on the title of some of my father's holding; it's what Mr. Sharp here calls a shadow on the title; so we thought if you would just sign us a quit-claim deed to a little tract of land in question we would make you a present of four or five hundred dollars just to show our appreciation."

All this talk about clouds on titles meant nothing whatever to Abner, but his hill instinct to trade made him say, "Is five hunderd as good as you could do on that, Mr. Northcutt?"

Mr. Buckingham Sharp leaned back and laughed roundly at this.

"If you had offered him a million, Perry, you would have got the same answer; it's automatic with them."

Mr. Northcutt likewise smiled his bloodless smile. "You forget, Abner, this is mainly a present in memory of your grandfather."

"What is a cloud on a title?" queried the youth shrewdly.

"Well, it is just some irregularity, perhaps your grandfather's signature was not witnessed; or your grandmother's signature does not correspond with the form it is written in the deed; some little misstep, you know," the banker waved his fingers and drew a legal-looking paper from the drawer. "Now here is a quit-claim deed which Mr. Sharp has drawn up, and if you'll sign it—you can write, can't you?"

"Y-yes, sir," hesitated Abner, deeply suspicious of a trap.

"Chester, just count out Abner four hundred dollars in ten-dollar bills."

Abner looked at the cashier quickly, "I thought you said five hunderd dollars?"

"You'll do, Abner," smiled the banker. "Make it five hundred, Chester."

The blond youth reached into a drawer and began counting green and yellow backs apparently out of an illimitable sheaf. A dreamlike feeling came over Abner. It did not seem that this money could be real or that he was going to get it. A violent emotion seized him and he arose with a shaken feeling to sign the paper when he glanced across and happened to see Mr. Ditmas frowning at him and shaking his head slightly but urgently.

It had the effect on Abner of a dash of cold water on a sleep walker. A certain kindness the engineer had shown Abner at the poorhouse had established the boy's confidence and this was something he felt for no one else in the group. He was advancing toward the table. Now he stopped still and drawled in his flat hill tones, "Naw, I don't reckon I'll sign that right now."

Mr. Northcutt was shocked and instantly angry.

"Won't sign it!" he cried. "Now, look here, Abner, that's no way for a man to do, balk like a mule right in the midst of an agreed trade. Why, you—you—what do you mean, shilly-shallying like this?"

The angry timbre of his voice aroused Abner. "I ain't shilly-shallyin'," he retorted obstinately. "I ain't goin' to sign it!"

Mr. Northcutt caught up the paper which he wanted signed and shook it at Abner. "My young man, I'll bring an action in chancery to clear up this title, and you'll not get a cent out of it! You are simply throwing away five hundred dollars!"

Abner moved wordlessly toward the door with a certain apprehension of an attack by Mr. Northcutt. The banker did take three steps after the boy and catch him by the arm.

"Abner, you idiot, listen to reason!"

The hulking youth flung himself loose with a feeling of being trapped. "Turn me go, Perry Northcutt, or I'll knock hell out of ye!" He had a fist swung back and his frightened eyes were blazing at the banker.

The cashier stepped back. "What a dolt! What a dolt!" he ejaculated furiously as he watched Abner pass into the lobby and disappear through the door. The banker was profoundly exasperated at this outcome. His rancour vibrated through his whole body. What had just occurred seemed to Mr. Northcutt impious, actually sacrilegious. It was absolutely sinful for an ordinary stupid drunken hill boy to thwart his designs in this fashion. Because Perry knew that he, himself, was going to serve God's purposes in every way he could whereas this youth would wickedly misuse anything of value that fell into his hands. Behind this he felt the villager's contempt for the hill folk, and for such a lout to frustrate his plans . . .

The cashier turned back to his window and by sheer will power restored the smile to his face and resumed the receiving of deposits from unwilling depositors. As he banked these deposits he felt vindictively righteous, and the parable of the good steward who put his money out at usury returned to his mind.

Presently Mr. Ditmas arose, excused himself, and walked out of the bank. Mr. Sharp watched the engineer go out and presently caught Mr. Northcutt's eye.

"I think our friend Ditmas played rather an odd little game just then," he observed, drawing a cigar from his pocket.

"How's that?" asked the cashier.

"He prompted the witness."

"What do you mean?"

"Well, I mean I've cross-examined too many witnesses not to know when a third party is prompting them by signals—I didn't glance around at Ditmas, but then I didn't have to."

The banker was thunderstruck. "But, my dear Sharp, why——"

Mr. Sharp lifted both hands. "Now, Perry, I'll be damned if I know why!"

Mr. Northcutt seemed to shrink visibly. "Sharp, I wish you wouldn't swear. Can't you realize that God hears your every word?"

"Pardon me, Perry," the lawyer laughed apologetically. Then he arose and moved leisurely and with a distinctly graceful carriage out of the enclosure, through the lobby to the door. He stood there a moment looking up and down the shabby street of Irontown. Then he saw something that caused him to nod in a sort of sardonic agreement with his own prescience—Mr. Ditmas was walking rapidly up the street after Abner and was obviously in pursuit of the youth. Buckingham Sharp took his cigar from his mouth and stood looking and smiling rather ironically after the two.

CHAPTER VII

WHEN Mr. Ditmas caught up with Abner, he explained to the youth that he had suggested a delay of the sale to the bank until the exact title Abner possessed could be ascertained. Abner agreed that this was good business but said the sight of so much money nearly had him going.

"I want you to feel," explained Mr. Ditmas carefully, "that I am not criticizing Mr. Northcutt or Mr. Sharp, but you were entering the sale in the spirit of a gamble, and it struck me that you were not in a financial position to indulge in that sort of thing."

Abner glanced at the engineer and listened to his sharply cut Northern sentences with a recurrence of that chronic suspicion with which all hill folk regard outlanders.

"Do you board here in town?" pursued Mr. Ditmas interestedly.

"Yes, sir," drawled Abner.

"Where?"

"At the Scovell House."

"What will you do to-morrow?"

"I—dunno," hesitated Abner, who nevertheless had a fair idea of the alternatives which would occupy him Sunday.

"I was thinking," went on Mr. Ditmas with his interested and helpful air, "that we might get up a game of baseball for to-morrow afternoon. We have plenty of men to make two teams, or even four or six. I don't see why we shouldn't get together a railroad league and play for a pennant this summer; it would be a lot of fun." Mr. Ditmas's voice warmed with the interest of an outdoor man in games.

Abner stared at the engineer. "Play on Sunday!"

Mr. Ditmas laughed. "Certainly, for a couple of years I was the physical director of the Y. M. C. A. in Akron, and I coached a 'Y' nine every Sunday afternoon."

The idea somehow shocked Abner, but perhaps for that very reason it attracted him; he agreed half-heartedly to the plan.

Mr. Ditmas was accustomed to half-hearted acquiescences so he said with the somewhat mechanical enthusiasm of all men who have been professional organizers of sports, "All right, you tell all the fellows you see to come out. I want our railroad boys to have as good a time as possible. We will organize to-morrow afternoon and will probably be able to get in a game or two."

"I'll tell 'em," agreed Abner dubiously.

Mr. Ditmas had a few more words for the boy, asked him how he was getting on, how he liked his job—the usual list of queries he had used in his "Y" organization work and was meant to found a friendly feeling between himself and his boys.

Abner Teeftallow was entirely unused to this mechanistic benevolence. He felt the spiritual automatism of it and could not make heads or tails of Mr. Ditmas. The two parted company at the intersection of the village streets, and Abner pursued his way to the Scovell House alone, his head filled with all sorts of suspicions as to what Mr. Ditmas might be up to.

The place where Abner boarded was a shabby two-story building with a spraddling mulberry tree in front of it, and nailed up to a limb projecting over the sidewalk was the sign, "Scovell House. Rates, $1.00 per day."

The Scovell House was the second-rate hostelry in Iron-town and its patronage came from farmers, lumbermen, book agents, and ordinary labourers. This hotel suited its patrons precisely. No farmer who put up at the Scovell House was ever embarrassed by the conventions of its dining room or its lobby. He could eat in coat, waistcoat, or shirt sleeves; he could convey food to his mouth with spoon, knife, fork, or

fingers, and no quiet zones were enforced for soup. It was
a very homelike place to persons who lived in that sort of
home. Physically it was as bare as a barn from cellar to
attic; the floors were uncarpeted and unpainted; the wall
paper in various stages of discolouration. The furniture
instead of appearing to furnish the rooms gave an impression
of further desolation. Two or three of the rooms leaked.

Abner Teeftallow was a boarder at the Scovell House and
Mr. Tug Beavers was another. These two young men occupied the same room and the same bed. Neither had
exactly wanted the other for a room mate, but the mere fact
that they had entered Irontown together had caught them
in the threads of a social entanglement which neither had
the deftness to escape. Unable to separate, they went to the
same hotel together, asked simultaneously for a room; the
landlady, a lank, grease-spotted woman, showed them upstairs to a room containing one bed under the impression they
were boon companions. She did suggest feebly that she
put in another bed, but hill courtesy demanded that the
boys protest, which they did, and the subject was dropped.

Abner was privately dismayed at the bedfellow whom circumstance had thrust upon him, and Mr. Beavers was privately disgusted.

On this particular afternoon when Abner entered his room
he found Mr. Beavers just preparing to go out. It was to be
a social call—Abner knew that, because Tug was oiling his
automatic pistol and occasionally he paused to whip it up
and snap it at some object in the mean room.

Tug glanced up from this work and asked with a certain
mockery in his drawl, "Did je git yore money, Abner?"

The youth silently drew out his three bills and two quarters
and displayed them.

"Didn't deposit none!" ejaculated Mr. Beavers, genuinely surprised. Then, after a moment with a hopeful
grin, "What did *you* say to him?"

"Nothin'; he jest handerd me the money right off an'—
an' offered me five hunderd more."

Mr. Beavers stared at Abner, then saw he was telling the truth.

"Godfrey's Cordial—didn't you take it!"

"Nope."

"Why didn't you?"

"Mr. Ditmas give me the wink."

"Fuh God's sake!" gasped Mr. Beavers, lowering his pistol laxly. "Did you let a man wink you out of five hunderd dollars! Why, Abner, with five hunderd dollars you could uh broke any crap game that gits started t'-morrer."

Mention of a game recalled to Abner the engineer's request.

"By the way, Tug, he told me to tell all you fellers that he was goin' to git up a big game of baseball to-morrer."

"Baseball—to-morrer?"

"Yeh."

"Why, to-morrer's Sunday."

"That's what I tol' him," declared Abner in a reinforced tone.

"Abner, he kain't keep as big a thing as a baseball game hid—where did he say he was goin' to pull it off?"

"In that open field by the railroad dump."

"Great Scots, ever'body'll see us!"

"He talked like he meant to jest come right out before ever'body an' let 'em see!" declared Abner roundly.

"My God, Abner, that wouldn't be right—desecratin' the Sabbath wide open like that. Why, hell far——" Mr. Beavers's observations dwindled away to murmured oaths and blasphemies and finally to silence as he pondered the right and wrong of it. Finally out of his reflections he declared with genuine conviction, "By God, I'm not that bad, Abner. I know I'm goin' to hell, but damn my riggin' if I'll go out an' play ball open on Sunday! I may have some influence in this world, Abner, an' I'm goin' to throw her for good no matter what I do myself." He paused and looked Abner belligerently in the eye. "Do you blame me?"

"No, I don't," admitted Abner, curiously moved.

A silence fell between the two room mates. Abner experienced a warm feeling toward Tug at this strong moral stand which his companion had developed so unexpectedly. To get away from the emotional topic he asked, "Where you goin' to-night, Tug?"

"Oh—out ramblin'."

A certain reticence in this expression told Abner that his room mate was going to Squire Meredith's for the evening. Tug began working at his automatic again.

Abner looked at the weapon and presently asked delicately, "D'reckon you'll need yore gun, Tug?"

"Never can tell, the boys may take a notion to rock me in," answered Mr. Beavers indifferently.

This referred to a custom in Lane County of the young men of the neighbourhood waylaying a suitor and chasing him away from his sweetheart's home with stones. The customary retort to this demonstration was for the swain to draw a pistol and fire it into the darkness. The assailants then ran away. If the suitor had no pistol, all he could do was to run and trust Providence to protect him from the stones.

Mr. Tug Beavers cleaned and loaded his pistol; then, having performed what one might call the drudgery of social life in the hill country, he brought up water and tub and bathed. He put on his Sunday suit, and for a moment hesitated between his green tie and his red one. Through some new-born reticence aroused in him by the charms of Miss Meredith he finally selected the green one and had Abner tie it. Mr. Beavers never could tie his own four-in-hand because he was used to tying hame-strings, which is like tying a four-in-hand from the front. His own tie was a four-in-hand as tied from behind. This reversed position always threw Mr. Beavers into the greatest confusion, and tying his own tie became an impossibility. By the same token he tied an extremely neat scarf around Abner's neck. The two young men exchanged these little services regularly.

When Mr. Beavers was gone Abner continued in the hot

shabby room filled with a faint loneliness and despondency.
He wondered again about Mr. Ditmas and the five hundred
dollars; whether he had done right in refusing the money.
This theme barely bordered his thoughts and drifted away
again. The motif which persisted was Tug Beavers going to
see the Meredith girl. Why this should persist, why it
should fill him with this faint undefined melancholy, Abner
had not the least idea. Nevertheless, it did.

Abner arose, raised the torn red window shade which
Tug had lowered when he took his bath, and then sat down
on the edge of his bed looking out over the shabby village
street. The hardness, the dirtiness of the scene recalled the
soft vistas of the poorhouse farm. At about this time
Beatrice Belle would start after the cows. He thought
wistfully of the Sandages; then he recalled Railroad Jones;
then Squire Meredith again. He remembered with a certain
sharpness that the Squire had said Nessie Sutton lived in
Irontown. This fact apparently had been the magnetic
centre about which revolved the vague whorl of his mood.
Nessie Sutton lived in Irontown. He looked out the window
with an irrational feeling that he ought to see her. But the
stores still faced him with their tobacco signs, with a few
ancient circus posters weathering from their sides; with a
loiterer or two moving across the lumpy street; and it
seemed to Abner that he had come to where Nessie Sutton
lived, and she had faded into thin air. He would never
see her again. And that was the poignant thing hidden in
tying Tug Beavers's tie and sending him off to see the Meredith girl—it was the vanished Nessie Sutton.

Abner drew a deep breath, stretched out his legs, humped
over, and stared fixedly into the squalid street. At that
moment a voice below at the Scovell House gate called his
name. An absurd hope twitched through him that it was
Nessie Sutton herself who, in walking past, had seen him in
the window. He thrust his head out hurriedly and looked
down. Leaning against the gate under the hotel sign stood
the tall angular form of Zed Parrum.

"Hey oh, Zed," called Abner rather blankly.

Mr. Parrum looked up with a grin on his rudely carved face.

"Jim Sandage is elected," he said.

"What?" Abner tried to straighten this news out in his mind.

"Jim's elected trustee of the county."

"He is!"

Abner was quite stirred at this change in the fortunes of his foster-father.

"Yeh, an' he's goin' to move to Lanesburg."

"Well, I declare!" exclaimed Abner.

"Yeh, an' Perfesser Overall has got the school down here in Arntown to teach."

Abner sat staring at Zed at this remarkable news. Presently he reacted hill-wise and repeated the stereotype which was being used from one end of the county to the other in describing Professor Overall and his new place.

"Well, they shore have got a smart man in books, Zed, even if he is a plum fool in all other respecks."

Zed shut one eye and winked solemnly and approvingly at Abner.

"Now they didn't skip it."

CHAPTER VIII

ABNER TEEFTALLOW joined Zed Parrum at the hotel gate and they strolled together down the street to the garage where they fell in with other labourers on their half holiday. These men whiled away the afternoon telling and listening to obscene jokes. Their thoughts played around women, drinking, and gaming, the three easements of their monotonous pointless lives. They smoked, chewed tobacco, spat on the cement floor of the garage, and enjoyed the human warmth of their oaths and verbal nastiness.

The men who supplied the jokes and anecdotes were called "liars." These primitive efforts at fiction always gave their hearers a kind of supercilious disdain for the narrator. He was such a "liar," they would say; for neither teller nor hearer had any conventional fictional frame upon which to stretch the woof of the "liar's" narrative and so maintain their mutual self-respect.

During the afternoon, the garage listened to the "liars" and made plans to shoot craps that night in a skirt of woods to the south of Irontown; a place given over to that sport or passion. Abner went back to the Scovell House and ate supper, full of hesitation about the coming night of craps. He was afraid of losing his money; and then he thought if he could win a few dollars . . . He was not aware that winning or losing was a minor detail of gaming.

When he finished his supper he went up to his room, drew out his week's wages, recounted it, and then stood in the middle of the floor with that drawn feeling in his diaphragm which marks profound hesitation. He did not want to go to the crap woods, nor could he endure to stay in his room. He fingered the money in his pocket. He made a move to sit on the edge of his bed, but instead, went to his window and peered out into the gathering darkness. The premonition of coming evil, which arises out of unsettled nerves, oppressed him. Zed Parrum had promised to call by the hotel for him, and now as Abner looked out of the window he saw Zed's angular form coming through the gloom. Zed whistled up, and Abner, immensely relieved that a decision had been made for him, put on his hat and hurried downstairs.

On his way down he almost collided with a girl coming up through the darkness. It seemed to Abner that this girl must know that he was going to a crap game. When he passed her he stood stock still, listening to her retreating footsteps down the long hall until his reason told him that she did not know his purposes.

Abner joined Zed at the door, and without a word the two went out the gate and set off down the street in the darkness.

Once Abner had embarked on the expedition he was very glad of it. It accelerated the whole tempo of the evening. A sense of adventure, a possibility of danger quickened his pulse. Their road presently deserted the main street for alleys among the Negro shacks at the outskirts of the village. These cabins merged gradually into the woods themselves. The alley dwindled to a path. As the boys walked along it other stragglers began to appear in the gloom moving toward the crap grounds. At two or three hundred yards' distance someone fired a pistol a number of times—a sudden hard hammering too rapid for Abner to count.

Some of the nearer stragglers whistled discreetly at the two youths and Zed answered them. Three men came up; one had a bottle. He passed it around with "Have a jolt." "Take a kick." "Bail her out." As each man drank he wiped the mouth of the bottle carefully on his shirt sleeve and returned it to the owner. There was a certain ritualism about it which impressed Abner as being urbane and cultured. These Irontown men certainly had a polish one didn't find in the hills.

A fire shining through the woods guided the gamesters to the crap grounds. A picket stationed some fifty yards from the fire identified the newcomers and allowed them to pass on. If an officer approached, this picket whistled a warning and the gamesters pocketed their money and dice and were found simply standing around a fire blackguarding each other in their usual social fashion.

The gambling place was a hard bare circle of earth, swept clear of twigs and grass, about fifteen feet in diameter. A fire of pine knots gave light. Half-a-dozen hillmen and two or three Negroes were already in the ring playing. A Negro squatted on his haunches had the dice and was shooting them out with a jerk of his hand and a snap of his fingers. As he shot he grunted, "Huh . . . hot dam, come up, Tom Paine . . . huh. . . . Come up, old Tom Paine . . . huh. . . . Come up an' look at yo' daddy . . . huh!"

At each "huh" he gave the dice a twitch which sent them spinning on their corners on the hard, smooth dirt. The pair would dance like tops, settle, and the Negro would whisk them up almost instantly and continue his monotonous chant.

Every player strained his eyes in the firelight to see what pips had rolled uppermost. Suddenly someone shouted, "Dough pips!"

The Negro stared at his seven, struck the earth with his fist. "Hot dam, old Tom Paine th'owed me down wid dough pips!"

Came a moving of the little piles of coins in the ring as they changed owners. The next player took up the dice and began the same sing-song, "Big Dick frum Boston . . huh. . . . Come uhlong, Big Dick. . . ."

Abner joined the circle and stood looking at the shooters weave their bodies about and spin out the dice. Other labourers were continually joining the ring. From the pickets came a series of guarded whistles which challenged each newcomer. Presently the crowd grew so thick that another

ring and a new fire were started, and a second circle of
players began shooting and betting.

In Abner's circle the men stood or squatted on their
haunches and tossed their stakes on the ground in front of
them. Those who stood raked the money into little piles
with the toes of their shoes.

This ring of money in the firelight fascinated Abner.
It appeared to be a kind of ownerless money engaged in some
hazardous adventure of its own. A squatting man edged
over and let Abner into the circle. The boy hesitated,
reached into his pocket, and fingered his money. Presently
he drew out his bills with hands that trembled so that he
could hardly unroll the quarters they contained. One of
these coins fell to the ground. He had a sudden flair
that this meant good luck. He squatted and pushed the
shining disc into the ring.

The dice were now in the hands of a white villager, one
of those dubious small-town Beau Brummels who exist without apparent labour. He was shooting with tremendous
esprit. His point was nine.

"Come on! Come on, you ninety days in jail! Git uh-
way frum here, feevy! What the hell! Goin' up thu Nashville! Ninety days in jail! Huh. . . .

> "Oh jedge I says, you cannot fail
> To gimme ninety days in jail. . . .

Huh! Stan' up, little ones!"

Abner watched this eloquent shooter and wondered
tensely whether or not he would make his point, Ninety Days
in Jail. If he could only know in time! Suddenly it appeared to Abner that such a devil-may-care must win. He
pushed out his coin and mumbled with a thick tongue,
"Quarter says he makes it!"

"Fade you!" said the man who had moved over and tossed
a quarter on top of Abner's. No sooner were the stakes laid,
than the shooter threw a seven.

"Crapped out!" shouted the Negro. The man raked Abner's quarter into his pile with a single gesture.

The sight of his quarter shifting to his opponent's money shook at Abner's nerves. He felt an angry necessity of winning it back. He got out another quarter with still unsteadier hands and flung that on the ground.

"I bet he"— then he hesitated not knowing whether to say wins or loses—"loses."

His neighbour covered Abner's coin with the quarter he had already won from the boy. He bet carelessly because he was betting inside Abner's pocket.

The shooter who was half drunk stood on his knees, weaving about, chanting at each shot, "Come up, Little Joe! Don't deceive yo' pappy! . . . huh. . . . Hot dam, Eights frum Decatur! Come up, you little son uv a gun . . . huh. . . . Hot dam, Big Dick frum Boston! . . ."

The succession of shots formed a continuous strain on Abner's nerves. He leaned forward, peering intently through the firelight to see what pips rolled uppermost. Every nerve in him vibrated. He did not know it, but the swift succession of suspenses and dénouements was a profound relief from the plodding monotony of his week's work. It was a spiritual refreshment. Hope and fear, gain and loss rushed past quickly enough for Abner to lose himself in the impetuous current of the game.

The dice whirled out, were snatched back, were whirled out again. . . . A Negro was shooting now, and at each sway and croon he might have been screwing up a string in Abner's head.

"Little Feevy!" Five was the black man's point.

Abner bet against him.

"Come on, little gal!" quavered the Negro, weaving about. "Stan up fuh yo' baby . . . huh. . . . Go way, box cars, come on little feevy . . . huh. . . . Thah you ah, honey chile, lookin' yo' baby in de eye. . . ."

A rake of his neighbour's hand swept Abner's wager into his own pile.

The youth bent down and trembled in the fellow's ear, "Gimme change fer a ten!"

"Throw it down an' shoot it out!" whipped back the man, who had no time for making change.

Abner tossed his ten-dollar bill to the earth.

"Much you want to bet?"

"Fifty cents he falls off," snapped Abner.

The gambler tossed a half dollar on to the bill; at that moment the black shot a three and a four.

"Hell far, a nachel!" cried someone.

The man picked up his half and tapped the bill, which meant a half dollar in it was his.

This was a fantastic thing; a bill which a moment before had been Abner's now was only partly his. It had been nicked; there it still lay on the ground, but would melt away, or grow. . . . Abner could feel his heart beating tumultuously.

"Dollar he makes his next point!"

The man threw the half dollar on the bill.

The Negro with his endless crooning threw eleven. Another natural. The ten-dollar bill had cured itself and had brought Abner a fifty-cent piece besides.

The play went on and on. Abner's attention focussed on the shooting with cataleptic intensity. His money grew and shrank. Now it was a greenback, now a pile of silver and two or three small bills. The blood pounded in his temples. The Negro won and won.

Suddenly above the profanity some player cried, "Crooks!" Instantly there came a thudding of fists, oaths. Abner saw two men rolling and pounding each other in the firelight. A moment later the Negro was thrown bodily from the ring by half-a-dozen hands.

Abner was conscious merely of extreme exasperation that the play was stopped. He crouched with his hands over his money, waiting for the game to be resumed. When the next shooter, a white man, picked up the dice, it seemed as if some intolerable gap had been bridged. Abner's nerves settled in their cycle of suspense, dénouement, pleasure, pain. He made his hazard concerning the future, even if that future were separated from the present by the merest tick of time. Still he was using his powers of forecasting a functioning his daily life did not hold. The boy played on and on.

The stars of the summer night wove slowly overhead as these devotees of the dark Goddess of Chance knelt at their devotions. Once in the syncope of his gaming Abner saw Tug Beavers come up to the firelight out of the darkness and join the gamblers. Near Tug sat Peck Bradley. The throw of the dice moved around the circle from man to man. Presently the cubes were in Tug's hands. Beavers was shooting when a voice snapped out:

"Lemme see them dice!"

Tug began, "What the hell . . ." when Bradley cut in, "It's that nigger's pair o' crooks!"

Tug cried out, "Damn it, look at 'em!" and threw them down.

"You've switched! What's up yore sleeve?"

Abner saw Peck jerk at Tug's sleeve and rip it open.

For a moment Tug seemed on the verge of smashing the face of his accuser, but Peck's hard animal face, his hog-bristle hair, and the fact that he was then on trial for murder must have halted Tug, for he said with a dry swallow:

"There, damn ye, I reckon you see I ain't got no dice 'cept them what was handed me!"

Bradley grumbled dissatisfaction but loosed Tug, and the next man took up the play. But the quarrel between the white men had broken up the spirit of the game. Three or four men arose and took themselves off through the darkness. Abner played for perhaps another half hour, when the last of the gamblers deserted the game and the youth was forced to quit. He took up his money, uncounted, and put it in his pocket. His bent knees were so stiff that he toppled over when he tried to rise. He straightened his legs with pain and at last stood on his feet and walked.

Tug Beavers joined Abner grouchily. "Damn fool," he growled, "accuse me of running crooks. . . . I kain't use crooks nohow. . . . I practised a lot with 'em, but I kain't run 'em. . . ." He continued his bitter meditations and finally said, "Don't know what's the matter with Peck Bradley, thought me an' him wuz the best of frien's."

A player walking through the darkness near the two answered, "You don't know. Where you been to-night?"

"Jess ramblin'," said Tug, trying to see his questioner. "What makes you ast that?"

"Nothin', cep' Peck Bradley used to ramble hisse'f in the direction you took tull he got into that trouble over killin' ole man Shelton; then Squire Meredith forbid his daughter from seein' Peck."

Mr. Beavers hesitated a moment, then said in another tone, "Oh—I see. . . ."

"Yep," agreed the informant, "I guess if you had made a move when Peck ripped yore shirt it would have been Katy Lock the Door with you, all right."

This was said very cheerfully, considering that the phrase "Katy Lock the Door" meant that Tug would have been killed.

"They ort to hang that damn rascal," denounced Tug earnestly.

"My dad," answered the voice discreetly, "told me to think what I pleased so long as I don't say nothin'."

Tug moved away from Abner over to the man and began talking in a lower tone.

Presently a stranger walked up by Abner's side and after a few words about the crap game ventured the remark that rich people could play cards in their own houses, but poor men were forced to go to the woods for their gambling. From this he went on to say that the rich took all the earnings of the poor, which was not right. After that Abner caught phrases about "class consciousness," "unearned increment," "plutocrats," and presently this strange fellow was saying that the labourers on the railroad were grossly underpaid. They were worth, he said, ten or fifteen dollars a day, they should receive this amount or strike for higher wages; it was shameful to allow Railroad Jones or any one else . . .

The unknown had a queer sharp accent, which reminded Abner somewhat of Mr. Ditmas. The fellow evidently was a Yankee—that is, a trickster. Abner wondered what was his trick? The youth walked on in a protracted silence, not understanding a word of what this Yankee said. The excitement of gambling still danced through his head and made the blood beat in his temples. When he reached the dirty alleys of the Negro houses, his grumbling companion left him and Abner walked on alone. Occasionally the strangeness of his recent companion's remarks came to him—the men ought to have ten or fifteen dollars a day—then he could see the dice spinning again before his eyes. . . .

The first gray of dawn glimmered in the streets as Abner turned toward his hotel; by the time he reached the gate, a delicate pearly light suffused the scraggy mulberry bearing the Scovell House sign and gave it a certain softness of outline. As he opened the front door the bells of the distant Catholic church began a solemn ringing for early Mass on Sunday morning.

CHAPTER IX

MR. DITMAS might have spared himself any effort in advertising his proposed Sunday baseball, for the news, once hinted, spread over the village with the swiftness of a fire alarm. A defensive reaction set up at once. The merchants discussed the new departure with confused disapproval. Some of them were afraid something would happen to their village if they played ball on Sunday, a storm, a fire . . . a bolt from Heaven.

The garage itself was undecided on the point. The boys who were to play this unholy game shuffled about, spat dubiously upon the cement floor, and would ask each other, "Air you goin' to play, Jim?" "I'm goin' to do what the rest of you do." It turned out that everyone, Abner included, was going to do what the rest did. Tug Beavers alone stood out against this flaccid unanimity. He swore he would throw his influence in the right direction no matter what he did himself. This was interpreted to be anti-baseball propaganda.

While the men of Irontown were vague and inarticulate on the point, the women were clear-cut. High-pitched denunciations of Sunday baseball were flung across backyard fences. The telephone wires buzzed with the outrage. For example, the bell tinkled in the home of a Mrs. Roxie Biggers, who before her marriage was a Northcutt. She was a tall, thin, humpbacked woman with a thin, hawklike face, a compressed mouth, a thin, humped nose with the lobes cut in the high triangles of temper and wilfulness. This good woman's husband, Mr. Timothy Biggers, a druggist, had not made a suggestion in his home since the day of his marriage, twenty years before. Instead he had taken quietly to the use of laudanum and other sedatives, thus escaping by way of the back door a hard and intensely religious world entirely dominated by his wife.

When Mrs. Biggers got the news over the wire she acted at once. She seized her hat off the bed, clapped it on her gray hair in any fashion, and hurried out into the street, her thin lips pressed together in determination. She set out walking in the direction of the home of her brother, Mr. Perry Northcutt, the banker.

When Mrs. Biggers reached this residence, she entered without the formality of a ring, hastened down a hallway, and then with the briefest rap entered the combined sitting room and bedroom of her brother and his wife.

When Mrs. Biggers entered she found the banker, his fat, rather sullen-looking wife, and their three children engaged in family prayers. At this sight Mrs. Biggers was somewhat soothed, a certain sweet satisfaction welled up in her bosom, for she was eleven years older than the banker and, during his childhood, had occupied toward him a maternal relation. Now to see her brother kneeling in prayer reminded her of their father who had been dead these many years, and she thought, "If there ever was a real Christian, brother Perry is one."

As Mr. Northcutt finished his devotions, his sister broke out abruptly, "Perry, did you know that man Ditmas is getting up a baseball game for this afternoon?"

The banker arose deliberately from his kneeling.

"I had heard it."

"What are you going to do about it?"

"It may not be true."

"You know it's so, ever'thing bad and wicked is so."

Mr. Northcutt hesitated, then said, "I don't know that I am going to do anything about it, Roxie."

This was a literal truth. He did not *know* what he was going to do. He had been worrying over the question all that forenoon, and in his prayer he had been silently asking

God what should he do about the desecration that threatened the village Sabbath.

His answer irritated Mrs. Biggers instantly. "You don't *know!* Do you mean you are not goin' to stan' up for your Lord and Saviour against the devil?"

The banker's wife, who was perhaps the most tactless woman in all Irontown, now said in her flat nasal tone, "Perry does a lot of business with them railroad folks . . ." and this was the truth.

Mr. Northcutt glanced at the fat mother of his children in sharp irritation. She had blurted out what he had meant to say by careful, self-respecting innuendo. The wife's answer set off his sister.

"Trade! Bankin'! Givin' over God's day to revellers for dollars! What good will dollars do you when you come to die?"

"Now, Roxie, I didn't say that; Nannie there said that!"

"You know that's the real reason," stated Nannie in her flat, matter-of-fact voice.

"There are a lot of things to be considered," pursued the banker, disregarding this interruption. "You must remember Ditmas is a Yankee, and Northern people don't look at these things like we do. I don't think they live quite as close to God as we do."

"What's that got to do with it? We've got laws against disturbing the Sabbath, ain't we, even if the Yankees ain't? No, Perry Northcutt, you know yore duty as well as I do, and if you don't go down and stop that game this afternoon, I'll do it myself!"

With that she started out of the room. The banker made a gesture after her.

"Now, don't you be flying off like that. If it's got to be done, I'll do it."

"Well, see that you do," and Mrs. Biggers left the house and went striding back to her home at her characteristic gait.

The contemplated action was thoroughly distasteful to

the banker. It threatened to break up his highly profitable relations with the railroad if he antagonized Ditmas; still, to violate the Sabbath was wrong; he shouldn't allow it. Moreover, he had been praying earnestly to God for direction in this crisis of his life and—Roxie had come. . . .

While the forces for righteousness were thus mobilizing in the village, a very half-hearted spirit moved the baseball players themselves. When the crowd gathered in the old field south of the railroad site nobody really wanted to play. All the players wanted to drop the matter but could not because they were victims of their own gregariousness. Even the score or so of spectators were uncomfortable.

Mr. Tug Beavers was the only man who refused point-blank to enter the game. He stated flatly, "When I do a wrong thing, I mean her to be wrong and I don't pertend she's right like Mr. Ditmas is tryin' to do. By God, no matter what I do myself, my influence is goin' to go in the right direction."

The players were impressed with this stand. There was something bracing about it. One or two others withdrew, there was a re-selection from the spectators, and the game finally proceeded.

During all this preparation a mere breath of persuasion would have broken up Sunday baseball in Irontown, but unfortunately, at this juncture, Mr. Perry Northcutt arrived.

The banker came walking over the railroad levee from the direction of the village; a thin figure clad in funereal black. From the moment he appeared the game halted automatically and all eyes focussed on Northcutt. When he came nearer the crowd saw he had a bloodless, placatory smile on his thin face and that he was rubbing his hands together in a most diplomatic manner. In his heart the banker earnestly wished to be diplomatic and agreeable. He knew that thousands of dollars in bank deposits and the good will of the managing engineer hung on the outcome of his venture.

He would have given it up most heartily if his conscience had permitted.

The banker came on until he was well within the circle of players. He nodded at those whom he knew with his conciliatory smile.

"Boys," he began in the voice of an elder speaking to children, "do you think it is quite right to be playing ball here on the Lord's day?" This phrase, "Lord's day," produced a clear-cut distaste in his hearers, whose mental associations with it were uniformly monotonous and disagreeable.

"Don't you think if He gives you six days to enjoy yourselves you might set apart one day to worship Him?"

Every man in the crowd took an antagonistic point of view at once. Somebody said, "What's the use in not playing ball? We ain't goin' to church noway."

It was characteristic of Northcutt that he could never brook the slightest opposition. Now he said in a sharper tone, "At least you won't be desecrating the Sabbath with your whoopings and shoutings!"

"Don't God like to hear folks have a good time?"

"He tells you how to have a good time! He doesn't say 'Play ball,' He says retire to your closets and seek Him in prayer. If you men would do that—eat the secret bread of life on your knees in your closets!" the banker's face lighted with eremitic zeal.

Another voice put in, "Well, Sunday ain't the Sabbath anyway, it's Sattidy. Do you keep Sattidy holy? Wasn't you doin' business at yore bank yestiddy?"

"Look here," cried the banker, irritated at this ancient thrust at the date of Sunday, "when Christ came to this earth, you know the old dispensation was finished and a new one began. They changed the day of worship from Saturday to Sunday. . . ."

The banker had launched one of those futile Biblical arguments characteristic of the hill people. That the banker should indulge in it amazed Mr. Ditmas; at last it moved him to speech.

"Look here, gentlemen, we know the purpose of either Saturday or Sunday—it was a day of rest; but for active young men rest doesn't mean doing nothing; their normal rest is play, a change from the routine of work, that's the spirit of the Bible."

The banker turned on the engineer tensely. "Mr. Ditmas, I'm surprised to find you encouraging Sunday sports! Do sports glorify God? The Bible says retire to your closets and pray! That's the way to spend the Lord's day, not in wicked sports!"

Ditmas was astonished at the banker's harsh hebraism, but was saved from saying anything more by Mr. Tug Beavers, who injected himself into the argument.

"All right, boys," he shouted, "let Perry Northcutt have his way. If it's plain-out wrong to play ball on Sunday, by God, I'll have a game myself. Come on, let's play!"

He waved his thick arms toward the diamond and a number of players followed him out into the field.

The banker was beside himself. "Stop it!" he cried in a high voice. "I try to be nice to you barbarians and you won't let me. I've got the constable right behind that railway dump waiting to take you up with a warrant if you don't stop desecrating this day! Now, you ain't going to do it, boys. I'm telling you!"

"Take us up!" exploded Tug. "I'm not skeered of you, you damned little spindle-legged, knife-faced hypocrite! You break the law ever' day chargin' eight per cent. in your damned ol' bank, then come out here tryin' to bust up our baseball game cause it's wrong! Bring your officer and be damned to both of you!"

The gratification of "cursing out" the banker extended to every man in the crowd when a dry voice said rather calmly, "Hold on, Mr. Beavers."

The crowd parted and a graying middle-aged man moved

toward the disputants. He held up a finger at the banker and asked in an assured and faintly supercilious tone, "Perry, you talkin' about God not approving of this and that—what makes you think there is any God?"

The whole crowd came to a horrified hush at this new departure. The banker looked at his new antagonist.

"Now, look here, Belshue," he said in a different tone, "I'm not going to argue with any infidel. Unless you believe in God, you—well, you just ain't human, that's all."

"You won't argue because you kain't prove it," said Belshue, staring at the banker with gloomy eyes.

"Prove it! I don't have to prove it, I know it!"

"How do you know it?"

"The same way I know I'm talking to you. I go to my heavenly Father and He speaks to me just as plain as you're speaking now. Once I was prayin' to Him when my little daughter died and He come down and touched my head and blessed me. Praise His holy name! Praise God! He brought me a peace you will never know, Andy Belshue, till you find God, too. Find Him, brother, find Him!"

The banker's thin face lighted up as he related these supernatural experiences.

"That was imagination," stated the jeweller, who knew every inch of the ground he was defending. "That doesn't prove there is any God."

"My imagination!" cried the banker, turning paler. "Don't you think I know my own Father's voice!"

The crowd was, by common impulse, turning back to the village now, the disputants with them. They would probably have stayed and played ball had not Belshue begun his shocking argument. Abner Teeftallow and his friend Zed Parrum followed behind the wranglers. Abner could hardly believe his ears.

"Zed, don't that man Belshue believe in no God?" he whispered incredulously.

"No, he's a infidel," returned Zed in the same tone.

"They say he can out-argue anybody. He reads Ingersoll and Tom Paine."

"Don't he know he'll go to hell?"

"He don't believe in no hell."

"He don't!"

"No, it don't make no diff'runce to him how bad he gits; he don't believe he'll git punished fer it. He thinks when he dies he'll jest be dead; that's all."

Abner stared after this fantastic man in horror. As the banker suggested, Mr. Belshue seemed scarcely human at all, but a sort of moral monster, ghoulish, unimaginable. At last a corollary struck Abner, and he asked Zed in a quick voice, "Look here, if he don't believe in no future punishment, why don't he rob and steal and jest raise hell generally?"

"Search me," grunted Zed. "I've often wondered why he don't myse'f."

Such a course of action seemed indicated to the young men because they held the hill belief that all wickedness was inherently pleasant, and all virtuous and right things were by nature unpleasant.

It was this same belief which had caused the banker to come out and break up the baseball game. If the workmen got pleasure out of it, it was sinful. All pleasure was sinful. Out of pure conscience Mr. Northcutt had placed thousands of dollars of bank deposits in jeopardy to prevent in the labourers the sinfulness of enjoying a pleasant afternoon.

CHAPTER X

IRONTOWN spent the rest of Sunday afternoon filled with that sense of monotony and endlessness which marked all Sunday afternoons. The villagers walked slowly along the hushed streets in their Sunday clothes; the merchants either slept away the time or sat about in front of their stores, like patient dogs ejected from their kennels awaiting the moment they would be allowed to return. The village girls yawned at home, wishing for beaux, for the telephone to ring, for a bit of scandal—anything.

Abner Teeftallow and the other labourers spent the afternoon in the garage retailing brackish anecdotes and inventing crude rural ironies about Perry Northcutt for breaking up their game. The energy bottled in their strong, dirty bodies moved them to some sort of reprisal for their defeat in baseball. They wanted something lawless, indecent, to set out their contempt for the whole churchly population. Their plans moved inevitably toward what was called, in technical legal phrase, "disturbing public worship." They meant to gather around the church during services that evening and fire pistols outside the house until the congregation became frightened and ran away. This would be exciting and retaliatory.

Abner went to supper at the Scovell House pondering whether or not to join the proposed batteau. The feature that restrained him was that he had no pistol and did not see how he could get one. He thought of going along with the boys and throwing stones at the church, but such pinchpenny methods of disturbing public worship made him ashamed. "No," he thought with decision, "if I kain't disturb 'em like a gentleman, I won't disturb 'em a-tall."

So it looked as if he would not be in the marauding party until he reached his second-story room and saw Mr. Beavers again preparing his automatic for a call on the Meredith girl. Abner looked longingly at the blued-steel firearm and at last said, "Look here, Tug, d'reckon you'll haff to use that to-night?" Mr. Beavers turned his eyes deliberately toward Abner with an effect of immense courage.

"Don't know, if anybody wants to try me out, this is a free country."

"I knowed you wasn't skeered," explained Abner quickly. "I was thinkin' about somepin else." He halted irresolutely.

"What else?"

"Well, the boys are goin' to run the folks out of church to-night, an' me not havin' no gun . . ."

"You ort to git one."

"Good God, don't I know that!" assented Abner fervently.

"A man goin' around without a gun looks kinder sissy."

"I ain't sissy, Tug; I've been jest dead pore all my life. I ain't had no chanst to fix myse'f up."

There was something plaintive in Abner's tone and position. Tug made inarticulate sounds and continued preparing for his evening call.

"If you wuz shore you wouldn't need yore gun, Tug . . ." resumed Abner hopelessly. "I hate like hell to jest set here till bedtime . . . nothin' to do . . . they don't go to bed here in town till nine or ten noway. . . ."

Now Mr. Beavers had developed a certain sympathy for this poorhouse lad he had picked up on the road to Iron-town. He looked at his automatic, pulled his face to one side, scratched his head.

"Ab," he drawled, "I hate like hell to discommode you, but why in the hell ain't you got a gun?"

"I told you already, Tug."

"Oh, hell, here it is, take it along. Know how to work it?"

"I'm going to git one of my own as soon as I lay by the money, Tug."

"A man's got to git his start in life," admitted Mr. Beavers generously.

Abner had no further preparations to make, and as soon as he could do so without unseemly haste, he got away and hurried to the garage where the hillmen had planned to fore-gather.

As Abner walked through the darkness, the weight of the pistol in his pocket gave him an exhilarated feeling of being a "bad man." This pleasure was connected in some obscure way with Nessie Sutton. It would be incorrect to say that Abner had set out to disturb a Sunday evening service to impress Nessie Sutton, but if there had been no girls in the congregation there would have been no boys with automatics on the outside.

When Abner reached the garage his gang was setting out in twos and threes for the church. Abner picked Zed Parrum for his companion, and Zed was a satellite of Peck Bradley's. So these three went together, the murderer, the fool, and the innocent.

As quickly as possible the trio deserted the village street and took to the back alleys, in order, as Peck explained, to set up alibis when the matter came up before the next circuit court, as it probably would.

Abner moved just behind his two friends in pitchy dark-ness. His enterprise gave him much the same sort of ex-hilaration that he might have received from the ball game that afternoon. His thoughts wandered about and presently reverted to Nessie Sutton; how she would open her blue eyes if she could know he was out with a man indicted for mur-der. She would certainly think him a hell-bent yaver—and he really was. There could be no doubt of that. He was a hell-bent yaver out of Yaversville!

Zed's pull at his sleeve drew Abner out of his musings.

"Huh, what is it?"

"Peck here ast if you had a gun." Parrum's voice was full of respect for the slayer of old man Shelton.

"Yeh, I borrowed Tug's automatic."

Mr. Bradley was interested at once. "What's Tug goin' ter use?" he asked in his hard voice.

"He ain't comin' here."

"Skeered?"

"Nope, goin' over to ol' Squire Meredith's to-night."

Came a silence, then Bradley said in a sneering tone, "I God, I see, runnin' after that Meredith gal. All I got to say is he's welcome to her, fur's I'm concerned. I wouldn't wipe my foot on a gal like her. She ain't fitten to be the wife of a sawdust monkey." After this hearty disapproval Mr. Bradley mouched along in the darkness for half a minute and then out of his reflections began a nasal ditty to a melancholy hill tune:

"Tell me you love me, give my heart ease,
  Then when my back's turned, love who you please."

He broke off his own song to say, "Well, here we air," and the next instant he must have lifted a heavy revolver, for six crashing flames spurted into the blackness. This was a signal for a fusillade all around the church. Shots roared in every direction, the flashes winking like fireflies.

Great excitement seized Abner. He got out his own weapon and with a trembling hand fired it at the skies. At every discharge the big automatic leaped in his hand.

The three disturbers came around a turn in a little alley and saw the church looking very large right in front of them. Through three open windows Abner could see the congregation rising in fright. The headiest excitement seized the youth at this milling of the people in the lighted interior. He fired his automatic in a roaring, leaping staccato. He rammed in another clip of cartridges. He was an Indian ambushing settlers; a soldier routing enemies. In reality he was a hillman putting on a demonstration of wildness before the possibility of a girl. His pistol roared at the girls inside, "What a wild man I am! Think of such a man as I for a lover!"

Inside the church the young hill women were shrieking, not in terror, for they knew they would not be hurt, but to let the young men outside know they were impressed by their firing and courage, that they were moved by this wild romance. It was a sort of tumultuous courtship; a roaring antiphony of sex.

The men in the church did not take kindly to the demonstration. They came running out, furious as disturbed hornets. Abner did not know the fine points of disturbing public worship. He did not know enough to run at this swarming of the men, but stood firing Tug's pistol in a kind of ecstasy. He did not realize that the flashes of his automatic were conspicuous in the darkness.

Flashlights blinked here and there. Came cries of "Halt! Stop! Throw up your hands!" The next moment a light was shining directly at him and seemed to be rushing at him at a rapid rate; a voice shouted, "Throw up yore hands, there, you country jake, or I'll shoot ye!"

A shock went through Abner. He whirled automatically and dashed up the lane. The roar of the revolver behind him seemed to shake the world. Bullets whispered by his ear, "Psst! Psst! Psst!"

Abner felt as light as a feather. He seemed to fly along the alley, just touching the ground here and there. Right ahead of him in the faint unsteady light that played over and past him he saw a tall picket fence. Horror swept through him as he dashed toward it. He was in a cul de sac. As he hurtled at the barrier a superhuman tightening went through his legs and chest. He dashed at the ghostly outline of the fence with his whole body screwed up for a terrible effort. Next instant he launched upward. A mighty power in his legs shot him high in air. His flight over the sharp pickets took his breath. He landed inside among the soft ridges of a garden. He struck the ground with the wild goose of fear still winging through his heart. He dashed ahead, clambered a fence on the opposite side of the garden, landed in a vacant lot, ran again, came to another fence. As he mounted this he saw ahead of him a twinkling procession of lights. It was the churchgoers on their way home.

A plan to give his pursuers the slip popped into Abner's head. The next moment he leaped off the fence and went legging it toward the twinkling line of lights. He meant to lose himself in the procession. He went as hard as he could run to within forty or fifty yards of the line, then slackened his pace and tried to control his gasping breath before he merged himself with the others. As he approached one or two flashlights turned on him, but as they did so he stooped as if he were picking up his hat which had somehow blown off in the windless night—that was the trick he had thought of—then he entered the line.

Everybody was talking about the hill billies who had broken up the meeting. Abner moved up the line, passing the marchers uneasily. He felt conspicuous. The angry talk disturbed him. He gained on the line, looking anxiously for a place in it where he could become a unit in the ranks. Now and then he looked behind him for a pursuing flashlight, but there were so many now, it was impossible to tell anything about them. Any of those lights might be an officer. Just then he saw a gap in the procession. A woman, or a girl, was walking alone. The manner in which she walked suggested it was a girl. Had it been a woman Abner could have stepped in beside her simply enough, but a girl was different. However, with a great effort the wild disturber of public worship took his heart in his hands and moved into place beside the young woman, and thus became entirely merged with the home-goers.

No sooner was he in place than he began speculating on how he could get out inconspicuously. It would be noticeable for a man simply to desert his girl companion when he came to the hotel. He thought of saying, "Well, so long.

I'll see you later," to make those behind think he had been to church, but this did not seem entirely natural.

They were now approaching the Scovell House, where he would have to do something. He could see the spraddling mulberry and the hotel sign illuminated by the lights passing under it. He thought he would simply turn in without a word. Then a wild notion came to him to walk on home with the girl. This might entail explanations at the other end, but it would be a postponement. He decided to risk it. He was nerving himself to pass his hotel, when to Abner's surprise the girl stopped at the gate. Utterly at sea, Abner opened the rickety gate for her and let her through. The flashlight procession continued on its way unaware that the most dramatic coincidence in the lumpy life of a hillman had just occurred.

The girl evidently was well acquainted with the Scovell House, for she entered the door, walked over and picked up a small kerosene lamp which sat on the newel post of the stairway, and turned up the wick. This low-burning lamp was the amenity which the Scovell House offered belated guests; it was, in fact, the one thing that differentiated the Scovell House from the private residences along the street.

As the girl turned up the wick the two silent companions saw each other for the first time.

Abner looked, then stared in amazement at the colourless oval face, the coils of pale colourless hair, and the large melancholy eyes that looked black in the lamplight. Yet even in the disguise of the yellow light he recognized her and gasped out, "For God's sake, Nessie Sutton, is it you I walked home with!"

The girl's hand trembled so she could hardly hold the lamp.

"Yes, it's me—I knew you were here the very first day you came, Abner. I knew it was you walking by me just then." There was a tinge of reproach in her tones.

Abner could not get on with his thinking. He stared at her.

"Well, I declare! Well, don't that beat a hoss a-flyin'!"

He could not take his eyes off her. He could not realize what had happened. She seemed entirely unlike what he remembered of her in the courthouse yard. Some mysterious change had come over every line and feature, yet through all this variation of memory, she was the same girl who had so held his attention and stirred his pulse at Lanesburg. That meeting seemed ages ago.

Nessie was first to break the long silence of staring.

"You was one of them pistol shooters, wasn't you, Abner?" Her voice carried neither surprise nor reproach.

Abner nodded in silence.

She regarded him solemnly. "Don't you know that's wrong, Abner—on Sunday night, too?"

"Perry Northcutt busted up our ball game; we thought we would bust up his church."

"You know it isn't Perry Northcutt's church—it's God's church."

The girl's tone was level enough, but she breathed as if labouring under some strong excitement; then she turned with the lamp and started upstairs.

Abner followed her in the grip of a growing depression. He felt that the night's enterprise somehow had failed. Nessie, apparently, had not thrilled at his wildness and bravery, although it was a fact the oil lamp shook so in her hands that she could hardly carry it.

They turned together down the long upper hall in the tensely strung silence. Evidently she knew what room he occupied; she paused before his door for him to enter. As he went in she said in her hushed, reproachful tones, "Goodnight, Abner."

The boy returned her good-night gloomily and went inside.

He lighted his own lamp, took out Tug's automatic and laid it on the rickety dresser whose cracked mirror gave him back a travesty of his own image.

He began taking off his shoes and trousers in great depression of spirits. Presently he drew a long breath and murmured aloud, "Well, good God Almighty, what does it take to please a damn gal anyway?"

Before Abner got into bed Tug Beavers came in. He, too, was sweating at every pore. Abner asked in surprise, "Was you shootin' aroun' the church, too?"

Tug explained amid long breaths that he was not. He had been coming back from Squire Meredith's place when a form arose apparently out of the road beside him. He had not been afraid, but simply had asked who it was. There was no reply. Tug then walked toward it, but the form floated back from him as if his air had brushed it aside. Tug then picked up a stone and threatened to knock the thing in the head, but no sooner were the words out of his mouth than a pistol fired and a bullet whizzed past Tug's ear. Then, Tug said, he had come on home.

As Abner sat on the side of the bed looking at his panting, sweating friend, it occurred even to that unsuspicious youth that Tug had eliminated considerable detail in the brief phrase he had "come on home."

CHAPTER XI

WITH the reëntry of Nessie Sutton into his life, the boyhood of Abner Teeftallow, one might say, ended. Thereafter, the texture of his thoughts was no longer the Pan-like dallying over the mere surface of things which constitute childhood. The girl brought a certain unity to his mental life. Take, for example, the smallish man who had grumbled to Abner on the night of the crap game about the injustice of the rich toward the poor. This man proved to be a labour organizer, and a few days later returned to his logical attack. He declared that Railroad Jones was oppressing the men on his construction works by not paying them a living wage.

Abner stared at Mr. Shallburger and drawled naïvely, "If anybody ain't gittin' a square deal, why don't he quit?"

"Quit!" snapped the organizer. "Labourers can't quit work; men of wealth own all the instruments of production; besides, it's the human right of these men to have a living wage."

This struck Abner as nonsense. He said he guessed the men must be getting a living wage—didn't see anybody dying.

Shallburger looked at Abner clearly, pondering whether or not to answer such a lump. Finally he did speak, slowly, as if teaching the alphabet to an infant:

"A living wage doesn't mean merely food and clothing for a man. It means enough to rear a family, to educate them so that they in turn can go on with life"—here a little enthusiasm warmed his voice. "Suppose all workers made just enough for their individual selves; then, so far as they were concerned, creation would come to an end when they

died.   A living wage means that life shall go on, Mr. Teeftallow, that it shall grow larger and better, not less and worse."

At the time Shallburger made this argument, it seemed the
veriest nonsense to Abner; men striking to-day so there would
be more and better labourers twenty years from now—
fantastic.

But it was Nessie Sutton who eventually vitalized the
organizer's theory.   After the youth's first accidental meeting with the girl, he now saw Nessie briefly every day.
Every afternoon at six o'clock he glimpsed her as she passed
across the piazza of the Scovell House.

Abner ate his own supper at five, along with the other
labourers, but instead of going immediately to the garage,
Abner loitered in the porch swing of the hotel until six, when
Nessie returned from her work uptown.

For a number of days he had confined his remarks to a
mere "Good-evenin'" as she passed in to supper, which she
ate with the Scovell family after the men boarders were
finished.   When she had entered the dark hallway, Abner
would get out of the swing, look after her as she disappeared
inside; then, filled with a queer faint pain, he would take
himself off to the garage.

For a number of days he spent an hour regularly for this
rather unhappy glimpse of her.   Then one afternoon she
quite startled him by pausing in the doorway, turning to look
out at the dilapidated village which lay in the yellowing
light, and saying that she was so tired she didn't want any
supper.

This sudden chance to begin one of the many conversations
he had planned startled the youth.

"Are you sick?" he asked in an anxious tone.

"My back hurts—I stoop over all day sewing."

"What do you sew?" asked Abner, following his frail clue
eagerly.

"Hats.   I'm Mr. Baxter's milliner."   She hesitated,
then added to assist this self-conscious conversation, "I'm
getting ready for our fall opening."   She drew a long breath,

as if the very thought of the fall opening wearied her, and her bosom lifted and fell beneath her rather deeply cut blouse.

The expressiveness of this bodily gesture brought home to Abner that the girl really was tired. A protective feeling toward her arose in the teamster and filled him with a dim trouble. It also took his mind from the thread of conversation which held them momentarily secure in each other's presence. The seconds ticked off. The silence arose like a wall, separating them once more. In desperation Abner was about to tell the girl that one of his mules had flung off a shoe that morning. He was on the verge of this when Nessie said:

"I saw you walk by the Grand to-day."

"Did you?" asked Abner gratefully.

"Yes, Mr. Northcutt was in there talking to Mr. Baxter about the boys shooting up the church Sunday night."

Abner became genuinely interested. "What did they say?"

"Mr. Baxter said if they found out who did it the lawyers up at Lanesburg would get them right out—I guess they would, too, you can't depend much on the law to help anything," added Nessie thoughtfully.

A trickle of uneasiness went through the teamster; he lowered his voice a trifle and asked, "Did you tell 'em what you knowed, Nessie?"

The girl was shocked. "Goodness, no! I was so afraid they'd ask me—I couldn't tell a story, and I wouldn't told who done it either. I was jest sitting there scringin', wonderin' what in the world I'd say if they ast me, when Mr. Northcutt said when the courts failed a community, God would help 'em."

The teamster stared at the girl blankly. "What did he mean?"

"He's plannin' to have Brother Blackman come over from Cypress Creek and hold a protracted meetin'. I hope he will. It would give a person somewhere to go, and then we need it."

This last phrase was said rather pointedly, but Abner

responded, "Yes, I guess we do," as impersonally as if he had not been one of the disturbers on Sunday night.

By this time the conversation was well launched, apparently, but somehow Abner's unprogressive "I guess we do," finished that topic completely and left the two young persons in another painful lacuna. Abner began thinking frantically for the next thing to say. The topic of his mule's shoe bobbed up again in his mind but was put down. However, it effectively held its own against all other themes.

The youth and the girl looked at each other, caught by this queer shy silence of hill lovers. Finally it became impossible to remain any longer in each other's company. Nessie said in a mechanical tone, "I guess Miss Scovell's waiting dinner for me," and went inside.

Abner drew a long breath as she disappeared. As much as he regretted her going, still—it was a relief. He got up from the swing, went out the gate and up toward the garage.

As he went he recalled every word of their conversation exactly as if someone were repeating it in his ears. Nessie had sewed till her back ached—she was a milliner and had to trim hats for a living—it made her tired. This fact filled Abner with distress. If he could only take this burden from her! If he and this blonde girl with the burnished yellow hair and blue eyes could only . . .

Now it was just at this point that Abner recalled the fellow Shallburger's dictum on the necessity of a man's making a living wage—a wage on which a man could marry, rear children, and keep the world going on. . . .

The "world going on" now meant for Abner, Nessie Sutton living in pleasant idleness in some pleasant home where he came after each day's work.

And Nessie should do nothing! She should rest from morning till night in a porch swing! He was emphatic in his thoughts about that. The æsthetic justification of mere beauty—of a delicate untoiling blooming—filled Abner with a tenderness he had never known before.

Later in his life, when the years must inevitably dim Nessie's corn-silk hair and fade the pansies in her eyes, Abner would look upon his household drudge with the stolid indifference of all hillmen for all hill wives, but just at this moment the thought of Nessie wearying her fingers by lifting so much as a cambric needle filled him with a melancholy as exquisite and aching as the dawn of first love itself.

CHAPTER XII

MR. ZED PARRUM came to Abner's room one afternoon to say that old man Elihu Warrington who lived three miles out on the Florence road was going to give a dance that night, and he insisted that his two friends should go.

There was something about Zed, his roughly chopped humorous face, that suggested country dances. Mr. Tug Beavers immediately began speculating on how he would send word to Mary Lou Meredith. Abner said he would take the note.

"Ain't you goin' to take yore gal, Ab?" asked Tug.

Abner warmed between embarrassment and gratification.

"I don't know whether she'll go or not."

"Do you mean she's one of them damned stuck-up town gals?" asked Zed drily.

None of the trio objected to the adjective Mr. Parrum applied indifferently to all village folk.

"I don't know if she be or not."

"For the love of sukey—don't know whether yore gal's a town gal or a country gal!"

"Go along and send her a note," counselled Tug, "and if she won't go with you, tell her to go to hell."

"We-ell," agreed Abner dubiously, and both the room mates began looking for paper and ink on which Zed Parrum was to write the notes.

This task fell to Zed because the awkward fellow possessed the queer accomplishment of being able to write a copperplate hand. Zed agreed good-naturedly, cleared a space on the boys' dresser, drew up a chair, and assumed what he explained was the "side position." Mr. Parrum had taught writing schools in Lane County, and never could write in the presence of any one without explaining how it was done— he rested his arm on the pad of muscles under his forearm, he held his pen so the nails of his little finger and his ringfinger glided smoothly over the paper, thus . . . here Zed broke into easy gyrations with his pen and drew a bewildering bird. The boys were in amazement at his expertness. Then on a page of pink notepaper he reproduced this form from the Ever Ready Letter Writer, or Epistolary Forms for All Occasions:

MISS NESSIE SUTTON, City.

MY DEAR MISS SUTTON, Mr. Abner Teeftallow requests the pleasure of your company to the dance at the home of Mr. Elihu Warrington at eight o'clock this evening. *Wednesday*.

ABNER TEEFTALLOW.

Without pausing he wrote a duplicate note to Miss Mary Lou Meredith. The two hill youths murmured oaths of admiration at Zed's performance. As a matter of fact, the only form of art ever practised among the hillmen is beautiful writing. This occasionally breaks away into the purely decorative and becomes a floridly drawn bird. It is only through handwriting that the pictorial art can form a liaison with the useful and practical and thus find any lodgment in the culture of Lane County. These narrowly hedged artists plead that calligraphy will be useful in book-keeping; but none of them ever keeps books. It is, in reality, a tiny tendril of pure art creeping up by subterfuge in that arid spiritual soil.

Abner was to carry Tug's note, and Tug, Abner's, to their respective girls. The two young hillmen set out at once, Tug to the Grand, and Abner walked on out of the village to Squire Meredith's place.

The poorhouse boy swung along happily out of the village into the country again. An extraordinary charm had fallen over the world for Abner. The colour of the light falling aslant the hills reminded him of Nessie's yellow hair. The musky smell of the weeds which the farmers allowed to over-run their fence corners foreshadowed his coming walk with Nessie through the perfumed summer night. Out of the gladness of his heart he began alternately singing and whistling the refrain of "The Cowboy's Lament":

> "'Oh, bury me not on the lone prairee
> Where the wild ki-yote will howl o'er me . . .'"

From the top of the higher hills Abner paused to look back at the village. He could see the dumpy steeple of the church where he had "disturbed public worship," and he reflected with a little thrill that he was indeed getting to be a hellion—gambling, drinking, shooting . . .

A little to the south of the village lay the new railroad, a raw red cut which extended in a level curve around the swell of a distant hill. Here and there were faint yellow cross-hatchings, which Abner knew were piles of ties ready to be laid. Close to the village the road was completed, and Mr. Ditmas was expecting a locomotive to haul material from the main line to the labourers.

As Abner looked he saw a feather of smoke on the southern horizon, then a distant shriek told of a freight train coming up the main line. To Abner there was always something wild and terrific in the blast of a far-away train, and now the thought struck him, suppose he and Nessie should find themselves in peril as they crossed the track going to Mr. Warrington's that night. . . . He could see himself seizing Nessie, swinging her to safety while, a second later, the locomotive struck him. . . . A sense of physical crash quivered along Abner's spine; he would be flung to one side, Nessie would rush to him . . . lift his dying head in her arms. . . .

Abner moved on, tears prickling his eyes. Around the turn of the road he made out Squire Meredith's house.

The old justice of the peace was throwing corn to his pigs

over his lot fence into the public road, and Abner received a fleeting impression that the old man had never left off doing this since he had seen him last.

Squire Meredith put down his basket and hailed Abner with pleasure. He began shouting questions in a large out-of-door voice asking Abner how he liked the railroad work, how he liked the town, how he liked his boarding house, did he get a good one, when Abner interrupted to ask for Mary Lou.

Squire Meredith changed from his cordial tone completely.

"Now, look here, you've got a note fer Mary Lou."

"Yes, I have," admitted Abner uncomfortably.

"Is it from that snake-in-the-grass Peck Bradley, or from that low-down, no-'count, whisky-guzzlin' windy-mouthed Tug Beavers?"

Still more reluctantly, Abner acknowledged it was from Tug. "Well, I don't want my gal to go traipsing off with none o' his kind," stated Mr. Meredith flatly.

"Squire Meredith," inquired Abner logically, "who in this neighbourhood can she go with, then?"

"None, I reckon! None a-tall!" stormed the old man, shaking his fist at a reprobate world. "Ever'body an ever'-thing's gone to the dawgs, and here it is right at the end of the world—it does look like we're all bound fer destruction to-gether. Oh, my Lord, young man, where air we bound fer! Where air we bound fer!"

Abner recalled with a little shock that the world was indeed to end in October—and he had forgotten it. He was amazed at his own feather-headedness. He said frankly to the Squire, "I be dad blame', do you know, Squire Meredith, I forgot what you tole me about that, shore as God made little apples?"

"You forgot it down in that wicked gamblin' city!" declaimed the old man, "and it's jest where you should have remembered it the most."

"That shore is right," admitted Abner, astonished at his own folly.

"Ay, Lord," sighed the old man, "and Lot prayed if they

wuz jest ten righteous people in the whole city would He save it, and God said He would, but they wuzn't ten—Ay, Lord! Same here, Abner, jest exactly the same here!" The old man thumped the top rail with his calloused fist and stood shaking his head in the fading sunshine.

Abner hadn't the faintest notion what he was talking about.

Miss Mary Lou Meredith must have heard the noise her father was making and divined its cause, for presently Abner saw her appear in the dark doorway of the farmhouse and then start to the gate with a certain curiosity in her manner.

Squire Meredith broke off his tirade to watch her approach. He remained quite silent until she reached the gate and had come to rest with her hands on its top, then he asked significantly, "Did you want anything, Mary Lou?"

Mary Lou made an unconvincing display of fanning her olive cheeks with her handkerchief. "I jest come out for a breath of air."

Abner began a movement to produce the note when the Squire said flatly, "Well, there is air in all directions, Mary Lou."

Mary Lou's dark brows puckered. "I declare, Pap," she ejaculated sharply, "air you an' Abner Teeftaller talkin' sich secrets I kain't stan' here at my own gate?" Then she changed her tone completely and asked cordially, "How air ye, Abner?"

"I jest come by . . ." began Abner, so embarrassed he could hardly get the note from his pocket.

"Put that right back in yore pocket, Abner," directed the old man sharply.

The girl flared up. "Now there you go ag'in! If the worl' ain't goin' to last but till October I don't see why I should be kep' penned up like fatt'nin' stock!"

The old man smote the top rail. "None o' yore high jinks aroun' me, Mary Lou! I simply ain't goin' to have that Peck Bradley comin' aroun' me!"

"Peck Bradley!" snapped the girl in sudden scorn. "Do you think I'd look at that murderer! After him killin' ole man Shelton over a pig! A stray pig!" Mary Lou flashed with temper, and it quite astonished Abner that anger could improve a girl's looks.

"Well, that other one, whatever his name is—is jest as bad, he drinks."

"Didn't you drink when you was a-courtin' Mammy?" flared the daughter, "an' would she ever got married to you a-tall if you hadn't been drunk—— Oh, that's what made a prohibitionist out o' you!" she pointed her finger scornfully at her father.

Came a pause. Even the leathery old face of the Squire grew duskier.

"You've been listenin' to that cat of a aunt of yours! You kain't believe a word she says, never could! Besides, Mary Lou, it was diff'runt in them days! Whisky was legal then. We had a legal right to drink what an' when we pleased! An' what did the apostle Paul say?—Take a little wine fer your stomick's sake——"

"Well, don't he still say it?"

"I—I don't know."

"Well, did he say git married on it back in them days?" cried the girl satirically.

"My Lord, Mary Lou!" cried the old justice of the peace bitterly, "that happened afore you wuz ever born!"

"I should hope it did!" flamed the girl.

Squire Meredith flung up his weathered hands. "Lord, Abner, what kin I say to sich a gal! You're modern, Mary Lou! You've got a lot of this all-fired modern information in yore head and it's goin' to drag you down to a devil's hell, that's what it's goin' to do. You better pray to God instid of traipsing off to these new-fangled wicked dances!"

"Didn't you go to 'em?" cried Mary Lou in exasperation.

"I'm a man, Mary Lou!"

"Who'd you dance with—other men?"

"Lord! Lord! Lord!" The Squire looked up at the heavens in genuine dismay, "What a daughter! What a daughter! I don't see where in the worl' you inherited such corruptness of heart—an' this present dispensation nearly finished, too!"

By this time it grew clear to Abner that he was listening to a quarrel which would go on indefinitely. He finally interrupted: "Well, I guess I better be goin' back. I jest come out fer a—er—little walk." He glanced about vaguely as if searching for one.

A moment's silence. Then Mary Lou asked belligerently, "When is it to be, Abner?"

"To-night," replied the youth in a hurried tone.

"Tell him yes," snapped Mary Lou.

"What!" shouted the Squire, outraged. "No, you don't, Abner Teeftaller!" He shook a finger wildly in the air. "You tell that young man if he shows up here, I'll—I'll—— Mary Lou! You go right back in that house! Go on back! You're not goin' off with that scapegrace Peck Bradley!"

"It ain't Peck!" screamed Mary Lou. "It's Mr. Beavers! An' he's a gentleman, ever' inch of him! I only wish *you* had half the polish an' manners . . ."

"You're not goin'!"

"You tell Tug I said yes, Abner!"

"Lord! Lord!" cried the justice, "this is goin' to be a purty howdedo! I saw that Peck Bradley hangin' aroun' my barn the other night!"

"Don't you bother yore head about that!" advised the daughter harshly.

"But there's goin' to be trouble over it, don't I know it!"

"Well, it'll be Peck's trouble! Mr. Beavers can fan out a fiel' full o' Peck Bradleys. He's ten times as stout as Peck ever dared be!"

This last came faintly to Abner as he walked rapidly away. He heard Squire Meredith make some angry answer; the girl replied; he left the feud in progress.

Abner walked on down the road, wondering at Tug's taste. What a noisy brunette sort of girl compared to the fairness and sweetness of Nessie! He couldn't understand Tug!

When Abner reached the hotel he entered his room and found his friend sitting gloomily on the bed. His first words were,

"I forgot to tell you, Ab, to sort o' shy aroun' the ol' man. I don't guess you got no answer."

"I got a verbal one," grinned Abner. "She said come on."

"What!"

"She yelled at me, 'Tell him, yes!' "

"Tell who yes?"

"Well, if she knowed who she was talkin' 'bout, I reckon you ort to!" and Abner began laughing outright.

Mr. Beavers's spirits improved somewhat, but even at that he fumbled gloomily in his pocket, drew out a very small envelope, and handed it in silence to Abner. With it came a whiff of perfume. It was directed in a girl's large wobbly hand to "Mr. Abner Teeftallow, City." It was unsealed, the flap turned inside.

Abner suddenly became so nervous he could hardly pull out the flap. This tremulousness swiftly spread over his whole body down to his very knees. At last he did have the note out and open in his fingers. He could barely read the unsteady page.

Mr. Abner Teeftallow, City.

Dear Mr. Teeftallow. Miss Nessie Sutton regrets her inability to accompany Mr. Teeftallow to the dance but she has a previous engagement.

Very sincerely yours,
Nessie Sutton.

Added to this was a woman's postscript, evidently not copied from the Ever Ready Letter Writer. The postscript said:

I couldn't have went anyway, I belong to the church.

Painful antithesis to Miss Meredith!

Abner continued looking at the fragrant paper for some minutes after he had finished reading it. Tug sat scowling on the bed. From the hall below came the opening and shutting of a door. Both youths involuntarily strained their ears and presently heard a faint careful tiptoeing of someone passing their door.

Tug nodded savagely toward this noise, "There she goes now," he whispered. "Jest step out there in the hall, Abner, an' tell her to—go—to—hell!"

CHAPTER XIII

A S ABNER opened his door the girl in the hallway glanced around at him, apparently on the verge of flight. This wrought up the teamster more than ever. He stepped out in the hall, moved by some irrational impulse to pursue her and make her retract something, he scarcely knew what. He called her name in a shaken voice.

Nessie paused, looked around at him, and asked in a tone as disturbed as his own what he wanted. Abner did not know what he wanted or what he meant to ask her to do. He moved her note which he still held in his hand.

"You kain't go to the dance?"

"Abner," she said breathlessly, "I told you in my note I belonged to the church."

The teamster's heart beat so heavily that the girl seemed to shake in little pulses before his eyes.

"But you said you had another engagement."

Nessie nodded almost imperceptibly.

An exaggerated apprehension seized Abner.

"Who with, Nessie?"

The girl flushed abruptly. "You mustn't ast me that."

For her to keep any of her affairs hidden from him seemed almost unbearable to Abner. He moved impulsively toward her.

"But you must tell me, Nessie. . . . Good Lord. . . ."

He seemed so imminent, so wrought upon, that the girl was almost afraid of him. She took a pace back, breathing unevenly.

"Mr. Belshue," she said in a scarcely audible voice.

Abner came to a stricken pause, staring at her.

"Mr. Belshue!" he repeated, stupefied.

"Y-yes."

"Not—the infidel . . ."

She nodded again with a whitening face and explained unsteadily: "I—I thought I—could help him—maybe."

Abner's mind jumped from the point of religious faith completely.

"Why he—he's—old. . . ."

Nessie took a sharp breath, pressed her lips together, then apparently ceased breathing.

"Why, Nessie!" cried Abner, as much now out of concern for the girl as for his own pain, "you jest kain't go with a man like that! Tell him he kain't come no more—and a infidel!" he stared at her aghast, then suddenly the irony of it struck him and he cried in scorn, "You kain't go to a dance with me on account of bein' a church member, an' stayin' at home to keep comp'ny with a *infidel!*"

The girl made a piteous gesture and seemed on the verge of tears. "Oh, Abner, you don't understand, I—I kain't jest stop him like that. I—he's been comin' to see me for three seasons. . . ."

Three seasons! This length of time spread before Abner with a devastating inference. He had thought Belshue was interfering in his courtship; now he saw that his own suit was very recent and that he was intruding on Belshue. The teamster was steeped in the hill convention of respecting another man's courtship as religiously as his marital rights. No two hillmen ever went to see the same girl at the same time. Abner himself was at fault. He had trespassed on the jeweller's vested rights.

He stood breathing through his open mouth, moistened his lips with his tongue. "You ought to of told me the first day you saw me settin' on the porch waitin' for you—some kind of a hint——" The hopelessness of his plight filled him with despair. "Do you shore 'nuff like him, Nessie?" he cried piteously.

"I—I don't know whether I do or not," shivered the girl.

"Do you like him better'n you do me?"

The girl shook her head with the tiniest and briefest of shakes.

"Then, fer God's sake, tell him he kain't come no more!"

"Please! Please! I kain't tell him that! I kain't do it, Abner. He's been so nice to me. Not another soul in town ever spoke to me 'cept him." Her eyes filled with tears. "He—he got me books, if—if it hadn't been for him I guess I'd gone plum crazy!" she broke off, biting her lips to control herself.

Abner felt the justice of this. "So you won't send him off?"

Nessie gave her head a little jerky shake, blinked, and turned away to her room.

Abner stood and watched her go down the hall, filled with that sense of profanation which an old rival always inspires in a young lover. For Belshue to come to see Nessie at all was somehow a monstrous thing. As Nessie turned into her room at the end of the hall she seemed to Abner a sort of human sacrifice offered up to Age.

He went back into his own room with his misery in his face and bearing. Tug Beavers looked up anxiously as his friend entered.

"Do any good?" he queried in a low tone.

Abner shook his head.

"She wouldn't go with you—after that!"

"Nuh-uh."

"Why?"

"She's goin' with somebody else."

Tug was shocked.

"Who?"

"Belshue."

"Belshue!"

Abner nodded.

"Well I—be—damn' . . ." A long pause, and Tug continued, "A infidel—why, Abner, that man'll drag her soul straight down to hell, don't she know that?"

"She thinks she can convert him."

"Convert hell! Don't she know he's the brainiest man in town? Of all little she-fools!"

After a while Tug came out of his amazement and began to prepare for the dance. He laid out all the appurtenances of a dance: tie, clean shirt, cartridges, buttons, automatic, Sunday suit. . . . It was high time he was setting out for the Meredith place, for no one knew what finesse he would require to get away with Mary Lou. In the midst of these preparations he glanced at Abner, who sat humped over on the bed, hands hanging between knees and staring at the straw mat which more or less covered the floor.

"Ain't you goin'?"

"No-ope."

"What you goin' to do?" he asked with concern.

"Don't know—Shallburger's goin' to have a meetin' to-night."

"A meetin'! Is Shallburger some kind of a preacher?"

"Naw, he says he's figgered out a way fer ever'body to live happy an' not work so much," explained Abner vaguely.

"Hell, if a man don't do nothin' he'd nachelly be happy; say, Ab, be independent, git another gal an' come on to the dance."

The very thought of another girl filled Abner with a sense of physical repulsion. "Good Lord—no," he shuddered.

Presently he got up, found his hat, and moved slowly toward the door.

"I'll jest see what Shallburger says—it'll beat settin' here listenin' to——" He nodded bleakly toward Nessie's room and moved out the door.

After her interview with Abner, Nessie Sutton went back to her bedroom a-quiver in every nerve of her body. She did not know what had happened to her. She entered her bare room with a sensation of being tall and giddily poised. She thought of Abner's face, the tones of his voice, the way he held her note in his hand. Back of these dancing pictures was the unhappy duty she must perform. She entered her room, went over to her dresser, and stood with her hands on the cheap scarf—she must dress to receive Mr. Belshue. With a deep sigh she went to her trunk, opened it, and stood thinking which of her two dresses to wear. She had two, a revealing lawn of pale blue, open of throat and with sheer sleeves, and a gray travelling dress. As she looked at the gray dress she was moved to swathe herself in it against Belshue, but that would have been absurd for evening wear. The conventions of women always override any impulse toward modesty which may untowardly arise in a particular member of the sex.

Under the gray dress lay a novel which Nessie had been reading. As she picked this up, the contrast between the pure-hearted heroine and her own ambivalent mood dawned on Nessie for the first time. She herself was pure perhaps, but not single-hearted. She was not perfect, impeccable, as was the heroine of the romance in her hands. The hero of the book was a handsome drunken gambler. It was the sort of fiction which flooded the South during a period just preceding the Civil War. All the heroes of this period were idle young men given to drinking, gambling, and venery. These novels, all written by women, represented the only point of view which a woman could take of such a type and still accept him for a husband. They were written straight out of a defensive complex and contained a bitter veracity beneath their high-flown sentimentalism.

Nessie laid out her blue lawn, and still feeling tall and insecurely poised, began taking down her yellow hair.

CHAPTER XIV

A T EXACTLY four-thirty-six of the same afternoon—precision in matter of time being almost forced upon one in the jeweller's repair business—A. M. Belshue, watch tinker and village infidel, sat at his desk with the light from his dingy window filtering down over him and with his magnifying glass screwed monstrously into his left eye. He was soldering together the broken hand of a tiny Swiss watch and was getting along badly with his work. He interrupted himself every few minutes by leaning forward and peering at an acute angle through his window down the street. The reason for this was that at some uncertain moment at about this time of the afternoon Nessie Sutton would walk out of the Grand, where she worked, on her way home. And if he could hit the exact moment of her departure, he could, by leaning forward and peering at an angle, get a ten- or twelve-second view of the milliner's assistant as she walked away.

Belshue's nervous straining after a glimpse of the girl told several things about the jeweller. One was that he did not feel at all sure of Miss Sutton; another, that he had never put his arms about her and kissed her, for just as marriage loses for the husband all those little eagernesses and ardours which go to make up the lover, so the ripening familiarities of courtship destroy those first gazings and wistfulness of the eye which serve as airy kisses and caresses until some solider demonstration takes their place.

As the time drew near when Nessie either must go, or else already had gone without having been seen—this last a painful possibility—Mr. Belshue abandoned his task altogether, got up, walked around the little railing which kept

the curious from meddling with his tools, went to the door
and looked out. He leaned against his dirty casement and
watched the village street as it lay in the afternoon light.
He looked and looked, apparently at nothing. Every person
who passed out of the door of the Grand delivered a little
shock, and, an instant later, a little disappointment to the
graying stoop-shouldered man who stood motionless in the
door of the jeweller's shop. He waited but for Nessie's
pleasant figure to fall upon his eyes. He knew she would not
so much as glance around at him as she went; she never did.
But there was something warming to the jeweller in the
mere view of Nessie, as if the sun shone upon him. The
fact that within three hours he would call on her, talk to
her, gaze on her to his fill, all that had no reference to this
immediate craving. He must see her at this very moment.
So he stood looking and looking with the demented patience
of a lover, afraid to remove his eyes for a moment from the
stodgy entrance of the Grand lest he miss her altogether.

Presently it became apparent even to Belshue that he
must have come to the door too late. He glanced into his
shop to verify this. Beside his desk stood a large board on
which were hung more than a score of watches which he was
regulating. The hands of all these watches, with a unanimity uncommon among timepieces, stood at precisely twelve
minutes after five. So he had missed her. Nessie always
left the Grand before five. That was the hour set for her
departure, and like all girl employees in all businesses, she
watched the clock and left the Grand on the dot.

Mr. Belshue turned back into his shop and stood by the
rail looking at the brace which held the tiny gold hand of
the Swiss watch ready for soldering. He had no heart to
return to his work. He looked again at the boardful of
watches as if somehow they had tricked him. The round-
faced chronometers returned his stare impassively. In the
silence of the shop their many tickings filled his ears as with
the flight of numberless tiny feet. As he listened to it with
fancies tuned to disappointment, it sounded as if Time might

be a Lilliputian army double-quicking (to what purpose?) down the endless slope of eternity.

Belshue gave up the shank of the afternoon altogether; he brushed briefly at any dust or glint of gold filings which might have clung to his clothes; then, glancing at his watches again, this time to calculate how long it would be before he really called on Nessie Sutton, he turned out into the village street.

Now, as a matter of fact, Mr. Belshue had nowhere at all to go. There were four or five places in the village where men congregated for whatever social life was possible in Irontown. "Loafing places," the villagers called them, and all the communal life they enjoyed was given this ungracious and derogatory name of "loafing."

There was rather an unexpected range to the village "loafing places" from the thoroughgoing obscenity of the garage up through Bell's Grocery, Bingham's Butcher Shop, to the religio-philosophical gatherings in Fuller's Drug Store. But in few of these places and only on rare occasions would any one debate with Mr. Belshue the existence of God, so the jeweller came and went, filled with a rancorous and unused dialectic.

On this particular evening Belshue did not stop or want to stop at any of these places. He walked along the tranquil street wishing that Nessie were with him, but she never would walk with him in the village. It was one of her notions which pained the jeweller at times, but she would get over that; at least, he hoped she would.

As Belshue passed Fuller's Drug Store he heard an aggressive voice inside demanding, "Gentlemen, see if you can get this 'un: If the half of nine is three what would the third of twenty be?"

Came a chorus of "But, perfesser, the half of nine ain't three. . . ."

At that moment, Mr. Ditmas, the engineer, came out of the door of the drug store lighting a cigar with a twinkle of amusement in his eyes. Belshue was moved out of his taciturnity to ask who was the man inside.

"That's Professor Lemuel Overall," smiled Ditmas. "I understand he is to teach the Irontown school."

The rather genial satire in the remark and the friendly way Ditmas dropped in at his side inclined the jeweller toward the Northerner. All the other villagers were rather stiff around Belshue—in fact, were a little afraid of him. The engineer, however, paid no regard to the cloven hoof of the village infidel but moved along smiling at the village professor. Presently he said quite gaily, "I really ought to have it in for you, Belshue. You are the one who broke up my ball game last Sunday." He offered the jeweller a cigar.

"I!' exclaimed Belshue in surprise. He took the cigar awkwardly, for such an amenity had been offered him hardly twice in his life.

"Yes, your espousal killed it. It was an instance of 'God deliver me from my friends.'" Mr. Ditmas laughed heartily. "How long have you been living here?"

"All my life," answered the jeweller, puzzled.

"That's odd. With your anti-religious views, somehow I felt you might be a Northern man."

"Are there lots of infidels up there?" asked Belshue naïvely.

"We don't exactly use that term," said Ditmas, his eyes resuming their faintly amused expression. "If we speak of the matter we say a man has liberal ideas. Life in the North doesn't seem to revolve around religious creeds as it does down here. One believes what he likes and nothing is thought about the matter."

"Queer state of affairs," mused Belshue. He could hardly conceive a state of society where religion was not the paramount topic. "What do you Northern folks discuss, what do you think about?"

Ditmas puffed thoughtfully. "Well, when you leave out

business, we are occupied with sports, fiction, drama, pictures, dancing, science, philosophy, and such things."

It was noteworthy that every single item in Mr. Ditmas's list was reckoned sinful by the hill folk. This religious pre-occupation had so seeped in around Belshue that the jeweller himself accounted such things, if not immoral, at least a wilful waste of time.

"Don't you Northern people believe something about eternity and a future life?" probed the jeweller out of this mental background.

The engineer glanced at him. "It is hardly ever dis-cussed."

"What do you think about it individually?" persisted the jeweller curiously.

"I—" The engineer paused to consider what he did think about it—"Well, I think we persist after death through our children."

The jeweller stared at him. "That isn't us."

"In a way it is. Our children were once part of us. Then the Old Testament suggests it. It says no man who is emasculated shall enter the Kingdom of Heaven."

Belshue was surprised. "I didn't know that."

"It does. You see, the Jews had an idea there was a close connection between reproduction and salvation. Of course, our modern life has broken up that feeling of solidarity in a family which permitted a man genuinely to feel that he was living on in his descendants. The American family is a far more casual assembly of individuals than was the old Hebrew family."

"But the Bible speaks of Heaven and eternal life," per-sisted the jeweller.

"That's true, but have you never observed that every religious injunction points directly toward the welfare of the young? Take the basic ten commandments. 'Thou shalt not commit adultery.' Why did Moses pick out the specific sin, adultery, whereas fornication is treated as a much lesser evil? There is no spiritual difference between the two.

It is simply because adultery corrupts the home and strikes at the welfare of the children; while fornication is very likely to found a home and protect the resulting children. You see the details of our religious thought are aimed at the preservation of the young. Our present moral code tends to the same direction. All of our novels and plays which exhibit life beyond kindergarten experience fall under the censorship of the Comstock society. The novelist who presents life as pap for babes is praised for his loftiness of purpose and purity of ideas. In fact, there has always been an effort in America to cut its artistic output to fit the nursery.

"Now, is it at all probable, if men possess an eternal soul, that its advancement in a future life would depend on exactly those acts and sentiments which assist in making the world safe for children? Would it not be quite the reverse? It would be a grasping of the actual complexities of life in order thoroughly to master it if we really had an infinitude of life bearing down upon us. No, the general tendency of human culture shows that our personalities cease at the grave." Mr. Ditmas thumped his cigar stump away.

"So you really are an atheist, after all," said Belshue.

"Not at all," denied Ditmas sharply, "if the whirl of nebulous gas can develop worlds which produce creatures of such profound sacrificial instincts that they refuse to look truth in the eye for the benefit of the unborn, creation cannot be dubbed Godless. Consider the pains and the trouble the human race goes to never to think coherently on any question; it is as beautifully pathetic as the stork which feathers its nest from the down plucked from its own bleeding bosom. All other animals see things simply as they are, but man has reached a point where he sees nothing as it is. Only a God could accomplish that."

The two men walked on through the evening with scarcely another word. The jeweller was offended. It seemed to him somehow sinful to speak ironically of nothingness. Belshue's feelings were probably the result of the hill life, where men are solitary with practically no object of thought save themselves. Hence their religious notions magnify the importance of each individual man. Mr. Ditmas, on the other hand, was a child of the Northern cities with their teeming impersonal millions.

CHAPTER XV

THE first faint star stabbing its pinprick of light through the spraddling branches of the mulberry tree held the jeweller's eyes as he pulled the doorbell of the Scovell House. He rang a second time when he heard a rustling of skirts in the dark hallway. He turned expectantly, but it was only the landlady, Miss Scovell, in a slatternly Mother Hubbard dress bringing the lamp to place it on the newel post for the night. She looked to see who was at the door; then, in a voice edged with distaste, directed, rather than invited.

"You go in the parlour—I'll tell her."

She stationed her beacon then went back upstairs mumbling audibly, "Middle-aged old fool—young girl—old enough to be her——" and then mercifully passed out of hearing.

Miss Scovell's detestation was aroused not so much by the jeweller's age as by what he believed. Her mutterings gave the jeweller's thoughts a painful twist. Belshue was two and a half times as old as the girl. Nessie was eighteen. Yet throughout all his forty-five years the jeweller had never deviated in his allegiance to eighteen-year-old girls. Even when he was a little anti-social boy of ten or eleven, young women of eighteen seemed to him the most beautiful, the most comforting creatures in all the world. During his early adolescence, girls of this age filled him with perfervid dreams and desires. In early manhood Belshue's affections were normally engaged. He had plighted himself to marry a girl, then, to his own dismay, had fallen in love with her younger sister. The heretic's love was a sort of fixed spotlight into which and out of which marched a procession of eighteen-year-old girls. In each instance his love had seemed eternal;

he felt he could never love another. Belshue was an artist.

So now, as the jeweller waited on the shabby piazza of the Scovell House, these mumblings of the landlady wounded him. He thought bitterly, "What difference does age make? If a man and a woman really love each other, nothing should come between them."

His heart quickened a beat as he saw the bottom of Nessie's skirt come into the light from the newel post; he marked the little motions of the sheer blue skirt caused by the touch of her knees as the girl lowered herself into view. She looked pale, paler than usual. Her fair hair was coiled in cables about her ears and at the back of her head; some of it was dark in shadow, some gleamed like pale silk. In the lamplight her eyes were very large and dark. She seemed unusually sober and a little strained. She gave him the faintest mechanical smile as she put her hand in his.

"Did you have a good day?" she asked out of habit.

His delicate jeweller's touch could feel the needle pricks, like fine sandpaper, upon the hardened ends of her fingers.

"So-so," he answered, and then turned toward the shadowy end of the piazza. "Let's sit out here in the swing where it's cool."

The girl answered hurriedly that she thought they "had better sit in the parlour" and moved determinedly into the warm dark room.

The jeweller was disappointed. He followed in Nessie's perfumed wake, obsessed with a nervous desire to sit with her in the swing. He even mentioned it again, but Nessie replied in her hurried manner that somebody might talk about them; Miss Scovell said folks had talked already.

The two entered the hot air of the room which Nessie and Miss Scovell called the "parlour." It was quite dark and stale from lack of ventilation. The jeweller swore mentally at Miss Scovell's intrusion in his affairs, then, as Nessie groped for a lamp, a sudden notion came to him to make the most of his opportunity. He would step forward, put his arms about the faintly visible girl, and all at once fling his hopes into the balance. He would ask her to marry him; if she loved him she would yield, if she did not . . . he would know. His heart began beating at his bold plan. He stepped forward, reached out arms that tingled to go about the girl, when there came the scratch and flare of a match. When Nessie saw the jeweller so near her she drew a little intake of breath and stepped quickly around to the opposite side of the table before she took off the chimney and lighted the lamp.

The jeweller watched the operation in silence. He was filled with a quivering sensation at what he had come so narrowly doing. But with the lamp lighted any such proposal became impossible.

Nessie stayed by the queer old china-bowled lamp until the jeweller was seated, and then chose another of the stiff green-plush chairs spaced along the wall at some distance from her caller. Belshue regretted his premature choice of seats. He felt instinctively that while a mature woman may be courted by words alone, a young girl, like other young animals, must be wooed by a series of slight physical contacts. The milliner's assistant seemed inviting. Even in the hot parlour she contrived to look cool. He could see her arms through her sheer blue sleeves, and her hands which lay demurely in her lap vaguely discovered the contour of her rounded thighs. Again he mentioned the heat in the parlour, implying the swing.

"It's been a hot day," she answered impersonally. "They're goin' to have a hot spell for their revival."

There was nothing for it except to make conversation about the dullnesses of village life with this girl sitting three chairs remote from him. He asked who would hold the meeting.

"Brother Blackman. They say he's a wonderful preacher."

Nessie would have liked to talk about the meeting and thus lead to the topic of Belshue's soul, which she once had a romantic notion of saving, but the jeweller let the opening drop. She forewent her plan for evangelization and thought hurriedly for another topic, for she was never at ease in Belshue's presence.

"Had you heard Mr. Ditmas was going to buy some land from Railroad Jones?"

"No, I don't hear much gossip."

"Some men were talking about it in the store."

The disconnection of this conversation was in odd contrast to the silent strife about the swing which was still going on beneath their words. The jeweller tried to break through this irrelevant patter by saying earnestly, "Why do you stick in that store, Nessie? That's no place for a girl like you—in a store—trimming hats."

"I really like trimming hats," she parried quickly. "I like working with colours. Then, it's hot everywhere—I bet it's hot at the dance to-night." This last speculation popped out because she was wondering if Abner had gone on to the dance without her.

"The dance where?"

"At Mr. Warrington's."

A faint jealous suspicion aroused in Belshue. He glanced at her aslant.

"Did you want to go?"

"I couldn't. I belong to the church."

Belshue continued studying her in faintly suspicious speculation. "Did someone ask you to go?"

She said no, no one had asked her. Then a faint colour came into Nessie's face. She sat extremely still, moistened her lips, and a moment later began talking rapidly of any topic that came into her head: of a hat she had sold, of an engine which Railroad Jones would bring to his new railroad in a week or two, of a new mortgage which Perry Northcutt was asking Railroad Jones to put on his property to protect the bank.

This scramble back to the irrelevant filled the jeweller with a kind of rancorousness. He explained with stony patience that no doubt the expenses of the railroad were overrunning the established quota at the bank and the directors wanted more security.

"I'm sure that's it," breathed Nessie, as if a burden had been lifted from her mind.

For the next thirty or forty minutes their conversation was a trying haphazard talk which covers the intimate jangle between illy paired lovers. The girl, three chairs distant from her suitor, still leaned away from him, and Belshue sat bent forward toward Nessie as if a rope were about his hips binding him to his seat.

As Nessie chattered of this and that, she was really thinking with dismay, "I have told a story. I can no longer say I am a truthful girl." Her sense of wickedness grew and grew; it interrupted her speech. At last she looked at the middle-aged man sitting bound in the stiff green chair and said with entire disconnection, "Mr. Belshue, I told you a story."

Her breathy tone, the wideness of her blue eyes gave a serio-comic touch to her confession.

"What was your story about?" asked the jeweller, with the first glimpse of humour he had known during the evening.

"About the dance—somebody did ask me to go with them."

Belshue stopped smiling.

"Who?"

"One of the boys here in the hotel."

The jeweller sat pondering this, also thinking with a thrill how exquisite a thing it would be to have a perfectly truthful wife. Out of his thoughts he said abruptly, "Nessie, I hate for you to stay here. There's no telling who you'll be thrown with. I wish——"

"Goodness, the boarders don't worry me, I'm in my room."

"Yes, but somebody asked you to a dance."

"He wrote me a note."

"A note!" The feeling grew that it really was unsafe for

Nessie in the hotel. "The idea of the fellow writing a note to a girl he has never met!"

"Didn't you?" asked Nessie with a faint smile.

"Yes, but we knew each other in a way—working next door to each other."

"This person works in Irontown."

"That's different," put in the jeweller sharply. "I'm a middle-aged——" He broke off his distasteful sentence to recast it. "I'm a citizen of Irontown and I'm responsible for what I do. You're just a young girl all by yourself in this musty hotel." In the warmth of his speech he somehow broke the invisible rope which bound him to his chair, for he got up and moved toward her. "And it's a shame, you staying in a dump like this, Nessie! And you needn't do it! I've got a place in the country where it's cool. A good place to stay, comfortable. The old Coltrane homestead, if you know where that is. . . ." He rushed on incoherently, passionately, making the middle-aged plea of property. "I bought it ten years ago for its taxes. I thought if I ever did want to marry, I'd have a big old-fashioned manor. . . . Look here, Nessie——"

She got up quickly, frightened at his speech and formidable approach. She put out a hand to ward him off.

"Wait! Stop!" she begged. "Don't talk so loud!"

He dropped to an unsteady undertone. "But I do want you, Nessie! I stand day after day waiting for just a glimpse of you. I want you more than anything on earth! I—I——" The girl's pale crown of hair undid the jeweller's self-control, "Nessie! Good God, you don't hate me!" As he stepped toward her she got quickly behind her stiff green chair with a whitened face.

"Stop! Hush!" she begged in a horrified whisper. "Don't talk so loud; somebody will hear you!"

She stood behind her feeble barricade, her heart pounding so that Belshue could see the pulse in the dimple at the base of her throat. As he approached again she quavered, "Please! Please, stay where you are!"

She was utterly without defence and on the verge of tears. Her novels, her criterions of conduct had never suggested that a girl might have to shield herself physically from a proposal of marriage.

The indignity of the girl dodging from him behind the green plush chair stopped the jeweller quite as much as her frightened whispers and white face. He put one of his hands on hers on the back of the chair and renewed his persuasions more coherently.

"Nessie, I know we will be happy together! You don't love me now but you will! I'd be so careful of you, Nessie, so devoted—at least the old Coltrane place would give you a—a home and a—a background. There's something aristocratic about the old house, just as there is about you! Old Judge Coltrane was an aristocrat!"

This time the name Coltrane set up in Nessie an obscure recollection, "Coltrane!" she thought, "Coltrane!" And it flashed on her that old Judge Coltrane had been Abner Teeftallow's grandfather!

Suddenly the tragic romance of the old-style Southern novel spread itself before the girl. Belshue was the villain; he had disinherited Abner!

But the jeweller caught the hand under his and was drawing her toward him.

"Nessie, I love you more than my life! I'm in misery without you."

At the jeweller's outburst of passion, he wavered in Nessie's mind between villain and hero. Her novel-reading had left her inextricably mixed. She had expected something clear-cut. Now she wavered between equivocal impulses —to jerk away and fly his reddened, middle-aged face; to yield herself, after all, into his arms. A vague something had awakened in her at his roughness: pity, tenderness, the dawn of passion, his patient, long-continued goodnesses to her when no one else even glanced at her. After all, why not? She let his arms go about her, but with a feeling mixed with shame, and somehow with grotesqueness . . .

A heavy noise on the stairs just outside the parlour door shocked the two like the crack of doom. They got apart, with frightened faces. The girl went to the door, straightening her hair. Through the glass she could see a form lying on the steps. In Nessie's overwrought state this seemed tragic. She beckoned the jeweller and whispered, "Who do you suppose it is?"

With a trembling hand Belshue patted the girl reassuringly. "Some drunken fellow, nobody . . ."

But a certain prescience seized Nessie. She opened the door and stepped out on the piazza.

"Bring the lamp!" she ordered sharply.

"Nessie," he remonstrated, "I wouldn't . . ." But he picked up the lamp and followed her. When he got out on the piazza, Nessie was kneeling by the figure's side, her arms around its shoulders. She gasped out incoherently, "Oh, Lordy! I done this! God help me!" She swallowed, and her face worked in the lamplight. "Pick up his legs! Pick 'em up! We got to git him to bed!"

As she seemed on the verge of carrying the bulk alone, Belshue obeyed. When he set the lamp on the top step it showed the white face of a youth drunken to insensibility. A single crimson streak where he had fallen against the step marked his forehead. He was the very hero of her novels come to life—a handsome youth flinging himself to the dogs for her love!

Mr. Belshue picked up the limp legs. He caught them high up on the thighs to take all the weight possible off the girl. Together they pulled up the stairs past the night lamp on the newel post. When they had struggled to the top, they lurched slowly along the hallway to one of the bedroom doors. They got inside and placed the powerful figure on a bed which had not been made up that day. Nessie laid her handkerchief on the wounded forehead.

Then the two samaritans straightened, drew weary breaths, and without speaking walked out into the hall and downstairs again.

On the way down the jeweller ventured an arm around Nessie's waist. The girl undid his embrace deliberately and without meeting any resistance.

"Mr. Belshue," she said with a newly found dignity, "I made a mistake down in the parlour. I am sorry if I caused you to think I loved you, for I do not. If you love me, I regret it very, very much, for I do not love you and I can never marry you—I don't think I shall ever marry. I'd rather you wouldn't come to see me any more. So good-bye and God bless you." She held the door open for him to go out.

A great peace had come over Nessie. Speech and action were in character at last. She could have cited one the gist of this scene and conversation from half-a-dozen novels packed away in her trunk upstairs had she been calm enough to do it.

CHAPTER XVI

A FEW days after Abner Teeftallow's rather justifiable
drunkenness, Mr. Tug Beavers sat on his bed at
the Scovell House filling the room with a strong
smell of iodoform. He was dressing a finger which had got
chewed during a fight at the Warrington dance. However,
Tug had licked his man, Peck Bradley, in a fair fight, so
Abner, Tug, Zed, and all the other denizens of the garage
counted it a finger well spent.

Abner Teeftallow was doing nothing that morning further
than waiting for a certain sound in the hall. To kill time he
was polishing his black hair as glossily as might be and was
trying to persuade it to make a large curl above his right
eye. Mr. Beavers was questioning Abner about what had
happened on the night of the dance.

"What did you fellows do at Shallburger's meetin'?"
he pressed. "He's a feller I kain't quite make out."

"We adopted Socialism."

"What's that?"

"It's a plan to divide up all the work into such little bits,
everybody will be out of a job most of the time."

"That's a hell of a plan."

"Yep, that's Socialism. . . ." Abner drew out his
nickel watch, noted the minute, then began listening more
nervously.

"Who'll support you-all?"

"The Guv'ment."

"How?"

"Pension us."

"Pension hell, don't you know the Guv'ment ain't goin'
to pension you-all unless you got hurt in a fight?"

At this moment Abner heard the sound for which he had been waiting, so began moving toward the door.

"I think Shallburger wants us to petition the Guv'ment to pension us."

"Hold on, wait—what will he say he wants it for?"

"So he won't haff to work—now I got to go."

"Fuh God's sake, hold on. What makes you so fidgety? You belong to 'em, don't you? How come you to join any such fool society?"

Abner opened the door and remarked briefly, "I was drunk," and stepped into the hallway, closing the door behind him.

His exit was accurately timed. Miss Nessie Sutton was just passing the door. He said "Good-mornin'" to the girl, and she said "Good-mornin'." Without further conversation Abner followed her down to breakfast.

The dining room of the Scovell House was dark and smelly as if air and sunlight were luxuries hardly to be arrived at in the country. The table linen was dirty and torn; the silver plating was worn off the spoons; the coffee cost thirty cents a pound. Yet Abner could never enter the dining room of the Scovell House without a certain embarrassment at the magnificence of its service. The Negro table boy in his dirty white coat always intimidated and irritated Abner with his hillman hostility to all Negroes. When the table boy asked Abner would he have his eggs boiled or fried, the white youth felt an inward tremor lest he should say or do the wrong thing.

A still greater hazard of a *faux pas* lay in the fact that Abner ate directly across the table from Nessie, so he was continually under her pansy and, the youth felt sure, critical eyes. Nessie herself unfolded her napkin and ordered her egg casually. She was in no trepidation whatever of the table boy.

Breakfast at the Scovell House began with about a three-fifths-cooked oatmeal, then bacon and eggs and coffee. Abner preferred milk but he felt coffee to be a more manly drink. Nessie herself drank it to keep from having a head-ache, she said. No one ever thought of the strangeness of Scovell House coffee preventing a headache.

Abner held his fork with his first and third fingers outside the handle and his second and little fingers on the inner or body side. His thumb opposed his index finger. This was the peculiar grasp of all hill youths as they clutch at straws of propriety when shipwrecked on social seas.

As breakfast proceeded in this unsure fashion, the table boy emerged from the kitchen, came up behind Abner, and said in a low thick voice, "Gemman wants to see you, Mistuh Abnah."

Abner looked around blankly.

"Wants to see me?"

"Yes, suh."

Abner was amazed. Never before in his life had he been called out by a gentleman. Now, coming on him like this at mealtime, he didn't know what to do. He made a move to go but corrected that as faulty. He remembered he should ask somebody's pardon, he didn't know whose. In rising he spilled his coffee. This unmanned him completely.

"I—I hope you'll pardon me," he stammered. Then, stiff with self-consciousness, he started for the door.

"It's de back do', Mistuh Abnah," said the Negro.

Abner was overwhelmed. To have a guest at the back door! He turned beet-red and started for the kitchen door. The floor seemed to wobble beneath his feet. When he reached the back door he had to stare for several seconds before he recognized the tall awkward form of Zed Parrum.

"Was you eatin' breakfast?" asked Zed in a contrite voice.

Abner nodded and cleaned his teeth nervously with his tongue.

"If I'd a-knowed it, I wouldn't of disturbed you."

"That's all right, Zed, this time, but fur God's sake don't never do it no more."

"This was a case of pushancy," explained Zed in an under-tone. He backed away from the door into the desolation of the back yard and nodded Abner to follow him. The mystery of Zed's manner calmed Abner's discomfiture. He followed, and when they were some distance from the house Zed said in a guarded tone, "I want you to do somethin' fur me."

Abner adopted the same tone, "All right, what is it?"

"I want you to go to the station an' buy me a ticket."

Abner stared, "Why, what fur?"

"That's all right what fur—will you do it?"

"M—yes." Abner stared at Zed in the wildest speculation.

Zed reached in his pocket and drew out a handful of bills and silver coins. He put it all in Abner's hands.

"All right, go ahead an' git the ticket," he hurried. "I'll stay in yore room tull you git back."

"But where do you want to go?" groped Abner, staring at the money.

"Jest as fur as that money'll take me!" snapped Zed. "Go ahead!"

"But, Zed, what direction!" Abner gazed at his friend in the utmost stupefaction.

"Toward Texas I reckon. Now, git out an' git back. I want to ketch the noon train out on the edge of town before it gits too fast fer me to jump aboard."

"Zed!" cried Abner, curiosity overcoming his hill reticence, "what in the worl' have you went an' done?"

"Not a thing in the worl'," interrupted Zed with awful intensity. "I'm jest leavin', that's all. I jest decided I ain't goin' to stay here no longer. Now, go ahead—talkin' ain't gittin' me out o' this town!"

There was a way through the hall which avoided the dining room. Abner chose this instantly and set out at a fast walk through the house, out the gate, then up the street to the station. At the ticket office he had a difficult time in purchasing seventeen dollars and forty-five cents' worth of transportation toward Texas. Abner did not know whether Zed wanted to go through Birmingham, Memphis, or Shreveport. However, the station agent in the edge of Lane County is accustomed to meeting vague demands. Abner received a ticket to Marked Tree, Arkansas, and twelve cents in change. The agent did not ask Abner if he had any baggage to check; Abner's type never had. When such a youth travelled, he travelled unencumbered.

When Abner returned to his room with the ticket he found Tug Beavers and Zed in a low conversation which they broke off when he entered. Tug arose with the air of a man making his farewells.

"Well, Zed," he drawled out, "if it so happens that I don't see you no more, we shore won't meet fer a long time."

"Be good, Tug," countered Zed, with the worn parting phrases of the hill country, "an' if you kain't be good, be keerful."

"So long, Zed," put in Abner, "don't do nothin' I wouldn't do."

"All right, an' don't you boys shoot craps with nobody that uses loaded dice."

"We won't. Good-bye, Zed."

"Good-bye, boys, an' I if don't git back the ol' gray mare's yo'rn."

So the three teamsters parted, glossing over the bleakness of their parting with mock moral injunctions after the manner of their kind. Abner and Tug tramped downstairs and started to work.

They were late, and as they hurried along the street, Abner was stung with certain jealous twinges because Zed had told Tug his real troubles and had not told him. He wanted to ask Tug, but pride forbade. If Zed did not trust him, then he didn't want to know. He was just as indifferent to Zed as Zed was to him. Then squarely in the midst of these thoughts he turned to his brooding companion and asked, "Tug, what's Zed havin' to leave town fer?"

Tug came out of a trance to say, "Oh—he jest took a ramblin' spell."

So that was the way the land lay—Abner was to be excluded completely from this intimate affair! The youth flushed under his sunburn. He felt bitterly toward Zed, and yet the fact that Zed was running away lay like a little lead weight somewhere at the base of Abner's throat. Clearly he would not see Zed again; Zed, with his good-natured wooden face and endless foolishness.

In the midst of this depressing mood, a sudden glorious view burst on his eyes which made him instantly forget the slight his friends had put upon him. The two companions were passing the L. & N. switch yard where the new railroad hitched on to the main line; there in the morning sunlight a small locomotive with two flat cars was puffing out of the switch yard on to the new track.

Tug saw it too for he shouted, "Look, Railroad Jones's injun's come!"

Instantly both youths set out at top speed after the puffing engine. The two flat cars were loaded with men who presently saw the boys running after them. The locomotives appeared not to be going fast, but Abner's best efforts gained nothing at all. He jerked off his hat and waved it for the train to stop. So did Tug. But the passengers began laughing at the two labourers trying to catch a train.

Tug bellowed desperately, "Hold on, you fools! Slow up! Let us on!" then gasped to Abner, "Missin' the first ride after we built the damn thing!" He bore ahead of Abner in a mighty effort to make this initial trip.

But the little locomotive steadily widened the gap. The men on the flats pointed and guffawed. Tug fell into desperate profanity.

At that moment a great fat man on the first flat went climbing over the tender at the risk of his neck. He got to where he could see the engineer and fireman. He gesticulated at them, then a miracle happened. The puffs ceased, came a wail of airbrakes, and a little later the train came backing toward the boys.

To Abner's amazement, the man who stopped the train was Railroad Jones. Evidently he had been off somewhere;

up North, no doubt, where such things are procurable; and had brought back this engine and the cars. How a man would set about buying such things, where they came from, who sold them, moved Abner with the same sense of mystery as did the glitter of the stars.

Railroad Jones himself, with his square yellow face, black mane, and birthmark, reached down and helped the boys up in his flat. "Well, Abner," he beamed down on his teamster, "we shore built her, my boy! Tug, we got her to goin' at last! When I seen it was you fellows, I says, 'Boys, we got to go back an' git them boys; they holp build her and they're intitled to a ride same as us.'" As the engine resumed its forward movement, he cried out,

"Watch her puff! Ain't she a dandy!"

As a matter of fact, Abner had been disappointed in the engine. He had expected a new glittering locomotive to run on the long westward curve of yellow ties and black rails, but this one was rusty, old, evidently second-hand. But this welcome by Railroad Jones, this backing the train to pick him up, filled him with the greatest enthusiasm. It undid all the preachments Shallburger had ever made or would ever make. The notion of striking against a genuine fellow like Railroad Jones was ridiculous.

The flat cars rattled and shook under their feet. The men held to one another to keep from falling down.

"Yonder's an auto!" shouted Jones gloriously, pointing at a motor car along a parallel road, "bet ever' man in the crowd a dollar we pass her!"

A number of voices took him.

"It's a bet! Whoop her up, boys! Monty, tell Henry to give her more coal; git this shebang under way!"

The man called Monty climbed the tender and began bawling at the engineer and pointing toward the motor to transfer the idea of a race. In a few minutes black smoke boiled out of the stack. The puffing increased in speed and intensity. A rising wind beat the men's faces. The rattle of the flats changed to a roar.

Unfortunately this demonstration attracted the attention of the motorist, who sensed a race, turned on more gas, and ran off and left the engine.

Railroad Jones roared with laughter at his defeat.

"Hey, boys, you tell 'em!" he shouted above the noise, "I ain't got the heart! But we got a railroad through old Lane jest the same-y! Here, come on up, boys, an' collect yore bets!" He drew out a roll of greenbacks as thick as his arm, and began peeling off dollar bills. Some of the men attempted to refuse the wager, but Jones would not hear to it, "Take it! Take it!" he shouted. "It's a souven-air!"

The whole trip became a love feast. Flasks of whisky began circulating among the men. The engineer ahead started a continuous ear-splitting shriek on his diminutive whistle.

"The name of this road!" shouted Jones, "is the Lane County Farmers' and Lumbermen's Railroad! That's what I name her now!" and he broke a bottle of illicit corn whisky against the tender.

The entire rolling stock of the L. C. F. & L. Ry. dashed along amid thin persimmon-grown hills, through narrow but rich creek bottoms; into pine woods; along desclate cut-over lands. Rabbits bolted out of the path of the monster; coveys of quails hurtled into air; half-wild hogs snorted and dashed off through the woods.

On the rear flat, two hillmen, who were old friends, and therefore could afford it, began fighting. Their buddies made a ring around them to keep them from toppling off the car to destruction.

After a run of two and a half miles, the excursion reached the end of the line where the men were working. The advent of the engine and of Railroad Jones disorganized everything. The men came flocking about the engine, all filled with a sense of proprietorship. They climbed over the locomotive and walked around it, examining its intricate mechanism. One of the men began telling a very old joke about how the train had chased a man along the track; how the engineer had shouted, "Get off!" and the farmer had yelled, "If I get off into the ploughed ground, you fellers will ketch me an' run over me!" All the men about the teller roared as if it actually had happened.

After about an hour of these felicitations, the foremen persuaded the men to go to work. Abner got out his team and hitched it to his scoop, but his work was so overshadowed by the fact of the engine actually standing there on the track, he could hardly think of what he was doing.

Lane County really had a railroad! How "smart" Railroad Jones was to build one! He recalled the suit about the heating stoves which Railroad had won in Lanesburg. A brainy man! A big-hearted man to back up the train and let him and Tug ride!

Out in front of Abner a small army of men was working on the right of way, levelling it, cutting away the hills, filling the valleys. The L. C. F. & L. Ry. was stretching westward into virgin country. The August sun climbed the heavens and looked down on this activity. It grew hot. Abner's mules danced with fretfulness; the youth jerked their reins and cursed. He went round and round in the heat, falling into the peculiar coma of labour.

A little before noon, Tug came to Abner and told him if he would take out his mules right away they could catch the train back to Irontown and see Zed off on the twelve o'clock.

Abner started at once for the stables. The foreman came up and wanted to know why Abner was quitting work at that hour. Abner told the foreman that all he, the foreman, had to do was to mark down his, Abner's, time, and if he didn't like what he was doing he could "chub" it. Thereupon Abner and Tug hurried to catch the cars for the return trip.

On the way back Abner rode on the last flat and watched the landscape spin back to Irontown. And as he rattled along it occurred to him that each day his work would be getting farther and farther away from Irontown, and eventually he would be forced to leave the village to get closer to his job and that would end his daily association with Nessie. This was a gray prospect; however, he hoped the change would not be soon.

Then he thought of Zed Parrum again; then of the time he had seen Zed and Mr. Ditmas and Professor Overall in the black jacks near the poorhouse farm. He remembered how he and Beatrice had hidden behind the plum bushes and yodeled. It all seemed a long, long time ago. He thought of Mr. Sandage who had been elected as county trustee and was living in Lanesburg now. How they had all split up. A melancholy fell over Abner at the instability of human associations. At that moment the little locomotive broke into a long furious shriek—they were entering Irontown.

Ten minutes later the two teamsters hurried along, filled with that queer human impulse to renew the pain of their parting with Zed. Because it was possible to see Zed again, they felt they must.

They kept a bright lookout down the village street, and also across side alleys for, if they had gauged Zed aright, he was likely to seek the outskirts of the village by the most inconspicuous paths.

As they walked they listened for the far-away blast of the noon train. It was due very soon, but it was nearly always late.

Abner's original curiosity returned concerning Zed's secrecy. He wanted to ask Tug again, but pride forbade him. Then he thought bitterly that if Zed had been as good a friend to him as he to Zed, Zed never would have refused to tell him, no matter what—— Here Abner lost track of his own meandering recrimination for a short cut—Zed hadn't treated him right! Neither had Tug! They had both used him pretty rotten, he called it.

In the midst of his reverie Tug ejaculated in astonishment, "Why, yonder's the damn fool walkin' along there big as life!"

Abner looked and sure enough, there was Zed walking down the village street with an old country man.

"Who's the old man?" asked Abner.

Tug strained his eyes. "That looks kinder like ol' man Tolbert."

The teamsters hurried forward, and as they drew near Abner noted that old man Tolbert held a gun in his hand, a long, muzzle-loading squirrel rifle. Abner had not observed it until it swung out of line with his eyes. Now, such an accessory was not at all uncommon among the hillmen who came into the village, but just at this juncture the squirrel rifle took on a certain possible significance to Abner. He looked sharply at Tug and suddenly realized that Tug had recognized old man Tolbert at an almost impossible distance. Then it dawned on Abner that there was something queer in the very way Zed was walking. The teamster forgot his jealousy and hurried on with a vague apprehension growing in his heart.

At some distance ahead two or three little boys ran out into the street and began whooping; still farther on, where the business section of the village set in, a crowd was gathering.

An impulse struck both teamsters to cut down an alley, run to the garage, and be there when Zed and old man Tolbert passed. It would have been undignified for them to come running after Zed right before the gathering crowd, that would not have looked right. The fact that this curiosity spurred flight did not comport exactly with the passionate friendship Abner at that moment had been vowing for Zed never struck the youth.

Both teamsters bolted down a by-way and ran stooping along a parallel alley and presently panted into the side door of the garage. Then they dodged among motors and spare parts, sharply afraid that Zed would pass the front door before they arrived there.

On the oily platform in front of the garage some half-a-dozen youths were grinning and staring fixedly down the street. The teamsters entered this group breathing deeply.

Zed and the old man were just coming past. Tolbert carried his squirrel rifle carelessly, in his left hand, on the opposite side from Zed.

Mr. Parrum moved along with a set and painful grin on his face with which he answered the multi-faced grin of his cronies in the garage. He even essayed to wink and nod at the old man stalking at his side; he meant this to show that no matter what happened he was still the same old devil-may-care Zed Parrum.

Old man Tolbert himself glanced neither to the right nor the left but marched straight on with the cheeks and upper parts of his bewhiskered face looking as if they were chopped out of gray stone.

Abner was amazed beyond all experience and knowledge. He twitched to ask questions concerning this unparalleled scene, but this was impossible with Zed so close. Everyone else knew. The moment the two had passed, the crowd broke into the most significant winks and grins, and immediately fell in behind the pair.

Old man Tolbert and Zed pursued their way past several doors, past the Grand, Belshue's jewellery shop, a grocery, and came to a little dusty one-room frame building which was the law office of Buckingham Sharp. It was also the office Squire Meredith used when he was in town. The mysterious pair entered this building, and then, notwithstanding the heated day, closed the door with a bang.

However, there was no curtain to the dusty window. The garage gang framed that window, like bees around a hive. Abner half climbed another man's shoulder and in turn had his own shoulders occupied. Abner's view of the interior was somewhat interfered with by reflections. He saw a blue sky, a rolling summer cloud, the peak of the storehouse across the street. But by disregarding this skyey scene, he dimly made out Squire Meredith inside while before him stood Zed Parrum and a girl with their hands joined together.

In the following weekly issue of the Irontown *Dispatch,* this notice appeared:

TOLBERT–PARRUM NUPTIALS

Last Wednesday at noon, the friends and acquaintances of Miss Pearlie Tolbert and Mr. Zedekiah Parrum were pleasantly surprised by the happy culmination of their romance in matrimony.   The marriage of this popular young couple was quite unexpected.   Miss Tolbert was attired in a simple travelling costume and is one of Lane County's most beautiful and charming examples of young womanhood, while Mr. Parrum is a prominent railroad man who played a leading part in the construction of the new Lane County Farmers' and Lumbermen's Railroad. May the Voice that Breathed o'er Eden never cease to wake to harmonious minstrelsy that divine tie of tenderness and yearning that writes across the firmament of this charming couple in letters of glorious emblazonry, that magic vocable, "LOVE."   Now is the time to subscribe.

It must be stated here in defence of the editor's eloquence that this last phrase did not really belong in the wedding notice.   The printer's devil accidentally mixed it in when he made up the form.

CHAPTER XVII

WHILE the Irontown *Dispatch* adopted this rosy view of a very untoward episode, Mr. Perry Northcutt did not follow any such slippery ethical practice. The state of his village lay, as he told his fat wife, Nannie, on his heart.

One night at the Irontown bank Mr. Northcutt remained in the building after a directors' meeting, thinking what to do about the moral state of his town. The directors' meeting had been a success. The board had decided to call on Railroad Jones for further security, and Mr. Northcutt knew this would be impossible for the magnate to advance. It seemed to Perry that the railroad was ripening, like a plum, and when it fell he meant to catch it. In fact, this request for more security was a very gentle shake at the plum tree itself.

So the banker sat at the directors' table, musing his projected coup, when his thoughts veered around to the immoral depths to which Irontown had fallen. Being a man of action, he drew pen and paper to him and indicted this letter to the Reverend Blackman at Big Cypress. It ran:

DEAR BROTHER BLACKMAN:

I am writing to ask you to hurry up your appointment in Irontown. We need a revival here right now. The new railroad has brought a disturbing element in our midst and the law is unable to control them. Nothing can help us but the blood of Christ upon the heart of Irontown. I ask you as a lover of lost souls to cancel any other appointment you may have and come on at once. Our streets are lined with drunks; crap games go on everywhere; our young girls are subjected to indecent remarks. The other day our town was disgraced by a shot-gun wedding. We soldiers of the Lord have got to break up these wicked practices. Sometimes I almost despair, but I know that the grace of God encompasseth all things. But you must come at once.

Our collection for a two-weeks' revival seldom falls under $300.

> Your brother in Christ,
>
> PERRY NORTHCUTT.

In the course of a few days came an answer to this very sincere letter setting a date for the meeting and enclosing circulars to be distributed in the village. In a few hours all the store windows in Irontown held posters showing the picture of a hard-faced man with a Bible in his hand, and below the picture was the catch line, "Keep the Devil on the Jump." Then came press notices:

"A power for good."—Smithtown *Herald*.

"Reverend Blackman cleaned up the bootleggers in our town in a red-hot revival of three weeks' duration."—Banksville *Express*.

"Reverend Blackman, the Big Bertha of Heaven, blasted hell out of Goodlettsville."—Goodlettsville *Inquirer*.

Appended was a list of the topics on which the Reverend Blackman would preach:

"The Dance Evil, or Foxtrotting to Hell."

"Evolution, or From College to Damnation."

"Novel Reading, or From Print to Perdition."

"Scarlet Women and Dingy Men." (For men only.)

"Bobbed Hair and Bobbed Morals." (For women only.)

"There Is a City Not Built with Hands." (Farewell sermon.)

When these posters appeared a flutter of anticipation set up in Irontown. In the meagre intellectual and emotional life of the hill country these annual revivals occupied the place filled in more liberal communities by the theatre, the symphony, the lecture, the fashion show, and the church. The only glimpse the hill folk ever received of philosophy, æsthetics, literature, science, art, and metaphysics was given them by such travelling revivalists as Blackman. However, the preacher touched these topics in a negative way; he spoke of them only to condemn them; to discourage any further thought or investigation of the subjects. Any human interest beyond the acquisition of money and how to please God by doing moral and spiritual works was derogated.

The posters stimulated Irontown to activity. The women came to clean out the village church; the choir began practising assiduously; every young man of the neighbourhood hastened to establish an entente with some girl because to enter religious excitement alone was dull entertainment. Human beings entered Heaven as the animals did the Ark, in pairs. The garage oiled up its automatics. Mr. Biggers, the druggist, who habitually consumed his own morphine, prepared to attempt once more to conquer this vice during the excitement of the protracted meeting; and queer to say, he could dispense with the narcotic as long as the revival lasted.

It would be difficult to put into words what the protracted meeting meant to Mr. Perry Northcutt. He did not drink, smoke, or curse. His wife was fat and obstinate. He compressed his whole emotional outlet into an annual protracted meeting. Mr. Northcutt went about his spiritual preparations for the revival with a concentrated earnestness. He prayed almost incessantly. He fasted two whole days. At the end of the second day, while praying in his home, he felt God stroke his thin hair and say, "My son, your faith shall be rewarded by the greatest revival Irontown has ever known."

He rushed out and told his wife, who received it with a sort of stolid credulity, but the miracle got scattered abroad through the town, and everyone realized that God was going to perform a mighty work in Irontown.

The first services of the revival found all Irontown wending its way to the church. The house itself was a large bare building as uncompromisingly cubical as a box. At one end of the room stood the pulpit, a square wooden pedestal painted white and topped with a large gilt Bible. Behind the pulpit, as a queer relic of vanished archiepiscopal

glories, stood three tall Gothic chairs made of black walnut.
What part these chairs ever played in rite or ceremony, what
prelates once occupied these great seats, neither the preacher
nor any of his congregation knew. That information had
vanished from the memory of the people after a century
of isolation among the hills.

The church filled rapidly—the church members choosing
the front seats, the unconverted taking places near the door.
These two bodies merged near the central row of seats. A
little later came a concerted movement as the choir went
forward to the stall on the right side of the pulpit. A pale
village girl took her place at the small reed organ. She
screwed the stool around to its proper height, then con-
ferred timidly with the song leader as to what songs should
be used. The two laid out the music on the organ desk while
everybody in the congregation leaned forward to get a song
book out of the rack on the back of the seat in front of them.
Then the organist began swaying from side to side, pumping
the organ with her feet, and the instrument set up a dolorous
wailing. Audience and choir then lifted a queer nasal cacophony of song. When it was finished the Reverend Blackman arose from the central chair behind the pulpit, came
forward in the midst of a spreading quiet, laid his own worn
leather Bible on top of the big pulpit Bible, adjusted the lamp
wick to suit his eyes, then for several moments stood looking
at his congregation with a long melancholy face. Then he
read his text of how Pharaoh hardened his heart, and after
the reading, nodded at the banker who sat on the front seat
and said, "Brother Northcutt will now lead us in prayer."

A strong gratified tremor went through the banker as he,
and the greater part of the congregation, slipped out of the
seats and knelt beside them. In the rear of the church a
number of sinners merely leaned their heads over the backs
of the next seats, and one or two contumacious spirits refused
to bow at all but sat bolt-upright.

Mr. Northcutt began his prayer in a conversational tone
but gradually became more vehement until near the end he

was shouting at the top of his lungs. He picked up the preacher's text, after the manner of an experienced deacon, and prayed that all the men and women in Irontown would not harden their hearts to the sweet impulses of the spirit. "O God," implored the cashier in a loudening voice, "help us not to harden our hearts! Help us to come to your altar like little tender-hearted children and bless us and save us!" [Interruptions of "Amen! Grant it, Lord" from the minister.] "You know we are sinful, Lord, You know we are steeped in wickedness! All of us are, but I pray especially for the young men of Irontown! They are sowing their wild oats, O God, and what a harvest they shall reap! They lie heavy on the hearts of their mothers; and they lie heavy on our hearts, too, O God! Save them from their sins!" ["So be it! Grant it, Father"!] "Keep them from a sinner's hell!" ["Do that, Lord, oh, save them!"] "And God, we have a man in our midst whose heart we pray for you to move. He doesn't believe in you, God! O, it's a pitiful thing for a son not to believe in his Father!" ["Help him believe!"] "It's A. M. Belshue, Lord; Belshue would be such a good man, Lord, if he could only come to you as a little child comes to his father! He's a money-making man, Lord, a moral man, but no man can be saved through his own works, but only by the precious blood of Christ!" ["Amen! Amen!"] "And there is Tobe Sanders, who kain't keep sober, and Caly Stegall, who bootlegs liquor, and my own brother-in-law, who has a secret sin he can't overcome. Help him, Lord! Put your great arms about him till he gains strength to be a man!" ["O, Lord, help Perry Northcutt's brother-in-law."] "And there's the boys in the garage, shooting craps, telling smutty yarns, using your name in vain; help 'em get rid of these dirty, filthy, indecent ways! They're good boys at heart, but their eyes are blinded by their wanton youth!" ["O Lord, what a blindness!"] "Help them; help us all, we need it. We are your feeble children. Do not destroy Irontown; save us, save our nation, save our President, we ask in the name of our blessed

Redeemer, Amen." ["Amen! God grant it; Blessed Master!"]

Came a sliding noise as the congregation got to their seats again. Mr. Northcutt had tears in his eyes and he wiped them without any concealment. The minister said, "Number fifty-four," and nodded at the choir leader. The pale girl at the organ flushed slightly, then began swaying back and forth pedalling, and the next moment the little reed organ broke into a harsh unmusical prelude which somewhat resembled a gigantic snoring. As the prelude ended, came a pause; the choir leader began beating time, and the choir of untrained voices, never quite together, several a little off pitch, arose in chorus. Certain nasal voices gave the whole volume of sound the effect of having sharp edges, but the effective feature of the hymn was the exaggerated beat of its time. Mrs. Roxie Biggers, who sat in the seat nearest the organ, marked this tempo with a sharp bobbing of her gray head. The bass voices accented it with a monotonous *tum-tum-tum*. Every long vowel was stretched out into a pounding polysyllable. The song ran:

"Holy *Bi*-yi-bul, blessed *Bi*-yi-bul,
Gift of *God*, and the lamp of life,
Beautiful *Bi*bul thou art mine.
I *cling* to the dear old Holy *Bi*-yi-bul. . . ."

The effect was a hammering on the tympanum which later in the meeting would produce clear-cut hypnotic effects.

The audience heard this first drumming with a foretaste of the fuller frenzy to come. The banker's eyes brightened as he was about to plunge into his annual orgy. Others dreaded it. Still others looked forward to it with a sense of high entertainment. Yet everyone in the village, except Belshue, sincerely believed that what would follow would be a miraculous manifestation of God's power. They prayed earnestly for this thing to happen.

When the singing was over the Reverend Blackman came

to the pulpit, repeated his text, and immediately began a long string of dismal anecdotes which related the tragic results of sinners hardening their hearts. Each tragedy had happened within the preacher's own knowledge.

He said that while he was holding a meeting in McMinnville, Tennessee, a beautiful girl had felt impelled by the spirit of God to come forward and join the church. But she had said to her mother, "No, Mother, not right now; just wait till after the Country Club dance, and then I'll give my soul to Jesus. Just one more dance."

"Brothers and sisters, just one week from that night I buried that poor girl in the McMinnville cemetery, and the mother was the most heartbroken woman I have ever seen. She cried over her daughter's grave, 'Oh, if Lucille hadn't waited—if she hadn't hardened her heart!'

"Brother Northcutt, I remember I was holding a revival in Lonoke, Arkansas, and the most brilliant member of the Lonoke bar, a young man, in the best of health, felt the influence of the Holy Spirit moving him to come to the altar and give his life to God, but he put it off, hardened his heart. I begged him to go. He said, 'No, Brother Blackman, I'm going to make the race for the Arkansas legislature, and a man can't be a Christian and get elected in Arkansas. Just wait. After this race is over I pledge you I'll come up here and give my life to God.'

"My friends, he never did come. Just three months after that night, I happened to be in Lonoke again, and I was called to the bedside of a dying man. It was that young lawyer. He was a drunkard, dying of delirium tremens. As I held his head in my arms, with his last gasp he moaned, 'Oh, Brother Blackman, if I had only listened to your warning!'—He had hardened his heart."

For some hour and a half the minister rehearsed an endless succession of tragedies, all, he averred, from his direct personal experience.

In reality Reverend Blackman had culled these stories from "Gunther's Handbook for Ministers," but this fact had no moral bearing whatever. He was telling the stories in the only moving way a man can tell a story, as having happened to himself. And then, no rational man could ever believe that the minister went about the country sowing death and destruction in his wake. No, he was simply telling moral allegories which pointed to the future and not the past. They were an artistic foreshortening and simplification of life, and the Reverend Blackman stood squarely within his rights as an artist to employ this realistic touch.

Then, right in the midst of these harrowing tales, came a sudden cracking of pistols outside the church. The women, already wrought up by the tragedies, began shrieking. The men leaped up ready to rush out and identify the miscreants. But the preacher held up his hands and shouted, "Brothers, sit quiet and watch the power of God!"

The next moment he picked up the pulpit lamp and strode down the aisle to the church door. He stepped out into the night and held up the lamp so he was in full illumination. At such an unusual outcome the firing ceased.

"Brothers!" cried the preacher, "bring your pistols into the church and use them for the glory of God! Long ago the Lord said unto David, 'Make a great noise for the glory of God!' Maybe our Lord meant pistols? I don't know, but anyway quit using them in the service of the devil and bring 'em to God! Come on in. You're welcome, pistols and all—nobody will report you. We love every one of you out there in the darkness of your sins. Get right, brothers, come on in!"

The Reverend Blackman walked back into the church holding his lamp high and waving his arm for all the world to follow him.

None of the garage gang really followed him, but the sport palled; only one or two more shots were fired; feeble affairs. The preacher had out-dramatized them.

The enthusiasm in the church was immense. The relief from the firing was accounted a miracle. A little old woman in black named Abigail Wendler began shouting, clapping her hands and crying, "Praise God! Bless his name!"

No one paid any attention to Mrs. Wendler. She was always the first to shout at the protracted meetings, but some person observed that they were certainly going to have a great meeting, as sister Abigail usually didn't shout till about the third night.

Indeed, when the service was over all the congregation filed out with the sense of a great victory stirring in their hearts. Mr. Northcutt squeezed the fat arm of his wife and said:

"What did I tell you, Nannie? I felt God stroke my hair just as plain as I feel your arm, and he spoke to me and said, 'Perry, my son, this meeting will be——'"

"Yes, you told me that before," interrupted Nannie, who required a very fresh miracle from Perry to hold her interest at all.

CHAPTER XVIII

ON THE fifth morning of the protracted meeting, Nessie Sutton was bold enough to walk out of the dining room of the Scovell House with Abner Teeftallow and see him off to work.

Nessie had a certain right to do this without being gossiped about because she and Abner went to meeting together every night, she had prayed for Abner publicly at the invitation of the minister, kneeling by his side and silently asking God to save him. This action had given her a position so that she could walk out on the piazza with him without arousing small talk.

At this moment she held to a button on his sleeve.

"And Abner, after you join the church, you could start readin' law of evenings. Mr. Sharp will lend you his books. . . ." She loosed the button and looked at Abner with soft possessive eyes.

"How do you know he would?" asked the teamster, to whom the notion of becoming a lawyer was both vague and repellent.

Nessie coloured slightly. "I—I asked him would he."

"You did!" Abner was surprised at the length the girl had gone. A thing like that Abner was accustomed simply to talk about.

Nessie went on: "Mr. Sharp laughed and said 'Certainly.' He said more Southern girls ought to go in for the professions. He said he would give me quizzes."

"Give *you* quizzes?"

"Well, y-yes," agreed Nessie, considerate of, and a little pleased at, this jealous note. "I thought I might read it too and remember what he said and sorter help you."

"Huh—I 'magine we can understand it by ourse'ves."

"So you do want me to get you the book?"

Abner pondered uncertainly and finally said, "Yes."

At this point Mr. Tug Beavers came out on the piazza and Nessie said, "Good-bye. Remember I'm going to pray for you an' Tug at exactly twelve o'clock to-day. (Individual prayers all over the village had been arranged by Reverend Blackman.)

Tug was picking his teeth. He manœuvred his jackknife to say, uncomfortably, "Much obliged, I'm shore," and went on out the gate with Abner.

When they were out of earshot, Tug swore an oath and immediately changed it to "By Gum"—for he was trying to stop swearing—"if this keeps on, somethin's goin' to bust shore's hell—I mean—er—now Mary Lou is goin' to pray for me at twelve, too, an' I God, I think that's wrong—doublin' up on a man!"

Mr. Beavers was clearly disturbed at these unfair spiritual tactics. He went on to complain, "I told 'em last night. I always tried to throw my influence on the right side, but Brother Blackman says, 'You got to throw yourse'f, too.— Hell—er, I mean——" He relapsed into a brooding silence and finally said, "If I don't cuss none I don't see how the hell I'm ever goin' to drive them mules."

Abner likewise was low-spirited. He had been able to elide profanity from his conversation without effort, but the idea of becoming a lawyer annoyed him. He looked upon lawyers from the hill point of view as subtle, rather awesome men who had somehow shifted the burden of life from brawn to brain; but who, nevertheless, were bloodless, leech-like, and unworthy to be classed as men. Now Nessie wanted him to become one of these—women had funny tastes. . . .

"Tug," he asked suddenly, "how would you like to be a lawyer?"

"Lawyer hell—I mean jest lawyer—why?"

"Nessie wants me to be one."

"Well, I be d——" He shut his mouth. (He did not

see how church members expressed themselves on any point whatever.) A suspicion entered his head. He looked at his friend meaningly.

"Is she ashamed of you bein' a teamster?"

"I hadn't thought of that," mused Abner. "Now, if she don't want to go with a teamster, she don't haff to."

When Nessie Sutton watched the teamsters go to their work, she ran back up the stairs to her room with an exquisite trembling in her breast. It was as if a mocking bird suddenly had begun carolling in her heart. As she went skipping down the long hall to her room she put a hand to her bosom for the sheer physical sweetness of the sensation there. She was so happy she could hardly go about the slight housekeeping duties in her room—sweeping and making her bed.

Abner was going to become a lawyer after exactly the romantic fashion of the novels. It would come about through her prayers and persuasions. After he had practised law for a year or two they would marry and live in a fine house near Lanesburg. Then Nessie's mind made an odd jump. She saw herself in this fine mansion with three children romping on the lawn; one was a boy with brown eyes like Abner's, and two were girls with blue eyes like her own. All biological necessities of bringing these children into the world her mind automatically skipped, but the bird of happiness warbled in her bosom again. She felt all her family would be intensely religious. Her children would kneel at her knees and pray.

In her heart Nessie was glad she was a country girl. She considered town girls more or less irreligious, selfish, and, with their dancing, impure.

She had been neglected for a long time here in Irontown, but she had gone faithfully to church, Sunday school, and prayer meeting, and now God had blessed her with this great happiness, this breath-taking ecstasy!

As she whisked off her bedclothes, she began singing the gayest of the hymns she knew, "Let a Little Sunshine In."

As she sang in her slightly nasal country voice, the real sunshine flooded her bedroom and burned along her floor like the light Moses saw burning on the bush.

At half-past eight Nessie went down to the Grand, and within a few minutes Mrs. Roxie Biggers came in with a scrap of pink calico which she wanted to match with thread. The old woman pawed impatiently among the spools in the coloured tray while she talked of something else.

"This dress is for one of the Skillern childern, pore little things; the Willin' Workers give it an' I'm makin' it." She glanced around to see if any other customer were near and sank her voice.

"You know Mr. Biggers has almost completely overcome his cravin'; ain't that a miracle!"

"He has!" Nessie selected another spool and placed it against the cloth.

"Yes, an' he tol' me this mornin' he b'lieved his faith was a-goin' to pull him through."

"I hope so, Miss Roxie," nodded Nessie earnestly.

"Nessie, in yore prayers, would you min' puttin' in my husban's name an' askin' God to make this cure permanent? I know you are a good Christian girl."

Nessie's heart expanded and tears came to her eyes. "You know I will, Miss Roxie."

Mrs. Biggers made her selection of thread and hurried out of the store compressing her thin lips and narrowing her eyes with the intensity of her purpose. In this instance her purpose was to clothe the children of a destitute family on the edge of town. She was thinking over certain dresses belonging to the children of well-to-do families and she meant to go to the parents and work those dresses out of them for the Skillern children. The old woman was ruthless when it came to forcing other persons to perform charitable deeds. She invariably left every donor angry.

Nessie, with a certain tenderness in her heart, watched her go. Then she went back to the hats Mrs. Peckham had laid out for her. She began sewing some silver lace on a wire hat frame and thinking of the time when she would live in a colonial home near Lanesburg with children playing on the lawn—she interrupted her daydream to think, "Dear Christ, have mercy on poor Mr. Biggers and cure him from eating morphine."

Forenoon and afternoon danced by for the happy girl, and at seven-thirty she and Abner set out for church through the limpid evening. Already an irregular procession of people was moving through the streets toward the meeting house, for by now it was necessary to come early to get a seat at all.

Among the line of churchgoers Nessie saw Mrs. Biggers holding her husband's arm and vigorously directing his feeble steps. As usual she was putting so much energy into her directing that she was making it uncomfortable for the invalid at her side. Mr. Biggers himself looked a dozen years older than when Nessie had seen him on the previous Sunday. His face was pasty; he shook, and Nessie sensed by looking at him that this clear pleasant evening was a world of confusion to him. She recalled, with a little pang of self-reproach, her promise to pray for the sick man, for she had forgotten it in her own joys; and now she again murmured fervently, "O Christ, bless Mr. Biggers and take away his cravin' for morphine."

But the intimate pleasure of walking at Abner's side soon swallowed up her concern for anything else.

She pressed his big arm with her fingers and whispered "I borrowed that book from Mr. Sharp this evenin'."

"Did you?" in faint dismay.

"Yes; I have it in my room for you—don't you want to be a lawyer, Abner?"

The mere thought of reading a book depressed Abner.

"Why—yes"—he agreed dubiously, "I suppose so." He recalled Tug's stricture of the morning and glanced around at her. "You ain't ashamed of goin' with a teamster, are you, Nessie?"

Nessie stared in amazement. "Ashamed of you! Me!

Why, Abner, I—I wouldn't be ashamed of you in the presence of the angels!"

The trembling flame of her affection for him, her pride in him, poured through the girl's fingers and shone through the look in her face.

Abner became suddenly and movingly aware that Nessie loved him. His heart began to beat. A film fell over the evening and blotted out for him the procession of people, the street, the whole village, and left just him and Nessie moving arm-in-arm through a sort of perfumed space. The touch of her fingers felt as intimate to him as the feel of his own flesh; the sentiency of their bodies seemed to pour through their linked arms so that she, in a way, became a very part of his own being; the sweeter, more exquisite part. Unconsciously their breathing fell into rhythm. They moved along through pellucid shadows in silence except for their faint sighs. A strange fancy crossed Nessie's mind, that Abner might, if he liked, walk over her prostrate body with his heavy feet.

A few steps behind them Miss Scovell, eyeing the mere walk of the lovers, whispered acridly to her companion, "Jest look at that—ain't they sickening?"

The spirit of the meeting on that particular night somehow was not so electric as usual. The congregation, perhaps the preacher too, had fallen into one of those slumps which sometimes overtake the most enthusiastic revival. The Reverend Blackman was irritated. Some of his most promising penitents who invariably had come forward to the mourners' bench for the last three or four nights, now, through some perverseness, remained stock still in their seats and would not budge on any proposition.

The minister always worked his hearers into action with "propositions." He would say, "Everybody who wants to meet their mothers in Heaven, walk up and give me your hand! Everybody who wants to see Jesus, come up and give me your hand! What, won't nobody come? Well,

then, anybody who wants to go to Heaven when you die
arise in your seats. Get up, folks! Get up! Everybody
that wants to go to Heaven when you die. Say, friends
what's the matter with you? Well, won't you bow you
head where you sit in your seats and by that act say, 'I wan
to go to Heaven when I die'? Brothers! Sisters, what i
the matter? Has the devil got you-all in his clutches?''

The real trouble was that the congregation had been over
preached. These village folk had been kept awake for fiv
nights until twelve or one o'clock, and they were accus
tomed to going to bed at eight. They were exhausted
Now an emotional backwash had set in, but it seemed to th
Reverend Blackman that his hearers had decided delib
erately to go to hell.

The preacher was as nerve-worn as any in his audience
and now he stood in the pulpit in his shirt sleeves, wet with
sweat.

"Brothers! Sisters!" he shouted. "Isn't there a single
person here who wants to keep out of the fiery torments o
the damned!"

The audience blinked in silence. The Reverend Blackmar
had a feeling that all these immortal souls were somehow
plunged into a trance by the power of Satan, and there they
sat, the only sign of life their blinking eyes.

A sort of agony went over the preacher; a kind of pro
fessional agony, good for one sermon only, which would dis
appear on the following morning, but which was, nevertheless
a bona-fide agony.

"Brothers! Sisters!" he yelled, flinging out his arms
"For God's sake break the spell of the devil! Kain't you
hear his deceitful voice whispering in your hearts, 'Set still
you'll have time enough yet! Go up another time!' Oh
my friends, how do you know there is goin' to be another
time?" The minister sobbed. "I know some soul is re
ceiving his last invitation now! I know somebody in this
congregation will never have another chance to accept Christ
God pity him! God pity him! Somebody is frittering away

the very last moment of their chance for salvation! O God, move their hard hearts!

"Brother Northcutt! Sister Biggers! Sister Wendler, get out and work among these lost souls. They are saying by their actions they don't want to meet Jesus in Heaven! They are willing to sink to a burning hell! O my God! What will become of these people! Brother Northcutt, I knew a man once, a doctor in Polk Flat, Alabama, a healthy young man . . ." The Reverend Blackman flung up his hands with a sense of the futility of relating the tragedy. He turned to the choir and motioned for a song.

For some strange reason the choir seemed always exempt from the preacher's maledictions. They were like the Greek chorus, a group explanatory of, but outside of, the dramatic action. Now they began a heavy drumming hymn,

> "'Come to Je-e-e-sus! Come to Je-e-e-sus!
> He will sa-a-ave you! He will sa-a-ave you!'"

The Reverend Blackman started up the aisle to do personal work. The dissipated face of Mr. Tug Beavers near the door attracted him and he made his way among the seats to Tug's side.

"My friend," he lifted his voice above the plangent uproar, "won't you give your heart to God?"

Tug became exceedingly nervous. "I—I'm goin' to, some day, Brother Blackman."

"Some day! Some day! Brother, don't you know it's the devil whispering that answer? He is standing right by your side lulling you to destruction!"

"I'm comin' up some day," repeated Tug emptily. "I always try to throw my influence on the . . ."

Tug's answers were in a very low voice while the minister meant himself to be heard all over the house.

"But, my God, brother, who knows you will live another day! We are worms of the dust! The least thing may kill you! You are not sure you will ever get home alive to-night! My dear brother, with life that uncertain, and torment stretching out for ever and ever, won't you come on now! Don't you want to meet your old gray-haired mother in Heaven? This minute she's reaching down over the battlements of Heaven pleading with you! Pleading, praying —*won't* you come!"

The minister himself was sobbing; responsive tears arose in Tug's own eyes, but through some strange spell, which he himself interpreted as the influence of the devil, he could not budge from his seat. All he could do was to shake his head, compress his lips, and mumble, "No—no—not to-night."

The minister paused and looked intently at Tug for several seconds.

"Brother," he said solemnly, "do you gamble?"

Tug sat silent.

"Do you get drunk and carry concealed weapons? Listen, God knows I love you! Give me that pistol in your pocket! Give me that bottle of rot-gut whisky in your pocket! Give 'em to me and go up to God's altar and say, 'Here I am, Lord, a sinner, take me and make me a better man!'"

Mary Lou Meredith at Tug's side was weeping openly now. She knew very well that Tug had both the whisky and the pistol.

"Do go, Tug! Please, please go, Tug!" she wept.

Tug blinked back his own tears and swallowed at the pain in his throat, but shook his head. He really wanted to go now but could not.

The preacher arose in deep frustration. "God have mercy on you," he intoned in solemn anger. "The devil has got you exactly where he wants you! God will not bear with you for ever, young man!" He shook a finger at Tug. "God will send some terrible calamity on you to break your stubborn heart!"

A wide silence fell on the congregation at this almost malediction. The singing stopped. Amid the silence Perry Northcutt's voice prayed, "O God, if it takes a calamity to lead us to You, do not spare us!"

The Reverend Blackman went back to his pulpit. He lifted his hands. He told the people that they sat and mocked him, that he could do nothing for them and that he would end the meeting that night.

The congregation sat in shocked silence at this extreme step. The minister dismissed them; they arose and filed queerly out into the night.

Abner left the church oppressed by the general feeling of coming evil. He peered ahead and saw Tug and Mary Lou walk out of the church into outer darkness. To the youth's fevered imagination this seemed a sort of symbol, and he wished from the bottom of his heart that Tug had gone to the mourners' bench when the preacher had asked him.

CHAPTER XIX

THE abrupt closing of the meeting spread an aura of evil over the dismissed congregation. One old woman, Mrs. Wendler, trembled out that she felt like she was walking home "under condemnation." Her very phraseology held a Biblical flavour because the hill folk are a remnant of that violent religious ferment in England during the time of Wesley, Calvin, and Penn. Among the homeward procession prevailed the same fearful psychology. In the darkness they sensed the presence of the Prince of Darkness.

This sentience of vast evil pursued both Abner and Nessie back to the Scovell House. On the way they exchanged a few dampened remarks in low voices.

Once Nessie said, "Tug Beavers broke up the meeting."

Abner said he reckoned he did, but what made the preacher pick on Tug?

"I guess he saw Tug was a hard case."

For Nessie to call his friend a "hard case" disturbed Abner. He was surprised that the girl, whose moods so exquisitely fitted his own, should form so erroneous a judgment.

"Tug really wants to do right, Nessie," said Abner in the gentlest remonstrance.

The girl looked around at her companion in the gloom.

"He picked a poor way to show it—breakin' up the meetin'."

"It wasn't jest Tug."

"Why couldn't he go to the mourners' bench when the preacher ast him?"

"Well"—Abner could think of no reason why any mortal man should not go to the mourners' bench and bewail his sins publicly if a preacher requested it—"I don't know—nobody else got up neither."

"But the preacher ast *him*."

"Well, as I say, I don't know, but I tell you one thing: Tug means to throw his influence in the right direction, he's told me that lots of times."

The girl was astonished. "How can he unless he does right?"

"Why, he jest wants to throw his influence, you know, no matter what he does hisse'f."

"But that don't make no sense!"

"Why, it does!"

"How does it?"

"Why, his influence, Nessie . . ."

Abner could simply stare at her because he had already reduced his proposition to its lowest terms. He was unaware that he was trying to expound a bit of masculine mysticism which the innately logical feminine mind would always reject. Abner easily conceived Tug as a bundle of influences, desires, acts, tendencies, in which his act might point in one direction, his influence another, and so on to infinity; but Nessie, womanlike, kept all these components of a man fused into one indissoluble personality; she could not possibly conceive of a man acting one way and wanting to throw his influence another. When Abner's explanation had dissolved on his tongue, Nessie said quietly, but with the deep satisfaction that the woman who is in love with a man gets out of his downfalls when pitted against her:

"You see—you haven't got nothin' to say."

Her little self-satisfied tone, her unjust reflection on Tug, and the fact that he really had nothing to say, because the emotion he felt was too delicate for words—this wounded Abner. It amazed him that she did not feel it herself, and disappointed him.

"Well," said Abner flatly, "Tug's one of the best-hearted fellows in the world no matter what he does on the outside."

This, of course, was a simple restatement of his paradox.

"I'm glad you think so," she said in a certain tone, and silence ensued.

Each knew that the other had been wounded. They walked the rest of the way to the Scovell House almost in silence.

Now, on their way home, under the gloom of a certain elm, Abner had not exactly planned, but a notion certainly had flitted through his head that he would kiss Nessie, or at least attempt to; but now, after this unhappy discussion and the way she had said, "I'm glad you think so," the caress had become impossible. He really did not want to kiss her now. He would not if he could. If she should put her arms about his neck and say, "I was wrong, kiss me and forgive me," he would coldly undo her arms and say, "No, not after you are glad I think so. . . ."

Nevertheless, when the two came to the gloomy elm, Abner walked under it in a state of deep depression. He felt somehow as if Nessie had vanished and a strange girl walked in her stead. Then a flicker of his former apprehension for Tug passed through his mind.

"I do hope nothing has happened to Tug."

"What makes you think anything has?" asked Nessie in her cold voice.

"Well, the preacher has been tellin' what awful things happen to folks who don't do like he says."

"That's so," agreed Nessie, a little impressed, but still unsympathetic.

The rest of the way to the hotel they maintained a strained silence. They let themselves in the hotel door as silently as they could and went upstairs past the light on the newel post.

At his door Abner said, "Good-night" in an unnatural voice, and Nessie returned it briefly and hurried on. While Abner neither loved her nor would forgive her on any terms, he remained looking after her with a shaken feeling, his hand resting on his doorknob. He could not see her, but he heard her enter her room at the end of the hall, then heard her moving around on the inside. A few minutes later he could barely make out a suppressed sobbing.

As Abner listened, his heart went down and down in the most melancholy fashion. He felt as if he had committed a crime.

He went into his room and was too depressed even to strike a light; but got off his shoes and trousers and coat in the darkness and tumbled sickly into his unmade bed. A great weight lay on his diaphragm. Certainly the congregation was right—the devil was at large on this ill-starred night.

He lifted his head from his pillow and listened intently for a long time, but was not certain whether he could hear Nessie still sobbing or not. It seemed to him all possible joy had gone out of life.

The woes of eighteen are absolute; untempered by philosophy, unsoftened by comparison. They are the worst that can ever befall any human being.

Abner did not know how long he lay in the darkness with his head full of dismal fancies, but presently he became aware of a rumour of distant voices. How long he had heard it he did not know, but when he noticed it, he knew it had been going on for perhaps a minute. It had arisen by the faintest crescendo out of complete silence.

But now that he had heard it, it held a certain overtone that brought him up instantly, sitting on the side of his bed, holding his breath and listening. Presently the confusion resolved into voices and a clatter of hoofs. Somewhere down the street he heard a window raised and somebody called, "What's the matter?" He heard a reply, but could not catch the words. The sound of hoofs grew louder, the voices came closer. Someone directed, "Go for a doctor!"

Abner jumped up from his bed, ran to his window, lifted the sash and looked out, letting the sash rest on his back.

Immediately the hoofbeats drew up at the hotel; out of the confusion a voice called desperately,

"Abner Teeftaller! Abner! Abner Te-e-eftaller!"

"What is it?" shouted Abner, shocked at the tone.

"Come on down here, quick!"

"What's the matter?"

"Tug's hurt! We got to carry him up to his room!"

A shock of supernatural horror shot through Abner and chilled his face. He knew now this was what he had expected. He whirled, struck the corner of the dresser, banged down the window sash, cursed, groped for his clothes, found only his trousers, huddled into them; the next moment went hurrying in sock feet through the hallway.

He could see the dark shape of the banisters against the reflections from the lamp on the stairpost below. He started to run downstairs when the lamp moved. When he got to the head of the steps, he saw the light held aloft by a hand and four men bringing up the body of Tug Beavers. In the yellow illumination the ghastly face did not look like Tug's. The four men bore the body with the shaky carefulness of untrained nurses. As they worked upward, one of Tug's hands slipped off his body and hung down at an awkward angle. The bearers paused to lay it back on the stomach again.

Among the crowd streaming up after the body, Abner could hear, "Is he dead?" "I don't know." "Shot in the back." "Picked him up on the road from Squire Meredith's!" "Know who done it?" "Hell far, ever'body knows who done it!"

Moved by some violent impulse Abner whirled and dashed down the hall. He knocked sharply at the girl's door.

"Nessie! Nessie!" he called urgently.

Already a light was moving on the inside. The next moment the door opened and Nessie, with a candle in her hand, her hair down and in her nightgown, stared at Abner with a pale face.

"You were right, Nessie!" gasped the youth in a horror-struck voice.

"What do you mean—what is it?"

"Peck Bradley shot Tug! I knew he would!"

Horror filled Nessie's face; she cried, "Oh, Abner!" and her shaking hand could hardly hold her candle.

Next moment Abner rushed back to his own room. The bearers were laying Tug on the bed, and up the crowded stairs hurried the doctor, the loiterers pressing to one side to let him pass.

The man of medicine had his bags. When he entered the room he called for more lights and a bowl of hot water. There was a confused passing of this message downstairs. Presently Miss Scovell appeared with her dress half fastened; in one hand she bore a plain lamp, in the other the flowered parlour lamp. Behind her, rather more than half asleep, dozed the Negro boy with a bowl of warm water insecurely held. Someone took it.

"Turn him over on his face," directed the doctor.

The four men turned Tug over. At the sight exposed came gasps and exclamations. Two or three of the weak-stomached left the room. The doctor stooped over Tug with probes and knives.

"Buckshot," he said in an undertone.

"Will he git well, Doctor?"

"How do I know! Get out of here, you folks who ain't doin' anything!"

There was a half-hearted movement toward the door. The doctor began cutting, and a number of the curious bolted from the room.

Among these was Abner.

CHAPTER XX

THE shooting of Tug Beavers precipitated a number of routine reactions in Irontown. Sheriff Bascom came from Lanesburg and telephoned to Florence, Alabama, for bloodhounds. On the evening train arrived an enormous dun-coloured bitch and a still huger dog, both grim as the crack of doom. The crowd around the station gave the two brutes a wide berth, awed by their ferocious aspect and their uncanny powers of trailing.

As soon as the dogs arrived, sheriff and constable started for the place of the shooting. A great crowd followed, Abner among them. The looks of the hounds, the fact that they were going to trail a man whom he knew very well, appalled the youth. He could imagine Peck Bradley flying futilely through the hills, wading streams, walking the trunks of fallen trees, putting pepper into his shoes, trying every ruse, and still these terrible animals would follow the scent he must inevitably leave behind him.

The constable had gone to Peck Bradley's boarding house and obtained one of the murderer's shirts. When the hounds reached the place where Tug had been found, the constable tossed the shirt to them, let them sniff at it, learn the peculiar odour which this man and no other man on earth bore. Then the sagacious animals started off, dragging their keeper and the constable at the end of their chains. They made wider and wider circles around the spot.

The handler of the dogs shouted to the crowd to stand back and not confuse the scent, but they would not do it. So the brutes circled about, casting over a hundred different trails, remembering by some unbelievable power a certain peculiar odour, searching it out among scores of other smells superimposed upon it.

Presently the bitch lifted her great muzzle to the skies and vented a prolonged and melancholy baying. The dog lunged toward her at her call. The hounds had struck Peck's scent behind a boulder some twenty yards down the road. Six feet away lay an empty shotgun shell. The sheriff picked this up and put it in his pocket, the first thread of the hemp to go around Peck Bradley's neck.

A minute later the hounds struck off through the hills, towing the handlers after them. The crowd followed; some trotting to keep up; others falling behind; all rather excited at being on the actual trail of a murderer.

Only once in a long while did the hounds give mouth in their basso-profundo baying. They settled to a steady pull up hill and down dale. The crowd got strung out in the long line of march; presently some of the men began dropping out of the chase by ones and twos and returned, walking more leisurely through the woods to the village.

Each straggler who returned was met by crowds eager to know exactly where the dogs struck the trail, which way Peck had gone, how long did it take them to pick up the scent? The telling of it was almost as exciting as seeing the dogs in action.

Peck had gone right through the manure pile behind Squire Meredith's barn, trying no doubt to throw the hounds off his trail. He turned up Grasshopper Ridge. He crossed this ridge and waded Big Ford Creek for about half a mile. Here the dogs split, one went up the creek, the other down. Half a mile up the creek the bitch again gave tongue; the dog came to her.

And so on and on and on, until the posse was reduced to the few men who actually saw the chase through. Then no more stragglers returned with their reports.

After that the village gleaned a general outline of the chase by telephone. Old man Darby heard the hounds on Piney Ridge. He had tried to go to them, but never could locate them as the sounds played tricks on him in the hills. Two of the Broadfoot girls had seen the men and the dogs pass through their cotton patch. The barking had scared them nearly to death. They didn't know it was dogs; thought it was some sort of varmints.

Then the chase bore so far away that only the flimsiest rumours drifted in: Peck was fighting the officers; he was not fighting the officers; he had begged something to eat at a Negro's shack; up on Harrican creek he had robbed an old man of his mule; he was making for the old John A. Murrell cave where, long before the Civil War, that noted desperado hid his stolen horses and Negroes before running them south to Louisiana. Everyone agreed that if Peck ever got into the Murrell cave, the officers would never get him out, it was so intricate and maze-like.

Three days later, Squire Meredith received a telephone message from Sheriff Bascom to get ready to hold Peck Bradley's trial at twelve o'clock, Saturday, that Peck was captured.

In the meantime sentiment in Irontown was being formed. On the morning after the shooting Mrs. Roxie Biggers paid a sort of visit of inspection to the Scovell House to see that Tug Beavers had what he needed. He had not. He lacked nightshirts. Now Tug had never worn a nightshirt in his life, but Mrs. Biggers held them indispensable to the recovery of health, so she would attend to it. She also found Tug's room unsanitary. It had a western exposure; the afternoon sun heated it up like a furnace and the bed was full of bugs. This was a great surprise to Abner; he had not seen any. Mrs. Biggers, so the village gossip reported, "laid into Miss Scovell about the room and gave her a piece of her mind." Then Mrs. Biggers started conscripting nightshirts; and while she was at it she seized enough for Tug and her husband, too. Mrs. Biggers never gave anything to charity herself except her services, but these services were dynamic.

When she had collected enough shirts to satisfy any and all uses, she worked out a plan what to do with Tug.

She bore down on Nannie Northcutt, her sister-in-law, and told Nannie she would have to have her best room for a while.

The banker's wife stared in consternation at the terrible chariteer and asked what she wanted with it.

She wanted to put Tug Beavers in it.

"The man that was killed last night!"

"He ain't dead, but he will die if we leave him down there in that hot cinch-y place!"

"That whisky-head who——"

"Nannie Northcutt!" cried Mrs. Roxie. "Don't you know this is the Lord's work to bring Irontown to repentance! If you don't do your duty in helpin' the afflicted, what do you think the Lord'll do to you?"

"But why don't you take him somewheres else?" cried Mrs. Nannie, with tears of outrage in her eyes.

"Because the Lord has called on you!" snapped Mrs. Roxie.

There was no getting around the point. Mrs. Roxie stood on the ancient Northcutt prescriptive right to enunciate the will of God. The Northcutt family always had done it. Undoubtedly, the old Hebrew prophets were some sort of distant relations of the Northcutts! At any rate, the prophets, according to reports, enjoyed the same sort of unpopularity as did Mrs. Roxie.

Mrs. Nannie evaded the requisition as hopelessly as a rabbit flies from a weasel. Finally and fatally, she aroused her large apathetic body to go into her cool dark front room and freshen up the bed to receive Tug Beavers. Mrs. Roxie immediately began to console her sister-in-law out of a genuine kindness of heart.

"Now, Nannie, you won't have a thing else to do. I'll have somebody else do all the tendin' to Mr. Beavers; all the settin' up; all the packin' of the slops an' feedin' him; an' when I git through I'll have somebody clean up yore front room an' leave it jest like I found it, so there." She patted Mrs. Nannie's shoulder.

By this Mrs. Nannie knew that her sacrifice had been accepted and that she had received absolution from Irontown's patron saint.

Mrs. Biggers hurried out on the street and commandeered the first four Negroes she saw to move Tug from the Scovell House to the banker's home. The physician objected at first, but Mrs. Roxie pointed out the bugs and the heat of the room. The medic yielded the point and went with the good woman to prepare the unconscious man for the journey on a stretcher—that is, a wire cot used for a stretcher.

The change was made that afternoon.

When Abner returned to his lodging he found his landlady, Miss Scovell, in tears. Upon inquiry he learned she had been insulted and abused by that meddlesome cat, Roxie Biggers. Miss Scovell controlled her sobs barely long enough to fling out these maledictions, and then she began her queer dry hacking again, without a film of moisture in her eyes.

Abner went out to the porch swing to await the coming of Nessie. So filled had the intervening hours been with shock and excitement, that it seemed to Abner he had not seen Nessie for months. When finally she came from her work and joined him, he felt he could never leave off looking at the glory of her pale glossy hair, her rose complexion, and pansy eyes. He wished he could put his arms about her and draw her to him, so sweet and intimate did she seem.

And Nessie kept glancing at him from time to time with her bosom rising and falling under her low-cut blouse, and a faint smile playing perpetually on her lips; a smile that had in it not the least hint of that inherently vulgar thing called humour or mirth; she smiled because of her happiness, her tenderness, her wistfulness for him, and because she was upon the verge of tears.

That night when Mr. Biggers was going to bed, he asked, in his shaking tones, "Roxie—i-is this my n-night-gown?" And Mrs. Roxie snapped, "Put it on an' don't worry me!"

But she was immediately sorry for her sharpness and asked, "Do you feel all right to-night, Mr. Biggers?"

The wrecked man sat down on the side of his bed picking at his unaccustomed nightgown but afraid to say anything more to his wife.

"What are you doin'?" she asked.

"N-nothing." He stopped his picking.

"Well—le's pray before you go to bed for God to complete yore cure."

"Y-yes, l-let's pray. . . ."

Mrs. Roxie was not sure from her husband's face and tones whether or not he understood what she said. She helped him to a kneeling position beside the bed, got on her knees beside him, and prayed determinedly for his complete recovery.

CHAPTER XXI

THE high pillars of the Irontown lock-up made it inconvenient for the boys and men of the village to climb up and peer through the barred windows into the cage where Peck Bradley was confined, but, nevertheless, this scrambling and peering went on all day long. There was something obscene and defiling in the spectacle of a mud-encrusted man locked up like an animal in a cage which stung the spiritual palate of Irontown with a kind of salty pleasure.

Peck, in all the mud and filth of his three-days-and-three-nights' chase, had been caged without even the comfort of a brush or a pan of water. Nevertheless, he sat on the noisome bunk in his cell with a certain air of assurance and habit. He had hung his woollen socks on one of the cross bars to dry. He pulled off his shirt and beat it against his cage to flail off the dried mud. He flipped his fingers through his bristly hair to get the dust out of it, and he begged cigarettes from his visitors. He made the most of the slender resources of the Irontown lock-up just as an experienced traveller arranges his things in a Pullman compartment and puts himself at ease for a journey.

To those who climbed to the window Peck talked freely and apparently quite casually, but, nevertheless, everything that he said held a certain expert-witness adroitness, so that if it ever should be repeated in a courtroom it would assist him to freedom and not to the electric chair.

"Why, yes," he told Tim Fraley, "I shot Tug—had to do it. I admit I was tryin' to skeer him. He pulled his automatic an' come at me spittin' far ever' step. I yelled at him to stop it, I was a frien', but he kep' comin' an' I had to

168

do somethin'—it was self-defence pyore an' simple. . . .
He went on to say he would get Buck Sharp for his lawyer.
He guessed Buck would pull him through. As a matter of
fact, when Tug's body was found his automatic had just
been fired and five cartridges were missing from the clip.

Now every person in Irontown knew those missing five
cartridges were *ex post facto* evidence. Peck simply had shot
them away. But the social centres of Irontown, butcher
shop, grocery, and drug store, conned this testimony which
Peck clearly meant to give in his trial, and all agreed that it
hung together. Whether or not the prosecuting attorney
would be able to pick it to pieces the gossips did not know.
They surmised not. At least, he had not in the Shelton case.
Besides that, Peck had been haled before the courts on two
or three cases of hog theft and he had always displayed a
curious ingenuity in coming off scot free.

The cunning with which Peck Bradley had planned his
crime and now was building up his defence excited a certain
admiration in the village. It was a parade in criminal violence of the same genre as one of Railroad Jones's coups in
financial trickery. In each instance the actor saw the law
clearly as an obstacle and evaded it. Such illegal technique
demanded its meed of admiration.

However, there was one fault with Peck's achievement:
he had ambushed Tug after his rival had whipped him in a
fair fight at the Warrington dance.

Tom Northcutt, the miller, in.talking about the matter in
Fuller's drug store, said he "didn't think after Tug had licked
Peck in a fair fight, Peck ort to of ambushed Tug—it didn't
look right."

Every man in the circle agreed by words or nods to this
sentiment, and a queer sentiment it was. The implication
being that if Tug had not whipped Peck, Peck's ambush
would have been justified.

Such a fantastic twist to hill morals was a relic of the old
Indian fighters who first settled the country. These Indian
fighters used the ambush freely, but when two white men

had a fist fight and one was whipped, then for the loser to resort to an ambush was dishonourable. Therefore, the village thought that Peck had done Tug a wrong.

On the other hand, every native of Irontown firmly believed that Tug Beavers's catastrophe was a direct dispensation of Providence brought on by Tug's refusal to go to the mourners' bench during the revival. Everyone had seen how stiff-necked the teamster was, and had heard the minister predict his downfall.

An old hillman in the butcher shop elucidated this mystery. God had used the criminal intentions of Peck to bring retribution on Tug. He had played one sinner off against the other. This was to the hill people's kidney. They could worship a deity like that, a celestial trickster, a kind of Railroad Jones of Heaven.

Mrs. Roxie Biggers, hurrying down the street from the banker's house, met Abner Teeftallow and stopped him with a sharp gesture. The two had come to know each other fairly well during Tug's sickness. Now something in Mrs. Biggers's manner alarmed the teamster. A fear shot through him and he asked in a constrained voice, "Miss Roxie—is he dead?"

"No, he ain't dead, he talked to me a little while ago." A quiver of wrath moved the old woman's high thin nostrils.

Abner was relieved that Tug was alive, but immediately was apprehensive as to what his friend had done to irritate Mrs. Biggers. It was quite within probabilities that he had sworn at the old woman and had offended the whole family.

"Wh-what did he say?" asked Abner, expecting the worst report.

"Why, I was talkin' to him about his soul!" snapped Mrs. Roxie.

"Y-yes," stammered Abner, who perceived that his worst anticipations had been realized.

"An' we've all misjudged Mr. Beavers; we've misjudged him bad, Abner!"

She uttered this with such feeling that Abner began to make plans to carry Tug back to the Scovell House. The youth nodded apprehensively.

"An' we've been too leenient with that stinking rascal, Peck Bradley! Do you know what Tug said to me? He said, 'Miss Roxie, I always meant to throw my influence on the right side,' he shore said it; he whispered it to me." Tears came into the old woman's eyes.

Abner caught his breath at this *volte-face* of what he had expected. All he could do was simply to stare at Mrs. Biggers, wondering what would come next.

"Did you know that?"

Abner nodded, "Yes, that's what he always tol' me, too."

"Why in the name of creation didn't you tell it!"

"Well, I—I don't know," stammered Abner now that her wrath apparently had switched to him.

"Why, that would uh *proved* this shootin' wasn't the Lord's work!" stormed the old woman, "because you know, Abner Teeftaller, God judges a mortal by what's in his heart, not by what he does!"

"Yeh, that's right," nodded Abner hastily.

"Well, don't that show you God didn't have a thing in the worl' to do with the shootin' of Tug Beavers! It's nothin' but the wickedness of that low-down murderer down yonder in the lock-up, Peck Bradley! It's him an' nobody but him!"

"Yes, I always thought that!" Abner nodded his head sidewise, which indicated great earnestness.

"You should of spoke up if you thought it!" she reproved sharply. "Here we are, lettin' that stinkin' Peck Bradley git up his plea of self-defence—an' he'll git out on it, too, as shore as you're a foot high, if we ever let his case fall into the han's of the law!" She shook a skinny finger under Abner's nose.

Certain nebulous but disquieting implications lurked in the old woman's phrase. Abner stared at her intently, breathing through his open mouth.

"If we let his case—fall—into—the—hands—of—the— law?" he repeated, very uncomfortably at sea.

"Shore! You know Buckin'ham Sharp'll git him out! You know that! That ain't no guesswork! When law comes in the door, jestice flies out the winder! Now, you look here, Abner," she wielded her finger again, "if us folks in Lane County don't use more jestice an' less law, this county ain't goin' to be fitten for decent, God-fearin' folks to live in! I'm not aginst the courts. I think they air fine in their places, but their place certainly ain't where they is a real crime and wickedness committed. 'Vengeance is mine, saith the Lord!' Well, how's the Lord goin' to git vengeance unless the childern of the Lord wake up an' do somethin'! God kain't come down out of Heaven, bust open that lock-up, an' hang Peck Bradley, but He can use the han's of the God-fearin' people of this town to serve His purpose! 'Vengeance is mine, saith the Lord!'"

The next moment she was off, past Abner, down the street on her way to the next person she met, even more wrought up than when Abner first encountered her.

The teamster felt as if he had received an electric shock. For the first time, Tug Beavers's shattered side called to Abner for vengeance. Like all his fellow villagers, the young man had fallen into a foggy notion that because it was customary to inflict merely the annoyance of capture and trial on a homicide, that custom necessarily was right. But Mrs. Biggers had been nursing Tug steadily since she had removed him from the hotel. She had fallen into a maternal attitude toward the wounded man, and now with ruthless feminine logic, she appraised the law for exactly what it was worth. And she had a woman's ability to burn her point of view into others.

Abner felt that he must do something. He moved along aimlessly, his wrath slowly kindling against Peck Bradley. Added to what Mrs. Biggers had said, there revisited Abner's thoughts the fact that Tug had whipped Peck once in a fair fight. And after all that, Peck had waylaid Tug and shot

him! The teamster began cursing softly under his breath,
"The God-damn yellow cur . . ."

Abner met Zed Parrum. Zed officially lived in the country, but he stayed in the village most of the time and visited
the home of his wife at intervals.

Abner passed a brief "Hidy" and then rapped out, "Zed,
what do you think about Peck Bradley?"

Zed was surprised at this question, but cocked his head to
one side, gave it consideration, and finally brought out the
information that he thought Peck was a "lallapaloosa."

"Do you think he done right shootin' Tug Beavers after
Tug licked him in a fair fight?" demanded Abner hotly.

"Now, Abner," philosophized Zed, "you see Tug hisse'f
had jest committed the unpardonable sin."

"Unpardonable hell!" flared Abner.

"You ain't mad at me, air you, Abner?"

"Naw, but where'd you git any sich idee?"

"Well—me an' Pap Tolbert was talkin' about it, an' he
said Tug had rejected the pleadin's of the Holy Ghost and
that was the unpardonable sin."

"What had ol' man Shelton done when Peck killed him?
He was a good ol' man, a deacon in the church."

Zed rubbed an unshaven jaw. "I don't know as *he* done
nothin', but God may of been jest whettin' Peck up gittin'
ready to land on Tug."

"By Geemeny, God's plan of punishment is mighty loose
in the steering gear, runnin' into ol' man Shelton first—a
good ol' man."

"His mysteries are past findin' out," quoted Zed rever-
ently.

"Well, of course, that's so," admitted Abner, who at heart
was as good a religionist as any of the hill folk. "But now
here I got ye, 'As a man thinketh in his heart, so is he.'"

"What you mean by that?"

"Haven't you heard Tug say many a time he wanted to
throw his influence on the right side?"

"Well, yeh, I b'lieve I have."

"Now, by God, I got ye!" He shook a finger at Zed. "It don't make a damn bit o' diff'runce what Tug done, whether he went up to the mourners' bench or not, he was thinkin' right in his heart, an' he *was* right! He was *right!* That shows Peck Bradley shot Tug out o' wickedness and cussedness, exactly like he shot ol' man Shelton, an', by God, me an' you as citizens of Lane County ort not to let him fall into the protection an' encouragement of the law, which will turn him go a free man."

Such an amazing conclusion took Zed off his feet. "My Lord, man, me an' you—me an' you not let him—how the hell can me an' you do anything a-tall?"

"Take him out an' hang him!" cried Abner, "or he'p do it! This ain't a case fer the law; there's been a crime committed!"

"Gosh, but you're talkin' batty!"

"Don't the Bible say, 'Vengeance is mine, saith the Lord?'"

"Shore."

"Don't the childern of God have to do ever' frazzlin' thing the Lord gits done down here? They build the churches, send off the missionaries, pay the preachers, hold the meetin's. God don't turn a finger for Hisse'f. Now, look here, if the Lord wants vengeance, who's goin' to haff to git it fer Him? Answer me that! Who's it up to?"

"Huh!" Zed fell into a surprised meditation. Presently he admitted. "I never had thought of that. . . ."

"An' Tug licked Peck once in a fair fight," clinched Abner.

"Le's walk down to the garage an' see what the rest of the boys think about it," proposed Zed.

At the garage Abner's bright flash of initiative was lost in a deluge of talk. All he succeeded in doing was to stir up one of those endless incoherent arguments, common to the hill folk, which rambled on and on to no purpose whatever. The question of redressing the wrongs of Tug Beavers was placed on the same impersonal plane as whether or not potatoes grew larger when planted in the dark of the moon; or the benefits of Shallburger's Socialism. The men at the garage argued like children, mixing their categories, using clichés from the law, the Bible, science, and folklore, with no sense of a lack of homogeneity.

Abner listened to them with a misery of frustration that they had completely sidetracked his plan of action. He broke into it, shaking a youth named Tim Fraley by the shoulder.

"Look here, le's do something!"

Mr. Fraley looked at Abner with the mists of speculation in his eyes.

"We kain't do nothin'. Willie Purvis there sounds to me like he's got the thing cinched, he says, the Bible says, 'Render unto Cæsar the things that air Cæsar's.'"

"What's that got to do with it?"

"Why, Willie says it means if Peck Bradley could waylay Tug legally so the courts kain't tech him, then we kain't n'uther . . . 'Render unto Cæsar the things that air Cæsar's'—that's what the Bible says."

"Aw, it don't mean no such damn thing!"

"Well, what do you say it means?" demanded Mr. Fraley with the elaborate politeness of the slightly offended. "Come, speak up, this is a free country."

Anger and despair filled Abner at the prospect of having to interpret the exact meaning of every Biblical text before he brought off his coup.

"I don't know what the hell it means!"

"Then, it seems to me you better find out," observed Mr. Fraley ironically. "Seems to me before you set up to lead the citizens of Lanesburg, you better find out jest what is right an' Scriptural."

That, of course, is the difficulty of combating child-logic. It is incontrovertible and betrayingly simple. It skips lightly from darksome premise to more darksome conclusion with a Gallic lucidity. It was far, far beyond Abner to answer

Mr. Fraley. He simply stood and looked at him and hated him and was balked by him—justice, righteousness, and the Scriptures. . . .

At that moment there entered the door of the garage a short stocky man whose felt hat and blue denim shirt were faintly powdered with meal. This was Tom Northcutt, the Irontown miller. Northcutt stopped in the sunlight, which fell into the square entrance of the garage, and made a peremptory gesture for the gang to come to him. They did not do this, but everyone stopped talking to look at him.

"Git ready, this evenin', three o'clock," he directed in the voice of a man used to shouting above machinery, "meet behind that lumber pile clost to the lock-up. Don't come a minute early, you might git identified; nor a minute late, for that'll be too late. Now you boys scatter out o' here an' git to yore homes. Don't be seen on the streets in crowds. I'm not sayin' nothin' a-tall about what's goin' to happen—I don't know. Now clear out, all of ye!"

He waved them away. A thrill went through the garage gang and they began to disperse. A certain note in this brief address was characteristic of the Northcutt oligarchy over the village, and this phrase inspired confidence in the hangers-on. This was Mr. Northcutt's assertion that he did not know what was going to happen. Every man recognized in this sentence Mr. Northcutt's legal alibi; the parry which would deflect from his bosom the keen rapier of evidence in the event that the doings of this day ever came before a grand jury. What had he done? Told the boys to go home and keep off the streets. It was the same sort of shrewdness that Peck Bradley had used, that Railroad Jones used, but on a slightly different plane from the shrewdness of either of those two.

The crowd dissolved at his advice; some wandered out the back door, some the front. Abner took himself out of the side door, the one by which he had entered, to see Zed Parrum walk past the garage with his bride-to-be.

This memory now flitted into his head and flitted out

again. Abner was deeply grateful to Mr. Tom Northcutt for taking the burden of redress from his shoulders. The teamster perceived now that he had been a tyro indeed in his effort to incite a lynching. He had gone to the garage arguing the right and wrong. That was not the crux of the matter at all; it was to avoid the law, not to argue about it. Nobody in the garage had sensed that until Tom Northcutt, with the Northcutt prerogative of leadership, had felt it instantly, had given directions in half a minute, and had vanished.

CHAPTER XXII

IN HIS hot little room on the west side of the Scovell House with the sun, a little past vertical, slanting into his window, Abner Teeftallow had immured himself until the appointed hour of three in the afternoon.

The fact that he was under instructions to secrete himself, that he was in hiding in his own room until the time came for him to hurry out and take part in a sharp and tragic and illegal spectacle—this filled Abner with his first sense of civic importance and, at the same time, kept him in nervous suspense like that of a new actor in the wings of the stage.

Time apparently had stopped in Irontown. The teamster glanced once more at the clock, a cheap tin affair which Tug Beavers had bought for their room. The hand seemed not a millimeter advanced since he had glanced at it before. In an hour and a half it would be time to start—an hour and a half. The timepiece ticked loudly in the hot little room; as Abner looked at it it broke into a startled double beat, ticketty-tick, ticketty-tick, as if it, too, somehow had become infected with the pervading nervousness.

At four- or five-minute intervals Abner would take his automatic from his pocket (he had bought one now) and reassure himself that its clip was full of cartridges. Then he would reinspect the bandanna handkerchief which he had cut into a mask, trying it on to see that the holes for the eyes and mouth fitted. He was apprehensive that in the moment of action the mask would not fit; that he would find himself working at it, adjusting it when all the other masks had marched out from behind the lumber pile to the lock-up, and he would be left. A vision of masked men hauling Peck Bradley out of his cell filled Abner's eyes. It reminded him

of pictures he had seen in the dime novels. He wondered if
Peck would fight. The alarm clock suddenly set up its double
knock again, as if the scene somehow had got into its wheels
and stirred it to violent action.

Abner paused with his mask to look at the clock. Its
miniature violence was the only sound he could hear. Indeed, the silence, now that the teamster noticed it, was extraordinary. He sat listening with mouth open to catch the
faintest noise, but could hear nothing at all. And yet there
seemed something strained about the stillness, as if on the
verge of an outbreak.

The teamster arose with a little shudder and walked to
his window. He did not thrust out his head as ordinarily
he would, but surveyed the street from the inside, moving
about, well back of the window, to obtain the whole view.
From one shabby end to the other, not a person was on it,
not even a child at play. This very absence of life reinforced in the youth his sense of an impending cataclysm.
The village in the still sunshine looked to Abner like some
sort of gigantic trap, baited, set, ready to clash into swift
and fatal action, but for the present, as silent and patient
as the very sunshine itself.

At this normally busy time of day for the streets to be
deserted advertised that every man, woman, and child in Irontown knew what was going to happen; that this solitude of
street was the collective alibi of the village to prove before
some future grand jury that Irontown knew nothing whatever about the tragedy it was about to perform. This was
the acme of hill-country finesse and social solidarity.

Amid this crouching silence it became impossible for Abner
to remain in his room. He glanced once more at the clock,
felt the mask in his pocket, then arose and took a turn in
the hall.

The hallway was faintly cooler than his own room and was
a kind of clearing house for the odours of the whole establish-
ment; smells from the dining room below, from the bedrooms,
the penetrating odour of an insecticide which Miss Scovell

had bought in consequence of Mrs. Roxie Biggers's defamation of her beds.

The thought flickered through Abner's mind that Mrs. Roxie had produced both these results: the smell inside, the suspended animation outside; odour and silence; maximal and minimal sequences of the visit of that dictatorial old woman to the Scovell House to see Tug Beavers.

This momentary glimpse of life in the round so foreign to the hill type vanished swiftly from Abner's mind, leaving him occupied with that never-ending stream of petty defensive and offensive thoughts which form the intellectual staple of his class.

He wondered if some future grand jury would really indict the whole of Irontown. Would it put the whole village in jail? Where would the grand jury come from?

This brought him squarely against the question of mob violence and communal lawlessness, but Abner, like millions of other Americans, could make no further step in his thinking. His questions stood out like figures against a fog and produced only a sense of grotesqueness, mystery, and danger.

As for himself, he would march with the others and take his share like a man. He felt in his pockets to reassure himself that mask and pistol were there, walked past his room to glance in at the clock, and continued his noiseless marching up and down.

At the end of the hall opposite his own room a door stood open, and as he passed it he saw to his surprise Nessie Sutton kneeling beside her bed, apparently in prayer.

Abner stopped short, staring at the girl, wondering what she was doing in her room at that time of the day. A suspicion that she meant to join the lynching party shot through his head and was instantly rejected.

The girl must have heard Abner pause in his soft pacing, for she looked around. Her face was white and frightened. After a mute interrogation in her wide eyes she began in a low voice, "Are you——" then broke off and moved her head in a mysterious manner toward the silent village outside.

Abner knew that she was asking him if he would take part in the approaching murder. He hardly knew what to answer. He could not in loyalty to his gang admit anything in words. Neither could he possibly deny Nessie any question. So, staring at the girl, an idea for an explanatory evasion came to him. He drew the edge of his bandanna mask from his pocket, displayed it significantly, and thrust it back. As he did so he thought, "That's enough to show her I'm goin', but she couldn't swear before a grand jury what she saw. . . ." And Abner felt he had done exactly the right thing.

"How come you at home, Nessie?" he asked curiously.

"Mr. Baxter sent me. He said I better go home, there wouldn't be no trade." She paused, then added with a touch of horror: "All the stores are locked up!"

"Fuh God's sake!" echoed Abner in the same voice. He was shocked, thrown out of his bearings. The whole town was locked up! The affair had leaped beyond his reckoning. He had thought it merely a coup of the garage gang, but the business men of the village must be in it: Mr. Baxter, Mr. Bingham, Mr. Fuller. Abner never before had known these men to do anything beyond attending the meetings of their fraternal orders on lodge nights. He had looked upon them as human machines whom nothing stirred, nothing retarded; nothing broke their steady money-making gait. Other men might fight, gamble, mob, but these pillars of village society would do nothing unusual whatsoever. They were standardized automatons of small-town respectability, and now—these mechanical figures suddenly had come to life, had locked up their stores and gone out to kill a man!

A shiver went through the teamster. "Look here," he whispered, dry-mouthed, "I got to go—my Lord, I kain't stay here!" He was spurred by a feeling that it was unsafe to follow Tom Northcutt's instructions and await an appointed hour. Such an unprecedented occurrence might break loose any moment. He turned on his heel when the girl cried out, leaped up, and was on him before he knew it.

"Don't! Don't!" she cried. "Oh, Abner, don't go out there! It's murder, Abner! Dear Abner!"

She had her arms about his neck and suddenly began a vehement sobbing.

The teamster was shocked, amazed beyond all experience. The perfume of the girl, her soft slender body pressing passionately against him, so shocked and confused him that he could distinguish nothing clearly. She was a blur of bluish dress, of pale cornsilk hair, of perfume. As she sobbed he felt her bosom pressing in spasms against his own.

"Why, what's the matter, Nessie? Little girl! There! There! Don't cry, honey." As he lifted a hand to pat her cheek a tear splashed his fingers. This somehow renewed his sense of shock. "What *is* the matter, Nessie, honey?" he begged.

"You'll be a murderer, Abner!" she gasped. "It's awful! It's sinful, wicked! Don't you know it'll send your soul to —the bad place!"

The last phrase was a horrified aspirate. She was looking up at him with tears on her lashes, her pleading lips within three inches of his own. As the person of the girl gained upon Abner, the imminent drama at the lock-up receded from him. One urgency slowly faded from his mind and almost imperceptibly gave way to another.

She was so slight, a mere wisp in his arms, and unbelievably soft. Never before had his arms been about a woman, and now, under the spell of the girl, the topic they were debating so passionately wavered and grew uncertain in the growing wonder of her appeal. He collected his thoughts with an effort.

"But, Nessie," he objected, "it—it ain't murder if ever'-body does it; it's—it's——"

She broke into his definition passionately.

"But it is! You *know it is*, Abner! To kill a man! You—you wouldn't help kill a man!" She bent back her lithe torso to her arms' length, her waist still held in his arms, and looked at him with horror in her eyes.

Abner scrambled desperately after the topic, confused by a twitching in his breast. "But—but he shot Tug Beavers. . . ."

"What of that! You're not the executioner! You're not the law!"

"I—no, I'm not the law—I'm not——" he tried to recall the arguments Mrs. Roxie Biggers had used in favour of mob rule. They flickered out under a queer compressed feeling in his chest. His heart began a steadily accelerated pounding. Almost unaware of what he was doing he leaned down and pressed his lips to the girl's mouth.

There came a motionless silence. He felt a little quiver go through Nessie. She moved her head away and breathed in a faint voice, "Oh—don't do that. . . ."

His fingers shook so that he could hardly control them as he pressed her face back to his own.

She tried to pull away and mumbled, "Don't, Abner—please don't . . ."

His voice came out, shaken by his heartbeats. "You—you love me—don't you?"

She said nothing to this but pushed away from him in the circle of his arms, shaking as if with an ague. Abner swallowed drily. "You do—love me—I know you do." Her continued opposition somehow inflamed him. He kissed her again roughly. Her lips felt so soft and warm. She still tried to move her head, but at his growing violence relaxed weakly in his arms. With his lips still pressed to hers one of the teamster's trembling hands began exploring the rondures of her form. He pushed her door shut with his foot.

Once, later, she half gasped, half sobbed, "Oh—oh—Abner—please, p-l-e-a-s-e——"

The teamster was fetched back to the drama of village life by the softened report of a distant volley of shots. A kind of slow shock travelled through Abner and delivered him from the swoon of his bewildering experience. He got up and said in a whisper, mainly to himself, "My God, they've already gone!"

He started for the door. This time the girl neither moved nor spoke but remained just as she lay with closed eyes looking as if someone had felled her at a blow.

A backward glance at her aroused in Abner a kind of questioning remorse. He had a feeling of coming out of some sort of whirling force that had betrayed and wrecked Nessie, and now it had passed and left in the room a kind of draggled evil. He felt an impulse to get away from this evil thing. He opened the door as silently as he could and left Nessie in the room.

More distant shots took Abner's mind from such dismal impressions and sent him tiptoeing down the hall, then down the stairs two at a time and so out in the street where he broke into a run for the lock-up.

The village street was still empty, and Abner's flying feet aroused echoes as if some invisible runner raced the teamster just behind the string of houses. As he approached the alley which led from the business street to the lock-up, the youth craned forward, trying to peer down it long before he reached the vantage of its mouth. When he did dash into it all he saw was the lock-up door standing open and Constable Gifford walking away from it with one of his shirt sleeves torn.

The teamster rushed down on the officer.

"Where'd they go, Mr. Gifford? Which way?" He drew down to a panting walk.

"Yander way!" the constable flung an arm toward the west. "My Lord, they all jumped on me at wunst—what could a feller do! Look here, how they tore my shirt! They'd uh killed me if I hadn't of give 'em the key!" He held up his arm to display more prominently the torn sleeve.

Abner had no time to waste on the alibi the constable was preparing, but struck out again, westward, toward the old Squire Meredith place at a long trot.

At every curve of the village street, and beyond town, at every curve of the country road, the running youth peered forward in hope of a glimpse of the violent melodrama. The road unfolded in yellow curves of summer dust.

Presently a fear began to mount in Abner's throat, which crystallized into an anguished certainty, that he had missed the lynchers altogether. He had missed their trail! They had turned off somewhere into the woods, for a stout tree, no doubt!

He now ran on miserably and hopelessly, but unable to stop running owing to the possibility that he might find them, that he might get to them. In his heart he damned his lingering with Nessie. The brief remorse he had suffered in her presence had vanished as completely as the reflection in a mirror when it is turned another way. He had missed the lynching! He could have wept!

As he mounted the long slope that led up to Squire Meredith's farm, running up grade became impossible. He slowed down to a heavy perspiring trot. He gasped for breath in the hot sunshine, but he could not walk. He could not endure the slow movement of a walk. Sweat stung his eyes. He thought expletives in mental sighs of frustration, "Oh damn—damn—damn that girl——" Then he was forced to give up even his poor trot. His legs were lead. The heat closed around him like a blanket.

He blinked up at the sun in despair when a swinging object on the right-hand side of the road transfixed his attention.

At the end of its rope the object turned slowly around until it faced the teamster standing frozen on the hot hillside. It turned on until it displayed three quarters of its back, then, gradually, it stopped, hung for a moment, and began slowly turning back again.

This slow passive exhibition of itself was the most gruesome thing Abner had ever imagined. It looked somehow as if it were dully summing up the whole matter—life had come to this. This was why he had been born, had laboured, stolen, and murdered—to this end. It was Peck Bradley, focussed to pure intellect at last.

The thing looked curiously shrunken and small. It seemed strange that the whole village should have made such a to-do over so trifling an object. It looked now as if one man—any man—might have done it. It was so small, shattered, and passive. The clothes were flecked with little round targets of dust where the bullets had struck. The thing never had got itself washed or combed after its three-days chase in the woods.

The head with its hog-bristle hair was bent at an awkward angle, and the face, rather badly shot, bore a certain messy grin as if there were a kind of jest in the fact that the very archtype of one stratum of hill-country illegal *savoir faire* should be seized upon by emulous fellow citizens and so sadly misprized. The body turned and returned to show the extent of its mishandling.

When Abner went closer he saw that one of its ears, two fingers, and a thumb had been cut cleanly off by souvenir hunters; men afraid, perhaps, they would forget this.

Abner stared and stared in a kind of mental syncope. It seemed to him as if he were peering through this body into another and a horrible world of which he had never even dreamed. The slowly revolving figure filled the earth with a terrible insecurity.

Then Abner observed that the mob had hanged Peck just above the place where he had lain in wait for Tug Beavers. With the melodramatic instinct of an uncultured folk, Irontown had brought Peck here. The implication was that this was not a dirty, hideous job, the sooner finished, the better; it was a processional, a rite, a holiday, a tidbit to be served with melodramatic sauce to the public palate. Abner himself, when he observed this, felt that it was a fine stroke.

A voice behind the youth shocked him profoundly.

"I'm glad to see you were not in this lynching party, Abner."

Abner whirled as if stung and saw a familiar figure at whom he stared for several seconds before recognizing Mr. Ditmas; then he repeated, "Glad to see I ain't in it?"

"Yes, very glad."

Abner looked at Mr. Ditmas, rather relieved to take his eyes off the thing.

"How do you know I wasn't in it?" he asked with a certain penetration.

"If you had been in it you would have run off with the others."

"Yeh, that's so, I guess—but now a jury would say I he'ped do it if they found me stan'in' here."

Ditmas glanced at the youth more sharply, seeking to fathom this extraordinary thought.

"Possibly—a jury's notions are more or less mechanical, a certain notion for a certain situation—funny thing, a jury, take 'em one at a time, each man seems to have ordinary sense, put 'em together and you've got twelve damn fools —but how came you to think of that at all?"

"I—don't know."

The teamster looked so stupid and stodgy standing there by the figure, the engineer gave up his questioning and fell into another line of thought. He said, more to himself than to Abner, "I wonder what period of human development this throws back to? Almost every grade and condition of man has some sort of form they go through with before executing one of their members. The American Indians held elaborate pow wows; African tribes possessed genuine courts; in the Fijis executions were the subject of religious ceremonials and ended by making a feast off the corpse. . . ."

"The people here do this," said Abner, proffering the usual village explanation, "because the law won't do nothin' to nobody."

"Certainly, that's the queer part; the law seems to function in Africa, in the Fijis, in every other place on the globe at least enough for the people to have confidence in it and depend on it, but down here in the South there seems to be no confidence whatever in the law. That's the puzzle, why is that?"

Abner turned around and looked at the corpse, spurred to a certain dim intellectual effort by its concrete question.

"Why didn't the law work in the South?" He pondered it seriously and finally said, "It jest never did, Mr. Ditmas."

At that moment, at a considerable distance among the trees, Abner received an impression that something had moved. His woodman's sense had marked the stealthy gliding of a man. He broke off suddenly to ask, "Who was that?"

"Where?"

"Out yonder behind that log."

"I don't see anything behind that log."

"Course not now, after I pointed."

"Is there someone?"

"Shore, le's go see."

Ditmas was really incurious about another spectator of the gruesome scene, but he followed Abner, who moved slowly and noiselessly toward the log. Instinctively the engineer followed his example. The teamster dropped his hand to the automatic in his pocket—not that he meant to use it; he habitually placed himself in a defensive posture when he walked up on anything like this.

When they were within fifteen steps of the log both men were startled by a fear-struck voice,

"Oh—oh, Mastuh Abnah, fuh God's sake don' kill me, Mastuh. Ah ain't done nothin'!"

And around the end of the log peeked an eye and the quarter of the head of a Negro boy. A second later this turned out to be the black chore boy of the Scovell House.

The chore boy had the misplaced appearance of a tame house cat in the woods.

"John!" snapped Abner, irritated by the strain on his nerves. "What the hell are you doin' here!"

John was the colour of ashes. He could hardly control his thick lips to speak.

"Ah—Ah jess come tuh—tuh see, Mas' Abnah! You won' kill me fuh—fuh dat, Mas' Abnah! Ah allus toted up yo' watah, Mas' Abnah. Ah—Ah——"

"No!" cried Ditmas sharply, "of course we aren't going to do anything to you. You have a perfect right to come out and look—what are you afraid of?"

"Wuh—well, Mas' Ditmas, when de white fo'ks k-k-kill one pusson d-dey usually k-k-kill all de niggahs dey can fin' too."

John eased himself up beside the log and stood wetting his dark lips with his red tongue, watching the two white men narrowly and a little sidewise, evidently ready to make one last bid for life with his heels if Abner drew his automatic.

Mr. Ditmas touched Abner's arm. "Come on, let's go back to town—this is one hell of a country!"

"John—you can go," said Abner slowly and enigmatically, though exactly why he should have to give John permission to leave him in the woods was a mystery. The black boy began walking away, taking quick cautious strides and most of the time looking back to see exactly what Abner was doing.

As the youth and the man returned to the village, Mr. Ditmas mentioned once more Abner's interest in the old Coltrane lands and said he had found out there was some claim on a tract of timber land he was trying to buy from Railroad Jones.

Abner answered more or less absently. The conversation was the veriest stopgap after the curious excitement of meeting the chore boy in the woods.

When the two friends entered the village again, they observed that all the Negro shacks at the edge of the village were deserted. Hardly a black person remained in Irontown. Some had fled to the woods until this white storm blew over; some were in the coloured church praying to God to preserve them; others had taken what few possessions they could carry in their arms and had deserted Irontown permanently for some other village. The experience of their race told them to fly a spot touched by the epidemic of lynching. Three or four of the most able of the Negroes drove their wagons, loaded with household plunder, up the railroad to the next station, bought tickets and shipped North, and so expatriated themselves.

CHAPTER XXIII

THE forthright removal of Peck Bradley from the scene of his cleverly planned but pernicious activities was considered an unqualified moral triumph in Irontown, and out of the sweet soil of the lynching flowered other blossoms of practical morality. For example, there was Caly Stegall, who advertised soft drinks and sold hard ones. It had been impossible to fix the misdemeanour of bootlegging upon Mr. Stegall, so many loopholes had the law, but about two weeks after Peck Bradley's sudden demise, a group of public-spirited citizens visited Stegall's home at midnight, rode him out of town on a rail and told him to stay out. He did, and that surely was another good riddance.

Then there were certain women in Irontown whose reputations were not the most honest, but every legal tribunal knows how difficult it is to prove such offences positively. These technicalities were cut short by a delegation of citizens waiting on the offenders. One Negro woman was stripped and horse-whipped as an example; the others fled; a commendable result.

Gambling places were raided, oddly enough by the very men who once had whiled away their time in them. In short, Irontown was in the midst of one of those acute moral reforms which sometimes seize upon a town, a county, a state, or even the great American nation as a whole; and it was working great observable good, as it often does.

As party to these reprisals Abner Teeftallow felt certain qualms in helping rid Irontown of bootleggers, gamblers, and women of ill repute, when he remembered that at irregular intervals he had gambled with Linters and had bought whisky from Stegall. As for the women, they were passive, shame-faced creatures, the pursued and not the pursuing. Now for the men of Irontown to drive these women out of their homes because they themselves had enjoyed whatever poor gifts the demireps had to offer—there was something grotesque and sardonic about it. It disturbed Abner, as youth must always be disturbed until custom and wont have lent their acquiescence to the odd face of human conduct.

At times the teamster was minded to stay away from these outbursts of village morality, but there was an excitement and go about them which always sucked him in. Then, too, the raids were in perfect consonance with the run of village taste; they were of a stripe with the novels they read, the melodramas produced at the commencement exercises of the village school, with the chromos of Custer's Last Charge and of a woman in a nightgown clinging to a cross in a stormy sea, which decorated the village walls, and with the hymns about the shedding of blood which constantly resounded in the village churches. In brief, they were so exactly of a piece with Irontown culture that the wonder was not that they started but that they had not always been.

It was Abner's fortune, or misfortune, to be sufficiently sensitive to feel this jangle in the village life. At times he tried to make Nessie see his point of view.

"How can it be right," he would argue, "for the boys to buy a man's liquor during the day, not pay him fer it, an' then chase him out of town that night?"

Nessie, notwithstanding her own violation of the village code, still reflected that code with perhaps an unequalled clarity.

"Abner," she replied gravely, "two wrongs don't make a right."

"What do you mean by that?"

"Just because the boys did wrong to buy Stegall's whisky, that doesn't keep 'em from doing right by driving him out of town. They can repent, I reckon. After all, nobody would get to Heaven if we couldn't repent." A melancholy tone came into Nessie's voice as she stared out of her window at a rectangular section of the shabby, unrelenting village outside.

Abner knew very well of what she was thinking. Their talk had been liable to these interruptions since the first of their sudden and passionate indiscretions. The most remote subjects brought up the condemnation under which they lived.

"I think the boys ort to of paid Stegall for his whisky before they rode him out of town," stated Abner briefly, and the subject was dropped.

Youth and girl sat silently in the hot little room filled with the same thought but moved by curiously opposed impulses. Abner was a little weary of this rather pointless sitting in the room which they had substituted for the swing on the piazza as less likely to give rise to gossip. Nessie, on the other hand, was nervously anxious for Abner to remain with her. She sat brooding unhappily for several moments and finally said, "I had such a dreadful dream last night; I have it every night."

"The same dream?"

"Nearly the same dream."

Abner felt his first tinge of interest in their afternoon tête-à-tête—dreams touched his hill superstition.

"That must mean somethin'. What kind of a dream was it?"

"Every time I go to sleep it seems like I walk through a big open door, but the minute I get through, the door disappears. I want to go back, but there is no way to get back, the door is gone. That doesn't sound awful, Abner, but oh, it feels awful. It seems to me I would give anything in this whole worl' to get back through that door, but there isn't any door; there simply isn't any. . . ." The girl was painfully moved at the mere recital of her dream.

Abner stared at her with foreboding.

"What does it mean?"

"My dream book says to dream of a door means a journey or a new acquaintance."

"A journey or a new acquaintance," repeated Abner, touched by man's age-old sense of the mysterious forewarnings bound up in dreams. "I wonder who it could be, or where you are going?"

Nessie exhaled a long breath. "I don't know. . . ."
They remained silent another space. Abner made an involuntary movement to get up from his chair but controlled it.

"Abner," interrupted the girl in a troubled tone.

"Yes?"

"Do you think"—she lowered her voice—"anybody knows about—us?"

Abner stopped the slight restless movements of his feet and hands and looked at her fixedly.

"No—why?"

"Well . . . I don't know . . . the way folks look at me . . . maybe I imagine it."

"I guess you must. Who?"

"O-oh, ever'body—Zed Parrum for one. He's been in the Grand two or three times lately pretendin' to want to buy ribbin—he keeps lookin' at me—I b'lieve he thinks somethin'. . . ." The girl heaved a deep sigh and searched the face of her lover.

"Zed Parrum," repeated Abner blankly. "What has he got to do with——"

"Abner," interrupted Nessie, "look at me and answer a question as you hope to save your soul. Do you promise?"

Her intensity filled Abner with misgivings.

"Y-es, what is it?"

She lowered her voice to a bare whisper.

"Abner, do I look like a—a—bad woman?"

The question shocked the teamster.

"Why, no! No! Nessie, you look like the dearest, sweetest——"

The girl gave a little shiver, arose, walked over to her wavering mirror and stood for half a minute perusing her dark-circled eyes. At last she turned away with a shake of her head.

"Well—no matter how I *look*——"

Abner made a gesture of protest. "Don't say that, don't!" He got up from his chair, went over to her and put his arms about her. He led her back to the chair and drew her down on his lap, snuggling her face under his neck and leaning his cheek on her pale hair.

"Nessie, you know you are not," he protested in a whisper. "You know we love each other. It ain't wrong for us to love each other?"

She whispered sadly in his ear, "You know it is, Abner —we ain't married. . . ."

Abner became still again, holding the girl in his arms, silently agreeing with her. In the eyes of the village, therefore in his own eyes, a marriage ceremony was of far more importance in a bodily union than love. Love and passion, he felt, were dubious things at best; his own for Nessie had faded away as mysteriously as it had arisen. He had reached the centrifugal moment of his honeymoon. The girl in his arms no longer moved his senses, and this brought a feeling of finality as if he could never be attracted to her again. He was aware that one of her elbows was uncomfortably sharp against his side; that she weighed one hundred and thirty pounds; that the room was small and hot; that her cheeks were disagreeably damp from tears . . . he wished he were at the garage.

And this was the moment when the girl most needed him; when she felt friendless and hopeless with the hands of all the village turned against her. She wanted Abner to stay with her at this moment because she could feel his indifference and it terrified her. She was not sure he would come back, once she let him go. Neither felt for the other any mental or artistic sympathy; simply their physical needs; and now that Nessie had assuaged that in her lover, she had lost him.

And thus together they stamped hill morality as irrevocably right in the hills.

The two lovers, silent and unhappy in this divided embrace, pursued their own thoughts to troubled inconclusions. At last the girl asked, "You didn't tell Zed Parrum, did you, Abner?"

A certain dismay went through Abner and he answered without conviction, "Good Lord, Nessie, you know I wouldn't tell nobody!"

At his tone she sat upright in his lap and looked at him with frightened circled eyes.

"What *did* you do?" she asked in a whisper.

"Why—nuthin' . . ."

"Yes, you did."

"Well," began Abner unwillingly, "the other day me an' Zed was eatin' our lunches out on the dump and I ast him if Peck Bradley put up a fight when the men went to pull him out of the lock-up. . . ."

"Ye-es?" queried Nessie, studying Abner's face with apprehension.

"He said, wasn't I there. I said no. He ast where I was. I said here at home. He ast whyn't I come. At first I said I forgot it. He laughed and said, 'Forgot hell—you was doin' somethin' else.'"

What little colour there was in the milliner's face vanished, her eyes widened.

"Then you told him!" she gasped.

"Good Lord, no. I spoke up like a man an' told him I stayed at home when I got good an' ready, and it wasn't none of his damn business!"

Nessie drew a breath of horror. "Oh, you told him! You told him! And now he knows! Ever'body knows! O-oh!" She arose in a sort of trance of terror and moved to the middle of the room, conveying a strange impression that she was utterly lost.

"For God's sake, Nessie, don't take on like that!" urged Abner in an anxious but somewhat irritated undertone.

"Oh me! Oh me!" She pulled her fingers through one another, looking about as if to find a way out of the troubles that encompassed her. Her eyes lighted on the teamster almost as if she had never seen him before. She wet her lips.

"Abner," she whispered, "will you marry me?"

At the expression that came over his face she put up her hands and involuntarily dropped on her knees before him.

"Oh, Abner, Abner, please, ple-e-a-s-e, if you don't, I'm lost, I'm lost. . . ."

At his instinctive step backward her forearms settled on the floor and her head upon them. Her bright hair sagged forward in an awkward manner as she sobbed on her arms. To Abner there was something painful and pitiful, yet profoundly repellent, in the scene. In Nessie's utter ignorance she had selected the most inopportune of all moments to make a plea of marriage to her lover—the moment of satiety.

The teamster mumbled something about not making enough money to get married—two dollars a day—somehow he spent it all as it was. . . .

Nessie got slowly to her feet with tear-stained face, apparently not aware that she had just proposed marriage in utter abasement and had been clumsily rebuffed. Her mind really was not on marriage at all, but was searching fearfully for a way out of her threatened exposure. She thought of another plan.

"Abner, you haven't told anybody but Zed, have you?"

"Good God, no!"

"Well, lissen—go to Zed and beg him not to tell, tell him you—you'll give him a—a hunderd dollars never to tell it. I got that much saved up in the bank. Tell him—— Oh, but I know he will tell!" She put her hands over her eyes and blindfolded herself in the hot little room.

"Lissen," said Abner hopefully, "all of us fellers, the whole railroad outfit, is agoin' to move out of Arntown an' camp about sixteen miles west o' here—then you'll be shut of Zed."

Nessie removed her hands and looked at her lover with a ghastly face.

"Oh, Abner, if just one man at the other end of the county knows it, he'll tell ever'body—ever'body. . . ." She shook her head with renewed tears silently running down her cheeks.

This was another truth which Abner knew only too well. The more appalling the injury which the hill folk could inflict on a woman, the more eagerly they bandied such defamation from tongue to tongue. But this injury was inflicted impersonally. It was merely interesting human gossip, and obscene—to their liking. It palliated their own repressions. Out of all the endless tongues that would wag perhaps not a dozen would realize that a woman's life was withering beneath their attacks. They had not imagination enough for that.

After a long pause, Abner could find nothing better than to repeat, "Well, we're goin' to move, an' that's somethin'."

"Are you going too?" she asked lifelessly.

"Why—yes, I guess so."

At the moment this seemed to make little difference to either of them.

"When?"

"Day after t'morrow."

The girl looked at Abner with exhausted eyes.

"Well—I don't know what I'll do. . . . You may go now—to the garage, wherever you want to go. You've been in a fidget to get away ever sence you come in. . . . I don't guess I ort to have kep' you."

She stopped speaking, looking at Abner as a soldier might look upon a battlefield which he has lost. Questions floated painfully before her mind, "if she had done this . . . or that . . . or the other. . . ." But, of course, the profound mistake back of it all was having given herself through impulse, tenderness, passion, and love. She had profoundly transgressed the code of village morals; that is to say, she had placed herself in the position of a victim of sharp practice, of one who gave much and received nothing. And that was something the village could never forgive.

Abner wanted to say something, but there was nothing to say. He turned and went silently out into the hallway, which was slightly cooler than Nessie's own room. Apart from his embarrassment, he was genuinely glad to be away from her. He walked as noiselessly as he could down the hallway and down the stairs.

At the bottom of the steps he saw, with a certain apprehension, Miss Scovell stationed with cap and duster. She had a look of having been standing there for an hour or more. Now she said with a kind of grim solemnity, "You stay up in yore room a good deal, Abner."

Abner was so disconcerted that all he could do was to answer with a bluntness he did not feel, "Well—it's my room."

Miss Scovell disregarded this. "Was you talkin' to somebody up there?—I thought I heard you talkin'."

"I guess I was talkin' to myse'f." Abner was so confused he could hardly continue down the steps past the woman into the street.

In her room above, Nessie listened with a bloodless face to this conversation which floated up the hallway.

CHAPTER XXIV

TWO days later the labourers of the railroad construction works, their families, and all their household goods were loaded into box cars at Irontown and were shipped to a camp site some sixteen miles to the west of the village.

The ordeal of parting brought Nessie Sutton to the station with Abner, and the two stood in the shade of the depot watching the trucks and wagons back up to the waiting cars and deliver their loads. The furniture of the labourers was shabby and seemed on the verge of falling apart. As it arrived in wagons, the two lovers would identify it mechanically as "That belongs to the Davises; that to the McLemores," but this was done without the slightest personal interest. It was a mere ticketing which went on mechanically in the strange trance of their leave-taking.

It seemed to Abner as if Time had paused, that it hung in a pool above the cataract of their parting. Down the line of cars sweaty labourers heaved and shoved at rickety furniture; the little engine of the new railroad panted intermittently; a brakeman in greasy overalls lay under a car wheel repacking a hot box with oily waste. The whole scene was laid on in pale yellow sunshine and soft bluish shadows. It seemed to Abner that he and Nessie would go on thus for ever, standing with their hands secretly clasped behind a fold of Nessie's skirt, watching the men, the wagons, the train, with all his senses wrapped up in the intimacy and sympathy of the girl. The touch of her small warm palm pressed against his own, their interlaced fingers filled him with a sense of unity with Nessie which he had never known even in moments of their closest embraces. A quietness, a steadfastness of affection seemed to emanate from her. It was an affection upon which Abner knew in his heart he could rely all the rest of his life; that she would always love him, always absolve his frailties, his intemperances and short-comings with the endless patience of the hill women for their men.

The thought that he was leaving such a largesse filled him with a great depression. To defend his own failing heart he pressed her hand and said to her, "But, Nessie, I can come back jest any time on the train; it makes a trip ever' day."

She nodded faintly, drew in her lips and bit them.

A pang went through Abner that he had not clung to the externals of the scene: the furniture, the labourers, a pet goat of one of the children.

Nearly all the men had wives; women who followed them everywhere. He and Nessie stood apart, alone in this eternal parting, this melting pain. He gripped the girl's hand till he hurt her.

"Nessie . . ." he began in a taut undertone.

At that moment the whistle of the locomotive deafened their ears. Amid the din they could faintly distinguish a dog howling. The blast swept the lovers out of their entranced security and flung them into the very moment of parting. They shrunk as best they could behind the corner of the depot and caught each other passionately in their arms. They pressed their lips and bodies together as if they could never tear away.

"Abner, good-bye. . . . God bless you. . . . O-oh, Abner . . ."

"Good-bye, good-bye. . . . I'll be back. . . ."

The teamster could barely make out her face blurred by his tears. It seemed to the youth as if he were tearing out a very part of his own body. His desire to marry her, to keep her by him for ever arose to an agony. Other men were not subject to these tearings asunder. He took his lips from hers.

"Nessie," he trembled, "I want you to be my . . ."

At that moment the last blast of the locomotive overpowered their ears. It shocked him into instant and violent action. He stooped, seized his paper suitcase and wooden box, and the next moment went running down the platform, jumped off the end on to the long cinder strip beside the track, and made for the last box car. Just as it clashed forward he swung his bags inside, leaped at the entrance, landed on his stomach across the bottom of the door. In an instant he wriggled, stood up, and began waving his hand at Nessie.

The girl waved back, gasping at this display of activity. For the moment she had been terrified lest he fall under the car and be ground to pieces. But the ease and supple- ness with which he had jumped and righted himself sent a thrill through her. It brought to her nerves the wild, passionate power she was losing. It was like so much strength being taken away from her own person; it left her a kind of shell of a girl, as if the stronger, more vital part of her were moving away on the box car.

She waved her handkerchief miserably, blinking her eyes so she could discern Abner's form in the square black door of the freight car. The youth, the door, the whole train rattled down the track, out of the freight yard, growing smaller and smaller. At the limit of the yard, the engine gave a final shriek, rounded a curve toward the west, and the tiny figure in the small black door was lost to Nessie's view.

After the train had vanished Nessie still stood wiping her eyes and staring down the track when a voice behind her drawled,

"Girlie, don't blubber so, when one's gone leaves room fer another."

In her pain Nessie did not understand the sentence or realize it was addressed to her. She continued wiping her eyes, made an effort to compose her face, and then turned to go home, holding her lips between her teeth.

"Hell," observed the voice behind her, "you ain't none too good to notice a feller. . . ."

But the man might as well have been talking to a patient under a surgeon's knife. Nessie walked on around the depot platform, then set out through the utter emptiness of the village streets.

The man continued looking at her with a sardonic leer on a face peculiarly adapted to this expression. His name was Nathan Bagley. In his pleasanter moments, Mr. Bagley's face wore a look of soiled cynicism as if he had learned thoroughly the dubiety of truth, the emptiness of chastity, the futility of kindliness, and the general inadaptability of the virtues to life as it is lived. He was a kind of be-smutted Nathan the Wise. No salacious rumour in Irontown escaped him, and he felt a personal interest in each report.

Now he stood looking after Nessie with a sneer on his face because she had not paused to fall into conversation with him. As she walked away he scrutinized the curve of her ankles, which was the part of a woman he always observed, and snarled loud enough for Nessie to have heard him, "Old skirt, if you think you're too good to talk to me, you've got another think coming!"

The overtures of Mr. Nathan Bagley toward Nessie Sutton at the railroad station were, broadly interpreted, an advance notice served on the girl of village excommunication. The fact that Nessie, in the pain of parting from her lover, did not hear Mr. Bagley's remarks was of little moment; the village could be depended upon to call the matter to her attention later.

It required a number of days for Irontown to formulate its position toward the milliner's assistant. By the different village groups she was discussed lickerishly, scornfully, philosophically; from garage to bank. The monotony of village life was stirred by this touch of colour.

The whole village readjusted its attitude toward the milliner's assistant under the conviction that she had turned out something different from what they had esteemed her.

The villagers immediately attributed a duplicity to Nessie's year-long church and Sunday-school going. "What hypocrisy!" they said. "The pretence she's been making!" Naturally, they could never suspect that the same emotional trait which caused her to tithe and give herself profoundly to religious observances might be transposed into as equally complete surrender to a lover. No one imagined she had remained consistent in character, so each village group readjusted itself to this new or "real" character which the girl had discovered.

When Mrs. Roxie Biggers heard the scandal, she was moved to take some instant action about it, as was her wont. Mrs. Roxie was sewing some sheets which she meant to give to a labourer's wife who had been brought down with puerperal fever. She had begged enough cloth from the stores to make four sheets, and she meant to keep two of them for her own use.

Now without looking up from the clatter of her sewing machine she spoke to the neighbour who was making an afternoon call upon her.

"It's the hypocrisy of the thing!" she denounced, glaring at her seam with thin, widely spread nostrils, "Going prissing down to my brother Perry's Sunday-school ever' Sunday; out to prayer meetin'; then to church; then workin' among sinners in the revival; and now turned out to be a strumpet! What will Brother Perry think!"

The caller at the Biggers' home, a Mrs. Gumerton, was a heavy, slow-motioned woman who went right on with the tally of her gossip entirely disregarding the angry ejaculations of her hostess.

"Kissed him right down there at the station before ever'-body!"

"Shameless baggage, advertisin' her sin! Flauntin' it in our faces!"

"Mister Bagley—you know Mister Bagley, the freight agent—he said they simply clung to each other—kissed fer three or four minutes. . . ."

"Didn't she have no sense of decency a-tall?" flared Mrs. Roxie, "Kissin' like that in public!"

"Outrageous!" echoed Mrs. Gumerton.

Gossip of this prolonged caress was peculiarly irritating to both of the good women, because it just happened that neither of them had been kissed in any sort of fashion for years and years.

Mrs. Biggers stopped her galloping seam to say, "I do think Brother Perry ort to be informed of how she's treated him—— Law, look here, this hemmer ain't been ketchin' for two yards! Well, that pore woman will jest have to put up with it. I'm in such a rush! Sally, would you min' goin' back over this while I run down an' warn Brother Perry—he ort to know it!"

Mrs. Gumerton, who also wanted to spread the news, began slowly getting up.

"I'm sorry, Roxie, but I jest haven't got time."

"Now, Sally," snapped Mrs. Roxie determinedly. "I don't know how it is that ever' bit of the work done by the Willin' Workers gits put off on me. There's not a thing in the worl' to hinder you from doin' a little. It won't hurt you none! Me, bent down to it all day long an' ha'f the night! Now you jest take holt here, and when you git this finished, here's another'n cut out"—she jabbed it at her. "I'll be down at Brother Perry's jest a minute!"

The force of her superior will moved Mrs. Gumerton unwillingly to the machine and seated her in the chair. The guest went slowly back to the point which the hostess, in her rush, had skipped.

Mrs. Biggers seized an old shawl, clapped it around her thin shoulders as protection against the faint autumn chill in the air, then with a final admonition to her guest to work diligently in her absence, she hurried out of the house. As she crossed her porch she saw her husband in an old armchair asleep in the sunshine. For some reason, the sight made her more rancorous still toward Nessie, and she thought to herself,

"That girl deserves to be drummed out of town exactly like all the rest of the prostitutes!"

This thought was still in her mind when she entered the bank and went into the directors' room, the only private room in the building. She called sharply through an open door into the cashier's department,

"Brother Perry, I want to see you a minute!"

Mr. Perry Northcutt detached himself grudgingly from the work of drafting a letter to Railroad Jones. It was a delicately poised instrument designed to mark the beginning of a fracture in the relations of the bank and Mr. Jones; or, in the event that the magnate had more property to hypothecate, the letter was intended to cement more firmly the friendship between the bank and the builder; a very diplomatic letter indeed. So now he walked into the directors' room with a projected sentence forming itself in his head.

"Well, Roxie," he asked in a professional tone, "what can I do for you?"

The sight of Perry as the controlling figure in the Irontown Bank always pleased Roxie.

"Perry, I just come to tell you about that Sutton girl in your Sunday-school class. . . . I thought it was my duty," she added as an afterthought.

The cashier looked at his thin gray-haired sister suspiciously. He knew when Roxie's duty moved her to make disclosures they were usually of a compromising nature.

"What did you want to say about her?" he inquired, transferring a little more of his attention from his letter to his sister.

"Perry, your confidence has been violated," she began solemnly.

"What are you talking about, Roxie? The bank hasn't advanced any money to Miss Sutton."

"It isn't money, it isn't as serious as that, but it's bad enough; she has disgraced herself with that Teeftaller boy —an' she's in your Sunday-school class. Such wickedness! Such ingratitude!"

The banker really was shocked. "You don't mean Miss Sutton has——" The pause in his sentence was eloquent and he stared at his sister in genuine dismay.

"That's exactly what I mean. It's all over town! Ever'-body's talkin' it!"

"Oh, that's awful! Maybe it's a false rumour—things get started. . . ."

"False rumour nothing!" cried the old woman. "Mr. Bagley saw 'em down at the station huggin' an' kissin' in a disgustin' manner!"

"Bagley's a lecher and a rake himself!"

"They tell that on Mr. Bagley, but I don't know—he makes a mighty good salary down there at the freight office."

Here the conversation came to a pause; the banker continued to look inquiringly at his sister and finally said, "Roxie, you didn't come down here simply to tell me that?"

"No, I didn't!" exclaimed the old woman, breaking into rancour again. "It's like this"—she shook a bony finger at her brother. "What right has Nessie Sutton got to stay in this town! Other loose women haff to git out!"

Mr. Northcutt was genuinely surprised. "You wouldn't treat a young girl as the boys did those old strumpets, Roxie?"

Mrs. Biggers compressed her thin lips. "The Bible says, God is no respecter of persons, Perry, and besides you know a young pretty girl can raise more trouble in less time than a house full of the other sort. Now sence Nessie Sutton has showed up in her true character, I think the people of Arntown ort to make her clear out along with the rest. No use bein' mealy-mouthed about it even if she is purty. We don't want her kind amongst us. So I say a delegation ort to wait on her jest like they did on old Mol Garraty!"

Mr. Perry Northcutt, who thought he knew his sister, marvelled for the hundredth time in his life at the peculiar ferocity of women toward women. A notion, due to his Biblical studies, flitted across his mind that if Christ had been a woman, Mary Magdalene would never have received absolution.

The banker came back to the topic in hand.

"Well, I couldn't sanction any such procedure as that, Roxie; Miss Nessie is entirely different. . . ."

"You mean she's prettier!" snapped the old woman.

"I mean it's her first offence!" retorted the banker sharply. "I'd like to know where your Christian charity comes in if a single misstep——"

"Single misstep! Huh! You're mighty innocent; her and that Teeftaller boardin' in the same hotel!"

"Anyway, I don't consider her habitually bad, and I personally won't do a thing to disturb the unfortunate girl. You and some other good woman ought to go down and talk to her, Roxie."

"Huh, I'm goin' down an' talk to Mr. Baxter an' tell him what sort of a girl he's got workin' in his millinery department!"

"Roxie!" exclaimed the cashier in alarm. "I wouldn't do that, it'll cost the girl her position!"

"It's somebody's duty to do it!" cried the old woman fiercely. "Somebody ort to tell Mr. Baxter what a hypocrite he's housin'. She'll run off all his trade! What decent woman would go there and trade with an unchaste woman! Take it to yourse'f, Perry Northcutt, suppose you had a crooked girl in your bank, would you keep her there a minute? Course not! Somebody ort to tell Mr. Baxter, an' I, for one, don't shirk my duty when I see it!" She wagged her gray unkempt head determinedly. "I'll tell it right before the girl if she's there! I'm not the one to say behind a person's back what I won't say to her face! So there!"

Mrs. Roxie snapped her lean jaws together, dilated her high thin nostrils, whirled about, and hurried out of the bank to discharge her duty as a citizen of Irontown. As she went she fired a last broadside,

"If your father, Perry Northcutt, who is dead an' in Heaven, can look over the golden walls and see you taking up for a whorish woman, I wonder what he is thinking this minute of his son?"

By this token the cashier knew that he had irritated his sister deeply; she never wondered what their father in Heaven would think of him unless she herself disapproved profoundly.

A vision of his father leaning over a wall of gold with a rather extra fine crown on his head and a harp neglected for the nonce while he surveyed the earth in general and Irontown in particular, to see what his son Perry was doing about the Teeftallow-Sutton scandal, flitted across the cashier's mind. He knew his dead father would approve his position, but he had a notion that his mother, who was also up there with a somewhat smaller and less gaudily ornamented crown and a less sonorous harp, would not approve if his father should chance to call her attention to the disturbance back in their old earthly home. The cashier trusted to the discretion of his beatified father not to mention the matter to his beatified mother because he felt sure that women are always a little unreasonable; as on earth, so they are in Heaven.

CHAPTER XXV

THE first notice of village condemnation was served on Nessie Sutton by a little yellow-curled toddler named Jabez Anderson who lived in a cottage between the hotel and town. Jabez played out in the street under an elm tree where he had a swing. Nessie heretofore had stood high in Jabez's favour because, as she went by on her way to work, she would give him a push. On this morning, the milliner waved at the little boy from the corner, but instead of settling himself on the seat and getting ready for the big push, Jabez continued doing what he could with his short fat legs to swing himself. When Nessie eventually helped him, he called out right at the top of his swing, in the clear impersonal tones of very small children, "Mamma says you are a mess."

The milliner watched him go and return to her.

"What is it, Jabez?" she asked, smiling.

"Mamma says you are a mess—mess," he strove to make the word as distinct as possible, for he had found the English language rather treacherous.

"Mess," repeated Nessie, ceasing to smile. After a moment she recalled having sold Mrs. Anderson an autumn hat the week before; then she added aloud more to herself than to the child, "I thought your mother liked that hat."

"Mamma says you are a mess," repeated Jabez simply, and that seemed to be the extent of his information.

At that moment the mother herself appeared at the door of the cottage.

"Jabez!" she cried sharply. "Come here this minute!"

"Mrs. Anderson," called Nessie, eager to protect her em-

ployer's trade, "if you don't like your new hat, I'll gladly
make any change . . ."

"I like my hat well enough.—Come here, Jabez Anderson,
this moment.—Will you please stop swinging him and let
him out?"

Mrs. Anderson's "please" was vitriolic.

"Why, certainly!" snapped the girl, getting angry herself at
this baseless attack. "Jabez said that you called me a——"

The housewife walked quickly down the path, seized the
hand of her baby as it came into the gate, gave the child a
shake, and rapped out in her irritation, "Now, you stay
inside, Jabez, and don't be talking to strangers!"

The little boy looked around at Nessie with frightened eyes
as he half trotted and was half dragged along at his mother's
side.

Nessie stared at the woman, and suddenly there came to
her a hint of what lay behind this extraordinary procedure.
She felt a constriction in her chest as she thought in dismay,
"Zed Parrum has told!" A rush of blood heated her face;
an instinctive impulse to defend herself seized her.

"Mrs. Anderson," she called in a strained voice, "what is
the matter? Why are you treating me this way?"

"You know!" whipped out the woman without looking
back.

"But I don't! I don't!" Nessie began trembling violently.

The woman flung over her shoulder on the very lash of
contempt, "You and that Abner Teeftaller . . ." and
hurried to the porch.

The world seemed to sway under Nessie. She held to the
palings. The blood drained out of her cheeks, leaving them
cold. She broke out suddenly, "But, Mrs. Anderson! I
—I didn't! Who told you? It—it's not true! Mrs.
Anderson, please believe me!"

Nessie had no conception of how trivial, how insignificant
Mrs. Anderson was in the village-wide condemnation. She
did not realize that to regain Mrs. Anderson's confidence
would be like making friends with one hornet in a nest.

The woman opened her door, got inside, and slammed it shut.

For a half minute Nessie continued clinging to the fence. Within the brief space of this scene the day, the village, her position in society had abruptly shifted about. A terrible sensation of nightmare fell upon her. Zed had told! She recalled her terrifying persistent dream of passing through an open door only to have it vanish behind her.

For the first time she realized that she was what the village called an "unchaste woman." She really was one. And the tragedy of it was, she seemed to herself to be precisely as she had always been. There was not a straw's difference between Nessie Sutton pure and Nessie Sutton impure. Oh, if the village only could know that she was exactly the same!

She turned away and moved mechanically along the shabby street with a beating heart. She got out her handkerchief and wiped her eyes covertly, and a little later dabbed her cheeks with her powder puff to remove the stain. She tried to walk on down to the Grand in a natural manner, but as she went she began wondering anxiously how many of the villagers had heard the rumour. For the first time she became nervously sensitive to the people she met on the street. She felt as if she were listening intently to hear what they thought of her. When she reached the business section she observed a curious zone of quiet formed about her as she walked. Everyone stopped talking and watched her intently. Once she saw a man motion to his companion with his eyes, and this companion very slowly and very casually turned and watched Nessie pass. It was an eerie sensation. The shabby village street stretched out before her to an amazing length. It was crowded with people, all silent, all watching. She was running a gauntlet of eyes, eyes, eyes, all staring at her. She thought of her dream again, with horror. She was walking physically into it.

The girl made a last effort to move along to her work as if nothing had happened, but her nerves were being slowly screwed up as if someone were tuning the strings of a violin. Suddenly she realized that something in her was getting past her control, that something would break, there would be a scene. Her habitual impulse toward prayer caused her to glance up and murmur piteously, "O God, help me! Help me!"

Then, like an answer to her prayer, she saw emerge from the door of the Grand the striding figure of Mrs. Roxie Biggers. At the sight of the old woman a sob of relief clutched Nessie's throat. The girl knew that this old woman was noted for her Christianity, her endless charity and good deeds. Now she had an impulse to fly after Mrs. Roxie and implore her help. The old woman would be her succour in this nightmarish scene; a motherly refuge to whom she could turn amid these silent staring men.

But Mrs. Roxie hurried so rapidly that Nessie would have become more conspicuous, if that were possible, should she try to run and catch up with her. The girl watched her disappear around a corner with tears of despair starting in her eyes. Her last hope of rescue had vanished.

After three endless minutes of walking, she entered the Grand. She met a village youth whose name she did not know. As he passed her in the narrow aisle between two counters of dry goods, he gave her an almost imperceptible wink and brushed his fingers across her hip.

Nessie gasped as if he had struck her with a lash. Such fear rushed upon her and weakened her that she did not know whether or not she could get to her millinery department at the end of the store.

Then she saw Mr. Baxter come angling toward her through the spaces between the ends of the counters. His face was serious and unsmiling.

"Miss Nessie!" he called to her in a queer undertone.

The girl stopped, holding to the cloth on the counter, waiting for him to come up. She noted his hair combed sleekly across his bald spot; his carefully trimmed mustache; his suave face which had the look of one accustomed to dealing with women. She heard him say solicitously, "You look ill, Miss Nessie."

"Yes—I'm not well."

"Perhaps you'd better go home for the day."

Nessie realized her own weak, shaken condition and agreed with a nod. There was a pause, the merchant glanced out the door, then back at her.

"And, Miss Nessie, you do look run-down, have been for several days. I believe a little vacation would do you good, chance to pick yourself up." He reached in his pocket and drew out a check book. "Why not let me give you a check for the rest of your pay this month and let you recuperate?" He smiled a strained, mechanical smile.

Nessie's face went very white; she moistened her dry lips and whispered, Yes, she would appreciate it.

Mr. Baxter produced his fountain pen and made out the check. On the notation line he wrote, "Payment of salary in full."

Nessie could feel her pulse in her neck, in her temples, her head was aching. Through her dry mouth she whispered, "Thank you."

The merchant drew a silent breath himself as if he had completed a disagreeable task. As he handed Nessie the check, he looked at her as if he was seeing her for the first time, and said quite ingenuously and with a remote sympathy, "You really do look sick, Miss Nessie—I'll send you home in the delivery wagon."

With a sinking feeling Nessie could see herself, more conspicuous than ever, being sent home in a delivery wagon, but she was too weak to walk. She went to the front of the store and shrank inside the recessed door of the Grand until the wagon came. Once a wild notion struck her to ask Archie, the delivery boy, to take her to the home of Mrs. Biggers. It seemed to Nessie that unless she could find some woman to whom she could unburden her grief and fear, some real friend upon whom she could rest in this nightmarish hour, she must go mad indeed.

But her head ached now with such a steady, throbbing pain, that by the time Archie came (glancing at her curiously and ill at ease himself) she was too ill to see any one, even the most perfect example of pious charity which the village afforded.

CHAPTER XXVI

THE telephone tinkled in the Scovell House, and Miss Lydia Scovell answered it. She began with the usual, "Hello—yes, this is Liddy.—What? What? She did?—You don't say so! You know I suspicioned something like that! I sure did! Oh, I seen enough! Plenty! I'll tell you when I see you. No, you can be sure she won't! Not a day longer! I run a respectable house. I do! Why, I'd see her in Jericho before I'd keep her a minute longer! I will, I'll go right up this minute an' give her her walkin' papers! Yes, I will! Good-bye, Roxie, an' much obliged for tellin' me!—Oh, I guess that's all right, me an' you didn't see exactly the same about Mr. Beavers, but now I know you are my frien'.—Well, I try to do right, too. Good-bye an' thank you ag'in," and she snapped up the receiver.

The old woman started up the stairs, thinking to herself, "I'll show her! The two-faced hussy!" She tramped smartly along the upper hall to the door of her boarder's room.

When she entered the door the hotel keeper stood, tall and gaunt, looking at the girl who lay prostrate on the bed with her hair about her face.

Miss Scovell had meant to fall into instant and violent vituperation, but now there was something about the forlorn figure on the bed which checked the bitterest of her thoughts. She cleared her throat in a menacing manner. Nessie gave a faint start and turned her face from her pillow to look with swollen eyes at the old maid.

The two women looked at each other silently for a moment, the young woman struck down, the old one slowly soured through causes fundamentally the same. Neither was aware of how near their grievances lay together, and they looked at each other with inimical eyes. Presently the elder woman said in a strained tone, "Miss Sutton, I'll want this room after to-morrer." She had meant to say, "I'll want this room to-morrow," but some weakening had granted an extra day.

It required, perhaps, two seconds for Nessie to understand that she was being turned out of the hotel. A last defensive impulse caused her to fall back on her legal rights.

"B-but, M-Miss Scovell," she protested unsteadily, "I—I paid for a week."

This faint opposition aroused the old maid's life-long sense of wrong. "It makes no diff'runce if you paid for a year!" she snapped. "A girl like you kain't stay here! Git yore things packed an' git out—prancin' off to church an' prayer meetin' an' Sunday-school ever Sunday, an' now this!" The old woman trembled from the implicit irony that this thing had happened here in her own hotel. "I'll have your trunk hauled off in the mornin', and between now an' then, I'll have yore meals sent up to you—you needn't come down to the dinin' room!"

The sentence revealed to the girl in a flash of illumination exactly how the village women looked upon her as something loathsome; something to be kept out of sight. And Nessie remembered that she herself had felt the same way toward other unfortunate women. It had seemed to Nessie then, and it seemed to Miss Scovell now, that some chemical change came over women who had sinned; their very flesh was not the same as other women's flesh; pollution was intrinsic in them; and yet now Nessie had no sensation of evil save that she was bayed at on every side; that every human being whom she saw reviled and despised her.

"Miss Scovell," she asked piteously, "where can I go?"

"Huh, you ort to know such places better'n I do!" and the landlady gave Nessie a look of hatred, turned on her heel, and with her thin dew-lapped neck held high, walked back down the hall with condemnation in her footfalls.

The milliner remained on the bed, closed her eyes, and moved her aching head. She tried to think. Where would she go? No matter where she went the "nice" people, the Christian people with whom she had associated all of her life, would have none of her. She could never speak to another "nice" woman, never help design another hat, never freely indulge in the simple pleasure of prayer meeting and Sunday-school lesson; and yet the thought of any other sort of association was terrifying to her. She was exactly what she had been before her passionate surrender to her lover.

A strange thought trickled through Nessie's throbbing head that perhaps all "nice" girls were merely fortunate girls, and "bad" girls merely unfortunate. This fancy itself seemed impure, not maidenly, and she thought with dismay, "Am I really becoming bad?"

Presently her thoughts came back to the problem actually in hand. Where could she go? How could she search out another boarding place, and then what could she do? The notion of walking out into the staring village and asking anywhere for board was impossible.

A profound shudder ran through the girl. A vision of those depths to which she knew unfortunate women did sink arose in terrifying detail before her. Tears trickled out of her eyes and wet her cheeks, and she prayed silently, gripping her hands and looking up at the fly-stained ceiling, "O God, don't let me come to that! God have mercy, I'd rather die than do that!" She grew chill with repulsion at the thought. She shook away the horrible imaginings and almost mechanically arose to her feet and set about her packing.

As she worked, her thoughts continued to skurry here and there like terrified rats seeking to escape from a trap. She saw Buckingham Sharp's law book still lying on her table and she thought of appealing to him. But she decided he would not hear her. She thought of going to other men of the village. She did not know that the essential thing in a woman's loss of chastity was a lowering of conventional masculine restraints; a loosing of the men upon her.

But presently her thoughts returned to Mrs. Roxie Biggers again, to the charitable old woman who had always befriended the stricken and the weak. Her fancy turned to the old Samaritan with a kind of yearning faith.

She was stuffing her slippers, hose, and underwear into her trunk, utilizing for the smaller articles the space between her novels; the pure benign novels which had never contemplated for their heroines any such desperate disgrace as this.

As she touched the books and sensed their tenor, her own falling away from the rôle of heroine filled her with shame and dismay. It seemed to Nessie that she would give her every possession on earth if she could reinstate herself in that perfect sphere where once her imagination moved. She still did not suspect that in essence it was an impossible sphere; that there were no such lives.

As she worked, the check for her month's salary which Mr. Baxter had given her appeared on her table in the mysterious way such objects have of appearing and disappearing in the hands of a careless person. It demanded some sort of disposal. Nessie took it up and looked at it. She needed the money on it, but the mere thought of taking it to the bank and getting it cashed daunted her. She could not take it to the bank with the whole village watching her and thinking that she had been first discharged from the Grand and then driven from her boarding house. The check was for seventy-five dollars.

Again Mrs. Biggers entered her mind as one who would assist her in getting the check cashed. She finished packing, pondering how she could get to the Biggers home. She could slip out of the hotel at about six o'clock when the village was at supper. The streets would be almost deserted then.

As she closed the lid of her trunk there came a faint tapping at her door. The girl looked around defensively and was surprised to see it was John, the Negro chore boy, who unaccountably had returned to the hotel. He had a dinner on a black oxidized tin tray.

She told him to put it on her table. John entered gingerly, rolling his eyes after the manner of a frightened Negro.

"Goin' away, Miss Nessie?" he asked in a low voice.

The girl nodded and looked at the food with throbbing temples. The black boy shifted feet and cap uneasily.

"Is dey anything else I kin bring ye, Miss Nessie?"

"I'm not hungry, John."

"Yessum," agreed the boy.

The girl thought he was waiting for the plates and sipped a little of the thick soup. Its greasiness made her shudder and almost nauseated her.

"You can take it all away," she said in a sick voice.

"Yessum." He moved again to the table and when he was nearest her he said in a low tone without looking at her, "Miss Nessie, would you min' if I tol' you somp'in'?"

"What is it?" she asked in the same tone.

"You won't tell I tol' je?" whispered the Negro, plainly frightened—" 'case, if you did, you sho will git me in Dutch, Miss Nessie."

"No, I won't tell. What is it?"

The Negro looked at her and barely whispered, moving his thick dark lips in the exaggerated manner of his race.

"Whitecaps gwinter git you to-night, Miss Nessie. I heared it down to de garage. Dat's why I tuk my ol' job back. . . ."

The girl's face went white.

"Coming for me?"

The Negro nodded, terrified; there was nothing under heaven which frightened him as badly as the whitecaps.

"Now I gotto go, I sho is gwinter git out o' dis town; an', please, if you don't want me hung up lak Mistah Peck Bradley, please don' tell I tol' je, Miss Nessie."

"I—I won't," promised the girl.

"Thank ye, Miss Nessie," the Negro whispered humbly, took up his tray, and passed silently out of the door.

A notion went through Nessie's mind that she should have given a last tip to the chore boy. The incongruity of tipping John for risking his life to save her the obscenity of mob violence did not strike her. The thought vanished instantly in the feeling of terror and helplessness which rushed upon her and snuffed out the last remnants of her courage and hope.

The girl sat with a beating heart, listening now with screwed-up attention to every sound in the street. A noise caught her by the throat. She looked out of her window at a long angle and saw it was a motor car. She was so nervous she could hardly endure to remain in the bare, dismantled room, and yet she dared not show herself on the street.

"Oh Lord! Lord!" she prayed incoherently. "Have mercy on me!"

The ticking of her clock called her attention to the flight of time. She stared at its round face, tried to control herself and think. The whitecaps would not come until night, midnight. She had planned to do something. She sat looking at the clock thinking intently, biting her under lip, trying to recollect what she had meant to do. She seemed on the verge of recapturing the plan, when the vision of the whitecaps chivvying her along the streets, down the road and out of town, as they had done the others . . . those others . . . She sickened at the inclusion of herself in this term; and for the first time in her life there dawned upon her the possibility that those others, the women whom the men of the neighbourhood had misused and then thrust contemptuously forth, had been, like herself, human beings, who grew hot and cold, felt shame and bruises . . . were women. . . .

As she sat peering out of her window, weeping as silently as she could, she received a hint of something grotesquely stolid and cruel in village existence—the "nice" folk, the church members; there was a mechanical, unimaginative quality to their functioning that inflicted ghastly wounds of which they knew nothing.

"Like horses . . . cows . . ." she whispered to herself; "kicking and horning. . . ."

She found herself again doubling and pulling at the check for her month's pay. She did not know when she had picked it up. As she stared at her check, she suddenly remembered her plan to get it cashed. This feeble plan brought her a little relief from the abject terror into which the thought of the whitecaps had plunged her.

She looked at her little clock to see how soon would come the supper hour when she could steal out of the hotel to Mrs. Biggers. The good woman would surely plan some way of escape for her.

In the vague relief this brought her she became aware that the afternoon was wearing away, and of the emptiness of the upper story of the boarding house. Suddenly it seemed that Abner must be in his room waiting to come to her. A profound desire for Abner to come to her and protect her rushed over the girl. If he would only marry her and save her as Zed Parrum did the Tolbert girl! If Abner only would come!

She went to her bed, fell on her knees, and prayed God to send her lover to her rescue.

"O God, put it in his heart to come to me to-night! O God, I need him, send him, put it in his heart. . . ."

But she felt as if she were trying to project her prayer into some hard, impenetrable space. The fly-specked ceiling seemed to cut off her pleas; in her memory swam the words of a text, "The prayer of the unrighteous availeth nothing."

It grew upon the girl with a sense of horror that even God had deserted her.

She got to her feet and ceased weeping. After all, she was bad. She wiped her eyes and looked with swollen, tear-bleared face at the clock. It was six o'clock, the hour when the village was at supper.

The necessity of action brought its relief. She bathed her face, powdered away the stains, then took her handbag, put the check for her month's salary in her purse, and tiptoed silently out of the room.

She met no one in the hotel, and a little later passed under the dingy sign hanging to the mulberry and so along the street in the direction of the Biggers home.

It had been a cloudy day, for purple and slate clouds covered the sky, but far in the west the sun set clear in a long strip of serene yellows and bluish greens. It seemed to Nessie as the cool autumn evening breathed against her face that the western zone of colour and light was the delayed blessing on her prayer. A little courage came to her. The west was of infinite depth and infinite tenderness. It forgave everything; it forgave even that Nessie had loved . . . unpaid and uncontracted for.

Not a person was on the streets. The village was at supper. The village devoted this single moment of the day when all the filth of its streets and all the moral cruelties and pettinesses of its life were forgiven in the solemn absolution of sunset; it devoted that single moment to eating. What cared the village for this pageantry of the west? Of what moment to them this tender forgiving hour; they, who had nothing to be forgiven? Let them eat hot bread in mean rooms beneath lithographs of dead fish, let them talk of the last scandal, or simply eat in silence. That miracle of jade and turquoise fades slowly into the sea-blue depths of night, but what have they to do with that?

Nessie paused at the Biggers's gate and her heart began beating again; but she embattled all her fortitude in her heart. She thought, "I know she will help me; she helps everyone, the weak, the poor, the broken, I know she won't refuse me. . . ."

A swift vision of herself being clasped in the old woman's arms and being allowed to weep out her aching heart flooded Nessie's emotions and softened the desperation of her mood.

The girl opened the sagging gate and entered the yard.

CHAPTER XXVII

NESSIE SUTTON'S tinkle at the Biggers's doorbell aroused Mrs. Roxie Biggers from her supper table where she sat eating with a sort of absent-minded voracity. As the good woman ate she revolved in her mind a fine stroke of charity. Now, at the ring of her bell, she arose from the table and started for the door still thinking over a detail of her plan. She was planning how she could get fifteen dollars and forty-three cents to buy a minister's Bible from a mail-order house to give to Mr. Tug Beavers.

But her charity did not stop there. Mrs. Biggers had conceived nothing less than the splendid accomplishment of sending Tug to a theological school and making a preacher of him. The thought warmed the old woman's heart with its glory.

The details of her plan and the glory she would receive mixed in her mind in a curious jumble! She now had twenty dollars and sixty-five cents in the Willing Workers' fund—every lost soul the future Reverend Beavers might succeed in winning to Christ would in reality be her work—with ice-cream suppers during the summer and chicken dinners during the winter, she could rely upon about thirteen dollars a month the year round—the people of Irontown would have to acknowledge she was a power for goodness after such a coup as this—the dues of the Willing Workers were eight dollars and a half a month—when she got to Heaven the stars in her crown, she supposed, would equal the sum of her own charities plus those the Reverend Tug Beavers might perform—she could count on about eight dollars from the Woman's Bazaar; then school entertainments . . . here she opened her door.

At first Mrs. Biggers saw nothing save the deserted street in the pale shadowless light of the evening's afterglow. Not a soul was abroad. She stood for a moment in her doorway, thinking that some of the village children had rung her bell and then had run away. These children hated the old woman with an odd intensity because she conscripted their labour for charitable and, often, for purely personal ends.

The good old philanthropist decided it had been some child; reflected generously that when it grew older it would come to appreciate her many good qualities, and was about to return to her table when she heard her name faintly called and then she saw a figure shrinking close beside her doorway.

Mrs. Biggers stepped out on the porch and looked at her visitor in surprise, then when she recognized who it was she stiffened with silent resentment that such a person should be on her piazza.

"Is that Nessie Sutton?" she asked, staring into the colourless light, as if doubting her eyes. "What do you want?"

The old woman's tone put an end to the milliner's fantastic notion that she might be allowed to weep out her wretched heart in the Samaritan's arms.

"Miss Roxie . . ." began the girl uncertainly.

"Yes, yes, what do you want, Nessie Sutton?"

The use of her full name, the tone in which it was pronounced, warned Nessie that the interview would not be long. It suggested that she go away as quickly as possible. In fact, it brought to the girl a realization, which was continually slipping away from her, of exactly where she stood in Irontown society, and indeed, in the whole world. A terrible thought seized her that perhaps this was the last chance she would ever have of talking to a woman of her own sort, of seeking forgiveness, of softening a little the universal condemnation. She began speaking with a rush:

"Miss Roxie, I come to you to help me! Miss Roxie, I hope you will! Oh, you don't know how sorry I am for what I—I done! It—it—Miss Roxie, it's like a nightmare! When I wake up at night I kain't believe it! To have ever'-

body against you; not a friend, nowhere, nowhere a-tall; I'd —I'd rather be d-e-a-d!"

Her voice quivered in a terrible intensity on the word "dead," and she broke into a stifled sobbing, trying to hold her lips steady and blinking the tears from her eyes.

"What I couldn't understan'," said Mrs. Roxie in a cold voice, "was how you could act that way after all Brother Perry had done for you."

"Oh, I know it, Miss Roxie!" responded the girl miserably. "All of you, ever' person in Irontown has been so good to me. Oh—oh, I can't tell why! I—I!"—the old woman could see her colour painfully in the uncertain light— "God knows," she wailed, "I would do anything in the world —anything, if I could be a pure girl again!" She extended her hands impulsively; then as the good old woman withdrew slightly, she pressed her clenched fists against her breast and stood looking at Mrs. Roxie with a tortured face.

Strangely enough the girl's wretched confession created a stronger repulsion in Mrs. Biggers; it brought the girl's undoing before her, visualized it. She wanted the creature to go away; to take herself off. Nessie seemed something unclean on her porch.

"Of course, there ain't no way to undo *that*," said Mrs. Biggers, controlling her distaste. "You ort to have thought of all this, Nessie, before you sinned."

The girl came to a pause in her weeping at this splendid but unfortunately retroactive advice.

"Ye-es," she agreed in a melancholy whisper.

Mrs. Biggers continued looking coldly and speculatively at her. The old woman really had a bit of very helpful advice which she might give if she were so minded; that was for Nessie to get out of town at once and escape the mob— but was she so minded? She did not know. She had a feeling that the obscenity and humiliation of mob violence were a part of the girl's just punishment. It would "learn her," she thought. She might even be interfering with God's vengeance. A Biblical text floated across her mind,

"If thy right hand offend thee, cut it off." But then, in the depth of her heart, Mrs. Roxie had a feeling that God's purposes were more or less like everybody else's, rather subordinate to her own. Now this girl was such a miserable wretch, such a come-down from the trim pretty Nessie Sutton of Sunday-school and church, that she decided Nessie had had enough. So she said laconically, "The best thing for you to do is to git out of town, or they'll run you out."

Thus, perhaps, the very kindest act, the single deed unaffected by religious vanity which Mrs. Biggers ever performed in all her life was when she violated her conscience, betrayed her accomplices, and contravened the will of her God.

Nessie stopped breathing, and then whispered, wide-eyed, "Yes, they told me that."

This somehow irritated Mrs. Roxie.

"Who did?" she probed sharply.

The name of the Negro boy was on the tip of Nessie's tongue, but she checked herself.

"I promised not to tell," she said feebly.

The old woman was furious that any one else had exposed her plans, so she simply repeated in a hard tone, "Well, the best thing for you to do is to git out o' town."

"But, Miss Roxie, where must I go?" trembled the girl.

The old woman withdrew into her door. "You know better'n I do where women like you go to, and that's all I got to say, so good-bye." Then she added in a less angry and more corrective tone, "I hope God'll touch your heart, Nessie, an' turn you away from your sins," and she closed her door in the unfortunate's face.

A violent trembling seized the girl at this implication of her class and forewarning of her future. She was so unsteady she could hardly get off the porch and to the gate. . . . "You know better than I do where women like you go . . ." Women like her . . . prostitutes. . . . Ah, to what bourne did prostitutes journey?

For several moments Nessie stood before the gate with her

imaginings of this repulsive lurid life rising before her eyes. At last she shook off the feeling of sickness it brought and addressed her thoughts to the necessity of escaping the mob. She let herself out the gate and stood listening with open mouth for the faintest rumour of a disturbance.

By this time night was come. She stood in the dark street trying to plan some course of action. Instinctively she turned away from the business part of town and began hurrying toward the outskirts; but after a little distance she reflected that every household within twenty miles had heard of her misfortune and not one family would take her in for the night. And yet she was afraid to turn back into Irontown again. She paused in suspense, listening intently. The only sound she heard was the faint faraway shriek of the evening train blowing for a crossing.

The eerie sound reminded the girl that she had not cashed her check and that it was impossible for her to buy a ticket on the train. This absolute necessity dispelled for a moment her fear of the mob. She turned and hurried townward again, hoping to get enough money from one of the smaller shops to pay her fare somewhere. She repassed the Biggers's home, a black mass outlined against a dark sky. In her conversation with Mrs. Roxie she had forgotten the check, the real reason why she had gone to the old woman. To enter the house again, after her ejection, was impossible. She would go to some out-of-the-way shop. But now at every step she took toward the centre of the village her fear of the mob mounted. It seemed to the girl that every tree along the street was the covert of some spy. She tried to walk silently, but her high heels would click. She peered into the darkness. Yet she wanted to hurry and catch the train which she could now hear murmuring in the south.

Then the old riddle confronted her again—where could she go? To what place could she turn to escape from her past? It seemed her only refuge was in a still more evil future.

Again the world of prostitutes limned itself before Nessie's shrinking imagination: vile districts, nocturnal debauches, drunkenness, lewdness, what a hell!

No matter where she went it would be to this. Everywhere women would avoid her, men beset her, she would become a prostitute, a haunter of shadowy streets, a painted creature of slinking defiance, an apprehensive accoster of men to be spurned in silence, or accepted and used carelessly. To what end should she endure all this contempt and obscenity?— to live? Was that all? To eat, to sleep, to breathe!

Out of the increasing murmur to the south she heard a louder shriek of the approaching train. Now, in her changed mood, she knew that no train would ever bear her out of her great damnation. Mrs. Biggers's treatment had shown her that; a good woman, a charitable woman . . .

"I would rather die than lead such a life," she thought desperately. "God forgive me, but I'd rather die!"

She was hurrying now toward the depot. As she passed the dim lights of the first shop she hesitated momentarily between the last force of her old purpose and the beginning of a new and terrible resolution. The next moment she walked quickly past. Her check suddenly had become of no more importance than a wisp of blank paper; even the mob itself was becoming something far away and unrelated to her. There was, after all, a way for the train to bear her out of her misery.

Now at the approaching noise of the engine a sudden fear of missing it set the girl running toward a cross street she knew. This street led down to the railroad track at a point two or three hundred yards beyond the station. She must get to this street, get down to the track before the train left the station. It would remain there only two or three minutes. Her heart began beating as her purpose grew upon her.

The strangest notions began to swarm in Nessie's head. She seemed to be running and stumbling in a nightmare; the occasional lighted door she passed, the mob which now had dwindled to a remote threat, all became part of this fluid unreality. It seemed to Nessie that she herself was somehow becoming unreal; her body, her legs running and stumbling through the dark, unkept street would presently slip away, out of the village, out of reach of the mob, out of any coming life of shame; it was all ending; she was ending; a leap, a crashing in the darkness—— She heard the express shriek for the station, a tremendous cacophony, stunning the night with its power.

Nessie darted past a shop that stood on the business street at the head of the cross alley she sought. She was running now in frantic haste lest the train roar past the other end of the alley before she reached it. She was hardly twenty feet down this thoroughfare before she heard a sharp running behind her. A new terror of capture by the mob filled the girl. She flew down the littered alley panic struck, but the footsteps of a man closed behind her and a moment later an urgent guarded voice called her name, "Nessie! Nessie! Is that you, Nessie?"

She tried to run faster with the terror of a woman before a man's superior speed. The voice cried out, "For God's sake, wait, Nessie! Where are you going?"

The lowered tones, the desperate urgency somewhat assured the panic-stricken girl. She checked her flight and stood gasping, her heart drumming, unable to speak. A smallish figure not much taller than herself appeared in the darkness. A moment later she recognized Mr. Belshue. She was neither surprised, relieved, nor did he move her tortured emotions in any degree whatever save to fill her with a violent impatience.

"What in the world do you want?" she demanded, with her heart shaking her husky voice.

"Thank God, I've found you!" panted the jeweller, coming up beside her. "I've hunted everywhere, at your hotel, the Grand, on the streets. . . ."

"What do you want? What do you want?" cried the girl tensely.

"I want to get you out of this town to-night, this minute.

right now!" He laid hold of her arm and began drawing her toward his shop at the end of the alley.

"Stop! Stop! I don't want to go. Where are you going to take me?"

"Where do you want to go?"

"Nowhere! There's no place for me to go! Let me alone!" She tried to jerk loose from him and her ears strained toward the station.

"Nessie, what do you mean?" cried the jeweller, frightened at her wild manner.

She tried to pull herself free. "Stop! Let go!" she wheezed in her effort. Suddenly she went limp and cried out miserably, "Oh, I've got enough of you and Irontown and ever'body in the whole world. Do please go away and let me alone. Let me alone! Turn me loose!" She whipped out the last in sharp cries and again tried to wrench herself free.

The jeweller ran his arm through hers and so linked her to him.

"Nessie," he warned, "they are going to mob you!"

"No, they won't!"

"But they will!"

"I say they won't. Turn me loose!"

"What'll you do?"

"I know. Turn me loose."

At the girl's tone the jeweller caught her other shoulder and tried to see her face in the gloom.

"Nessie!" he cried in a shocked voice, "you don't mean . . ." he broke off in horror at her implication.

The girl stood silent save for her fluttering audible breathing. The fingers on Nessie's shoulder became a palm drawing her pityingly toward the jeweller.

"My poor dear child, what a horrible idea! Poor girl, don't let them drive you mad! I'll do anything, all I can to help you, Nessie, anything in the world I can do. I've got a car in front of my shop. I've hunted you all afternoon. Now, come along, Nessie." His arm linked through hers, slipped down around her waist. He was drawing her to him, and Nessie recalled with painful clearness that other night in the Scovell House, ages ago, it seemed, when he had kissed her and when Miss Scovell had warned her against him. Now his pity, his sympathy, his caresses wrung at the overwrought girl, but still she pushed away from him, moved now by her inherent truthfulness.

"But—but, listen, Mr. Belshue—what are you going to do with me?"

"Marry you, Nessie, if you will let me."

"Marry me!" she echoed in a ghastly tone.

He patted her shoulder gently.

"Mr. Belshue—Mr. Belshue—you—you kain't marry me. . . . I—I'm a ruined girl."

Came a silence; the pressure of the jeweller's arms on her shoulder and waist did not relax.

"You are not, Nessie," he said in a moved voice, "but you may become so unless somebody helps you."

"Oh, but I am, I am!" sobbed the girl piteously. "I—I—he—Ab——" but at the first syllable of her lover's name something seemed to lock in her throat.

The lonely man drew her to him with a profound tenderness, caressing her cheek, her hair.

"No man can ruin a woman, Nessie," he whispered in her ear. "The people do that."

At the entrance of a little side alley on the main street of the village a man and a woman entered an automobile just as the locomotive pulled away from the station that evening. As the puffs of the engine smote the night, came the whirring of the car's self-starter; a moment later the motor whispered and the headlights spurted up the dark shabby street. Automobile and train moved off through the night on their separate ways.

CHAPTER XXVIII

IN THE camp for the construction men Mr. Tim Fraley and Mr. Zed Parrum were talking lightly of a light matter. Mr. Fraley winked.

"Ab Teeftaller showed a better head in his little kick-up than you did, Zed—his gal ain't got no daddy."

Mr. Parrum put little heart into his return wink. His involuntary marriage was a sore point with him.

"Yeh—live an' learn. . . . Have you talked to Ab lately, Tim?"

"Nope, I seen him walking around the camp here pretty offish, figgered he'd got the big head over this sheracketty an' didn't want to talk to a common feller like me."

"You done him wrong," defended Zed at once. "He ain't stuck up, he's worried."

"What's he got to worry about?"

"Tim, he's got the derndest fool idyah I ever heard of."

"What's that?"

"Why, he's figgerin' on marryin' that Sutton gal, after all that's happened."

Mr. Fraley stared, finally blurted out in slow bewilderment, "The—hell—he—is!"

"Yep. I tried to persuade him out of it, but you know that damn fool Ditmas is backin' him up in it."

"I thought Ditmas was his frien'."

"I reckon he is a frien' accordin' to his lights, but I shore say, 'Damn his lights.'"

Tim agreed profanely, then assembled his information about the engineer.

"It's like this, Zed. Ditmas is a Yankee, an' you know them Yankees ain't got no sense of honour like we got here in Tennessee. They tell me a Yankee'd as soon marry an unvarchuous woman as look at 'em."

"Ditmas was arguin' that bein' it was Abner hisse'f that done it . . ."

"Hell far, if a feller tries one out an' she shows up bad . . ." Here Mr. Fraley recalled that his companion had not lived up to the strict Tennessee code of honour; he stumbled in his speech, and finally muddled out, "Well—down here we do our damnedest. . . ."

"Uh-huh," mumbled Zed uncomfortably, then he remembered that he had to see a fellow and started off rather awkwardly through the tented street. He had not gone far when he heard Mr. Fraley behind him wheezing with a stifled laughter, and he thought in disgust, "Damn fools won't never quit laughin' at that."

Which was quite true.

This same hill feeling of what was honourable halted Abner Teeftallow on his way to the unsheltered platform which served as a railway station for the construction camp. The youth did not know whether he wanted to go to Irontown that afternoon or not. Everyone except Ditmas advised him against it. Nessie was in trouble. He would better stay away. No telling what might bob up. All his friends, except Ditmas, considered any other action mad.

As a matter of fact, all the gossip about the girl seemed to change her from the simple, affectionate creature he had known into a woman whom he could not quite trust. The scandal was like tinted glass, which gave the girl, viewed through it, a new and disturbing colour. But Abner's natural fondness and tenderness for Nessie kept breaking through this feeling, and for a moment he would remember her as gentle, trusting, with an affection for him as enduring as her life. At such moments he would take a few determined steps toward the platform where a half-dozen persons awaited the afternoon train.

Then he would grow undecided again and walk up and

down the track, harrowed between the clash of his impulses. Finally he decided that he would not go to Irontown. He could do nothing for Nessie. He could not marry her—he would not dare to. A hill adage popped into his head, "Who faithless is before she wed, will faithless be to marriage bed."

This decided Abner. No, he'd be damned if he'd go!

Here the shriek of a whistle caused him to look down the track. The construction train was coming. Then something deeper than his adage seized the youth and moved him toward the platform. But his rebellion toward Nessie was still in progress. And a plan popped into his head how he could, as it were, both go and not go at one and the same time. As he passed the caboose he shouted to the engineer, "Hey, cap, lemme ride, won't ye?"

"What the hell you want to go to Arntown fer?" growled the engineer. "Looks like you'd be goin' t'other direction."

Evidently the whole world knew of his affair.

"That's the point," explained the youth earnestly. "I wanted you to kinder slow up an lemme off before we reached town—got to git my clothes," he lied, to conceal all trace of his tenderness.

"It's against the rules. All I can do is to tell you to keep off."

This meant Abner could ride. He climbed up into the caboose and a few seconds later a voice shouted, "All aboard!" The grimy one moved levers and wheels; the mass of iron came to life and started panting down the new uneven track.

Abner stuck his head out of the caboose window, and the cold rush of air somehow comforted him. He thought to himself, "I won't go plum into Arntown, I'll sorter scout aroun' an' see how the lan' lays, an' then . . ." Here his thoughts drifted vaguely and wistfully toward Nessie. He caught a vision of himself holding the girl in his arms, fondling her, weeping over her, saying, "Nessie, did ye think I wuzn't comin' back? Why, honey, I'd wade through fire

an' watter before . . ." Here he blinked the moisture
out of his eyes and shouted across the cab to the engineer,
"Partner, I wish you'd kinder slow down about even with old
Squire Meredith's place. I want to git off there."

The greasy one gave a wooden nod.

Some hour later the teamster jumped from the cab and
landed with a jar on some freshly turned earth alongside the
track. He waited till the train had gone and then set out
across the field in the direction of the Meredith home. As he
walked he could see the gray gable of the old house and the
slender column of a pear tree above the shoulder of the hill.
In the yellowing sunshine this formed a picture, but its line
and colour were lost on Abner. To him it was simply Squire
Meredith's old house which he could see from the foot of the
pasture hill, and he veered off at an angle toward the high-
way.

Once Abner placed himself on the familiar road a dozen
memories of Nessie Sutton arose in him and filled his heart
with a sharp desire to see her again, and with an anxiety about
her welfare. The Meredith house recalled the time he had
carried Tug Beavers's note to Mary Lou, and the row the old
justice had raised. He remembered how he had stayed all
night with the Squire and had cried for homesickness. He
recollected talking to Nessie in the Lanesburg courthouse
yard—how beautiful and unattainable she had looked standing there silently on the lawn. . . .

Now he was passing the hill where the mob had lynched
Peck Bradley. He would have seen the tragedy had it not
been for Nessie's surrender to him. The mere thought of
this moved Abner to an exquisite tenderness and desire for
the girl.

Suddenly, he decided he would marry her. He would
rent a car at the Irontown garage, go to Lanesburg with
Nessie, marry her, and end this gossip at a stroke.

He was striding down the hill now, filled with this warm
impulse composed half of generosity and tenderness and half
of desire. He felt it was distinctly a generous thing to do, to

marry a girl after she had given herself to him. Somehow it was a condescension on his part, a stooping. But he loved her. The thought that he could sacrifice himself by marrying her filled him with a sort of high pleasure. He really was a noble fellow. The villagers might jibe, as they were sure to do, but he would stoop and rescue a weak girl from their clamour!

He strode along in quite a cavalierish mood, when he saw a Negro coming up the road at a slow trot, head tucked down, arms drawn up for long-distance running.

Now it is the invariable practice of any white man in the rural districts of the South to stop any running Negro and question him closely as to why he is running, whence he came, and whither he means to go. It is a relic of the apprehension of runaway slaves.

Abner acted according to this custom. He put aside his own anxieties, placed himself in the middle of the road ready to fight or chase as the exigency of the occasion might demand; then he called roughly, "Hey, nigger, where you goin'?"

The black boy started as if someone had fired a gun under his nose; flung up head with white eyes.

"N-nowhere, suh!"

"You're in a hell of a rush to go nowhere——" Then he broke off. "Well, I be damned, it's John! John, where in the hell are you goin'?"

At this turn the chore boy's fright changed to delight.

"Well, 'fo' God, if it ain't Mastuh Abnah! Mastuh Abnah, Ah sho is glad to see you!" He came up to Abner, apparently on the verge of embracing him.

"What's the matter?" asked Abner, stirred and somehow uneasy at John's emotion.

"Mastuh Abnah, Ah jess seen Miss Nessie packin' her trunk." The chore boy's face was sorrow-stricken.

"Seen her packin' her trunk?"

"Yes, suh, she's goin' tuh haff tuh step out."

Abner stared. "The hell she does—where to?"

"She don' know—jess some'er's. She's all tore up about hit. Ah jess carried huh huh dinnah."

"Is she sick?"

"No, suh."

"Look here, who the hell's goin' to make her get out?" demanded Abner furiously.

"De"—John glanced up and down the empty road and whispered—"de whitecaps."

Abner stared at him. "Whitecaps!"

The Negro nodded, white-eyed, and whispered, "Don' you tell Ah tole."

"What for?"

"Er—uh—um——" swallowed John, then blurted out, "You knows what fuh, Mastuh Abnah."

Came a silence, then, "Of all damned outrages!"

"Yes, suh—yes, suh," bobbed the chore boy rapidly, "white fo'ks sho is supuhstitious 'bout dat, Mastuh Abnah."

"And besides that," raged on Abner, "they can't do it. Why, damn it, I'm the daddy of them whitecaps. I got 'em to hang Peck Bradley. They can't do nothin' to my own gal!"

"Th-they say they is gwi'n' do it, though," stammered John.

"But I tell you I started 'em!"

"Yes, suh, Mastuh Abnah, but startin' 'em ain't stoppin' 'em. Ah started a pair o' mules once . . ."

Abner did not wait to hear the conclusion of the story. He strode off down the road, cursing, and determined to take a strong hand in the matter of the whitecaps. And this determined him positively to marry Nessie.

The black boy watched the hillman leg it down the road, then he turned and resumed his endless trot in the other direction, placing as many miles as possible between him and Irontown before nightfall.

The road entering Irontown from the direction of Lanesburg leads within two or three hundred yards of the crap-

shooting grounds, and Abner decided to make a detour and
see if he could find any of the village reformers and deter-
mine, if possible, their plans for the night. So when he
neared the Negro huts on the outskirts of Irontown, he
turned out through the woods to the bare circles on the
ground used by the gamblers. He had not gone far before
he was rewarded by a warning whistle from an outpost.

Abner looked about until he discovered the fellow and
then approached him with a fraternal wink.

"Anything on for to-night?" he inquired.

"They usually is," returned the fellow distrustfully.

"Big game?"

"Of its kind."

This alarmed Abner and he asked in a different tone, "What
sort o' game is it?"

"I reckon you've heard the rule, 'Ast no questions an' hear
no lies,' " returned the fellow with sour philosophy.

Abner passed by him to a circle of gamblers who were very
elaborately doing nothing in the presence of a stranger.
Abner glanced over the group and was relieved to see two or
three faces he knew.

"Willie Purvis," he nodded at one of these, "lemme see you
a minute."

Willie arose from his haunches stiffly and followed Abner
into the bushes. They paused behind a huckleberry bush.

"Look here, Willie"—Abner's tone was serious and con-
fidential—"have you boys made up to do anything to my gal
to-night?"

Mr. Purvis became ill at ease. "Look here, Ab, I ain't
got a thing in the worl' to do with this. I think it's tom-
foolishness. I say if you chase all these women out o' town,
the men'll jest foller 'em."

"Good God!" exploded Abner in a hot undertone. "You
ain't puttin' my gal in that class! She's a nice gal,
Wlllie!"

Willie waggled a sophisticated head. "They're all nice
gals to somebody. If you don't give up yore nice gal an'

me mine, an Tom, Dick, an' Harry their'n, this town never will git cleaned up."

Abner was amazed at such a view. He always had felt so profoundly the innocence of Nessie's yieldings to him that Willie's view dumbfounded him.

"By God!" he cried in an ill-coördinated effort to refute, "if—if you think that—you're no friend o' mine!"

"Why, Ab, you know it ain't right. Now, I leave it to you, is it?"

"All I got to say is, it looks damn funny to me! That's all I got to say!" He turned and began smashing his way through the bushes.

Mr. Purvis, peace-loving by nature, hung on to the teamster's flank.

"Now, look here, don't git mad at me. But you know it ain't right. And besides that, Perry Northcutt's kinder talkin' agin' you, too. Says the boys would make a good job if they chased you out, too."

"By God, try it, if you feel like it!"

"Hell, I'm jess tellin' you. I tole 'em if you start chasin' the men out for that, they'd haff to move 'em in gangs, an' the last man would haff to march hisse'f off."

But Abner was not conciliated by this cynicism. He tramped on off through the woods, determined to marry Nessie Sutton out of hand, and to hell with what anybody thought about it. He wouldn't let any spike-headed bank cashier tell him what he could do or where he could stay. Here his soliloquy fizzled out as he entered the purlieus of the village again.

By this time the sun was down. Against the flare of the sunset the woods which Abner had just left were picked out in a gamut of textures from the lace of willows through the progressively darker spotulations of sycamore, elms, maples, to the solid blacknesses of cedars and pines.

Unmindful of all these traceries against the scarlet west, Abner hurried into the silent village streets which were deserted during the supper hour. His object was to find Nessie, take her away, and marry her.

As he turned toward the Scovell House he heard the faint shriek of the evening train as it blew for some distant crossing. It brought to Abner its habitual implication of danger and uncanniness and hurried the youth's steps. Then he formed a plan for him and Nessie to catch this train and so escape the rising mob. He thrust his hand into his pocket, felt some bills. That would be enough to start them somewhere.

Under the urgency of his thoughts he began trotting through the silent thoroughfares, between rows of gray houses tinted with the yellows and reds of the evening sky. Presently he sighted the scraggly mulberry before the Scovell House. The teamster slowed up, entered the gate, and without pausing to knock at the door, walked on into the dining room.

There were a number of guests at the table and Miss Scovell was waiting on them. When Abner opened the door he saw the landlady's ungainly figure leaning over the table offering her guests hot biscuits. The chore boy was gone again. A glance showed that Nessie was not at the table, and this sent a quiver of apprehension through the teamster. Amid the clinking of knives and plates, he blurted out anxiously, "Miss Scovell, where's Nessie?"

The landlady looked around and broke into instantaneous wrath.

"Look here, Ab Teeftaller!" she began in a tense undertone which implied that her guests were not supposed to hear or mark what she was going to say. "Don't mention no disreputable names in my house, an' don't come hangin' aroun' here yo'se'f! You jest git out o' here! You've done enough dirt to this hotel already!"

"B-but, Miss Scovell," stammered Abner with lips stiff from embarrassment, "I—I got to see her! It—it's important!"

"Well, she's up in her room, but you kain't go up there!"

"I—I'll call her from the hall!" stuttered Abner, turning brick-red.

"We-ell . . . I reckon you can do that," she acceded grudgingly.

The landlady gave the youth a look of hatred as he turned swiftly to the hallway. A constriction passed over her thin face. As she turned to the kitchen she trembled in an undertone, "Scan'alous! Him to have the face to come an' ast for her!" It was a cruel thing, this tragic love affair in her loveless hotel.

A moment later she could hear Abner calling Nessie's name from the foot of the stairs in edged tones. He tried to restrain his voice not to disturb the diners.

"Nessie! Oh, Nessie! Nessie Sutton! Oh, Nessie Sutton!"

At last Miss Scovell could endure these anxious trembling cries no longer. She came angrily into the hallway.

"Do shut up! I'll go tell her! You've made my place the talk of the town as it is! What do you want with her?"

"I—I want to m-marry her," shivered Abner.

"O-oh, you——" A shudder went through the withered woman as she hurried stiffly up the stairs. She had no idea why this moved her with such a sense of her own frustration. She could but sense, not analyze, the logic of these facts—if an illicit love finally could be rewarded with peace, then her own solitary inhibited life had been in vain. The punishment of evildoers was a sort of negative dividend that fell due on Miss Scovell's negative investment in morality. If that failed, she would be a bankrupt indeed!

She hurried up the stairs and very quickly came down again with anxiety and yet a sort of malicious pleasure in her face.

"She ain't in her room, Abner! I don't know where she went to—well, no matter where; it's good riddance of bad rubbish!"

While the landlady and the teamster stared at each other,

both really anxious about Nessie, there came the shriek of the evening train and a moment later, the rumble of the cars slowing up for the station.

A solution of their riddle flashed on Abner.

"She's goin' off on the train!" he cried, and the next moment dashed out of the hotel, up the dark street toward the station.

The teamster sprinted along at top speed because he knew that the train tarried at Irontown only two or three minutes. If he did not reach it in time Nessie would be borne away from him for ever. Now that he was about to lose her his whole desire focussed on marrying her. He ran down the block full tilt, whipped around the corner at the garage. Here four or five voices shouted at him, but he paid no attention to them. The street from the garage corner was unpaved and sloped down an incline. Abner drove down it at enormous strides, his feet plopping against the ground. As he ran he could hear the slow panting of the locomotive as it stood at the station; then a turn in the dilapidated street showed him the brilliant glare of the headlight washing the track in front and a string of faintly illumined car windows behind it. Against these lights moved silhouettes of people. Forward on the platform he could sense the movement of freight and baggage. He was running harder than ever when he heard the conductor shout, "All aboard!" and the bell began ringing.

Abner was halfway down the hill. Without realizing what he was doing he began yelling, "Wait, conductor! Hold on! For God's sake, wait!"

The measured puffs of the engine answered him. The glowworm of the cars moved off after the brilliant torch of the headlight. As the train gathered speed the rumble of the cars reasserted itself. Abner came to a halt.

He stood panting in the darkness, feeling tremulous and empty as if someone had torn out his bowels by some painless but numbing operation. There seemed to be nothing further for him to do—or think. Presently he realized that from his first step toward the train in the railroad camp he had meant to marry Nessie. Every movement of his mind or body had been directed to that end. Now Nessie was gone and their marriage impossible.

He stood watching the tail lights of the express diminish, draw close together. At last they coalesced into one faint light, and presently this vanished in the night.

When the noise of the train fell to silence, Abner still stood in the poor street, feeling numb and stricken. There was nothing at all to do. He might as well stand there in the street as to do any other useless thing.

Up on the main street of the village he could hear someone starting a car. The self-starter purred at the cold engine. At last the unwilling motor began a rush of coughing and was presently throttled down to a slower tempo. Came the rasp of a clutch let in by some unskilful hand. Then the car also murmured away into the night. This sound increased Abner's impression of loss and desolation.

CHAPTER XXIX

ABNER TEEFTALLOW turned back toward the dark business street of Irontown hopeless of ever seeing Nessie Sutton again. When the train had borne her away it was as if she had entered the tomb. He moved slowly back up the hill, robbed of any further purpose in Irontown, or indeed in life itself.

When he reached the garage, habit caused him to gravitate toward the faintly lighted place, but in his mood a thought of its obscene life caused him to veer slowly away. He did not want to speak to any one, he did not want to see any one; he wanted merely to get away from Irontown, which was redolent of Nessie's presence, like some dirty box still fragrant of flowers that are gone.

A thought crossed his mind that now was the time when he ought to go drink himself into stupefaction, but alcohol was not habitual to him and this thought was a mere intellectual moment and lacked all executive force. Then he considered the notion of going to a crap game, or to a bawdy house and spending the night, but all of these distractions were uniformly repulsive. Finally he decided to go back to the railroad camp and his work. He could walk the sixteen miles in four or five hours. He would get into camp sufficiently tired to sleep. The next day he could work himself to weariness again, and so on and on; each day a laborious avoidance of the thought of Nessie Sutton.

As the teamster passed the garage a voice hailed him from the dark building. Abner almost replied, but knew that he would be called back and talked to, so he continued on his way in silence.

The voice lifted in menace.

"That's you, Ab Teeftaller, I know you!"

As Abner still did not reply the unseen person snarled out, "Go to hell, then!" and Abner heard the same person insist to someone in an undertone, "Yes, it is Ab Teeftaller. He's jest a damn coward, skeered to face the music. . . ."

When Abner reached the woods at the edge of the village the darkness became so intense that he could keep in the road only by looking up and walking under the path of stars cut out by the inky masses of the trees along both sides of the thoroughfare.

In the woods the night was very cold and still. At the tops of the elevations in his road he entered slightly warmer strata of air. These warmer areas were sometimes perfumed with wild cucumbers or mown clover, which gave him a sense of mounting into some fragrant ethereal pool whence he fancied himself shaking off the earth and rising and rising, perhaps to rejoin Nessie in some purple chamber of the night.

He walked on and on with that vague balm welling up out of his lover's pain, with the poetry of the girl hovering over him sweet with grief.

Far to the south he could hear the rumour of a fox chase which swelled or faded with the configuration of the distant hills. At last the chase was lost to his ears, and he began speculating on how different this night might have been had he gone to Irontown on the preceding day, or if he only had gone in with the train that afternoon. Right at this moment they might have been walking together in the sweetness of this night, with their arms locked about each other's waist, with the perfume of her pale amber hair in his face and her lips and embraces free to him. It seemed fantastic that a few minutes' delay, a hesitation should have erased all this joy utterly and finally. If he only had ridden on into the village on the train, if he had saved even the few minutes he spent talking at the hotel . . . a kind of anguish gripped him at the heaven he had so barely missed. He flung up his hands in the darkness, "Oh, good Lord, why didn't I hurry! What made me git off the train!" An intolerable loneliness seized him. He stared up at the distant lights, and a bright star caught and held his eyes. He thought Nessie, gazing out of her car window on the northbound train, might also be looking at this shining star. He hoped she was, and that she grieved for him as he was grieving for her.

A motor car thrumming somewhere in the darkness behind him aroused Abner from his reverie. The machine drew closer, and presently a beam of light flickered past the teamster, making the road ahead of him visible in sharp blacks and whites. Without glancing around Abner got to one side to allow the motor to pass, when to his surprise there came a rasping of the brakes and the car came to a halt behind him. The teamster looked around into the dazzling headlight just as a voice called out sharply, "Hey, there, Ab Teeftaller, stop there, will ye?"

The menacing tone, the unusualness of a motor stopping behind a man on foot, sent a tang of apprehension and anger through the youth. He flung back over his shoulder the usual hill snarl, "Go to hell," and continued his plodding.

The next moment a shotgun roared behind him and the load splashed into the roadbed a few yards in front of him. In the ringing silence that followed another voice ordered, "Now, damn ye, stop, or do you want us to stop ye?"

Abner whirled and stared into the blinding light at this unexpected challenge. He instantly decided that he had to do with drunken men and called out angrily, "Look here, you damn fools, shootin' aroun' a man like that; don't you do that no more!"

"Then you come on back here," replied a voice, coldly sober. "We've got a little business with you to-night."

This phrase, "little business," in that hard sober tone could mean only one thing, that Abner had committed some wrong which was to be settled by force. The teamster thought swiftly over his recent doings for some insult or grievance he had offered any one, but found nothing at all. As far as he knew not one of his acts merited censure from any person. He turned and walked slowly back into the light.

"I guess you fellers have made a mistake," he said in a different tone. "I'm Ab Teeftaller. I run a dirt scoop at the railroad camp. I don't guess I'm the man you're lookin' for."

"We know who ye air all right an' what ye done," returned the flat voice. "Jest come on an' git in this automobile with us."

"Well, by God," said Abner, pausing, "if you know what I done, I want to know it too; so spit her out. What you fellers got agin me?"

A third voice answered, "Damn you, we're goin' to take you back to Arntown an' marry ye to that Sutton gal!"

Such a surprise flooded Abner that he felt weak.

"What in the hell!" he ejaculated blankly; then a terrifying possibility smote him. "You-all ain't a passel o' her relations, air ye?"

"That's all right what *we* air," returned the voice. "You ruint that gal, an' now you got to marry her."

As Abner stared at this amazing mission, all his ardour to have Nessie for a wife vanished and he recalled with gratitude that she had gone away on the train. He moistened his dry mouth.

"Why—er—gentlemen," he stammered in a frightened voice, "they ain't no use takin' me back to Arntown. I jest been down there on purpose to marry her, an' she left on the northbound about an hour ago."

"That's a damn lie," returned a snarling voice, "for she didn't buy no ticket. Come on, you kain't lie out of it. You got to marry her an' then both of ye got to git out o' this country."

This was a strange view for Nessie's kinsmen to take. A moment later, when Abner stepped out of the glare of light, he made out, with a still deeper sinking of the heart, that all the men in the motor wore masks. Then they were not Nessie's kinsmen. If they had been, they would not have worn masks. It is the undisputed right of the kinsmen of a seduced girl in the hill country to capture the lover, take him anywhere without any legal process whatever, and force him to marry his mistress. Such kinsmen had no need of masks. Abner knew they were whitecaps and had taken unto themselves new and unpredictable powers.

"Climb in!" repeated a voice sharply.

Abner stepped on the running board. There was something unearthly and inhuman in the expressionless masks. The black eyeholes were like monsters seen in a nightmare and suggested danger and horror. A sudden desperate plan went through Abner's head, to climb in and while he was in the seat with the men suddenly to draw his pistol and begin shooting. When he put his hand on the door of the motor to step in, the man nearest him slipped a seagrass loop over his wrists and drew them together with a jerk. The masks on the back seat made room for their captive between them. The car manœuvred around in the narrow road; the headlight swept a circle among the trees and then the motor started back to Irontown.

Abner looked from one to the other of the dimly seen masks in an effort to identify his abductors. The small seagrass rope pinched his wrists. He held up his bound hands and complained to the man who held the ropes. The fellow eased the cords a trifle, but not enough to stop all pain. Abner endured the lessened pain without further protest. This slight charity gave the teamster courage to argue.

"Look here, fellers," he began, "you ortn't to do me this way. I'm the man who begun this whitecap business; I got up the first gang. Now, you ortn't to take me out like this. It ain't right."

A figure who had not spoken heretofore now answered Abner in a sepulchral tone, "Remember, poor mortal, that Judas who betrayed Christ was a disciple."

"Damn it!" cried Abner angrily, "what's Judas got to do with me? I ain't done nothin'."

"Judas," repeated the deep voice, "also betrayed an innocent."

The teamster felt he was being made sport of, a sort of ghastly sport.

"That ain't no way to answer a man!" he cried.

A mask in the front seat asked sardonically, "Do you think you're fit to live in the same county with decent men, Abner Teeftallow, after what you done?"

The question discomfited the teamster. He wanted to defend himself, to plead that other men had done the same thing, but all he could say was, "You ain't goin' to run me out of the country fer that, air ye?"

"Isn't that enough?" droned the deep voice at his side. "A woman is the noblest handiwork of God, Abner Teeftallow. Her station is above man and next to the angels. Beauty adorns her head, tenderness reigns in her heart, and innocence dwells in her soul. If your vile flesh were fed to the dogs, would that atone for the degradation of one of the handmaids to the Most High?"

The teamster grew more frightened than ever at this rhetoric, for the deep voice was intoning what may be called the Southern oratorical view of women. It was what Southern speechmakers always say of woman in the abstract, and somehow Southern men believe these dithyrambs, although not one of them ever knew an actual woman who approached such a seraphic being. Still, that never shakes the Southern credo. The country stands in the droll position of worshipping woman, but entreating their women rather hardly.

However, since the whitecaps repeated this jargon, such is the force of custom that its rolling measures gained on Abner. His heart sank when he thought of having dragged down one of these heavenly creatures. All that he had done now appeared to him unqualifiedly evil and corrupt where a few minutes before it had seemed sweet and innocent. And the whole dark sin was saddled on him alone. Nessie, as abstract woman, had no share in it at all, although, as one of the concrete women, the whitecaps meant to chase her out of the country along with the other baggages without ever taking into account the genuine simplicity and passion of her yielding.

But all this was far, far too involved for any defence from Abner. He sat silent with some dim baffled feeling of the contradiction in the whitecaps, but what could he say?

Presently the motor emerged from the woods and the headlight picked up the house and barn of Squire Meredith, standing like wraiths against the black sky. Then, as the machine droned down the road between these two buildings, Abner saw coming up the hill from Irontown the light of another automobile.

One of the men in the car said in an undertone, "There they are," and Abner suddenly understood that this meeting of the motors had been planned.

The youth's heart began to beat and he leaned forward staring intently as his car whirled down the hill. He saw three other motors parked by the roadside at the spot where Peck Bradley had been lynched. These cars were arranged in a semicircle so that their headlights were focussed on the tree which had seen the bushwhacker's end. This tree stood out against the night in pallid greens and intense shadows. It looked like the spectre of a tree, and Abner could visualize Peck Bradley once more slowly revolving under its limb.

Beyond the motors, in a faint reflected light, Abner could make out a group of figures. Here and there in the group he could see a cigarette tip glow and fade. With a tremor he realized this crowd in the darkness was awaiting some sort of entertainment; they waited as complacently as spectators at a circus for something to pick up their nerves, something that would break the monotony of their hill lives, something that would afford them a thrill and a spectacle.

By this time Abner's wrists were swollen and the ropes were cutting him badly. He moistened his dry lips and asked his captor to loosen them again. But under the influence of the crowd the kindliness that once had moved the man deserted him. He simply snarled, "To hell with yore wrists, stay where you are!"

All of the men in Abner's car got out and left their captive tied to one of the stays of the motor top. The teamster sat for a moment watching them go. He knew very well that in a few minutes some indecent or terrible thing would be perpetrated on him. He began trying to free himself. He stooped over in the seat and tried to get his mouth to the knot around his wrists, but the rope had sunk too deep in his swollen flesh. He ran his puffed and throbbing fingers along the steel support and found the bar was held on its post by a spread rivet. He eased himself out on the ground, circling the stay with his arms, bent his mouth to the flared rivet and began trying to bite it together. He fitted his canine teeth against the two flanges and bit carefully and powerfully. The iron ground loudly against his teeth but slowly closed together. He tasted rust. He could hear the whitecaps talking, a number of voices at once. He chewed on the iron again. The voices were saying, "We didn't git her. . . . She must have run off with Belshue—he hired a machine at the garage this evenin'. . . . No, Bagley says she shore didn't go off on the train. . . . They ain't no way to git that damned infidel, Belshue—he's gone. . . . Nothin' left but make an example out o' this'n. . . ."

Abner began a frantic jerking at the key in the post. The last phrase he heard meant the crowd would have no other amusement than what they could get out of him. Just as he had the key nearly out, two men came briskly up to the motor. Abner made a desperate pull; his throbbing fingers slipped. The men took hold of his rope. One of them cut the segment that went around the standard. Then without a word they led him between them into the beating focus of the headlights.

The teamster walked toward the spectral tree preceded by three long inky shadows. About him arose a dreamlike sensation of unreality and horror. He thought again of Peck Bradley and a prickly sensation swept his scalp.

"Say, men," he wavered in a strained voice, "what air ye goin' to do to me?"

His captors walked on in silence and Abner moved his tongue about his slimy mouth. The masks by his side were inhuman, horrible. He said again, huskily, "I—I wush you'd tell me, s-so I-I'd know what to expeck . . ."

At the tree the masks tied the ends of the rope around the bole with the teamster's back to the light. Then Abner, peering over his shoulder, saw a number of masks, looking black against the headlights, come forward with rope ends, leather straps, and heavy hickory limbs which they had cut in the bushes while they waited.

When Abner saw them coming with these weapons he knew that in a few moments he would be unable to stand, so he knelt beside the bole with his arms held up at a painful angle by the rope. With hill doggedness he determined in his heart that he would not yell. They would probably beat him to death, but he would die silently as his forbears had died silently, a century before, under the tortures of the Indians.

And he did endure it in a sort of rending silence. The teamster received an agonized impression of fire, of tearing flesh, of knife stabs, and of blinding light and a struck gong when a stray stick hit eye or ear. He writhed uncontrollably, swinging by his hands, turning up his belly, his sides, then his back again to the bastinado. He floundered doubled up his legs, kicked, but he did not groan. There was no sound at all save the swish of straps and sticks and leather and the clatter of impacts on his tortured flesh. At last Abner hung limp and motionless and silent beneath their blows.

The teamster did not know when the mob quit or whether they had quit. He was still wrapped in fire, but his hands were free and now filled with lancinating pains. Somebody was kicking him and telling him to stand up; others were saying, "Oh, let him lay," in the disgusted tones of men who have taken some vile satisfaction and who then hold the instrument of their pleasure in disgust.

But the man kept prodding Abner with his toe. "Now we want you to git out o' this country!" said a voice which sounded far off, a mere thread of a voice amid the booming of the blood in Abner's ears. "If ever you set foot in Lane County agin, you'll ketch it right, this won't be a breakfus' spell. We're goin' to make this a decent moral county if we haff to . . ."

The mob turned away and left Abner at the roots of the tree. A few minutes later the cars whisked away and left the teamster in utter blackness. After some time had passed the youth made shift to pull up by the tree. He stood whispering oaths and obscenities. He loosed the tree and tried to walk, but stumbled. He got back on his feet again and staggered forward with pioneer endurance through the benighted hills.

BOOK II. ADELAIDE

CHAPTER I

M R. JAMES SANDAGE, one-time overseer of the poor farm, now triumphantly elected trustee of Lane County by an overwhelming Republican majority, which the election returns invariably and uncritically present, was worried.

On this morning his daughter Beatrice Belle drove the new trustee from his new bungalow in Lanesburg to his office in the courthouse. As she manipulated the car she complained that there was a knock in the motor and begged her father in a discontented whine to buy a new automobile.

"I think we're lucky to have as fine a car as this, knock or no knock," said the new trustee absently.

"Makes me ashamed when I drive Adelaide Jones in it, havin' a knock. Now, lissen when I drive off."

Mr. Sandage's thoughts drifted in a slightly troubled, slightly disconnected fashion as his daughter drove away. . . . The car did have a knock. . . . Beatrice Belle certainly was getting grown. . . . When the railroad at Irontown paid its state and county taxes, he would have another seven thousand dollars with which he could assist his political godfather, Railroad Jones, in his new railway enterprise. Railroad paid him eight per cent. on these loans. . . . Eight per cent. on seven thousand . . . Sandage wondered if these investments were entirely safe?

He had heard a rumour that Perry Northcutt was beginning a suit to press Jones for the money the bank had lent him. He would ask Jones about that. The new trustee wanted to keep the county funds perfectly safe—also bearing eight per cent.—because that percentage was his own honorarium.

Then Sandage recalled a disagreeable rumour that Abner Teeftallow had got into trouble with Perry Northcutt's daughter and that Perry had run Abner out of the county. This report disturbed Mr. Sandage. He had always been fond of his foster-son. He knew, of course, that young bucks would be young bucks, but it troubled him that his boy, Abner, had fallen into this ever-waiting pit. Cheek by jowl with this disapproval, Mr. Sandage was a little gratified that it was with the banker's daughter. Evidently Abner had been getting on in society . . . with a banker's daughter. Still, it was bad business, bad business. He should have warned Abner against it. Only it was impossible for a man to warn a lad against that sort of thing and keep his own face. The best any man could do was what he had done: pass over the topic in silence.

The county trustee walked through the main passage in the courthouse to one of the smaller rooms in the northeastern corner of the building. The place was empty and his steps echoed through the corridor. He produced a key, unlocked his door, and opened it, still thinking of Abner. He went around to hang his hat on a nail behind the door when he heard a noise. He glanced around and saw a tattered figure rise up from behind the trustee's desk.

A combative thrill went through the trustee. He thought of the money in his vault, a pistol in a drawer near the robber. He took a stride toward the fellow.

"What in the hell do you mean——"

"It's me, Jim," interrupted the figure in a low hurried tone. "I come to borry yore gun!"

The trustee's advance was checked to an astonished staring. The face before him seemed to change from that of a stranger to the strained worn countenance of Abner Teeftallow, the boy he had reared. The reappearance of this Abner in the place of the simple Abner he had known amazed the trustee. He could scarcely credit his eyes.

"Abner!" he ejaculated incredulously. "Is that you? How did you get in here?"

"A feller showed me yore office. I prized open the winder an' got in last night."

"Why in the worl' didn't you come to my house?" cried Mr. Sandage, with outraged hospitality.

Abner's face twitched. "I didn't want nobody to see me; they"—he nodded in the direction of Irontown—"they think they run me out of the county—" his eyes narrowed vengefully—"but, by God, they ain't! I'm goin' to heel myse'f, slip back down there, and kill a lot o' them damn skunks, an' then I'll prove a alibi."

Mr. Sandage was horrified. "You don't mean that, Abner!"

"Yes, I do. I want you to len' me a couple o' guns. I lost mine the night they beat me up. But I'm goin' to slip back down there an' git that damn Perfesser Overall an' Tom Northcutt—I know a lot of 'em." Abner nodded grimly. "They're welcome to that skin they tuk off'n me, damn 'em!"

"But, look here, Abner, you kain't do that, my boy," cried Mr. Sandage. "My Lord, you don't want to be like old Rodman Sikes, who spent his whole life killin' off a gang of bushwhackers."

"Jim, you ain't never been beat up like I have," said the youth in a monotone.

Sandage began to realize that the boy he had known was indeed gone and he had a man to deal with, a vengeful, obstinate man, but still one with courage and fighting ability, and this aroused a certain admiration and satisfaction in him. He began arguing with the youth.

"Look here, Abner, whyn't you git the law on them fellers?"

"Law hell!"

The trustee knew that his foster-son was right on this point. He tried another tack.

"Now, look here, if you've been foolin' aroun' Perry Northcutt's gal, didn't he have a kind of right to beat you up an' drive you out o' the county—now, man, to man, didn't he?"

The younger man straightened indignantly.

"Perry Northcutt's gal!"

"That's what I heard."

"Why, he ain't got no gal!"

"He ain't!"

"Naw, if he has I never saw her in my life."

"Then what the hell did Perry mean by runnin' you out o' the county!" cried Mr. Sandage.

"I didn't know he done it!" cried Abner, growing bewildered himself.

"Well, he done it all right!" declared the trustee, waggling a finger in the air. "He done it shore as God made little apples. Now we got the straight o' that!"

"What made him?" cried Abner, losing his anger in his amazement.

"Wasn't he kin to yore gal a-tall—didn't he collugue with her kin folks?"

"Hell, no!" shouted Abner. "I tell you they wasn't none of her kinfolks in the gang that beat me up! They was jest outsiders who had no rights whatsoever. I was goin' back down there to marry the damn gal on my own account, an' they grabbed me an' beat me like a dawg!" Tears of rage filled Abner's eyes; the muscles in his square brown jaws worked as he clenched his teeth.

"Well, by God," cried Sandage, catching his passion, "that's a hell of a way to treat a honest boy. Damn little 'Parson's Delight' of a town. Ought to be wiped out! Ab, my gun's right here in this drawer"—he thumped on his desk—"I don't say git it, but damn it, I ain't goin' to stan' here guardin' it for ever—an' they's a box of ca'tridges right by it, too!"

There was a pause in which Abner and his foster-father slew crowds of imaginary whitecaps. At last Mr. Sandage said with a little more composure, "What I don't understan' is how Perry Northcutt come into this? Did you have any business dealin's with Perry?"

"Nope, in fack, I refused to trade with him a-tall."

"Uh-huh. . . . Suppose we step over to Railroad Jones's office an' ast him about this little matter. I got some business with him, an' he's a mighty level-headed feller anyway. What he don't know usually ain't happened yet, an' ain't a-goin' to happen."

Mr. Sandage turned behind the door for his hat while Abner watched him uneasily. When the trustee was ready to start, the younger man said in an embarrassed tone, "Jim, I—I kain't go out in the street with ye."

"Why kain't ye—what's the matter with ye?"

Abner flushed under his tan, but for answer turned his back. His coat was stained and stiffened and made of shreds patched together. The garment might have been run through a mangling machine. The county trustee stared at his boy, astounded.

"You don't mean them God-damned scoundrels . . ."

"That's what they done all right," Abner relapsed into his savage undertone, "an' my back was the same way. It was two weeks before I could walk!"

"Where you been all this time?"

"Some niggers took care of me. A old nigger woman patched up my coat so it would hold. They wouldn't git me no gun for fear of gittin' into trouble theirse'ves, damn 'em!"

"That's like a nigger!" sneered the trustee. He thought a moment, went behind the door, and brought out another coat. "Pull that off an' use this'n—doggone my skin, I b'l'eve you're bigger'n I am."

As Abner gingerly permitted the new coat to be slipped on him, the trustee asked, "If it ain't givin' away no secrets, Ab, I'd like to know what actually went with the gal yo' knowed in Arntown?"

"She married a damn infidel," stated Abner briefly.

"The hell she did!"

"Yep."

The two turned out of the trustee's office side by side for an interview with Railroad Jones.

When the two men reached Railroad Jones's office they

found the magnate overflowing his office chair as he pressed against his flat table thumbing through a stack of papers and making some sort of calculation. For while the fat man could neither read nor write, he had worked out for himself some sort of mathematical system by which he computed his problems with accuracy.

The financier looked up abstractedly as Sandage entered, his little burnt-out eyes blinking in his yellow expanse of face

"Mr. Jones, this here is Abner Teeftaller."

The railroad builder became aware of Abner. "Yes, I know Abner, worked for me—mighty good han' too."

The trustee cleared his throat. "Well, now, Abner—er— got in a little trouble over in Arntown, Mr. Jones."

"Yes," nodded the magnate benevolently, "I believe I heard it mentioned."

"So we come to see you about it. I been listenin' to what Abner says, an' it looks to me like there has been some sculduggery worked on the boy."

The fat man became attentive. "You think they might be somethin' behin' them fellers chasin' Abner out o' Arntown?"

"Yes, I do," nodded the trustee, using the hard tone of resentment. "It ain't usual for men to git drummed out of town for what Abner was drummed out for; if they did, most of the towns here in Lane County would be empty."

"Of course, they is usually politics behin' ever'thing," generalized the magnate, "but jest answerin' you by an' large, I shouldn't be supprised at nothin'."

At this vague statement, Sandage turned to the young man. "I told you so, Abner." Then he continued to the financier.

"Now, Mr. Jones, you're a better lawyer than half the bar here in Lanesburg, what do you think of Abner's chanst of makin' Perry Northcutt an' them whitecaps pay damages?"

"Knowin' Perry as I do, I shouldn't say he had much chanst."

"Well, he's been damaged!" cried the trustee. "They ain't done him right down there, an' somebody ort to pay him fur it."

"Well, Jim, you know the criminal law very seldom applies to individuals an' never does apply to crowds. Abner there will find out if he wants to do business in a big way he'd better keep his private affairs straight an' above board; otherwise some competitor will bushwhack him an' claim he done it for private reasons. That's what morality is, Jim, livin' so if anybody bushwhacks you, ever'body will know it was fur business reasons."

During an impressive pause, Mr. Sandage would have been more than a human father had he not turned on his foster-son and sought to impress this great and valuable moral.

"Now, you hear what Mr. Jones says, Abner. It shore is worth while listenin' to a man who has made a success like he has—live so when you git killed ever'body will know it was a business deal. Well, we're much obliged for your advice."

"Not a-tall," nodded the magnate solemnly.

"An' by the way, Mr. Jones, may I ast one more question? I've been hearin' that Perry Northcutt is goin' to sue you on some loans he made you."

The magnate nodded. "I don't want it talked, but I b'l'eve he is."

"In that case—now I hope you won't take no offence, but —er—it makes me a little juberous about the county funds I loaned you."

"You needn't be a-tall uneasy, Jim," soothed the magnate with a gesture, "he's suin' merely because I overdrawed the security I give him."

"Yeh," agreed the trustee vaguely.

"Well, if a careful financial institution like the bank thinks they can make their debt by a suit outside the mortgages I give 'em, that shows I must have a lot of resources, don't it? It shows I'm solid, all right."

"Well—yeh, I reckon it does," admitted Sandage, who did not follow this very clearly.

"An' besides that, you know nobody ever has got a court judgment off'n me, an' Perry Northcutt ain't got no better show than nobody else; so, since he kain't collect his debt till I'm good an' ready to pay it, it simply shows I'm one of the solidest institutions in Lane County, don't it?"

"Well, ye-es," dragged out Sandage, "it does look that way. So you don't consider your business the least bit shaky?"

"Firm as a rock, Jim, firm as a rock! An' if you want yore money back, jest ast for it. You can git it right now or any other time. I wouldn't give you a uneasy minute." Here Mr. Jones reached, one might say boisterously, after a pad of checks, got out a fountain pen, and pushed them toward the trustee. "Jest write out what I owe you an' I'll jest pay you off now!"

The trustee retreated from this sudden threat of payment.

"Oh, no, no, Mr. Jones, I jest wanted to talk it over with you! Lord knows, I kain't put my money out at eight per cent. with nobody but you. I want you to keep it!"

"Well, all right, but I don't want you to be uneasy about it."

"No, I won't be, an' much obliged for your advice, Mr. Jones."

"Not a-tall, Jim, not a-tall, an' jess come to me any time an' spit yore mind right out if you want to know anything."

"I shore am much obliged," repeated the trustee.

At that moment the door was darkened and Abner turned to see Mr. Ditmas, the engineer, standing in the entrance. The Northern man glanced at Abner in surprise, and then at Railroad Jones.

"Why, you did find him for me after all, Mr. Jones!" he cried.

"Yes, yes," nodded the magnate. "I got him to the office for you."

"That's fine—Abner, I've been combing three counties looking for you."

The youth stared at the engineer blankly. "What for?"

"It concerns a little timber deal between me and Mr. Jones. I've been investigating the records, and it seems, Abner, that you have to sign the deed before I can get title to some timber on one of Mr. Jones's farms."

"What have I got to sign it for?" cried Abner in astonishment.

"Because your grandfather, old Judge Coltrane, owned it years ago. After his death it was sold for taxes, but your mother, being of unsound mind, held a right of redemption, the statutes did not run against her during her life. When she died you were a minor heir, so the limitation did not operate against you. You still hold a right of redemption at any time you see fit to redeem. That's why you have to sign the deed to conclude the sale."

By this time the trustee was staring at the engineer.

"Look here, is that so about any of old Judge Coltrane's land?"

"I suppose so."

"Then, holy smoke, Abner, if that is so, you own nearly all the north end of the county. Why, I shouldn't be surprised if you wasn't the richest man in Lanesburg to-day."

"Where is it all?" cried Abner, looking about as if he expected his acres to appear in the magnate's office.

"Look here," interrupted Railroad Jones, "when Lydy Coltrane married Linsey Teeftaller, didn't the time limit begin to run against her then? Her husband wasn't crazy."

"No, Judge Coltrane left his will to prevent Linsey Teeftallow from having any control over the property."

"What can I do to get this property?" inquired Abner in a maze.

Mr. Ditmas laughed. "All you have to do is to sign my deed and I'll pay you eight hundred dollars now. I think your equity against my timber is worth about that."

"I take you!" cried Abner, shaken by such a sum.

"You—you better see the place first," advised Sandage in an unsteady voice.

"Yes, that's a good idea," agreed Ditmas. "We'll look at it and then go over my figures together."

"An' I own the whole north en' of the county!" cried Abner in a daze. "Who's got it now?"

"Oh, different persons," answered the trustee cheerfully, "but their claims ain't good."

Railroad Jones spoke up from where he had been sitting motionless at his table during this colloquy.

"It may happen, Abner, that I own one or two little pieces of yore land, but of course we can make any little adjustment that's right."

Abner was further amazed that he should have a claim on any of the magnate's land, but Mr. Jones said this so amiably that the youth nodded, "Sure, sure, I want to do what's right. Now, Mr. Ditmas, if we could look at that tract you're offering me eight hunderd dollars for . . ."

The three men turned out into the cheerful sunshine, when, coming around the court square, the trustee saw his motor driven by Beatrice Belle. He immediately shouted to his daughter in his big out-of-doors voice and waved his hat at her. Beatrice had a companion with her, and as the two girls drove up they shot lively glances at Abner. When Beatrice Belle recognized the youth, she flung up her hands and almost lost control of the machine.

"If it ain't Abner Teeftaller!" she cried in amazement.

"Beatrice!" laughed the other girl, catching the wheel. "Don't smash me up just because you see a man!"

The two girls, by jointly kicking the clutch and the brake, stopped the car. Beatrice slammed open the door, leaped out, rushed up to Abner, seized him around the neck and kissed him.

"How glad I am to see you!" she cried. "Goodness, I didn't know it was you! Abner, how you have growed! When did you come back? Here, let me introduce you to Adelaide Jones. Adelaide, this is Abner Teeftaller, the boy I've told you so much about!"

Miss Jones leaned forward with a fluttery movement.

"If you're half as wonderful as Beatrice says, Mr. Teeftallow, this is my lucky day."

"He's a sort of brother of mine," beamed Beatrice.

"I hope so," laughed Adelaide.

"But he's wonderful, just the same!"

"All men are wonderful, dear, and the bigger they are the more wonderful they become." Her glance complimented Abner's size.

Beatrice tipped her head at her companion. "Now, you aren't going to vamp him under my nose, Adelaide."

"As if I could! Do get in here between us, Mr. Teeftallow"—she moved to make room—"we're just going out for a drive."

Abner, who had received his introduction, compliment, and invitation to ride without the chance to say a word, now mumbled out an awkward "Much obliged," and got into the front seat by Miss Jones. He was at once enveloped in an atmosphere of perfume. Beatrice Belle took the wheel again and was about to start when her father called, "B'atrice Belle, I want you to take us out to the old Coltrane place."

"All right, Dad, anywhere," and then she added cheerfully, "I hope I can knock the old machine to pieces so I'll get a new one."

"If she does," stipulated Miss Jones in a low tone to Abner, "you must hold me in. I'm so little I'll bounce out."

"I—I will," agreed Abner, with awkward seriousness.

The motor moved eastward with a faint knocking in the purr of its engine. The girls continued their chatter and laughter. Beatrice Belle asked Abner a dozen questions without giving him time to answer one. Now and then she would call absently over her shoulder, "Is this the right road, Pappy?" and then would not wait for a reply.

Miss Jones was explaining with vehemence how she adored literature, especially Poe. She said she was a regular Poe fan, and her teacher in the girls' seminary in Nashville where she had been to school was as nutty over Poe as she was.

"You ought to hear her read 'Ulalume,' Mr. Teeftallow it's just wonderful—is this boring you?"

"No-o," said Abner, bewildered but not bored.

"Miss Stebbins was so brilliant. She knew everything. Beatrice, don't you think Mr. Teeftallow looks a little bit like Poe's picture?—the same mane of black hair and the same sad, suffering face."

Beatrice said she didn't know how Poe looked.

"Well, let's run around to my house and look at it."

When they veered from their course to see Poe's picture, Mr. Sandage objected, but he was not heard. Miss Jones was saying of her idol, and to her conquest,

". . . to think he died of a hopeless love. I wonder, Mr. Teeftallow, did you ever almost die of a hopeless love? Somehow, you look as if you had. . . ."

CHAPTER II

TO ABNER TEEFTALLOW the effect of his new life was sheer legerdemain. Here he was lodged with the Sandages again, but instead of the bare poverty of the old poor farm, the young man found himself in a bungalow so garishly new that it still smelled of paint and plaster. A low piazza surrounded three sides of the building with heavy square-cut columns. The lawn, bare as Abner's palm, had been levelled, manured, and seeded, and cement strips were laid down for Beatrice's car to cross to a garage in the rear.

To Abner the most extraordinary feature of the building was the bathroom. Sandage had installed a private light and water system run by a little gasoline engine. It always amazed Abner to hear the engine burst into a feverish pumping on its own accord, and a few minutes later give a gasp and stop when the compression tank was full or the batteries charged. It was an oddly human sort of thing, a little entity which knew how to do perfectly just two things, but all else was excluded from its queer electric intelligence.

When Abner moved into his room Jim took him covertly to the bathroom and explained in a low tone the manipulation of the bowl, bath, and commode. He turned the water on and off with a naïve delight in seeing it work.

"All the modern improvements, Ab," he boasted in a whisper, "right here in the house, too. I don't come here much myse'f; seems to me like it's more for women an' the sick."

All these conveniences in the Sandage ménage did not originate with Jim or his wife, but came through Beatrice Belle under the inspiration of Adelaide Jones. Adelaide was just returned from a girls' seminary in Nashville and possessed a girl's memory for house furnishings. Mrs. Sandage gave Miss Jones full credit for what she had done. One morning, in her white-enamelled kitchen, she said to Abner, "Addy told me about th is dreener," pointing to the wire hold-all in the sink, "great convenience. She's one of the smartest girls I ever see, Ab. They ain't no kind of a dish she don't know how to make; scientific, too. Domestic science, they call it. I wonder you don't notice her more, Ab; she certainly will make some man a good wife."

At this the Negro girl whom the Sandages had hired for a cook but to whom Mrs. Sandage had never been able to resign her pretty kitchen, gave an audible titter. It irritated the two white persons.

"Aline!" snapped Mrs. Sandage roughly, "mind your work!"

Aline, who was peeling turnips, continued her task in silence.

But the woman so recently from the poor farm could not correct her servant briefly or with dignity.

"Snickerin' like that before your betters—if I had my way I'd run ever' nigger——" She meant to add "out of the county," but realized in time that this sentiment characterized only the very poorest class of whites. She turned to Abner again.

"I think Addy is the liveliest girl; always in a flutter. Jim says it's put on, but I think it's nachel. She picked out all this chiner. I wanted some with more flowers, but she said I'd git tired of it, an' this does look sweet. I tell Jim I feel like some sort of a bride agin—an' it all come through the railroad."

"How did that do it?" asked Abner curiously.

"Brought business in the county. Made the trustee's office a very payin' job." Here she paused in her speech to adjust her new false teeth with her tongue. These teeth were too white, too broad, and too long. They gave her a corpse-like look when she smiled, so that her mirth was ghastly rather than merry. The plate was the work of the village dentist.

"Yes, the railroad shore made the trustee's office pay good.

Jim feels like he mighty near owes all he's got to Railroad Jones. He certainly is a good man, an' so sharp—brainiest man in Lane County, an' his daughter's jest like him." She paused in scolloping a pie crust. "There's Addy now, blowin' for B'atrice. Abner, step an' tell her B'atrice's gone. She went to carry our washin' to niggertown."

The young man went out on the piazza and saw Adelaide Jones in a big yellow roadster in front of the gate. The girl leaned forward and waved.

"How are you this morning, Mr. Teeftallow? Where's Beatrice?"

"She took the clothes to the washerwoman."

Adelaide pouted. "I'm so peeved. What made you let her go?"

"I didn't have nothin' to do with it," said Abner heavily.

"Well, I suppose you want to go to town, you've developed into such a business man; come on and climb in.—Well, say, do you want to ride with me, or don't you?"

"Yes, yes," hastened Abner, starting abruptly for the car as if Adelaide had touched off a spring.

"You didn't seem very enthusiastic."

Abner, who never possessed a syllable of light chatter, reddened faintly and said, "I wasn't expectin' a invitation."

The girl stared, then dimpled into sudden laughter.

"What do you require for them—a nerve tonic?"

"Why, no-o——" dragged out Abner, growing more uncomfortable; then he remembered the cook Aline's titter and he thought with a certain resentment, "She thinks she's better'n me. . . ."

Abner entered the motor in silence. The girl pushed forward a lever and the big car whispered off.

"Where do you want to go?" asked Adelaide.

"Why, nowhere in particklar."

"Then evidently we're out for a joy ride?"

"That suits me," agreed Abner stiffly.

"I declare, Mr. Teeftallow," cried the girl, "do you always let your enthusiasms run away with you like this?"

Abner suspected the irony, but it was so much lighter than what he had been accustomed to in the Irontown garage that he had no answer at all. So he sat uncomfortable and faintly resentful in the rush of cold air. Now and then he gave a side glance at Adelaide and at her small square-cut hands on the wheel.

Abner did not like this girl, and he wondered why he had ever got into her motor, but his glances gave him a confused but pleasant impression of her yellow wool sweater, amused brown eyes, and curly brown hair against the yellow leather upholstery of the car. He did not observe these details consciously but the ensemble had its effect on him.

Adelaide no doubt noticed his pique, for presently she said soberly enough, "I hear you have placed your land claims in the hands of Buckingham Sharp."

"Who told you?"

"Why, Buck himself."

This astonished Abner so much that his mind was diverted.

"Do you know him?"

Miss Jones shrugged. "Rather; he was the only eligible man in this town until a few days ago, when a certain very melodramatic young landholder exploded into our midst as the long-lost scion of an old and noble strain." She glanced at Abner with quizzical bright eyes.

Abner did not follow the details of this raillery because Adelaide had used words unfamiliar to him. However, he knew in a general way what she had said. He stuck to his own text of Buckingham Sharp,

"Do you like him?"

"A drowning girl doesn't quarrel with her life preserver, Mr. Teeftallow, when she is going under the third and last time."

This figure was so whimsical that Abner burst into loud laughter. He looked at her frankly.

"You're the funniest girl I ever saw," he stated simply. "You don't act a bit like I'm a man."

Adelaide whistled in amazement, "Aren't I taking you motoring?"

"Why, sure."

"And didn't I see Beatrice Belle well on her road before I drove around to your place? My dear Mr. Teeftallow, if I'm not acting as if you were one of the opposite sex, then I'll quit trying—there isn't any way to do it."

Adelaide's little gusts always caught Abner up in the air and left him without any footing whatever. He grinned rather emptily now and repeated, "Well, you're a funny girl, anyway."

"Do you know why I decided to drive with you this morning instead of with Beatrice or Buck Sharp?"

"I don't know," admitted Abner, looking at her curiously.

"Can't you guess?"

"No, kain't guess."

"Your agility is surprising. Well, I'll tell you. Buck is too—too slippery. I never know what he really thinks by what he says, and what's worse, I can't tell by looking at him."

"Is that the way you usually tell?"

"It's the only way, Mr. Teeftallow. Men don't know what they mean themselves. A girl has to look and see. They all put their arms around you and kiss you in the same way, and you've got to find out why, and you haven't much time to do it in, either."

Abner had a shocked sense that Adelaide was a very improper person.

"That's what I like about you," concluded Adelaide; "you're so frank and open."

They were well out of the village now and around them lay the colourful autumn woods. Abner harked back to the original subject of their discussion, which interested him somehow.

"If you don't like Buckingham Sharp, what makes you let him come to see you?"

"He is a sort of Romeo to my Juliet. You see, he is suing

Dad for the debt Dad owes the Irontown bank. That makes Dad despise Buck. He has told me a hundred times not to let Buck come to our house again. I suppose that's the only reason I keep on doing it."

Abner knew now that Adelaide was indeed the worst girl he had ever seen. He glanced at the depraved creature and was surprised to find her face still gay and her bobbed hair still blowing about in merry ringlets.

"By the way," proceeded Adelaide after she had smiled to herself in silence, "your putting your claims in Buck Sharp's hands works rather a hardship on Daddy. You see, since Buck represents the bank that is trying to take Dad's railroad from him, he will use these claims to embarrass Papa. Of course, Buck wouldn't compromise for anything, because your claims will help freeze Dad out—you see that, don't you?"

"Yes," nodded Abner, surprised at this sudden change to seriousness.

Here the girl's attention skipped to the scenery around them. "Look at that old crow," she pointed, "with the martens after him!"

Abner looked across a new ground of ripened corn. Over the tops of the dead black trees a crow winged his way with awkward haste, harried by the darting attack of two martens. Now and then in its flight the crow gave a lugubrious call.

"Now, that's what I don't like to see," declared Adelaide, "two birds fighting one; two anything fighting one. It isn't fair!"

"Well," suggested Abner guardedly, for they were both thinking of something other than birds, "a crow really ort to be run off. A crow's a pest."

Miss Jones had slowed her motor to a crawl to watch the chase.

"You're like everyone else, against the crow because he takes what he can. I'm not against him. I'm for him. You are bound to admit he's the wiliest bird we have."

"He's that, all right," agreed Abner.

"And besides, those martens really can't do anything to him when they catch him. They're too *little*."

They sat and watched the chase until the martens were reduced to black specks, and then became invisible. The crow hurried on and on, its distressed caws growing fainter and fainter until at last it, too, became a mere dot and then melted into the wind-swept sky.

CHAPTER III

THAT night, when Abner went to bed at the Sandages', his thoughts and emotions were filled with Adelaide Jones. Certainly she was the most unusual girl he had ever met. Her conversation with him had been as one man with another. She had not said anything particularly reprehensible, he pondered under his blankets, but still she had an air about her. On the drive back she had mentioned casually the number of children she meant to have. "That was a hell of a thing for a girl to say," he thought, more than half insulted, "'goin' to have six children'."

The young man fell asleep thinking about Adelaide, and after the irrational fashion of sleep drifted into a disagreeable dream of Nessie Sutton. Once or twice he started awake during the night and thumped the hot pillow under his head in an effort to beat away the vision of this woman who haunted him. Why did he dream of Nessie? It seemed to Abner that the milliner had died when she married Belshue. Nessie Belshue—he mused on her new name in the darkness. There was something funereal and bitter in it. The change of name was symbolic of the change in the woman. Nessie Sutton, the sweet simple girl whom he had known and whom he had loved so passionately and confusedly, was dead to him indeed.

He fell asleep in the gray of the morning and was awakened, it appeared to him, but a moment later by Aline, the Negro maid, calling through the door, with disdain tincturing her tones, that the telephone wanted him.

Abner arose and hurried on his clothes without bathing, for, like Jim, he instinctively avoided the bathroom.

276

He got down to a desk telephone in the hall with a clear-cut sense of adventure because he had never used a telephone before. He placed the receiver to his ear without knowing quite what to expect. For several minutes he heard a simple buzzing, then said aloud to the maid, "I can't understand anything." The next moment a queer metallic voice said in his ear, "Is that you, Mr. Teeftallow?"

"Yes," exclaimed Abner in surprise.

"Buckingham Sharp talking. Will you kindly call at my office at about ten?"

"Yes," said Abner, keeping his voice elevated and expecting the conversation to run to the indefinite length of all colloquys in the hills.

"I'll expect you, then, good-bye." There was a click, and the quality of the buzz against which this conversation had been cast changed somewhat.

"I declare," thought Abner, hanging up the receiver and looking at it, "he was pretty damn short. . . ."

At ten o'clock Abner entered Buckingham Sharp's office in the court square wondering what the lawyer wanted. Mr. Sharp sat at his desk, a short, rather heavy young man, with a round pink face and a soft pulpy look to his body. He would have appeared a nonentity with his round face and fat body had it not been for his eyes. These were slate-blue, shrewd, informed, and appeared to be appraising the world, planning how to use it to the best advantage for Mr. Sharp. The lawyer was always polite and impersonal. This morning he arose to meet Abner, smiled faintly as he shook the youth's hand, seated him in a chair, and then said in the softly accented English of the aristocratic Southern plantation owners, "I have just found out something about you, Mr. Teeftallow, which interests me."

"What's that?"

"Your grandfather, Judge Coltrane, came up here from Talledega, Alabama."

Abner nodded indifferently.

"He was one of the North Alabama Coltranes. He must

have eddied up here in the hills just as I did—he married up here."

"Where did you come from?" asked Abner simply.

"I'm one of the Tuscumbia Sharps. You must have heard of Governor Sharp, Senator Dalrymple Sharp, and Horse-Racing Bob Sharp?"

Abner dragged out a "Y-e-s" in a tone that meant "No."

Mr. Sharp understood him to mean "no," for he smiled and said, "Well, there are such persons in the world, at any rate. Now to get down to business, what I wanted to see you about, Mr. Teeftallow, was your claim on the old Coltrane estate. The timber on this tract adjoins that which Mr. Ditmas bought, and he would like to arrange to work it off together with his own."

"I thought he had all he could handle in his new tract?"

"No," said Sharp drily. "There was some confusion about the amount of timber he was buying from Jones."

"How was that?" asked Abner with interest.

"There was less timber than Ditmas thought. He will have to purchase more now in order to work profitably what he has."

Abner became very interested, as all hillmen are in a business deal. "Just what did Railroad Jones do?" he asked, scenting one of the financier's coups.

"I'm afraid I'm not informed enough to give you the details, I merely wanted to tell you Ditmas was in the market for more timber, and you might do well to see him."

"I'll see him," nodded Abner. "I'll look him up right away."

Abner arose, and Sharp got up with him and accompanied him to the head of the steps, where he stood ceremoniously until Abner reached the street below.

The ex-teamster moved off in the morning sunshine with his whole curiosity aroused within him. He wondered what Railroad Jones had done. He knew it would be something dramatic. It would be a new act in the life-long vaudeville which the wealthy man was spreading across the stage of

Lane County—a new act, a striking act. Abner moved aim-lessly along, smiling in anticipation of whatever it might be.

A group of hillmen were standing on a corner of the square, watching a man in their midst draw a figure in the dust with his whipstock. The whole group had the gnarled, almost grotesque faces developed by generations of illiteracy; the way the man in the centre stooped to the dirt and made his designs upon it spoke his familiarity with it. He was not finical about it. One knew he worked in it, turned it over, hoed, ploughed, scraped it. His companions were guffaw-ing and wheezing in awkward hill laughter.

For the first time in his life Abner felt there might be a difference in the quality of these men and the more sophisti-cated county-site folk, such as Sharp and Jones and Ditmas. This critical feeling of difference vanished almost as quickly as it came, and Abner went up to the group. Already he was beginning to smile through sympathy with their mirth. The man with the whip was saying:

"This here line is Turkey holler. Here it heads into four other little hollers, like this"—he made marks in the dust at an angle to the main line. "They air all growed up so dang thick with trees, it's dark in there all the time: white oaks, poplars, black walnuts, purtiest you ever see. Well, what did ol' Railroad do but walk this damn fool Yankee up one side o' Turkey holler into one o' them little hollers headin' into it here at the top; then he clumb the hill, got over into the next holler, an' walked back down through Turkey agin. They turned around, went up Turkey agin, got into the next little holler, clumb another hill, started down it a third time . . ." Here the narrator became so convulsed he could not go on. His hearers were reeling around him wheezing, whooping, and gasping for breath.

"Well, I be dad-snatched—jest showin' him the same thing over an' over!"

"Yeh, ever' one of these little head hollers counted the whole thing! Made that damn fool Yankee b'lieve he was dropped into eight or ten square mile o' solid oak an' walnut!"

"Thought he was buyin' the whole yeth!"

"Yeh, an' the nicest lot o' hollers to snake logs out of he ever did see."

All other explanations were lost in the yawping and whooping of the hillmen.

"What did it set him back?"

"Seventeen thousand dollars!"

This was the barb, the tang of the jest. The men stumbled over each other pounding backs, dashing away their own tears of merriment.

"God'lmighty! That Railroad Jones! He won't do! Oh, Lord!" the gasper went into convulsions again.

"We ort to send that man to Congress!" panted another, his face set in the mould of laughter, "brainy, wide-awake man, stid o' these little two-by-four lawyers."

"By heck, inside of a month he'd come back with the capitol buildin' under one arm and the guv'ment mint under t'other."

Abner was haw-hawing with his companions from the time he gathered the simple efficiency of Railroad Jones's ruse. There was something grotesquely humorous about it—the fat man leading Ditmas up and down one valley of trees, time and time again, making him think he was covering a wide territory of timbered hills and hollows. It was an exquisite game, this slipping up on the blind side of a purchaser and picking him off as the first pioneers had crept up on the Indians and picked them off! No wonder with such a father Adelaide was the smartest girl he had ever seen. The youth's heart warmed to Railroad's stratagem because he was Adelaide's father. There was something personal, intimate in this victory. Why he, Abner, could have done it himself if he had only thought of it in time!

He turned away from Railroad's admirers with an elated feeling and continued moving about the square with the restlessness of a man too excited with pleasure to remain still.

Since Abner was walking without any objective at all, the little suggestion that Attorney Sharp had given him to see Ditmas presently took control of the youth's automatism and Abner found himself walking eastward from the square, down a rocky lane toward the engineer's boarding house. It was not until Abner came in sight of a drooping willow in the front yard that he realized this place was his destination.

"Why, sure," he thought to himself, "that's where Ditmas boards." He scrutinized the house. It was one of those self-respecting little cottages with a tiny front porch and two doors opening on to it, so that the guest room was entirely cut off from the rest of the household. A man sat on the porch in the comfortable sunshine, and as Abner drew nearer he was surprised to see that it was Zed Parrum. Abner stared at Zed for several moments before he agreed with his eyes that it really was Zed. Then he wondered why the teamster should be there. He could not imagine any business Parrum could have with Mr. Ditmas.

"Hello, Zed," he called. "What in the world you doin' up here?"

The labourer replied in the guarded tone one uses in the hearing of the sick, "I jest come up from camp with Mr. Ditmas."

A shock travelled through Abner. "What's the matter with Mr. Ditmas?"

Zed drew a long face. "Overwork."

"Overwork! An edjercated man overworkin'?"

Zed winked solemnly, "Overwork from drawin' corks."

Abner stopped at the gate, staring fixedly at Zed's rough-hewn face as the teamster's amazing implication seemed to swing around in his head.

"You don't mean to say—Mr. Ditmas is drunk. . . ."

"I didn't meant to tull you ast me."

"Well, I be dern—drunk! Mr. Ditmas drunk!" Abner stood at the gate, staring at Zed.

"Yep," grunted Parrum noncommitally.

Abner opened the gate and came slowly up on the porch beside Zed.

"Where is he?"

Zed nodded toward the spare room.

"Can I see him?"

"Why, shore, jest walk in."

But Abner did not approach the door. He stood on the porch, looking out over the village, at a spire over the roofs, at the barred windows of the county jail which he could see in another direction. These were narrow windows in a blank brick wall and looked grim and sinister, although now and then prisoners broke jail and escaped.

"Why don't you go in?" asked Zed at last.

"I don't want to," said Abner, for at the thought of seeing Mr. Ditmas drunken and degraded a queer pain had arisen in the youth's heart. In reality an idol of Abner's had fallen, and the young man shrank from looking at its prostrate form. Why he had set up Ditmas for an ideal, when he had done it, he did not know; but now, somehow the thought of Mr. Ditmas drunk was as harrowing as would have been the thought of a drunken sister.

"How's ever'thing in Arntown?" asked Abner in a mechanical voice, to hide his strange and surprising pain.

"All right. Of course, you know Perry Northcutt's suin' the railroad."

"Yep."

"They all say he'll shore git it. They say Railroad Jones is squirmin' like a eel tryin' to git up the money, but they say he kain't make it; no other banks won't let him have no money."

"When did you bring him up here?" Abner nodded toward the room in which Ditmas lay.

"This mornin' frum camp. We ain't more'n four mile east o' here now. We jest about got her connected up."

"Why won't the other banks let him have no money?"

"Well, they kinder stan' in with each other. When one banker decides to cut a man's th'oat, the others gin'rally lend a han'. If a man had any heart he nachelly wouldn't be a banker."

"Naw, of course not."

"He'd go broke if he did."

"Nachelly."

"You kain't blame Perry for cuttin' Railroad Jones's th'oat if he can an' when he can."

"No, of course not."

"Railroad would his, I guess."

"Nachelly."

The two hillmen stood a moment staring at the windows of the jail after this exposition of finance as it was known to them.

"By the way, Abner," said Zed, gravely in one of those flares of intimacy which come at such moments as this, when you see how yore lan' claims air workin' out an' air certain to disaccommodate Perry Northcutt like they air shore to do, can you blame Perry for gittin' you flogged an' tryin to run you out o' the county? After all, Ab, a man's got to look after his investments the best he can."

"Shore, I'd thought of that. I guess it whets him the wrong way that the boys didn't hang me."

"'Magine so. After all, a man plays his han' fer what it's wuth."

"Nachelly. I've 'bout quit bearin' him any grudge."

After another moment Abner nodded at the room again.

"Him, was it losin' his money that made him?"

"I reckon so."

"It was Perry pinchin' Railroad that made Railroad pinch him?"

"Oh, I guess he'd uh pinched him anyway," suggested Mr. Parrum generously. "By the way, Abner, had you heard that Tug Beavers is a-preachin' now?"

"The hell he is!"

At this moment a voice from the sick room called out Zed's name.

"Want anything?" inquired the teamster.

"Is that young Teeftallow out there?" asked a thick voice.

"Yes, sir."

"You boys—come in here."

With a last flinching that he must see him after all, Abner followed Zed inside.

The room was darkened by green blinds drawn to the bottom of the windows. Mr. Ditmas lay in bed, white and drawn from his debauch. He looked at the two men with unfocussed eyes.

"Abner," he began in his thick tones, "you—surprised at me, I fancy. . . ."

"A little, Mr. Ditmas," said Abner, pained and embarrassed.

"M-m, I can't acchept the loss of sheventeen thousan' an' not feel it, Abner. Had frien's back up—Ohio-way—went in with me—losht their money too. Man can't get his frien's in trouble an' then—then——" He lay staring at the two men at the foot of his bed, apparently pondering deeply; finally, with difficulty he asked, "Wh-what was I talkin' about, Abner?"

"Losing your money, Mr. Ditmas," said Abner in growing depression.

"Oh, yes, money—trouble down here in the hills, Abner, business methods barbarous—game of tricks. Contrack never means what it says—ever' sentence ambush these fellers hide behin' to—to waylay somebody. Tain't right, still, it—it's the way the game's played—down here. . . ."

Again he lay thinking, staring past the heads of the men with a swimming gaze, then with an effort he went on:

"Law's the same way, Abner—civil law, a game of sand-bagging between the clauses of a contrack. Criminal law —a sieve of tec-technicalities that lets ever'thing through. No wonder there are whitecaps; no wonder you got beat in inch of your life, Abner. In land where there's no law people must use other and less precise methods of ret-retribution. S' necessary." He wobbled his head solemnly at the boys.

"Would you like a drink, Mr. Ditmas, to pick you up?" offered Zed.

"N-never drink, Zed, sank ye—t-t-teetotallar.—What was I about to say, Abner?"

"Something about the law, Mr. Ditmas."

"Law. . . . Oh, yes, yes. I see, and I want to—to impress this on you, Abner, 'press this great fack on you. This—dis-this—disingenuous method of l-law and business here in South been a long gradual development, Abner—ver' long, an' ver' gradual. I see it all before me, Abner—hist'ry of the South." Mr. Ditmas made a weaving gesture. "Look at slavery. Slavery committed the South to stress the ex-exact words of a contrack above the ax-actual human rights it contained, Abner. Declaration of Independence did-didn' 'clude niggers. Constitution Newnited States didn' 'clude niggers. Property rights in a human bein', Abner, p-prevailed over natural right of man to his own life. You—you see, in the ver' beginnin' the South obtained unfair advantages through con-contrack. What result? She made a great point of ad-adhering to the letter of the law, not the spirit. What result? Her laws are a maze of technicalities that won't convict anybody for anything—technicality—get out on technicality. What result? Whitecaps, mobs, posses, lynchin's, burnin's, beatin's. You've seen 'em; you know, Abner. . . ."

He lay staring with uncoördinated eyes past the boys at his sinister vision; then he went on thickly: "An' it's spreadin' all over our nation, Abner—ever'where—technicalities —precedent—losin' the spirit of the law in the letter—an'—whitecaps. But—but nobody's to blame. Since there's no law of right, there must be one of might. Mobs and whitecaps, all over our nation. North and South, East and West, anywhere, ever'where—but there's nothin' to do. That's what I want to 'press on you, Abner; nothin' to do. You're a citizen of the South, and of the United States, Abner, and don't you do nothin' a-tall about it, Abner—f' th' ain't nothin' to do. . . ."

His hands dropped and his eyes closed. His message was delivered. Sweat stood out on his white face. The two hillmen stood looking at the figure.

"He shore is drunk," said Zed slowly.

"Shore is," agreed Abner in a gray voice.

So this alcoholic candour passed away with the words that formed it, and no one was the wiser or the better or the worse.

CHAPTER IV

THE impending Northcutt-Jones suit in chancery became, during the next few weeks, the chief topic of gossip and speculation in Lane County. It was a dramatic situation with two of the cleverest and shrewdest tricksters the county had ever produced embattled against each other.

To Abner Teeftallow the coming legal action held no especial interest except that he personally liked Railroad Jones and particularly hated Perry Northcutt. The railroad, no matter into whose hands it fell, promised eventually to enrich Abner by enhancing the value of his indeterminate holdings in the county. The details of that enrichment, Abner left, through inclination and necessity, in the hands of Buckingham Sharp. In fact, Abner did nothing at all in Lanesburg except sign an occasional legal document for Mr. Sharp. He had fallen, by great good luck, into that goal of the hill people, a state of complete idleness. Indolence was not only the hill idea of earthly bliss; it was their notion of Heaven. Heaven was a place where nobody worked or created anything. Up there everything was furnished free from a celestial ready-to-wear department: robes, crowns, jewels, etc.

By way of amusement, Abner spent some time with Beatrice Belle learning to dance to jazz records on a phonograph. His progress was not rapid, as Beatrice entirely failed to inspire him with a gusto for dancing. As she whirled him around she was tantalized by the absence of any spiritual response in his mechanical efforts.

"Why don't you sway with me?" she would cry out waspishly. "When I step back you step forward so we'll stay together."

But Abner lacked that physical sympathy with Beatrice which takes the place of finish with the ordinary run of dancers. He could never dance with Beatrice Belle, he could only practise dancing.

"You'll make a pretty out over at Adelaide's next week," she would sniff.

"I thought Adelaide's party was a social?"

"We call it a social so people won't know, but it's a dance. She's goin' to have a nigger band from Columbia."

"I'll come out all right."

But Abner did not feel the confidence in his words. He had the hill fear of making himself ridiculous.

Once during such practising, Adelaide came to the Sandage home. She stood in the hallway and clapped her hands.

"I bid for the next dance, Valentino," she cried, and burst out laughing so immoderately that Abner stopped with a reddened face in the midst of a braying passage from the phonograph.

"Oh, go on, go on!" she insisted.

"No, you an' Beatrice Belle can dance if you want to."

"Now don't get peeved; everybody has to learn; why don't you let yourself go? Watch me and Beatrice."

She spread out her arms, floated over to Beatrice in rhythm to the interrupted strain, then entwined herself in her companion's clasp, and struck into a florid step, whirling herself this way and that, flinging her torso over Beatrice's arm. Then she floated away from her partner until only their fingertips were engaged; closed again and came to a gay halt, leaning backward with her head down laughing at Abner with an inverted face.

"That's the way you do it," she cried, twisting herself lithely upright again. "Just imagine there's not a bone in your body, that you're a flame blowing in the wind."

"Why, Adelaide, I didn't know you could do that!" cried Beatrice in astonishment.

"That's æsthetic dancing, my dear; æsthetic dancing is meant to be seen by men who don't know how to dance. It's a kind of last arrow in a girl's quiver which may bring him down when he's gone too far for ordinary weapons—it's expensive to learn."

"I should think it would be," agreed Beatrice, who did not follow these innuendoes.

Abner looked at Adelaide seriously. He thought she was the limberest girl he had ever seen. An impulse came to him that he would like to dance with Adelaide, but he said nothing about it. After she had gone away, a vision of her swaying over Beatrice's arm, taking high, pointed steps to the music, lingered with him and became a part of his growing amorousness for the girl. After this brief dance he never looked at her again without sensing in her the possibility of her limberness, her pointed tread, and the swaying of her delicately modelled torso.

Notwithstanding these symptoms it was not until the evening of Adelaide's dance that Abner discovered whither his emotions tended. As Beatrice Belle drove over to the Jones residence she warned Abner as to what he was about to see.

"What was the last dance you went to, Abner?" she began diplomatically.

"Old man Warrington's, clost to Arntown."

"In the country?"

"Yeh."

"Well, of course they don't dance town dances in the country. Town dances may look a little funny to you at first—ever'body dancin' like they do, lots o' times with perfect strangers—jest git interduced an' go to dancin' with their arms aroun' each other tangoing and charleston-ing.'"

"It won't look funny to me," protested Abner, disliking Beatrice Belle's patronage. "I guess I'm hard-boiled, all right. I seen things at the railroad camp. . . ."

"Well, it looked funny to me at first." Beatrice Belle swerved her car to avoid a rut. "I felt the funniest when

Mr. Pratt, that new drug clerk at Ransom's, jest said, 'Glad to meet you, Miss Sandage,' an' next minute put his arms aroun' me and his cheek against mine an' went to dancin'. I kinder gasped inside myse'f, but I'm used to it now. I hope he asks me again to-night; he's a wonderful dancer."

"I imagine the wickedness you folks carry on ain't up to much," disparaged Abner, implying a wide criminal experience of his own.

"Well . . . no . . . I guess not," admitted Beatrice, a little abashed, recalling the lurid tales which accompanied Abner from Irontown.

But later that evening in the ballroom of the Jones residence, Abner forgot the vaunt of his hard heart. The dancers actually on the floor, swirling and jiggling to the blare and clash of the jazz band from Columbia, filled him with a feeling of impropriety. From the first dance he had realized that his own efforts would be clumsy, and a painful self-consciousness kept him prisoner on a settee. This settee was behind two artificial palms which Adelaide had borrowed from the Ransom drug store through the good will of this same Mr. Pratt who had danced with Beatrice Belle. The palms formed a little retreat behind which Abner was gratefully concealed. Girls and men circled past his eyes in a never-ending stream. In the opposite corner the jazz band neighed away in feverish syncopation. The leader, a yellow Negro, had a mephistophelian cast of countenance which he kept moulded in a satanic grin. This grin was as mechanical and as much a stage property as the saxaphonist's waving of his instrument up and down, but Abner did not know this: it looked wicked to him.

After the fashion of non-dancing men at a ball the youth gradually grew more and more melancholy and despondent. Whether he would or not quotations from the travelling evangelists concerning dancing floated through his head . . . devil's trap . . . road to hell . . . palace of shame. . . . And behind this was the hill-born instinct in Abner to associate wickedness with everything pleasant, graceful, or beautiful. It seemed to him that he was committing a subtle sin merely to sit and look at the dancers, although he disapproved. He thought if he should happen to drop dead in this ballroom—a fatality which, according to the evangelists, often occurred—he would very certainly go to hell. He felt far more wicked now than when he hurried after the mob in Irontown to help lynch Peck Bradley. And he knew this to be a true moral judgment because his conscience was whispering it to him; that still small voice in his heart, which according to the hill belief is the actual voice of God, and is therefore infallible.

Out of this generalized disapproval of the dance Abner's attention was drawn to certain particular objections. Beatrice Belle and her Mr. Pratt were the greatest of these. Abner could see Mr. Pratt's sleek black head dipping among the dancers as he pressed a perfectly strange jowl to Beatrice's cheek. As they dipped past the palms, Abner noticed a misty, unseeing expression in their eyes, a set seraphic smile on Beatrice Belle's lips, while Mr. Pratt's face wore the strained look of one clinging to the fringe of paradise.

Abner regarded this bliss with suspicion, suspecting some connection between it and the sex of the dancers; and, reverting to the evangelists, to possess sex at all was wicked, much less to enjoy it.

"I'm goin' to speak to Miss Haly about this," he thought, "the way B'atrice Belle's carryin' on."

He watched Pratt with the disgust a boy feels when he sees another boy kissing his sister.

"It wouldn't take much for me to tell that damn little drug clerk where he heads in—and a perfect stranger to her . . ."

In the midst of this brotherly mood another pair of dancers floated past the palms and a sharp constriction went through Abner's chest. He caught his breath, staring after Adelaide Jones and Buckingham Sharp. Both danced well; they were the most graceful dancers on the floor.

Oddly enough Abner's feeling of the wickedness of the pastime evaporated completely in a stab of jealousy that Sharp's arms should be around Adelaide. He felt a sick envy of the lawyer. He watched the couple with little waves of cold and hot running over his skin. Sharp was in evening wear, and his black arm around Adelaide's waist; his white plump hand placed delicately sidewise against her shimmering green gown was the most exasperating spectacle that ever gnawed at Abner's patience. The girl's waist looked so slender in the revealing silk; her shoulders so white. Abner believed Sharp wanted to press in feverishly on that *svelte* waist, and then to hold his hand just so—"The damned hypocrite!" cursed the teamster under his breath. "He sha'n't have my land suits any more. I'll take 'em away from him!"

The united movements of the dancers suggested some profound sympathy between the two, some exquisite intimacy from which Abner felt for ever excluded. Adelaide was a sort of celestial creature whom his own arms might never encompass. If he might embrace her, put his arms about her—the voluptuousness of the fancy sent tremors through him.

The dancers swayed along languorously, but at intervals broke into a little running step which ended by swinging their feet lightly about and turning in a new direction. How Sharp managed his bulk so deftly, Abner could not imagine. The softly swaying bodies, masculine black, feminine green, were maddening. They were talking to each other, apparently lost in a dream. He saw Adelaide lift her brows, nod happily, her eyes scintillant with happiness.

And suddenly Abner knew that Sharp had asked Adelaide to marry him and had been accepted. His heart went down and down. His resentment at Sharp's embrace trailed off into sheer unrelieved misery. She was going to become Sharp's wife. The teamster thought he would go home.

At this point the palpitations of the jazz ceased; the dancers came to a standstill with a great clapping of hands.

A few moments later the leaves of the artificial palms were pressed aside and Beatrice Belle and her Mr. Pratt stepped into the embrasure hunting a seat. Pratt murmured a "Pardon" and was about to take his partner elsewhere when Beatrice Belle saw who occupied the covert. She straightened indignantly.

"Abner Teeftaller, why wasn't you dancin'?"

"You know I kain't dance good enough for this place!" growled Abner.

"Why, he can, too!" cried Beatrice. "He dances very well, Sim."

"You must try, Mr. Teeftallow," encouraged Mr. Pratt earnestly. "It isn't hard when you get the hang of the thing."

"I didn't want to ball up the dance," said Abner, with his dislike of Mr. Pratt considerably diminished by this bit of sympathy.

"Oh, you won't," smiled the drug clerk. "We're used to collisions."

They were so kindly and considerate toward him that Abner's world brightened measurably. He decided that perhaps Sharp had not proposed and been accepted after all. It was possible Adelaide had nodded to some other suggestion.

"Adelaide thought you had gone home," reproved Beatrice Belle. "She was all cut up about it. I'll tell her you are here."

"No, don't!" cried Abner, with an irrational terror at being found.

"Why, the idea, you're not a hermit or anything . . ."

At that moment the roar and rattle of the jazz burst out anew. Mr. Pratt received Beatrice Belle in his arms, adjusted his blue-shaved cheek to her own, and wobbled rapturously out of the palms and away.

Abner, watching them, decided that Pratt was not an emissary of Satan as he had at first suspected, but that he was merely a sissy; one of those watered youths who go about with girls on purely feminine terms. Perhaps he placed his cheek against Beatrice Belle's in sheer girlish effusion—it was hardly worth while to mention the matter to Mrs. Sandage.

Amid the plangent jazz Abner began looking for Adelaide again when there was a rustle of the palm leaves and he glanced around to see Adelaide holding her green skirt aside and letting herself into his retreat. She smiled at him as she eased through the leaves.

"Is this a game of hide and seek, Mr. Teeftallow?"

A little thrill travelled deliberately through the hill youth, whether of pleasure or embarrassment he did not know.

"I kain't dance good enough to come out; ever'body would laugh at me, Adelaide."

"You don't want to dance with me?" She held out her arms, pouting her lips and shaking her head as if talking to a child.

The lifting of her arms, the temptingness of the girl, her faint perfume filled Abner with a sharp desire.

"I wish I could dance!" he cried.

"You don't do so badly. I've seen you try."

"But not here, before ever'body."

"Well—if you just won't . . ." She seemed about to go.

He was on nettles to keep her. "Look here, Adelaide, if it wouldn't be askin' too much, would you min' stayin' here an' talkin' a little?"

"You mean sit out a dance?" she smiled.

"Yes, if you wouldn't mind."

"Well—all right—strangle holds barred." She sank at his side, giggling at her impropriety. "I suppose you think I'm awful wicked?"

"Why, no-o," denied Abner, a little hazy as to what she meant.

"Anyway, it's nice to talk to such a cave-looking man after the usual dancing partner."

"Don't you like your partner?" asked Abner hopefully.

"Why, Abner, they're my guests!" She regarded him with amused, speculative eyes. "You're awfully strong, aren't you, Mr. Teeftallow?"

Abner had difficulty in disregarding the white modelling of her neck and bosom and clinging to the thread of their conversation.

"I—guess so," he answered vaguely.

"You look as if you could hold a girl up in one hand— when do you do your daily dozen?"

"Look here," ejaculated Abner, entirely bewildered by this attack. "What are you driving at, Adelaide?"

"I'm not sure I'm driving at anything yet; this is probably a tour of inspection.—Papa says you're awfully wealthy."

Abner withdrew himself sufficiently from Adelaide's décolleté attire to answer in his country drawl, "You mean you're looking me over to see if I'll do?"

"Well, a girl has some idea of what she wants—after she falls in love the first time and lives over it."

"But she don't know the first time?" inquired Abner curiously.

"Of course not. Were you aware of any faults in your first sweetheart, Abner? No, life sends everybody just one paragon straight down out of Heaven, and that's the last one you'll ever see no matter how long you live. . . ." Adelaide broke off a tip of the artificial palm. "How old are you, Abner?"

"Nineteen."

"That's very young. I'm eighteen; that's very old. Such an old woman as I am oughtn't to rope in a kid like you, but if I don't—some other ancient will. How many farms have you got, Abner?"

Abner flushed slightly at Adelaide's chaffing air. She was certainly the most unladylike girl he had ever seen. She sat regarding him with a little smile, presently began again: "I saw you watching me dance with Buck Sharp; you didn't seem to enjoy it as much as we did."

Abner reddened. "I thought you didn't know where I was?"

Adelaide shrugged a smooth shoulder. "When I'm interested in a man I would hardly lose him in my own parlour. —You haven't said how many farms you own——"

"I don't know. Buck Sharp is finding out."

"Buck Sharp!"

"Yes."

"Poor child, you do need a guardian."

She reached over, took one of his hands, spread it on her silk knee palm up, and perused it after the manner of a fortune teller.

"What's wrong with you, Mr. Teeftallow, is, you have a long tapering hand. It is calloused from work, but really it's the hand of a dreamer and an idler. I venture you sit around and dream all sorts of things and do almost nothing, don't you?"

"No-o," denied Abner, unable to recognize this description of himself.

"How came you to leave the poorhouse?" probed Adelaide. "Weren't you turned out?"

"No-o, not exactly."

"Yes, you were—exactly. Beatrice told me all about it. It was right pathetic, I call it. I've thought about it a lot."

Abner sat with his hand on the girl's knee, flushing uncomfortably. Adelaide placed her own small square palm on Abner's and looked at him with a kind of tenderness in her face.

"That's why you are so appealing, Abner," she continued. "When a man just constitutionally can't help himself, some woman feels like she's got to do it for him. The reason you are so wishy-washy is, you feel instead of think—and that's appealing. You know these thinking brains are terrible, Abner. They go straight, straight—you can coax, sob, implore, but you can't change their course because they're going somewhere. Most men are not like that, Abner. Most of 'em are like you, easy, wishy-washy fellows, and we

women ought to fall on our knees and thank God for it."
Her bosom lifted with a little irregular breath and she
smiled faintly in his face.

"Papa wants to see you," she said unexpectedly.

Abner gave a little start as if coming out of a daydream.
"Where is he?"

"In the library. I'll take you in."

Alarm touched Abner. "Won't I get to see you any more
to-night?"

She laughed. "You'll have to come thank me for my
party afterward."

She arose, and Abner unwillingly concluded the most
intriguing and confusing tête-à-tête he had ever known.
They passed out of the palms through the dancers. "This
door," she directed, and opened a door into a small room
in which a single electric bulb was burning. She closed the
shutter behind them and the music was muffled to a palpitant
wail.

Adelaide seemed to listen to it. "You really ought to learn
to dance, Abner," she advised in a queer tone. "You could
if you'd try."

"I don't much believe I can."

"Try! You can try!" She caught his arm, slipped into
it, wound her own arm about his body and began swaying
to the subdued music. "Here, like this," she directed urgently, "swing with me . . . like this . . ." She
pressed herself to him, bending back and forth.

Abner began swaying with her, self-consciously at first,
but presently the beat of the jazz, the intimate feel of the
girl's body, the curves of her bosom moving against his own
changed from an awkwardness to a rising intoxication. The
hot syncopation of the jazz band filled the room. The girl
became part of the music. The cornet skirled, the saxophone
wailed, the drums pounded—the voice of Africa, of burning
suns and passionate bodies hurled them along in the provocation of its swift tempo. Abner gripped her to him with
a strength he was not conscious of; Adelaide followed his

lead limply, her eyes shut, her face against his, her limber body curving in and out with his own.

Very abruptly the jazz ceased. The dancers stopped writhing and stood clasping each other convulsively.

"Here," panted Adelaide, with her heartbeats shaking her voice, "let's sit down."

They moved together carefully to a seat as if afraid of breaking the intimate contact. The girl still clasped Abner's neck with her bare arms and the perfume of her corsage enveloped him with its provocation. He sat down, taking her in his lap, and her weight filled him with a sort of maddened despair. His hand crushed her bosom, but she caught her breath and pulled it away.

"No, no," she gasped.

"But you love me!" he whispered unsteadily.

"No—I don't know—I don't think so."

"You don't—my God!" Abner was stricken.

She pushed his hands away from her with decision and slipped out of his lap on to the seat beside him.

"N-no, you just attract me physically, Abner, I think. There are two parts to love, you know, physical and—what you call spiritual—now don't be angry. Here, you may kiss me. You haven't kissed me. The idea of doing a girl this way without kissing her first." She held up her lips with a shaky smile.

Abner kissed her. The caress was colourless after the feel of her whole body pressed to his, and he gave the kiss with a vexed feeling.

"How spoiled you are already," she said thoughtfully, staring at him as he withdrew his face. "Goodness, some girl has made a rotten job out of you, Abner. You have no feeling whatever for *crescendo*, just a wild explosion." She leaned happily against his chest again and reached an arm about his neck. "You are an old bear, dear, but you certainly have got pep." At that moment the jazz music brayed forth again. "Do you want to dance to this tune?"

"No."

"Suit yourself. I'm your hostess and at your disposal, within limits. However, I have other guests and I'll have to go back to them after this piece. Conventionality is my synonym."

"Are you going to dance with that Sharp man again?" growled Abner, who found himself in a very bad humour indeed.

"I don't know. Why?" she glanced up at him sidewise.

"Suppose we go back in there and dance together?" suggested Abner, on an impulse.

"Oh, no, dear, you won't do to dance in polite society for several generations yet to come. Now, your great-great-grandson may be able to dance with a lady in a perfectly gentlemanly manner, like Buck."

For some reason this little speech whisked away Abner's dourness. He grinned and patted Adelaide's shoulder and this tempted him to another embrace, but she moved away.

"No, that's enough. I suppose the village would think this much perfectly awful, but it's necessary. How can you tell whether a person really attracts you or not?—You have to try it—that's what hugging and kissing are for. It's a try-out for passion. Folks make a great hullabaloo about passion, Abner, how wicked it is, but if you haven't got it it's S O S at the matrimonial altar. You can complain of petting parties all you please, Abner, but they are bound to save hundreds of divorces in the end. My room mate and I talked that over in the seminary."

Adelaide sighed and sat for a few moments following some thought. "Of course, dancing is a formal way of petting. That's why jazz has such a hold on everybody. I think young folks instinctively want to be frank and open in their love-making, Abner, but the old folks don't like to be reminded that they are old, so they make a great sin out of youth—that's what my room mate said."

She seemed so pensive and at sea that Abner was moved to tenderness. He took her hand and gently quoted the hills.

"Don't you think love comes from God?"

Adelaide smiled sadly and shook her head. "Our first love comes from God, but after that He puts too many and too contradictory impulses in our hearts. Look at me: you attract me terribly physically, Abner; Buck Sharp entertains me mentally. And there was a theological student up at Nashville who, I believe, attracted me spiritually. Abner—now you wouldn't think I had a soul, would you? You think I am a very bad girl, don't you, Abner?" She looked at her companion, blinking her eyes a little.

"Why, no, I don't," said Abner with a queer feeling.

"You see the trouble is with God—as you call it—God divides your husband up among maybe half-a-dozen men, and then you've lost him, of course—only a few moments ago Buck Sharp was begging me to marry him. . . ."

Abner looked at her.

"Adelaide—is that why you—came in here with me and —danced?"

Miss Jones nodded faintly.

"Yes. I wanted to know how I felt toward you. I didn't know. G-God, as you call it, is such a bungler at making a g-girl's dream come true."

Abner was moved unwontedly. He leaned over and caressed the girl's naked shoulders for once without thinking of her flesh.

"Will you marry me, Adelaide?"

"I don't think so," she said sadly.

"Oh, Adelaide—I wish I was smart, like Buck! I wish to God I was what you wanted, but I haven't got much sense; I'm very ordinary."

He leaned toward her in his humility. The girl suddenly put up her arms and clutched his leonine head convulsively to her bosom.

The music stopped.

She put him away abruptly, arose. and began powdering her nose and eyes.

"This is what you call sitting out a dance," and she gave a choked giggle.

"Are you going back in?" asked Abner, aghast.

She nodded swiftly, erasing the traces of her emotion.

"What are you going to say?"

"I don't know."

She was turning away.

"Wait! Wait!" cried Abner in despair. "Tell him no, Adelaide, tell him you love somebody else."

"Oh, I do! I do!" cried the girl with wide eyes. "I've already told him that!"

Abner followed her to the door, gripping her hand.

"T-tell him——"

"Good-bye for to-night, Abner; come to see me to-morrow. Go through that door and you'll find Dad; he wants to see you. Now, kiss me good-bye."

He kissed her with a certainty that she was lost to him, and it filled him almost with a physical weakness. She disengaged herself gently from his arms, opened the door, and slipped through it. As she entered the illumination of the ballroom, Abner saw her face light up with a bright practised smile.

CHAPTER V

ALONE in the dimly lighted room, Abner Teeftallow, even if he was, as he admitted, "ordinary," still realized that a remarkable thing had happened. A girl of the hills had asserted the validity of sex along with the other values of life. When in doubt as to her own emotions, Adelaide had frankly experimented. Reared as Abner had been amid the shamed and secretive treatment of sex, Adelaide's attitude toward it was like a fresh breeze blowing through a swamp. Clearly she belonged to herself and would find happiness in any way she could.

Very probably at this moment she was in the ballroom, making a decision against him, promising to marry the other man. This thought brought a twinge in Abner's chest. The notion of losing her was painful. Yet while Adelaide dazzled him, still, after all, the stolid hillman felt there was something absurd about her gesture. A courtship could not be conducted like a shopping tour. A girl could not go around trying on man after man, like gloves. . . .

In this mood Abner crossed mechanically to the door which Adelaide had pointed out and entered without knocking. He did not think of knocking. In the hills intramural signals are not used. When a hillman enters a house—he is in it.

The teamster found himself standing in a large library looking at the huge back of Railroad Jones. The magnate was in his shirt sleeves wearing a fresh striped shirt that puffed up between the cross of his suspenders and gave him a freshly bathed look. He was standing beside a cabinet filled with mineral specimens and held a reddish-looking stone in his hand. The fat man dominated his library com-

302

pletely; beyond him Abner barely distinguished some sectional bookcases; an electric spray overhead shining down on him, and at the farther end of the room a library table with a shaded light.

For several moments Abner stood awkwardly looking at the puffed shirt between the braces, and finally attracted the fat man's attention by saying, "Mr. Jones, Adelaide said you wanted to see me."

Railroad Jones turned his bulk with the waddling movement of the very fleshy.

"Why, yes, I wanted to see you, Abner; glad you come in." He replaced his specimen and explained in his burring voice, "Addy put these rocks in here—they've all got names —you kain't find a single little rock out in the hills, Ab, but what it's got a name"—the fat man gave an abdominal chuckle at the absurdity of the thing—"another fool way of weakening the brain, Ab, namin' the rocks." The great square-cut face with the small eyes burnt in it took on such a droll expression that Abner laughed outright.

"I suppose they have to teach girls things ordinary folks don't know," opined Abner, "so folks'll realize they are educated."

"Mostly show," agreed the magnate from deep in his throat. "Have a cigarette." He moved to the table.

Abner followed him and had one. It had a cork tip, an oval shape, and a flavour Abner had never tasted before.

"Sit down," stewed out Jones, and Abner sank into bottomless upholstery.

The rich man waved a puffed hand. "This is all Addy's idyah: books, rocks, pictures, things to git your mind off yore business. I tell her she'll never be a business woman. She says she's goin' to marry an' turn that over to some man; says she's goin' to raise childern herself. I told her to hit her pace. I didn't keer what she done so long as she kep' on livin' here with me. I don't propose to have her leavin' this house, Ab. I want her to keep on livin' here, married or single—I like to watch her."

The magnate stewed all this out between deliberate cigarette puffs, opening and closing his eyes, which were fixed on Abner.

This pointed discussion of Adelaide's matrimonial future brought a certain suspense and suggested very enticing possibilities to Abner. He glanced around the handsome library and felt a dawning proprietary interest in it. The youth almost said—he had it on the tip of his tongue to say, "Mr. Jones, I wouldn't think of taking Adelaide away from you," but an indeterminate atmosphere about the rich man suggested that Abner wait a little further, which the youth did, leaning back in his chair, and letting go the breath with which he had meant to talk.

"What I wanted to see you about," rebegan Mr. Jones, "is a little trouble I'm having with my men in winding up the railroad work."

Abner looked his disappointment at this abandonment of the theme of Adelaide.

"What's the matter with your men?" he asked without interest.

"Well, they've been tryin' to engineer a strike for a long time, but now Perry Northcutt's got behind it an' it's goin' through."

"I hadn't heard it."

"No, you've been pretty busy in society here in Lanesburg lately." This was said in Railroad's usual burring voice, but Abner thought he detected a faint sarcasm in it. He looked at the broad yellow face.

"You wanted to see me about that?"

"Yes."

"What can I do?"

"I thought maybe you would be inter*ested* in this family keepin' some of the value my railroad is bringin' into this county, Abner. Ever'thing I've got now is in that railroad. If it was finished I could git a line of credit on it an' pay Perry off, but if it's tied up in a strike I kain't do it, an' nachelly

Perry will git it all. Then me an' Addy will be down jest where I started fifty years ago."

The fat man stated his position impassively, scrutinizing the young man in the chair opposite him.

"An' what do you want me to do?" questioned Abner with more interest.

"Well, bein' as you was a frien' of Addy's, I thought you'd be inte*rested* in seein' her keep the proputty her daddy got together for her. I allowed you'd be more inte*rested* in seein' it go to Addy than to Perry Northcutt. The fact is, Ab, I'm old. I kain't start at the bottom agin an' set Addy up where she is now. If I could make it a-tall, I wouldn't be in time. She's a young lady now, an' anything that money can do fer her happiness has got to be done now. Like all right-minded gals, Ab, she'll marry soon. With money she can have her pickin' choice of whoever she wants, and I want her to have that feller, whoever he be. Any man she picks will be all right with me. That gal's got more sense in a minute than most folks has in a year. She's got too much sense to pick for mere book l'arnin', Abner. He's got to be a man!" His guttural voice came down on the word "man" with an emphasis that picked Abner out and nominated him for the position.

"Look here," said the teamster earnestly, "what can I do in this business?"

"If the strike comes off like it's billed, we'll need men to take the strikers' places. You've already worked down there; you'd be a valuable man to break in raw labour. Sheriff Bascom is goin' to be with you fellers; so are most of the deputies in the county."

"You mean there's liable to be a fight?"

"I hope not, nachelly, but when one set o' men steps up an' says nobody can work unless they say so, seems to me it's time to decide whether we're all rabbits or bulldawgs. I thought I'd speak to you about it. I shore don't think it's right fer me to spen' my life makin' a fortune for Addy, an' have Perry Northcutt git it. I thought you might feel like doin' somethin' to keep Addy from bein' beat out o' her right; specially as Northcutt has already done you a pretty mean turn."

At the prospect of rescuing Adelaide's fortune for her, something quivered in Abner's chest. He nodded earnestly.

"Now you've said it, Mr. Jones. I may have a little money, but I ain't forgot how to do a honest day's work, nor, by God, how to put up a fight, neither."

"Of course, I hope they won't be no fightin'," said Railroad, waving a hand, "but what is to be will be. I'm Babtis' enough to b'lieve that; an' sence it shore is goin' to happen, my plan is to hit fust an' make it happen to the other feller."

"I do, too," said Abner to this commendable creed.

The magnate arose and came forward, extending a puffy hand to his guest.

"I'm glad you feel like that. I knowed yore gran'dad when he owned putty near all this county. I was jest gittin' my teeth whetted to do a little bitin' myse'f then—a fine ol' man—an yore mammy goin' crazy, too—you come from fine stock, Abner. I thought I'd find a man when I put my han' on you."

"I'll go down with Bascom any time an' up agin anything," said Abner with a slight swagger.

"Much obliged. I appreciate that, Abner, an' Addy will, too."

They moved together to the outer door of the library. Before Abner went out on the porch, Railroad Jones paused again.

"By the way, Abner, if I was you I don't b'lieve I'd push them partic'lar lan' claims you got agin my estate right now. Me an' you can make a settlemint, any time, you know that." He nodded intimately at the youth. "You don't want to force a sale o' my lan's just before the railroad makes 'em jump in price. I haven't the money to settle off with you right now—if you ever do want a settlemint with my estate."

"Why, s-sure," stammered Abner, thrilled at this intimate suggestion. "I'll do anything in the worl' I can to accommo-date you an' Adelaide, Mr. Jones."

"I knowed you would, Abner, so I jest wish you'd tell Buck Sharp to lay off them lands which belong to me. When you need money you can proceed aginst the other places aroun' here. Yore gran'daddy owned the old Coltrane place, the Beshear place. I understan' Ditmas is wantin' the timber on the Coltrane place. You ort to be able to compromise an' sell it to him straight out."

The mention of Mr. Ditmas introduced a discordant note into the sacrificial mood of the youth.

"I saw Mr. Ditmas a few days ago, an' he seemed mighty cut up over a trade he made with you." Reproach coloured the ex-teamster's tones. "He was sayin' somethin' about the South's not tradin' fair and whitecaps, or somethin' like that."

"Whitecaps an' the South not tradin' fair?"

"Yeh, somethin' like that."

"Well, now, Abner, I was lookin' out for my side o' that trade, an' nachelly I supposed he was lookin' out for his'n. When I trade with a man, Abner—I mean a man outside my own fambly—I nachelly make as good a trade as I can, an' I mean fer him to do the same. I thought that rule was understood North, South, East, West, an' ever' other direction."

"Sure," agreed Abner, for Railroad's logic was as clear and convincing as Mr. Ditmas's had been cloudy and involved. "Well, I don't guess Mr. Ditmas really meant anything by what he said, he was drunk when he said it."

That ended the Ditmas analysis of the South and the nation. It passed from Abner's mind and never returned.

The young man and the old one stood talking a few minutes longer in the chill autumn night. Then they shook hands again and Abner crossed the porch and started down the gravelled path to the front gate. He would walk home.

In the Jones parlour the jazz band still caterwauled, and Abner gradually left it behind.

As he walked he looked up at the cold stars and saw himself rescuing Adelaide's fortune. He imagined himself standing beside Sheriff Bascom and the deputies, defending the last of the railroad construction. Also, he would be defending Adelaide in her fine home, with her fine car, and her fine, unashamed passion seeking happiness for herself, and for her children who were yet to be.

"If I knowed I'd git killed an' never git to marry her a-tall, still I'd do it for her," mused Abner, "because—because . . ." His thoughts lost the form of words and became a feeling of what Adelaide was to him; a fresh heartsome breeze, blowing on him amid the exhalations of a swamp.

CHAPTER VI

ABNER'S high sacrificial mood which prompted him to hazard life and limb for Adelaide Jones lasted no longer than the night. He awoke next morning gloomily certain that Adelaide had accepted Buckingham Sharp's proposal of marriage, and he had become indifferent to the threatened strike and the wreck of her fortune.

He sighed heavily, sat up on the side of his bed in the cold autumn morning, yawned, and began pulling on his shoes and trousers. One reason for Abner's lapse from idealism was that he had slept in a small, tightly closed bedroom in order to exclude the unhealthful night air. His chamber was now filled with stale air and the odour of his body.

Another yawn was interrupted by his door creaking open; he covered himself hastily and growled, "Keep out!"

Mrs. Sandage's voice said in her flat country accent, "I'm not comin' in, I'll jest stick in my head," thereupon her head appeared around the edge of the door.

Abner looked at it resentfully. "I'm not dressed," he repeated.

"Well, I'm not comin' in.—Say, what's this I hear about you goin' to work on the railroad ag'in?"

"Who told you that?"

"Aline."

"Well, you tell Aline—— No, don't tell her nuthin'. I don't like that nigger nohow."

"Well, I couldn't see no sense in you workin' after you got money. I told Aline they wasn't no sense to it."

"You told her right."

Another brief silence; the head in the doorway gazed past

Abner in an effort to recapture some escaped thread of thought.

"Oh, by the way, Jim's awful worried."

"What about?"

"They say Perry Northcutt's goin' to start an investigation of what Jim's done with the county's money."

Up to this point Abner had been trying to drive Mrs. Sandage out of his room by the expression of his face; now he put his feet under the cover for a prolonged conversation.

"No sense to that, Miss Haly. What would Perry start an investigation for? He's the one that's finally gittin' the money."

"That's a fack," assented the head, staring at Abner, "but I bet it's so; nearly all bad news is."

"You're jest skeered, Miss Haly. A man wouldn't quarrel with his own pocketbook."

"No-o. . . . I reckon not. . . . If he was to, Mr. Jones would haff to git the county's money up for Jim mighty quick so he could show it."

"Well, of course he would. Jim would hand it right back to him as soon as the investigation was over."

"Now, d'reckon he would? Did je ever hear of Mr. Jones payin' anything?"

"My Lord, that wouldn't be payin' it—handin' it out, takin' it back. How much is it?"

"Over thirty thousan' now."

"Why, Miss Haly, his railroad costs a quarter of a million; thirty thousan' would jest be his pocket change."

The woman pondered. "I guess Jim's worried about nothin'," she agreed uneasily. "Anyway, Abner, if you can help break that strike I wish you'd do it. Anything to help Mr. Jones on his feet again will help all of us."

"Oh, I don't min' workin' some more," agreed Abner good-naturedly.

The head withdrew as unceremoniously as it had entered. Abner got briskly into his clothes and went down to the breakfast table. Jim and Mrs. Sandage had eaten and the table was disarranged. The breakfast of fried chicken, boiled potatoes, cabbage, and apple pie had become cold. Presently Aline entered with a cup of lukewarm coffee and marked her contempt of the meal with an audible sniff. Aline had worked for Judge Stone; she knew what a breakfast ought to be.

As Abner ate, Beatrice Belle came into the dining room with her pale hair wound up on curlers. She rubbed her puffed eyes and regarded the table with a hostility equal to Aline's.

"Mammy makes me so tired," she whined. "Cabbage and potatoes for breakfast to suit Pappy's whims."

"He got used to it on the farm," defended Abner absently. "I like it myself."

"You an' Daddy will always be country," stated Beatrice disagreeably.

"Looky here," growled the youth, "I'd ruther be from the country than one of these sissy town johnnies."

The girl made a little *moue* and became silent; presently she asked, "Where did you go last night?"

"Home. I couldn't dance."

"Well, you ort to of stayed instead of runnin' off an' gittin' me insulted," reproved Beatrice sharply.

"Insulted!"

"Yes, I couldn't find you, so I picked up that Sim Pratt."

"You don't mean that he——"

"He certainly did. I was drivin' an' he put his arm around me. I pushed him away but purty soon he done it again."

"Whyn't you make him git out an' walk?"

"I tried to but he wouldn't git out. He said it was dangerous for a young girl to be drivin' alone at night; somebody might do somethin' to her."

"An' him settin' there doin' it hisse'f!"

"He was jest tryin' to be smart."

Abner bit off the end of his chicken bone and crunched it in his teeth. "I'll fix him for that—he won't bother you no more."

Beatrice's expression changed. "What are you goin' to do to him?"

"I'll mop up his drug store with him!" Abner leaned over his plate, dropped the shreds of chewed bone on it.

Beatrice watched him apprehensively. "Look here, Abner, they ain't no use fightin' about it. Besides, he's so little you could lick him with one finger. That's what I don't like about him; he's so little and puny. One night I ast him did he ever gamble or git drunk. He got so serious; he said, 'Miss Beatrice, upon my honour, I never did.' I thought, 'You little sissy!'"

Abner got up and pushed his chair from the table with a backward motion of his knees.

"Where you goin'?"

"To see Pratt."

"No, you don't," protested Beatrice. "You let Sim Pratt alone. I can manage my own affairs."

At this moment Mrs. Sandage entered the dining room. "What's this about Mr. Pratt?" she asked suspiciously.

"He was tryin' to hug her last night!" snapped Abner.

"You permitted it, B'atrice Sandage!"

"Naw!" cried Beatrice at this new outrage. "I was tellin' Abner to leave him be!"

"He ortn't to be left be! Abner ort to settle with him!"

"Oh, Mammy, you're so countrified! Adelaide says as long as a girl can breathe she don't need protection."

Abner left the two in the midst of a quarrel, with the maid Aline standing to one side with down-drawn lips and lifted brows.

Abner Teeftallow set out for the drug store. He was irritated at Pratt for the brotherly reason that he could not sympathize with the drug clerk in his desire to caress Beatrice Belle; therefore he would put the young man in his place.

Then the lawsuit and Jim's money, Adelaide Jones and Buck Sharp, all drifted through his mind, each bearing its own savour of gall. He sighed heavily. He certainly had got up on the wrong side of the bed that morning.

Another thing that vexed him was that somehow he felt restless with nothing to do. He couldn't understand it. Here he was with money and idleness, the two goals of a hill-man's life, and yet he was not half so contented as when he was working on the railroad—damn funny thing! Well, he would just go back and work on the railroad, since Jim and Haly seemed to want him to. . . .

Here Abner turned into Ransom's drug store.

The store appeared empty of persons. Abner became suspicious that Pratt had seen him and had slipped out of some rear entrance. He was about to call Pratt's name when he caught sight of the round top of a sleek black head over the prescription counter. The mere sleekness of this head incensed the teamster anew. He strode silently to the back of the store, staring fixedly at the obnoxious hair as men and animals do when they stalk their enemies.

At his step Mr. Pratt came to the entrance of his den holding a large-sized bottle in one hand and a small one in the other.

"Good-morning, Mr. Teeftallow," he saluted in clerkly fashion. "Glad you come in. I was just wishing I could see you."

"Well, by God, you're goin' to see me all right!" snarled Abner.

Mr. Pratt was so wrapped up in his project, whatever it was, he did not observe Abner's angry tone.

"Sure glad of it," repeated Pratt earnestly. "Say, look here, are you goin' to be at the head of the men?"

The drug clerk put down his big bottle and came up to Abner, shaking the smaller one.

"Head of what men?" growled Abner.

"Why, the strike breakers!"

Abner deferred his attack for a few moments.

"Hell, no, I ain't the head of no strike breakers!"

Mr. Pratt appeared disappointed. "I heard you were. Do you know who is?"

"No, I don't," reflected Abner, "unless it's Bascom."

Mr. Pratt came closer, lowered his voice, and reddened slightly. "Anyway, when you join, d'reckon you could get me in with you?"

Abner looked at the little clerk with surprise and distaste. "What in the hell do you want to join fer?"

Mr. Pratt became more embarrassed and stammered in an undertone, "Uh—to tell the truth—it—it's Miss Beatrice. . . ."

Abner could do nothing but stare in amazement. The drug clerk went on more confusedly than ever:

"She—you know—don't like a fellow who—er—just stays in a drug store—where nothin' happens—I mean like mobs and gambling an' shootings—something that appeals to a girl—I mean in a man. Mr. Ransom said he would give me a week off, and I—I thought if you could get me in with the strike breakers, and—and there was some—some fighting and shooting and drinking or—or something, it—it"—Mr. Pratt swallowed—"it would please her. . . ."

"Fuh God's sake, what an idyah!" ejaculated Abner.

However, the idea effectually stopped Abner from slapping Mr. Pratt's jaws as he had intended. It left the teamster a little at sea. He decided quickly, since he could not beat up Mr. Pratt, he would "bawl him out."

Abner cleared his throat and began his bawling out.

"Look here, Pratt, whether you go or don't go, I don't give a damn. I come here to see you about what you done to Beatrice Belle las' night."

"What was that?" asked the drug clerk, quite astonished at this turn.

"Well, you—er—kep' huggin' her after she tol' you not to."

"They all tell you not to," he said, still mystified.

"Well, by God, Pratt——"

"An' besides, we'd been hugging all evening."

"You had!"

"Dancing."

"Dancin's one thing and huggin's another. You knowed

that was wrong, Pratt!" Abner shook a finger at the offending drug clerk. "If a man don't respect the virtue of a pure woman, Pratt, he ain't fitten for the decent men of the county to wipe their feet on." Abner was mounting a high horse whose riding comes natural to all Southerners. "I say if a man don't hold the honour of his sweetheart closter than he does his own life, he ort to be beat up an' run out of the county! He ort to be——"

At this moment a voice from behind the prescription counter called out curiously, "Ain't that Ab Teeftaller out there?"

"Yeh," ejaculated Abner, startled into ending his harangue.

"By gum, Ab, I ain't seed you for a long time. Heard you got rich as a cattle pen all of a sudden."

Speaking these words, a man in overalls appeared at the entrance of the prescription department. Abner stared a moment and then exclaimed cordially so as not to appear stuck-up, "Why, hello, Tim Fraley, what you doin' up here?"

But the man who has to think not to be stuck-up is stuck-up, and Mr. Fraley saw through Abner's pretence, so he said with a slightly sardonic air, "Oh, camp's jest a mile or two out o' town where us hill-billies stay."

Abner felt the innuendo; there was a moment's hesitation, then, from Abner with renewed cordiality, "Arntown 'bout the same as usual, Tim?"

"I guess so—they're all stirred up over the railroad suit —I guess you don't keep up with sich little things sence you come into yore own."

"Sure I do," protested Abner uncomfortably.

"Well, we've got some little news back there—Tug Beavers is comin' back to hold a meetin' there before long."

"Is that a fack!" cried Abner, pleased at Tug's extraordinary progress.

"Yep, an' they say Professor Overall has landed the winter school here in Lanesburg."

"Now, by God, there's a man of learnin'," praised Abner

warmly. "He learned me all I know or ever expect to know."

"Yep, an' I suppose you heard about Nessie Sutton—Nessie Belshue, she is now?"

A tickling came over Abner's scalp, as if someone had douched him with cold water. "Why, n-n-no-o," he said.

"She's a proud mammy now—her an' Belshue's got a little gal."

"She has!" ejaculated Abner, oddly moved again.

"Yep, an' the quare part is, it's a four-months baby. She's been married to Belshue that long, but it's alive an' kickin' all right—quick action, I call it," and here Mr. Fraley burst into a roar of laughter, leaning against the prescription counter in his mirth.

Mr. Pratt stood looking from one hillman to the other.

It seemed to Abner that the floor was sinking under him. He was thinking with an overwhelming sense of pain and pathos, "A little gal—a little gal . . ." Something constricted in his throat and he heard his own voice saying in a strained tone, "Well—that—that's nice—er—Mr. Pratt—yes—I—I'm goin' with the—the strike breakers—g-get you in if I can—I got to go——" He was getting out of the drug store on shaking legs.

As he went he heard Fraley gasping out some explanation half choked with laughter. This faded to silence as Abner passed out the door. He walked unseeingly into the chill sunshine that lay over the unsightly square. The courthouse clock began slowly tolling an hour. Abner moved on with an aching throat, repeating in a whisper, "A little gal—a little gal—to bring a little gal in a worl' like this 'un."

CHAPTER VII

AFTER that first moment of sheer pathos when he heard of the birth of his natural daughter, Abner Teeftallow's thoughts were drawn, in time, to the position in which he now stood in Lanesburg society.

The gossip spread over the village with the speed usual to small-town salacity. In reaction certain girl acquaintances of Abner's grew distantly polite, while others "stopped speaking"; a misnomer, since both distant and silent ones now discussed Abner incessantly. The youth's invitations to parties and dances dropped away to nothing. Such criticism discomfited Abner. In the garage at Irontown his liaison with Nessie had been admired, but the feminine world of Lanesburg censured him keenly. Abner never before had dwelt in a feminine world.

The men of Lanesburg sympathized with Abner in a semi-humorous way. The man who came in for their serious contempt was Nessie's husband, A. M. Belshue. The jeweller had broken that unworded law forbidding any easement or comfort to the enemies of society. In marrying a social outcast, Belshue weakened the village discipline and imperilled its whole structure. His sin was, in reality, subtler and more insidious than was Abner's in deflowering the girl. The village folk would forgive Abner in time, but they would never forego their bitter contempt for the jeweller because he had rescued the unhappy girl from degradation and utter destruction.

One day Abner was complaining to Jim Sandage about his social boycott.

"It's jest freshened up for a while," philosophized Jim

easily. "It'll die down an' that'll end it—tull you do somethin' else."

"I don't give a damn for the rest of 'em," proceeded Abner gloomily. "What I'm worried about is Adelaide."

"Think she's goin' to hold it agin' you?" asked Jim with concern.

"Don't know."

"I don' imagine so. No matter what man she gits it'll be the same thing. A sensible gal like Addy ort to know that."

"Wish you'd give her a hint."

"She'll find it out fer herse'f, if she don't know it already. Have you seen her sence the news got aroun' town?"

"No, I'm kinder skittish of her."

"That's no good," declared Jim roundly. "You ort to go an' git married to her. It's ridickilous, a man of yore age havin' troubles like this. This here scatterin' idyah ain't no good. A man ort to keep his childern where he can lay his finger on 'em; he gits satisfaction out of his fam'ly same as anything else he owns. Thing for you to do is to marry Adelaide, an' that'll end up all this gossip. Gals never talk about what a married man done when he was single."

But Abner could not accept this broad, easy view of life. He could not marry Adelaide Jones out of hand; neither could he dismiss his relations with Nessie Belshue in such a cavalierish manner. Their baby girl would remain their baby girl no matter whom he married; and then his old tenderness toward Nessie, his effort to marry her which had been frustrated by the mob, moved him.

Several times he nerved himself to go to Adelaide and try to explain himself—if only she could understand how he felt she might come to sympathize with him and even love him in that strange mixed way women have of loving the very wounds of another love. But he never went to Adelaide. He was afraid. Not so much that she would take the cold attitude of the other village girls who had no compassion for any frailties except their own; but that she might not take him seriously at all; she might pass flippantly over his tragedy, coin a cynicism about it, laugh at him as Tim Fraley had done; only with that more polished and subtle mockery indigenous to a modern young ladies' seminary; that place where nothing is sacred, not even unchastity. Abner felt he could never endure that.

The conversation veered from Adelaide to Railroad Jones and the strike of the construction gang. The two men were sitting in Mr. Sandage's office in the county court-house watching the country people who were beginning to gather for another quarterly court.

"I shore hope Railroad gits his new gang together to-day," mused the county trustee, watching this fresh supply of raw labour.

"Jest what did the old gang strike for?" asked Abner. "More money?"

"No, some money."

"What you mean by that?"

"Perry Northcutt quit advancin' wages, an' nachelly the men quit work."

"How's Railroad goin' to finance his new gang?" inquired Abner curiously.

"Tell you the truth," said the trustee in a low tone, "I'm goin' to do it myse'f."

"You!" Abner stared at his foster-father.

Jim moistened his lips. "I got to, Abner. I got so much invested in that railroad, I got to put through these last few miles, then I'll git all my money back."

"You goin' to pay off the old gang, too?"

"No, Railroad said we didn't have enough money to pay off the old gang; said we'd jest start in with a fresh gang we didn't owe nothin'."

"That's playin' it purty low down on the others," mused Abner.

"Once the road's a-runnin', Railroad says he can pay off ever'body. . . . You know sometimes I wish I hadn't got into this damn business a-tall." He sat staring at the crowd. "You might go around to Railroad's office to-day, Ab, an,' if you keer to light in an' do a little work with the new gang, it would he'p that much."

"Shore, if I can be of any he'p," agreed Abner with the easiness of his kind.

Abner left the courthouse and started toward the yellow office on the west side of the square. As he went along he did not pause to gossip with the country folk as he once would have done. Too many perplexities were in his mind to permit such aimless conversations. He was acquiring the focussed attitude of the town. He heard somebody drawl, "Money has turned Ab Teeftaller into a stuck-up town johnny. I guess he's forgot his daddy died in the county jail."

A group of men were already forming below Railroad Jones's high porch in anticipation of the magnate's new draft on labour. They were talking about the lawsuit, about what wages Jones would pay. As Abner came up they turned to him.

"How's this suit goin' to turn out, Ab?" asked a black-bearded man. "I hear Perry Northcutt's got ever' foot of Railroad Jones' lan' tied up in mortgages."

"Don't worry," said Abner in an oracular manner, "the only way to beat Railroad Jones in a lawsuit is to kill him."

At this reply the hillmen burst into raucous laughter, which fell into silence as Railroad Jones waddled out on his porch. There was something grim in his square jaundiced face, purple birthmark, and little burnt-out eyes. He caught and held the attention of the crowd.

"Boys," he began in his spewing voice, "you know what we're up ag'inst here in Lanesburg."

"Yeh, Railroad, we know."

"Arntown wants to grab our railroad after we got it built. I ain't callin' names, but the man I partnered with has gone back on me and says he won't allow me to finish the road I promised you folks."

A murmur from the crowd at this.

"I told him to take his money an' go, that us Lanesburg folks could build our own road an' we wuzn't beholdin' to no little razor-backed banker from Arntown."

The crowd roared raucously at this. "You said it, Railroad!"

The magnate shook his fist and swung his mighty jowl. "Yeh, an' I'll say more. You boys stick to me an' I'll finish this road if it takes the las' cent I can scrape an' the las' breath I can draw. I say you farmers in Lane County ain't goin' to be shut off from the markets of the worl' no longer. I say if the little two-by-fours of Arntown injoy a railroad, why in God's name shouldn't the broad-gauge citizens of Lanesburg, the county seat, have the same advantages? Ain't we as good as they air? Ain't we better?"

Came a drawling cheer. "By God, we're with ye, Railroad!"

Railroad shook his big head. "Stay with me an' we'll have a express train whistlin' in the courthouse square. Don't let no silver-tongued orator turn you away from your own intrusts, boys. All the money I ever made I made workin' for you, an' damn near all you ever made, you made workin' for me." Laughter at this. "United we stan', divided we fall. Walk up, boys, sign the payroll, and begin to draw yore pay this minute, an' we'll build a railroad in spite of Perry Northcutt an' the devil! Come on up!"

At this the men looked at one another, and when Abner climbed the steps everybody followed him. Railroad Jones waved them into his office, where a clerk took their names on the payroll.

The magnate shook hands warmly with Abner. "I 'preciate this, Abner," he said in his closed voice. "I haven't seen you sence the night of the dance, what's the matter?"

"I—jest haven't been aroun'," said Abner awkwardly.

"Me an' Addy's been sorter expectin' you."

Here the conversation was interrupted by some of the men beginning to file out.

"When do we report, Mr. Jones?"

"Right away—Sheriff Bascom is goin' down with ye."

"We heard he was.—Not goin' to be any trouble, d'reckon?"

"Reckon shorely not. They ain't nobody big enough fools to tell a set of men like you they won't let ye work. If so, you boys know what to do?"

"Hell, yes."

The black-bearded man winked. "There's one feller in this crowd who stopped two revenuers from raidin' his still one night."

"Nobody ort to disturb a man at work," returned Railroad, and winked solemnly.

Another gust of wheezing and hacking laughter. The men filed on out, leaving in the office the rank odour of their unwashed bodies. As they were going out, a motor honked outside, and a little later Adelaide came in among the outgoing stream of men. As she passed them she spoke to some, nodded brightly to every individual workman. They all knew her and gave her "Good-days," "Howdy, Adelaide?" "Howdy do, Addy?"

Her bright cordiality to them might have been timed.

"Dad," she called, "got those blanks ready for me?"

Railroad turned to his table and drew out a drawer.

"Come an' see if these ain't them, Addy."

In passing she flung at the youth, "Hello, Abner!—Yes, that's them, Daddy."

"As you drive over to Arntown, you might give Abner a lift to the camp, Addy," suggested the magnate.

The girl gave Abner a swift glance. "So you *are* going to be with us after all?" she said with a warm inflection.

Abner stood by the big goods box full of papers.

"Yeh, I told yore daddy I was," he said, a little constrained.

"Well—we hadn't heard anything more. . . ." She stepped over, took the bundle of papers from her father's hand, then started past Abner to the door.

"Ready to go?" she asked, smiling.

Abner acquiesced and went out with her to the yellow roadster. They got into it and eased away into the square without a word. Owing to the crowd, the girl had to sound her horn constantly. Half-dozing countrymen would come awake at her blasts, look around, and then with a movement that was slow, and yet somehow appeared to be startled, would get awkwardly from in front of the big machine.

Once Adelaide smiled and said, "He needs dancing lessons, but I suppose he would think it a sin to take 'em."

Abner was faintly amused at the idea; then for some reason he thought of Nessie Sutton and his amusement vanished. They said no more until they were out of Lanesburg, rushing silently down a hill. Beneath them lay a small creek valley glowing with the red and yellow of autumn. Adelaide glanced at the scene from time to time in the midst of her driving.

"Isn't it gorgeous?" she admired.

"Yes, it is—yonder's a lot of mighty good white oaks." Abner pointed out a great length of russet foliage.

Adelaide laughed. "I declare, have you got so you see so many white oaks and chestnuts, so many cross ties and so many saw logs every time you look at the woods?"

"Well—they're there, ain't they?"

"Not unless you have a kind of sawmill in your eye, so that every tree you look at falls into logs, lumber, and cross ties. You never see the trees at all . . . that's the kind of person my husband will be, I suppose, no matter whom I marry." Adelaide pressed her accelerator and increased the gale about their ears.

Abner hardly knew what to say. He looked at Adelaide's half-ironic, half-wistful smile with a feeling of how essentially alien she was to him. The thought of marrying her seemed vague and impossible. He tried to think of himself possessing the Jones mansion with Adelaide in it; this pretty, cynical, poised girl for a wife. The more he thought of it the more impossible it appeared.

"Why didn't you come to see me the day after the ball?" asked Adelaide, breaking her silence at last.

Abner hesitated. "I wasn't sure you wanted to see me."

"Why—on account of the gossip?"

Abner was surprised and a little shocked at her coolness. "Well—yes—the other girls turned aginst me."

Adelaide shrugged a shoulder. "They're silly—in this world a girl may get her frocks made to order, but not her husband."

The implication in this careless phrase caused a lifting sensation in Abner's midriff which marks a joyful surprise. He was on the verge of putting an arm around her very self-assured little waist and asking, "Do you love me, Adelaide, and will you marry me?" but she was so self-poised and self-contained that to mention love to Adelaide seemed somehow incongruous. He substituted in a slightly tense voice, "Did you see Buckingham Sharp that night, Adelaide?"

The girl glanced at him with a faint smile. "Certainly I did."

The youth grew more nervous.

"Well—are you—er—going to marry him?"

She shook her head in a slight negative.

Abner looked intently at the curve of her cheek over her furs. He had a nervous feeling of having come to the brink of a sharp turn in his life. He was half afraid she would laugh at him as he asked in a tone that caught somewhere in his throat, "Are—you—going to marry me—after all?"

He watched breathlessly, fearing a smile, when to his relief, her small bosom lifted in a little spasm.

"I—I think so, Abner," and she went on immediately as if justifying herself. "At least you are not conceited; and you don't think I'm just waiting to tumble in your arms. And you really are good-looking, and you will soon learn to dance, though, of course, I won't want to dance with you when you're my husband; and you have farms. . . ."

Abner put an arm around her and leaned over to kiss her with a jubilant relieved feeling.

"You don't have to apologize, Adelaide!" he cried, and pressed his lips toward her mouth.

Adelaide laughed, but turned her face quickly away. "Let's don't spoon here on the road. I was just counting your good points aloud. Goodness knows I've counted them a thousand times to myself.—You like to hear them, don't you?"

"Shore I do!" cried the youth, but in his heart he felt the lack of that intimate feeling which he had known with Nessie. This girl, somehow, was so self-contained she excluded him completely.

"Abner, let me ask now, if it will be all right with you, after we are married, for me to dance with other men?"

"Why—yes," drawled Abner, surprised, but not feeling the slightest jealousy of anticipation.

"And I want other men to call on me and be nice to me, just as they do to other married women in other places. Why, I think it's awful the way the Lanesburg women do. When they get married they bury themselves. They have no mixed social life at all. They never really talk to anybody except other women and their husbands. Why, Abner, that's not civilized! No wonder they grow into a lot of tittle-tattles and backbiters; women just naturally get that way unless they see a lot of men—just as men get profane and vulgar if they don't see a lot of women. If folks would just use their sex right, it would keep them sweet!"

During this outburst Adelaide gradually had stopped her car. Now they were standing still and she stated her position with more passion than she had spoken of their marriage.

"Why, ye-es," agreed Abner, "I guess that's right."

"I want to lead a human life, even here in Lanesburg. Of course, I'll have to stay here. Daddy's property is like a great big ball and chain. It will be one around you, too, Abner. Neither of us can ever possibly get away. Nobody ever gets away from Lanesburg—we're either too rich or too poor."

Abner began to smile. "Maybe they can when the railroad is built?"

"Yes, yes, no doubt—well, run along and build it. Goodbye."

Abner observed for the first time that the motor had stopped.

"Do I get out here?"

"Of course, silly, this is the old Coltrane place. The camp's right over that hill past the house." She pointed and Abner climbed out of the car.

"Now, don't let the strikers get you," she cautioned, leaning over and touching one of his hands on the door.

On the impulse she moved to him quickly. "Kiss me, after all," she said, lifting her face and holding out her arms to him.

Abner put his arms about her and kissed her lips. He caught the faint fragrance of her face powder, and his arms were about furs which felt exquisitely soft and warm. The curve of her torso seduced an extra heartbeat, and he would have lifted her against his chest, but this was Adelaide Jones, and the open country and chill October sun forbade. He stepped back from the car.

"I'll watch out for strikers."

Adelaide looked up the road and whispered, "Look—that man saw us guzzling."

Abner laughed. "What he saw was all right."

Adelaide gave a little shrug. "It was more than all right, it was positively virtuous. You know the great virtue in this county, Abner, is iciness to the opposite sex—well, come to see me when you get back to Lanesburg," and laughing at her own irony, she sent her car forward at gathering speed.

CHAPTER VIII

ABNER TEEFTALLOW stood on the hillside brooding over the sinfulness of sex, yet mixed with this in an alternating current was the thought of the value of the timber which he could see on the old Coltrane place. As he stood thinking now of sin, now of value, a perfect epitome of all hill thought, a voice with a foreign accent asked, "Were you looking for me, Mr. Teeftallow?"

Abner turned to see the man whom Adelaide had pointed out down the road. He recognized the intense studious face of Shallburger, the labour organizer whom he had known in Irontown.

"Well, no," ejaculated Abner, surprised at seeing Shallburger on a country road. He looked out of place.

"Then it's luck," said Shallburger in his quick accents. "I sent out a call for every loyal member of the union to come and resist the heartless encroachments of the pluto-crats of labour." He dropped his voice. "They're goin' to bring a bunch of scabs here."

"They are?" echoed Abner, grasping the situation with the slowness of his kind.

"Yes, a bunch of new men to take the place of the old men. I understand the sheriff's coming with 'em.—Have you got a gun?"

"Nachelly."

Shallburger squeezed his arm. "To-day you can stand up for the cause of labour. You'll be a soldier in the army of human liberation! It's a glorious opportunity, Teeftallow, to carry on the battle for social progress, the uplifting of men!"

Abner became more and more disconcerted; he cleared his throat and wet his lips.

"Er—hadn't you heard about me?" He hesitated, although he knew that Shallburger had not heard of his good fortune. The organizer never talked of anything except the wrongs of the working men. "I inherited a lot of farms from my gran'-daddy."

The foreigner's face lighted up. "Fine! Magnificent! You can be an example; a beacon on a high hill!"

"How?" asked Abner, mystified.

"By throwing your influence on the side of labour, by fighting the battles of the working men!"

"But look here," persisted Abner, thinking the fellow must not have understood, "I tell you I ain't a workin' man any more. I'm well fixed, Mr. Shallburger."

The organizer stared at him in turn. "What difference does that make?"

Abner was more confounded. "What dif'runce! Why, my Lord, man, it's jest like quittin' one job an' workin' at another. I'm on the side of money now 'cause I got money!"

"Does your money change the human right of life?" demanded Shallburger in amazement. "Is it a reason why the children of these poor crackers around here should grow up in poverty, ignorance, and crime?"

"You're damn whistlin' it is!" cried Abner, answering the spirit and not the letter of the question. "To git a man to work fer you is jest a trade, that's all. When I work fer somebody I want the highest price, nachelly, but when I har somebody I want to pay the lowest price. That's plain common sense. If a man don't do that he'll bust hisse'f."

"Would you turn traitor to the cause of humanity for money?" shouted Shallburger. "You're not worthy the name of——"

"You damn fool!" yelled Abner. "When a man's a workin' man, then workin' is his side, but when he's got money, then money's his side. If I've got a pocket full of money an' flop to the workin' side, then I'd be a traitor for leavin' my side. Let the rich man stan' by the rich an' the pore by the pore! Now, by God, I'm rich an' I'm stan'in' with 'em, an' if you don't like it you can go to hell!"

An invitation to go to the place of eternal punishment is usually the end of all arguments in Lane County. Mr. Shallburger seemed not to realize this. He stood looking distressfully at Abner, and presently began again with persistent persuasiveness, "But, Mr. Teeftallow, let us look to see which side has right and justice and charity on it——"

"Well, we've got the Bible on our side," interrupted Abner. "Didn't you ever read in the Bible about the feller who lent out his money first here and then there, an' they all got to tradin' with it—I forgit jest how it went; I heard Perry Northcutt tellin' it—but anyway, the idyah was to skin 'em when you can, an' that's in the Bible, Shallburger, an' there's no gittin' around that!"

Shallburger underwent such facial contortions that Abner thought he was about to have a stroke.

"The Bible! The Bible!" he spewed. "Record of an obsolete morality of a barbarous society. What does the Bible know about the complexities and injustices of our proletarian world or the rights of labour! There was no labour in those days."

"Now, look here," interposed Abner solemnly. "When you butt yore head agin the Bible you're buttin' agin a stone wall. Moreover, I won't lissen to you, because God'lmighty might send down a streak of lightnin' to kill you an' hit me by mistake. So it's fare you well if you're goin' to talk like that."

With this the hillman climbed over the rail fence which bordered the road and walked up through a field of scrawny corn stalks toward the old Coltrane place on the hill.

Abner walked quickly, uneasy, because Shallburger by his blasphemy had exposed them both to a bolt from Heaven. The hill youth bristled at the recollection of Shallburger's stupid theories—they were so dead against common sense.

He could not conceive how a sane man could think like that.

As Abner hurried to escape any carelessly directed lightning bolt the deity might hurl, a rabbit leaped up before him and ran across his path from right to left. The young man stopped and regarded it with a mental oath.

"Damn that rabbit," he thought; "it'll bring me bad luck. It could jest as easy have run the other way."

He stood several moments, perturbed over the course of the rabbit. The omen of its direction brought before Abner the purpose of his journey and predicted for it an unfortunate outcome.

In this grayer mood he approached the dilapidated old manor on the hill. From the side Abner could see the weather-beaten columns of the piazza which were two stories in height. A little balcony which marked the second story was stuck halfway between the floor and ceiling of the piazza. A long ell of rooms ran back from the front chambers. Here and there a piece of weather boarding had fallen down or was hanging by an end, displaying a black opening in the gray wall. Several windows needed reglazing; others had been recently mended, to judge by their yellow, unpainted sashes. The old house was in its last stages, but it still had the bleak dignity of that old South which Abner had never known.

Abner had been born in this manor. In it his mother had spent her lonely and finally unbalanced life; his grandfather, old Judge Jefferson Coltrane, had built it; and his ne'er-do-well father, Linsey Teeftallow, had lost it. Now this melancholy family history recurred to Abner's mind as he approached the house on the hill. Certain salient features reasserted themselves from the misty memories of his childhood. He recalled the little balcony thrust out above the great door of the central hall; and the epic arc of the well sweep which thrust its pole, it had seemed to his childish eyes, quite to the sky—and there it was now, surprisingly shortened by the years.

The well sweep, the little balcony, an old horse-apple tree, and his mother, a thin sallow woman, not quite a hillwoman, moving in settled melancholy about the gray old mansion; such were his memories.

Abner meant to walk through the Coltrane farm on his way to the railroad camp and look at the timber on the estate. So now he directed his steps toward the lower side of the garden fence which was screened with elder bushes and blackberry briars and was set at irregular intervals with candelabra of sumac burning with flames of brilliant red seed.

As he walked through the corn stalks the gauze of spiders continually tickled Abner's cheeks and eyelashes and the hairs on the back of his hands. The youth must have been walking amid a bewilderment of webs. Every step he took brushed away this enginery of destruction, gins and traps, spread by the aristocrats of the insect world with indomitable patience and endless cunning.

As Abner passed this tangled fence at the back of the house, the creaking of the old well sweep caught his attention. He looked up, saw the long wooden arm coming down, and then with that rural instinct to see and identify every person in one's vicinity, the teamster moved about, peering through the hedge until he made out a woman pulling on the sweep rope. A few paces farther on he turned into a little weed-choked gate which would open a bare foot at the bottom, but the rickety top would press back perhaps a yard. He let himself through, meaning to ask for a drink, and as he rustled the small growth, the woman at the well turned.

For perhaps thirty seconds the two stood perfectly still looking at each other; the woman with her arms extended upward to pull down the sweep. At last she whispered, framing the words with her lips with difficulty as persons do under great stress, "Abner—what you are doing here?"

The teamster nodded across the hill, "I was goin' to the railroad camp."

"To fight?"

"I—don't know—we want to finish the railroad."

Nessie let the rope slip back up through her fingers.

"I heard you were interested in the railroad," she said in a pathetic voice.

"How d'je mean?" asked Abner uncomfortably.

"I heard you were going to marry Mr. Jones's daughter —are you?"

The youth straightened, on the defensive. "Look here, Nessie!" he cried, "you sayin' that to me, an' you already married to Belshue!"

The girl stood silent with her hand resting on the bucket which swung at the edge of the well curb. It seemed to Abner that an almost invisible film of age had settled over Nessie; her features were sharpened; her blue eyes appeared larger and sadder. Her bosom had ripened and the lines of her body were a little changed from child-bearing. The dress she wore was somewhat soiled about the bosom from suckling her baby.

"I hear you really are rich," began Nessie again; she hesitated a moment, then, colouring faintly beneath the almost imperceptible roughening of her skin, "Are you still studying to be a lawyer, Abner?"

"No, I'm not doin' nothin' now—jest collectin' on my land." Here he remembered that he had come to arrange a settlement on this very house and farm.

The girl gave a deep sigh. "I wish you could have made some great somebody, Abner . . ."

"Well—I'm goin' to be rich, Nessie."

"Ye-es . . ." Her tone was dissatisfied, freighted with the unrealized dreams of her novels. Presently she began on a new tack. "You know, Abner, this is the sort of house I always meant," nodding at the decaying manor, "only, of course, kept nice."

At this moment a thin cry, repeated in an expressionless monotone, like some little animal in pain, came to Abner's ears. Nessie stooped swiftly to a basket on the ground and out of it picked up the tiniest bundle of a baby he had ever seen. He moved toward her with a catch in his breathing.

"Nessie," he gasped, "is that it?"

The girl glanced up at him in affirmation and then gazed tenderly at the little morsel at her bosom. Abner bent over the wry little face with a gauze of dark baby hair on its head and its staring dark slate eyes which would change later into the brown of Abner's. Its tiny face was wrinkled against the weak sunshine and its doll-like fists made aimless motions about its breast. Abner touched it and felt a tiny hand grasp the end of his thumb.

"What's its name?" he asked in a shaken voice.

"Nessie Teeftallow Belshue," whispered Nessie, still looking at the baby.

"Teeftallow!"

Nessie nodded at her baby.

"Then he—knows?"

"Certainly, Abner, I—I told him before he—married me. I—I couldn't do anything else."

The irony of the situation swept over the hillman with a sickening effect. He looked at the mother of his little daughter.

"Jest to think! Jest to think, if you had waited two hours longer. . . ."

Nessie looked at him with a paling face.

"What—what do you mean?"

"Why, I—I come to Arntown that night, lookin' for you."

"Lookin' for me, to—to—marry me?"

Abner nodded. "But you had gone."

Nessie steadied herself with a hand on the well curb.

"I—didn't know—the men, the whitecaps—I was so scared, Abner . . ."

"Yes, I know—they beat me."

The young mother gazed with horrified eyes at Abner. She sat weakly down on the curb, looking as if she might fall into the well with her baby. She began weeping silently, her tears falling on her baby's clothes.

"Oh, oh, Abner, what a terrible thing! What a cruel thing! If they had only let us alone!"

The pity of it; the tragedy of it; the nearness with which her girlish dream had skirted her life, broke her heart. She got to her feet with her baby, picked up her basket, and moved unseeingly toward the ruinous old manor.

Abner turned and walked on amid confused and painful emotions; the sad tender change in Nessie which motherhood had brought; the tiny baby, his own baby to be reared and cared for by Belshue; and now Nessie was really living in his old ancestral home, while he was an outsider—he could still feel the tiny hand of the child, like a peach petal coiled about the end of his thumb—and all this was because of the mob; the flounderings of the great moral mob; his life and Nessie's and their child's had fallen apart in confusion. What if his little daughter's hand did curl about his thumb, and about his heart, too, the sensibilities of the mob, who had flayed him in bloody agonies, must be respected. And presently the queer fact came to him that thanks to the mob he was the father of a little girl by a woman whom it melted his heart to see or even to think of, and he was betrothed to Adelaide Jones.

The teamster walked on through the long unkempt manor yard meaning to climb the fence at the end and get into the road to the camp, when an old man, who apparently had formed out of the air, came meeting Abner. With a little qualm the young man saw that it was Mr. Belshue, the jeweller whom he had known in Irontown.

The man had gone gray and withered during his few months on the Coltrane place. Time, apparently, had taken the jeweller's own burin to engrave his face. He stopped Abner with a gesture.

"That's Teeftallow—Abner Teeftallow, isn't it?"

"Yes," said Abner, defensive in air and tone.

"What did you do to my wife to send her to the house crying?"

Abner thought quickly what he could say.

"I—was talking to her . . ." he began, trying to frame something.

"Yes—did you insult her?" trembled the old man. "Did you do like all the folks around here—insult her by word or act?"

"Insult her! Insult Nessie!" Amazement filled Abner's voice.

Belshue stared at him. "But she was crying—I saw her—you hurt her somehow!"

Abner studied the gray, angry old man and wondered what would be the best thing to say; the best thing for Nessie. If he simply said Nessie had shown him her baby and wept, that might arouse his jealousy and make the girl's lot harder.

"I—I come up when she was drawin' watter, Mr. Belshue, an' I guess I must uh give her a start, the bucket swung aginst her hand and hurt her. I was mighty sorry. . . ." Abner's mind always worked in concretes.

Neither the jeweller's anger nor suspicions were allayed.

"Well, I don't know what you did, but, Teeftallow, I tell you for your own safety, as well as my wife's comfort, to go away from here and stay off this place." His voice rose a trifle. "Don't enter my lands; don't ever set foot on this plantation again."

Abner reddened at being ordered off the farm. It was the kind of insult in the hills that has caused more homicides than any other one thing.

"All right, Mr. Belshue, I'll git off now—I was jest takin' a nigh cut to the railroad camp, I wasn't expectin' to see your wife, wasn't thinkin' anything about her—but I tell you now, I own this farm, and the time's goin' to come mighty soon when you're goin' to haff to git off yorese'f!"

"When you get possession by law, we'll leave it to you, but don't persecute me and mine till then!"

Abner nodded angrily. "You'll be leavin' soon!" he blustered. "I'll—I'll——" and then at the thought of Nessie, he hesitated, then stammered,

"N-no, Mr. Belshue, I—I won't do that. I'll stay off. I won't give you no more trouble. An', honest, I didn't know I'd meet Nessie. If I had, I never would have clumb over the hill."

The teamster turned and walked self-consciously down the long eminence. Past the brow of the hill there came into his sight the tents of the railroad camp, the long shanghai stables, the line of track, and the little unsheltered platform where he had stood months before waiting for the train to take him to Irontown and to his torture by the mob.

CHAPTER IX

AFTER his altercation with Abner, A. M. Belshue hurried to the old manor, filled with anxiety for his young wife whose sobbing retreat from the well he had seen as he came up the private road toward his home.

Notwithstanding what Abner had said he persisted in an uneasy and a kind of insincere belief that Abner had insulted his wife and this had caused her weeping. He told himself that Abner had spoken to her with the contempt, the crude hill irony, or the cold reserved manner which the hill folk use toward a woman who mothers a child altogether out of love and not out of foresight. Undoubtedly Abner Teeftallow had so used his wife, and that was why she wept. But even while the jeweller repeated this assertion to himself, in the depths of his mind lay a questioning, a repressed doubt, which wrought on his nerves. From this subconscious depth a phrase came to Belshue precisely as if another person had spoken the words inside his ear. The voice said, "She ought to be very grateful for all you've done for her." And with this desolate comment, the voice disappeared again somewhere within the sunless caverns of his being.

The jeweller hurried in through the pauperish magnificence of his piazza into a stately hallway whose tinted stuccoed ceiling had faded and fallen away in places to be renewed by smooth whitewashed plaster; and this in turn had grayed and cracked and fallen. The jeweller's inner voice had been put back where it belonged and he was thinking, "Insulting a woman after his conduct—I ought to have run him off the place with a Winchester. . . ." He would next time.

Belshue passed into a large living room which he had furnished for Nessie, but she was not there. She seemed

337

to have been out for some time. The autumn wind rattled the great French windows and flung out the muslin curtains which Nessie had put up. Yet with all its draughtiness, the odour of infants, which careless hill mothers allow, permeated the air. Three drying diapers hung on chairs before a great fireplace in which a log smouldered. As an ironic touch, the capstone of the fireplace was carved with an old coat of arms which must have belonged to Abner Teeftallow—the coat of arms, the unfragrant cloths of the baby, an unmade bed, a hearthstone scattered with ashes and bits of kindling. . . .

Belshue went through an adjoining room which once had been a legal library. All left of it now were some private acts of the Tennessee legislature; two volumes of Blackstone; an early copy of Kent—books which had daunted the eloquence of the auctioneer who had gutted the old judge's library. Cheek by jowl with them in their walnut shelves were towels, napkins, hammers, wrenches, buckles, brads, harness, dried peppers, cured onions, a tuft of mullein to make medicinal tea, gourds of seeds from flourishing gardens; a kind of illiterate *hoi polloi* elbowing the last remnants of the old aristocracy of law books.

The jeweller went through one deserted room after another with a growing fear in his heart, when finally he passed out of the dining room along a covered brick walk about twenty feet long to the detached kitchen. In this dark room he heard a rattling and entered, expecting to see Lizzie, the Negro cook. Instead he saw Nessie herself bending over the stove besmudged with pots. Belshue looked at his wife in surprise.

"Where's Lizzie?"

Nessie answered, with a long breath, "She was afraid to stay here—I don't mind doing this."

"Afraid to stay here, why?"

"The neighbours have been talking to her."

Belshue felt an impulse to ask angrily, "What did they say?" but he hesitated for fear it would bring up the old unpleasant subject, but finally he did ask the question in a colourless tone:

"What did they say?"

"They told Lizzie they saw a light moving about your second-story windows at night."

"Why, certainly!" cried the jeweller, surprised and irritated, "that was me regulating my watches."

"I told her that, but Lizzie wanted to know why you were regulating watches at night; why you bothered at all to regulate a lot of old watches. I never could make her understand it was just your pastime. We talked about it for a long time." Nessie gave another long sigh. "Finally she said she had to go because her sister was sick; she hated to leave me—niggers always say that."

The middle-aged jeweller stood looking at his young wife with a sort of frustrated tenderness for her and a desire to shield her and keep her looking fresh and flowerlike. The faint veil which maternity had spread over her had been saddening to him; whereas had the child been his own, this change in her appearance would have been pensive and sweet, like the air of an old song.

"I'll get you another cook." Then, after a moment, he said, "if necessary I'll—quit tinkering with the watches."

Nessie shook her head without noticing his renunciation. "I don't think any of them will stay."

"How about a white woman?"

A look almost of fright came into the young woman's face.

"No, Mr. Belshue, don't get a white woman, I—I——" she controlled her voice and gave a reason which was not the real one, "I'm used to nigger servants. . . ."

Her disturbance brought up again to the jeweller's mind the isolation that spread over their two lives and left them marooned here in this old manor, cut off from all companionship.

"Can I do anything to help you now, Nessie?" he asked.

The girl looked around with that lack of administrative ability which reduces work to drudgery.

"No-o-o, I don't see——" Here, to her surprise, she saw that her water bucket was dry. She had believed it full.

"I thought I had some water. You may bring some if you will, Mr. Belshue."

Her notion that she already had water stirred a painful suspicion in Belshue which he could not analyse. He stepped across to the bucket, but hesitated, exploring his uneasiness and trying to define it. Some impulse caused him to ask abruptly, "Nessie, did you hurt your hand at the well while ago?"

She looked at her hands. "No—why?"

"Nothing," he said in a kind of uncertain relief. "That Teeftallow boy said you hurt your hand at the well while ago, that was what made you cry."

Nessie looked at the jeweller with widened eyes, drew a breath, then said in a low tone, "No—he was—mistaken— I didn't hurt my hand."

By this Belshue knew that Nessie meant Abner had told an untruth. She never said any one told an untruth, but always softened it into a "mistake."

The husband thought quickly and gratefully, "That proves Teeftallow lied; then he must have insulted her." He had it on his lips, was drawing in a breath to ask, "Did he insult you, Nessie?" when a certain thing stopped him. He shifted his question to, "Why did you cry, Nessie?" when again he paused with the shaken feeling of a man with one foot slipping over a precipice. The inhibiting thought was this: he knew that his wife would hesitate, pale, but finally she would tell him the exact truth. A chariness of intruding into his wife's confidence had grown on him in the few months of their married life. She would tell him the truth. Now, as he stood with his unuttered question on his lips, "Why did you weep?" a sudden discomforting analysis dawned on his mind for the first time. He had made a mistake when he had searched out and married his ideal, a sincere truthful woman. He had always imagined he wanted a completely truthful wife, but he had not anticipated that she might have some unpleasant truths to tell him. Nessie never thrust her truths upon him, but when he pressed her she told him honestly what she thought and never made any allowance for his sensibilities in her religious adherence to verity. She would not feed him comfortable untruths, which if repeated often enough and earnestly enough, might in time become truths. And there occurred to Belshue the disquieting fact that an ability and willingness to lie with emotion and conviction were perhaps the most precious traits of character which any wife could bring to any husband.

The jeweller came out of these odd reflections to the matter in hand.

"Anyway, he won't make you cry any more, Nessie. I ordered him off the place."

The girl looked at her husband with widened eyes. "You didn't, Mr. Belshue!"

"Why, certainly, I did; do you want him to——" Again he broke off his natural exclamation to avoid a frank answer and substituted, "You don't want him to make you cry, do you?"

"No-o," hesitated Nessie, "I suppose it is best." Then, plucking up her resolution, "But nobody ever comes here, Mr. Belshue, now that Lizzie has gone. . . ."

"I'll get you another cook!" exclaimed the jeweller, annoyed. "It seems I'm no company."

"Yes, you are, but—but it's lonesome for both of us, and —and when somebody comes, once in a long while. . . ."

The jeweller was exasperated. His wife practised shifts and evasions well enough when it came to—well, what had it come to?—to something she herself desired; but for him, she had nothing but flint-like truths. The torment hidden in Belshue's soul suddenly rose up.

"Nessie," he cried, "I should think mere gratitude for what I have done for you would make you see—make you feel——" He paused a moment with a spasm twitching the muscles of his face. "You—you still love him," he said in a throaty tone, "that's the trouble!"

Nessie stared at the jeweller with her own face whitening.
"I—I told you I loved him long ago, Mr. Belshue!"

"But you always will!"

The girl was painfully moved. She pressed a smudged
hand against her full breast. "I—I don't know, I—suppose
so."

"A man who would mistreat you—seduce you!" cried the
jeweller, "leave you helpless, about to become a mother, in
the hands of a mob! drive you to the point of suicide! And
I——— My God, I gave up everything I had on earth for you
—a business, a sort of friendship among the men. I was the
only person in Irontown who did not spit on you, but somehow or other, I still felt you were pure and fine, and—I
loved you, Nessie——— Oh, Nessie, it seems to me mere gratitude———" He paused, miserably holding out his hands
to his wife.

But the jeweller was middle-aged and had that inhuman
remoteness which middle age always has for youth. The
girl could not enter into his emotions at all. She began
defending her lover at once.

"But you are not fair to Abner, Mr. Belshue," she gasped,
"he—he was coming to Irontown to—to—take me away
the night the mob wh-whipped him." This last phrase she
whispered, and then began weeping again at this exquisitely
edged misfortune, sobbing, drawing her breath in gasps, wiping her eyes on the back of her wrist to avoid her smudged
hand.

The simplicity of her grief filled Belshue with utter despair. All the fears and forebodings which had lain uneasily
in the depths of his heart rose up and were realized. It
seemed to Belshue that this sweet, sincere, untidy girl was
at that moment withdrawn slowly from him, that she moved
physically away from him never to return.

He faced about and went slowly out of the kitchen door,
forgetting the bucket. He walked slowly and with a tottery
effect of age into the great house and up a flight of curving
stairs into a room he had set apart for his own. In it, over

by a great window, was a rack of old watches which had never been called for by their owners. They were the accumulation of years. Their running filled the room with a faint myriad-voiced ticking.

The jeweller mechanically compared his master watch with the others, turning his eyes from one dial to another in regular order. As he did so he whispered through gray lips, "It seems mere—gratitude . . ." He did not complete his sentence even mentally, but sat down in his chair and listened to the ticking of the watches.

The sound suggested once more to Belshue that Time might be a Lilliputian army double-quicking down the long slope of eternity into nothingness.

CHAPTER X

AS ABNER drew near the railroad camp he saw that Sheriff Bascom's labour gang was already in possession of the stables and tents. Men were coming and going; teamsters chivvied mules out of the stables, and their oaths came to Abner through the hazy autumn air. Now and then other sounds were overpowered by the sudden churring of some big tractor, which roared for a few seconds and then coughed into silence after the manner of cold machinery.

The stir, the movement, the purposefulness of all these activities brought to Abner a renewed feeling that life was solid and real; a motif which his own existence in Lanesburg lacked.

He walked down the hill, drawing in deep lungfuls of air. He was going to do something at last. For the next month or two he would work, sweat, swear during the day, and tipple and gamble at night.

He strode on toward this final taste of life with joyful strides when he saw ahead of him a little black-haired fellow with two buckets dipping water out of a great spring. This man or boy wore the neatest overalls that Abner had ever seen; in fact, the legs of the overalls had been pressed and the creases stood out clear cut in the sunlight. The fellow rinsed his buckets with great care in the lower part of the spring, then swished water in his barrels, threw that out, and finally began filling the barrels from the undisturbed upper part of the pool.

As Abner approached this finical labourer, his foot rattled a stone, and immediately the little man started up, jerked a pistol from his pocket and drew it on the teamster. A shock went through Abner.

"Hey, what the hell!" he shouted, stopped in his tracks by the moral influence of the revolver. "Put down that gun!"

The little man stared with dilated eyes, but presently recognition dawned on his face, and he cried apologetically, "Oh, is that you, Mr. Teeftallow? I thought you were a striker. Come on down."

"Hell far," exclaimed Abner nervously, "what were you goin' to do—shoot him?"

"No, but I was going to make him go away."

Then Abner recognized Sim Pratt in creased overalls and buckskin gloves to keep the bucket handles from skinning his palms. He had a tan four-in-hand around the collar of his blue working shirt; and it all set Abner laughing.

"So you fin'ly got to come with the boys, Sim?"

"Yes," said Sim soberly, "I got to be water boy."

"I see you air. What kind of a weapon was that you pulled on me—wasn't it a thirty-two?"

"Yes, one I kept in the drug store."

Abner took off his hat and broke into large laughter.

"Got a thirty-two. Why, man, you shoot one of these country jakes with a thirty-two an' it would make him 'most mad enough to hit you. Out here in the country we use little dinkusses like that to throw kisses at the gals with." Abner laughed again, disregarding the brain storm which Mr. Pratt's thirty-two had just given him.

"What do you use?" asked Sim with a pink face.

"Somepin' when she barks you don't haff to strain yore years to find out whether she went off or not." Abner drew out a blue forty-five, swung it about in an expert manner, and put it back in his pocket.

"Well, how's ever'thing gittin' on, Sim?"

"All right, I guess."

"You made a hit with Beatrice Belle—goin' off to kill strikers with a great big gun like that."

"She—seemed to like me very well, last night," coloured Mr. Pratt.

From the drug clerk's manner Abner knew that the two had made an emotional scene of their parting. However, notwithstanding the friendly irony of his thoughts, knowledge that Pratt had reached terms of intimacy with his foster-sister had a sobering effect on Abner. He wondered if Beatrice would marry the little town johnny. . . .

"Well," he said at length, "let's fill up these barrels and get back to camp. I want to get strung out scoopin' dirt again." He took one of Pratt's buckets and the two men set to work filling the barrels.

In camp, Abner found the talk mainly about what the strikers would do; speculation ran all the way from Indian ambush to moral suasion.

From what Abner gathered, Shallburger had stopped the men about a mile up the road and had harangued them about humanity and the rights of labour.

"That Shallburger's a smart man," confided one of the caterpillar operators to Abner. "He made ever'thing sound mighty nice, but we had the law with us." By this he did not mean any abstract legal right, but the sheriff and deputies in person. These men were the law and what they did was perforce right.

In camp Abner was able even to get back the pair of mules which he had driven before on the plea that they understood his "cussin'," and that he hated to break in another pair. As he put the harness on them in the stable one of the mules, called Bud, bit at his hand, just as he had always done, and Abner warped Bud over the head with the bridle bits and kicked him in the belly, just as he had always done. It seemed to tone up both man and mule for the work that lay ahead of them.

Within half-a-day's time the new men were broken in and the whole crew were working smoothly. The long red level of the railroad levee began reaching through the last few miles to Lanesburg. However, the men worked in a kind of suspense; they were not altogether sure they would not be fired upon from the bushes. As the scoop men jerked their sweating mules around in a great circle they called to each other when opportunity offered, "Well, ain't nothin' happened yit?"

"Naw, guess it was mostly bluff."

"Well, by God, they ain't got a sign o' justice on their side. The idyah we kain't take a job they throwed down!"

"That Shallburger feller talked 'em into it—they won't do nothin'."

"Jest you fellers wait," grumbled a pessimist, "the meetin' ain't over till the shoutin's done."

After he had got into the swing of his work again, Abner went around and around through the loose dirt with the inner voices of his mind pursuing their different interests. It was odd to think that Nessie and Belshue lived in the old manor the tip of whose chimneys he could see over the brow of the hill. Then he mused that all this slowly lengthening railroad would one day belong to him. His thought of marriage with Adelaide always took the form of property.

Presently Sim Pratt came by with his water wagon and Abner pondered Beatrice Belle and the little drug clerk. His thoughts drifted on and on. When a man is at physical work out of doors all themes are on a parity in his mind. They are like suits before a bar of justice: the most trivial causes are heard as gravely as the most momentous. Philosophy was born out of doors. Yet in the midst of this mental meandering, Abner swore at his mules, jerked their bits, and occasionally snatched up a stone and flung at their heads, in a word, "fought them."

That night Sheriff Bascom posted guards about the camp; and as he had no authority to detail his men for any duty, he was forced to go about asking this one and that one to "sit up" during the night and watch the camp.

A number of men told the sheriff that they did not consider a guard necessary that night; others said they were not a good hand at sitting up; still others declared they were paid to work, not to watch. However, there were enough volunteers for the duty; and Bascom divided the night into two watches: from sundown till midnight, and from midnight till sun-up.

Along about sundown there was a great to-do in camp about the men who were to watch during the latter part of the night. An early supper was made in order that these men might go to bed early and obtain a half night's sleep. The other men in camp were cautioned to keep quiet to promote their rest. Sure enough, when supper was finished, the appointed men got up from the benches in the mess tent and filed off to their bunks. There was a certain sacrificial air about it which impressed their fellows. They were giving up their nightly gambling, drinking, fighting, and cursing for the benefit of their comrades and the good of the county. Among those who retired at this early hour was Abner Teeftallow.

All this parade about going to bed effectively banished sleep for Abner. He was not tired from his day's labour. He was in his rubbery teens and was keyed to days of toil and nights of carousing. So he lay on his bunk, listening to the flap of his tent in the windy night, and the occasional outburst of some excited crap shooter who forgot the camp pledge of silence and invoked a return of Little Joe or Big Dick from Boston.

Somewhat later in the night Abner heard a bootlegger and a customer just outside his tent chaffering over the price of a pint of moonshine liquor. Abner reflected that a pint of whisky might get him to sleep before midnight, and later, when he went on watch, it might help him stay awake till morning. So he got out of his blankets, put on his shoes, went around and bought the pint from a man in the black shadow of his tent wall.

He took a swallow of the fiery liquid; rubbed the top of the bottle, gave the vender a drink, and went back to bed with his purchase.

After his mouth and throat stopped burning, the current

of his thought grew pleasanter and more interesting. The fact that he was going to marry Adelaide Jones and live in the Jones mansion appeared in rosier colours than it ever had before. As for Adelaide, her strangeness would naturally wear away after she was his wife. He visualized her as he had last seen her that morning, driving over the hill to Iron-town—she was perpetually driving to Irontown; he spent a moment wondering why.

Here he had an impulse to reach out in the darkness and have another drink, but he thought he had had enough. That was the thing about drinking whisky, to know when you had had enough. Then he did take another drink, after all; the merest sip, which again set burning his mouth and throat.

Outside somebody fired a pistol very rapidly five times, and Abner heard a voice expostulating, "Let the men sleep!"

A little later somebody drew aside the flaps of his tent and told him it was time for him to come on watch. Abner arose, put on his shoes and trousers, took his bottle, and went yawning out into the night. The man who had come for him preceded him through the dim line of tents and came to a place on the levee overlooking a long shanghai stable. Here, seated on the levee over a little pile of coals, was the first watch of the night, mending his fire with some pieces of pine boxes. The fellow handed Abner a flashlight and apologized for the dying fire; he said he had gone to sleep "accident'ly."

Abner produced his bottle and offered the departing watch-man a swig to make him sleep well, while he himself took another to keep from getting drowsy during the long stretch till dawn. The men went away and Abner sat down by the freshly burning fire to watch.

The wind nipped him chilly after the warmth of his blankets, and the big fellow turned his collar up about his ears and reached into the inner pocket of his coat and felt the bulk of his pistol. A wide rustling of dead leaves filled the whole dark valley, and against this came an occasional squeal of a mule in the long stable, or the hard kicking of hoofs against the walls. From far off in the direction of the Coltrane place he heard the howl of a dog mourning the evil of night.

The howl made Abner think hazily of ghosts, of hobgoblins, of the eerie things that endanger the darkness to men. A shiver went through his chill frame. He bestirred himself and kicked the pine fagots so that they burst into flame and guttered down the wind.

He thought of Nessie and his child again with a queer detachment, little Nessie Teeftallow Belshue; and presently he would be living in the Jones's manor in Lanesburg, married to Adelaide. In what a queer way life worked! There was no justice to that; there was nothing supervising such things as that: it was just luck.

Abner drew out his bottle again with a feeling that here at least was something dependable in an unstable world. He took a draught of the liquid, then breathed through his open mouth while tears started to his eyes from the fiery stuff. He hoped his little girl baby would never marry a drinking man. A song started in Abner's head, and he began crooning aloud the words of a doleful tune.

He did not know how long he had been singing when a sense of movement among the bushes beyond the shanghai stable caught his attention. He had been, one might say, only tentatively tipsy, now this movement near the stable sobered him for the time being.

He arose swiftly from his sitting posture, took two long strides out of the firelight into the darkness, then moved silently down the levee toward the stables with his automatic ready. For some reason he was growing angry. He leveled on the dark bushes and snarled out, "Come out o' there, you damn snake. I'll blow hell out of ye!"

He was on the verge of shooting when a voice quite to one side of the suspected spot said, "Wait a minute, partner— you ain't shootin' peaceable men, air ye?"

"You're a striker, ain't ye?" snapped Abner, shifting his gun in the new direction.

"I'm a labour union man," returned the voice with dignity.

"Then the quicker you git out o' here the fewer holes you'll have in yore hide!"

"But, look here," argued the voice, "you're open to reason, ain't ye?"

Abner considered, and as all hillmen avow fealty to reason, he said that he was.

"I know you got yore gun on me," said the voice. "I'll hol' my han's up agin the sky so you can see 'em. An' le's git over there by the far an' talk this thing over. I ain't tryin' to do you no dirt, but I take it if you are ackshelly doin' me a wrong you'll be man enough to change over an' say I'm right."

This was fair speech, in fact, too fair and too glib; it sounded recitative.

"Well," agreed the guard suspiciously, "hol' 'em up where I can see 'em; come up slow an' lemme search you fer a gun an' I'll talk with ye."

As Abner made his proposition, a form with arms elevated arose against the sky.

"I got a gun," said the figure, "in my front breeches pocket on my left side. I could 'a' shot you when I come up if I wanted to, but I ain't wantin' to hurt nobody."

"Well, come on," said Abner, and the two walked together back up the railroad embankment and sat down by the fire.

"Well, what do you want to say?" asked Abner. Then peering through the dim light he saw he was talking to Tim Fraley, the man who had laughed at Nessie and her little baby girl. A regret went through the guard that he had not fired when he first heard Fraley's voice, but the next moment his vengeful mood passed, and he sat looking at the striker with an inactive dislike.

Mr. Fraley cleared his throat and asked, "Got anything to drink? It's purty cold."

Abner produced his bottle.

Mr. Fraley took some, wiped the neck, and returned it to

Abner ceremoniously, who lifted it to his own mouth out of politeness.

"It's like this," began Mr. Fraley, smacking his lips and blowing out gently, "if us workin' fellers don't stand together, the rich fellers will git richer and the pore, porer."

"I'm rich already," said Abner flatly.

Mr. Fraley came to a dead halt. "Why, by God, that's a fact," he admitted, quite taken aback; a moment later he excused himself by saying, "Of course, I couldn't tell it was you in the dark."

Abner was gratified at this common-sense view that Mr. Fraley took. This man admitted frankly that the rich were for the rich and the poor for the poor; a most pleasing contrast from Shallburger's muddled argument which Abner had heard that morning.

"But, after all," said Fraley, "we might as well set a spell. I was detailed to talk to jest one guard, an' if I tried another'n, I might git shot next time."

"Sure," agreed Abner, rather pleased with Mr. Fraley now, "set as long as you please—kinder lonesome watchin' the stables by myse'f." He produced his flask again.

Mr. Fraley helped himself.

"After all, Abner, you boys ain't doin' us right—takin' our job when we ain't been paid for what we done."

"I don't know—Railroad Jones is goin' to pay ever'body as soon as he gets a line of credit."

"Yeh, I see him payin' us—Railroad never paid nothin' to nobody."

"You fellers can sue him," counselled Abner.

"Sue hell," snarled Mr. Fraley bitterly. "I see myse'f with a debt of eighteen dollars an forty cents suin' Railroad through the Circuit Court an' the Supreme Court."

This personal reasoning moved Abner in a way no labour-union argument ever could have done.

"By God, that ain't right," he admitted, impersonally.

"I say it ain't," nodded Fraley.

Abner felt that such wrongs deserved another drink, so he

gave Mr. Fraley one. Then he suddenly and unaccountably began telling his companion about his little girl baby, her dark film of hair, her slate-coloured eyes which eventually would turn brown, and her name, "Nessie Teeftallow Belshue."

"Looks like Belshue would raise hell about that."

"Looks like I'd raise hell about him keepin' my little gal."

"Oh, well, a baby nachelly goes with its mammy. Then you're goin' to marry Adelaide Jones anyway; you'll have some more."

"Yeh, that's right, too," admitted Abner, growing more despondent than ever. He felt so bad he was forced to take another drink. It was for such crises as this in a man's life that Adam distilled the forbidden fruit and invented whisky.

Presently Abner broke off this wandering conversation to listen to a certain change in the overtones of the noise among the mules.

Mr. Fraley listened, too. "They're puttin up a hell of a fight," he suggested.

But Abner's country ears diagnosed the screams of the mules with more precision than did his companion's.

"That ain't a fight, somethin's botherin' them mules."

"Hell, what could be botherin' 'em?" yawned the striker.

"Don't know, guess I better step down an' see."

Abner got up lazily and stretched himself in the cold night air.

"Hell," disparaged Fraley, "you drink too much liquor, Abner; if you prance down there ever' time them mules whicker, you'll be on the jump all night long."

"No, I tell you there's somethin' the matter with them mules," insisted Abner, with a faint suspicion edging his tone.

By this time the stable was a bedlam of noise, and Abner set off down the railroad dump. Fraley tried to discourage him but remained by the fire.

Abner found the outer rank of doors all closed. He unfastened a hasp and jerked open a door and entered just as he heard the peculiar scream of a mule in the act of kicking. The youth crouched instantly and the iron-shod hoofs crashed into the wall just above his head.

"God's little hell!" thought the teamster, switching on his flashlight and leaping into the adjoining stall. But the next mule was as infuriated as its mate. In the ray of his light Abner glimpsed the swift balling up of enormous haunches. Next moment the hoofs crashed past him. He flattened against the stall bar shouting, "Tobe! Sam! Be quiet, boys! Whoa there, whoa!"

The sweep of his light showed him a long row of mules, all kicking or standing trembling and flocked with sweat. While farther up toward the end of the stable two mules were lying down.

Oddly enough these quiet mules shocked Abner's nerves more than did the lunging furies. He climbed along the stall partition to the nearest door, loosed the hasp and jumped outside. He ran to the end stalls and entered the rank ammoniacal darkness again.

His flashlight showed him the two mules on the dirt floor of their stalls. At his light, they lunged helplessly, getting their hind legs under them only to roll against the stall bars. The animals had been hamstrung. Pain from their tearing muscles covered them with lather; and blood and ordure stunk from the ground. A plank had been pried off the back of the stable to permit the entrance of the miscreant. Through this same hole, no doubt he had fled when the kicking of the mules had stopped his cruelty.

A tide of fury seized Abner, tightening his belly, lifting his chest and setting two hot coals behind his eyes. The mules were as near to him as human dependents. He strode past one trembling, prostrate animal, patting its wet hide with unsteady hands. The next moment he was out through the gap into the bushes behind the stable.

"God damn ye!" he yelled at the top of his voice. "Come here, you damn yellow houn'. I'll beat hell out of ye. I'll——"

Then he realized the insanity of shouting and cursing in

the blackness. He hushed and stood holding his breath, listening intently, but could hear nothing except the frantic mules and the drum-drum of the pulse in his ears.

Abner pushed forward in the undergrowth with every nerve stretched ready to lunge at the first moving thing, when he suddenly remembered Tim Fraley.

The duplicity of Fraley detaining him by the camp fire while an accomplice slipped into the stable and hamstrung his mules poured the last drop into Abner's vial of fury. He turned from his futile search in the bushes and crashed out of the growth, passed the stable, and saw the fire on the top of the levee. In its light Fraley still sat.

Abner went running up the slope with clenched fists. Fraley saw his threatening form, moved to get up crying, "What the hell!"

Abner rapped out the bitterest expletive of the hills, and lunged. Fraley had not time to get to his feet but kicked at Abner's flying form. The next moment the two men were grappling on the levee, rolling over and over, choking each other; pounding each other's faces; panting, sobbing, cursing. . . .

Blows on the head filled Abner's eyes with red flames of light. Abner beat Fraley's head and face with all his strength; even receiving the fellow's blows was a sort of satisfaction. Once in the rolling Abner struck at Fraley's head and hit a stone.

With his skinned hand he clutched at his enemy's face and succeeded in sticking his fingers in the striker's eye and mouth. He clamped down digging his fingernail in the tender eyeball. Fraley bit savagely on Abner's thumb.

The most excruciating pain of the fight filled Abner's thumb and flowed up his arm in a hot jet. The teamster beat the prostrate man's face with his left hand, but Fraley recognized his advantage and lay doggedly biting off the first joint of the thumb. Amid a lancinating agony, Abner gouged his middle finger deeper into Fraley's eye, and with his left hand seized and choked the striker's hairy throat.

They were floundering about under these torturing punishments when a voice near the embankment cried out:

"Turn him on top an' I'll shoot the God damned ——"

Instantly both fighters began trying to whirl the other on top. A sudden realization filled Abner that he was about to be killed. He made a terrific effort to turn Fraley, flinging himself to one side and lifting with his throttling hand and chewed thumb. He could hear other voices shouting. He made a last desperate lift. A man was over him. Came the crash of a pistol almost in his eyes. The blaze of fire seemed to fill the whole world, and the next moment, the fight, the night, the shouts were no more for Abner Teeftallow.

CHAPTER XI

WHEN Abner Teeftallow next became conscious of the flow of life he found that it was full day and he was lying on a bunk in a tent crowded with men. The high uplifted voice of Sim Pratt argued and ordered the labourers out of the tent, but to no avail. The crowd was held together, not only by a wounded man, but also by a miracle. A miracle, a providential wonder had saved Abner's life.

After that first pistol shot had inflicted a scalp wound and rolled Abner over unconscious, the assailant had fired another shot into the teamster's prostrate body, and this bullet had been stopped by the forty-five automatic in Abner's coat pocket. The shot had smashed one of the steel sides of the pistol and had ruined its mechanism. The hillmen inspected the wrecked firearm with a touch of awe. That was why Abner's tent was jammed with men and still others were outside awaiting their turn.

There was a general opinion among the labourers that this "meant something." They tried to interpret God's intention in saving Abner's life. It was clearly an anti-strike gesture on the part of Divinity, and linked up with Shallburger's avowed irreverence for the Bible. The incident in itself was enough to kill the strike.

One old fellow said he had heard of pocket Bibles saving men from pistol shots, but he had never before known the Lord to make use of an automatic, which was against the law to tote.

This introduction of the theme of pocket Bibles spread among the wonder lovers; first, as an odd thing that the pistol had not been a Bible; then among those outside the

357

tent, as an alternative for the automatic; later the pistol was successfully transformed into a pocket Bible, and was triumphantly used by the Reverend Blackman as an illustration showing the marvellous care of Providence over the lives of men who read one chapter of the Bible each day and three on Sunday, which he said Abner always did. In a fiery evangelical sermon, the Reverend Blackman shouted at the top of his voice that the bullet had penetrated to the exact verse, "Not a hair of his head shall be harmed," and these precious words had stopped the missile.

However, in the midst of this wonder and admiration, Sim Pratt, the drug clerk, insisted on getting Abner instantly out of the crowd and the unsanitary camp. As Pratt was known to be the beau of Beatrice Sandage, Abner's foster-sister, this gave the drug clerk a certain authority over the sick man; so eventually six men started with Abner on a litter for the old Coltrane manor, while the ruined automatic was left in camp for the men to look at and marvel over.

Abner went up the hill on a stretcher made of a blanket and two poles; not because he was so badly wounded, but because he was so dazed he could not walk. The bullet had administered quite a thump and now, as a result, Abner saw the heads of his litter bearers far above him; their arms reached down from enormously high shoulders, and he seemed to be borne through space on some sort of Aladdin's rug. The only mental connections Abner had with such a scene was a memory of pictures of angels bearing away the souls of the dead to Heaven. Abner stared intently at the far-away faces and came to the conclusion that these enormously tall creatures were angels, and since they were clearly lifting him upward, he decided he was on his way to Heaven. And this surprised the teamster as much as his dazed wits could encompass because he had always been morally certain that his final destination in eternity was hell.

When Abner reached the Coltrane manor, his senses were cleared sufficiently for him to recognize the weeping face of

Nessie, to feel her arms about him and his head drawn to her soft bosom. Then he knew he had gone to the abode of the blessed, for Nessie completed his Heaven. A marvellous sweet weakness flooded him. He lifted rather hazy arms about Nessie's neck, drew her face down to his own, and murmured her name.

She was sobbing:

"Oh, Abner, are you badly hurt? Do you feel better? Oh, I heard the shooting last night! I knew it was you! Oh, Abner! Abner!"

The men had placed the wounded man on an ancient bed—it may have been the very bed Abner was born in—and Nessie was sobbing and bending over him as if she could not take her hands away from caressing and loving him.

Mr. Sim Pratt said he would go and telephone to Lanesburg for a motor to come after Abner.

Nessie immediately thought it would not be safe for him to be moved in a motor.

"Sure it will," assured Pratt in a cheerful voice. "It's nothing but a scalp wound; as soon as it's dressed he'll be up and all right."

By this time Abner's Heaven had become badly diluted with the earth, and a few minutes later resolved itself into the living room of the old Coltrane place with half-a-dozen labourers in it, with its big fireplace, the carved arms, and some unfragrant diapers strung before a blazing log.

Nessie was still frightened and chafing Abner's hands when Mr. Belshue entered the room, and he in turn was bewildered by the novelty of so many guests. One of the men began explaining to him what had happened.

Abner became uneasily aware that Nessie was still half lying on the bed beside him, with one arm under his neck, and stroking his hands with the other. He saw that the jeweller's entrance made no difference at all in her anxiety and tenderness for him. The wounded man looked steadily at the jeweller's gray face, and finally, with much effort to control the movements of his tongue, he mumbled thickly,

"I— didn't— come— back— my— se'f— they— brought— me——"

The effort produced beads of sweat on his forehead.

Nessie cried, "Oh, Abner, dear, don't try to talk!"

And the men said, "He's gittin' all right now."

Mr. Belshue invited with a pinched-looking face, "You can let him stay here till he's all right. Have they caught the man who shot him?"

The men didn't know. They had caught Tim Fraley, but Tim's gun hadn't been fired.

Mr. Pratt reiterated his offer to get a motor for the sick man, when one of the workmen who had wandered out on the big piazza shouted, "Here they come now, Beatrice Belle an' her mammy in her car. I guess they telephoned to Lanesburg from the camp."

Abner was sufficiently recovered to make a movement to sit up on the edge of the bed. Nessie helped him and so did Mr. Pratt.

At the same time everybody began persuading at once, "You needn't go home now, Abner; stay here till you're all right." Even Mr. Belshue offered his home for Abner's convenience.

But as Abner's wits and strength rapidly returned he recalled the jeweller ordering him off the plantation, and that is an unforgivable insult in the hills. He could sit up quite well now, and he said with a kind of stolid politeness, "Much oblige' to ye, but I'll be gittin' on. Yes, much oblige', but I'll be gittin' on. I don't want to put you out any."

Nessie was so unstrung that she began weeping at this dull formal refusal of all her favours. The young mother felt if she could only keep Abner in her house and nurse him and dress his wound she would be ecstatically happy. But Abner would go, and presently he was up again; Pratt at one arm, a workman at the other, and Nessie behind him blinking back her tears. They began a fairly steady progression to the front door.

When the group reached the piazza, they saw Beatrice

Belle and Mrs. Sandage flying up the gravelled path of the unkept lawn. These women, when they saw Abner surrounded by helpers, shrieked out, "Oh, Abner, what's happened to you!"

Mr. Pratt stared at the Sandage women in turn and cried out, "What's happened to you all!"

Beatrice Belle, oddly enough, flew across the porch into Mr. Pratt's arms. The drug clerk hastily deserted Abner for this new charge.

"Oh, Sim! Sim!" wailed Beatrice Belle, sobbing on the clerk's neck.

Mr. Pratt enfolded her.

"Belle, darling, what is the matter? Has anything happened to you?"

Mrs. Haly Sandage was putting her arms out to Abner and crying in a shaken voice, "Oh, Abner, you mustn't be sick now! We need you! Come home at once and see Railroad Jones—Jim's in jail!" The poor wife fell to weeping so violently that she had to lift a hand and hold her ghastly false teeth in her mouth.

CHAPTER XII

IT TRANSPIRED, when the motor reached the Sandage bungalow in Lanesburg, that the coloured maid, Aline, was the only member of the household who knew precisely what to do under the untoward circumstance of Mr. Sandage being clapped in jail. On Mrs. Sandage's return she found a note from Aline in the crack of the front door saying that her mother was sick and she would not be able to come back any more. She would send her little brother for the money due her on the week's work. This note, correctly interpreted, meant that at last the Sandages had sunk to a social level to which Aline could not descend.

Mrs. Sandage read the perfectly clear writing with difficulty. It was always hard for her to understand what she read, owing to the length of time she had to devote to spelling out each word. At last she said in a lifeless tone, "Aline's quit us."

"Well, I'm glad of that," said Abner.

"Ever'thing'll go fin'ly," said Mrs. Sandage, staring at the bungalow as they entered it. "I know Jim'll lose his job after this."

"I don't think so," said Mr. Pratt helpfully. "Jim's awful popular."

"If we could git him out right away," wavered Mrs. Sandage. "A man's popularity goes down awful fast in jail. You must drive right over there, Abner, Jim wants to see you. He wants you to git Railroad Jones to git him out. You've got influence with Adelaide an' she's got it with her daddy." Here the good woman began sobbing again and holding in her spectral teeth. As she went weeping down the hall to her own room, she gasped, "I—I knowed I was

362

goin' to lose this purty house—c-come easy, g-g-go easy
. . ." and she disappeared, sobbing broken-heartedly.

Beatrice Belle drove Abner immediately to the jail, and its
heavy walls and narrow barred windows struck Abner with
dismay. It seemed impossible that his foster-father, the
trustee of the county, could have come to this sinister place.
Tears trickled slowly from Beatrice Belle's lashes to her
cheeks. Mr. Pratt, who sat on the rear seat, leaned forward
and put a hand on her shoulder.

"That's all right, Belle, it's unjust. Everybody knows
your father is honest—it's all owing to Perry Northcutt's
trying to cripple Jones. . . ."

Abner got out and went in.

The first floor of the jail was given over to Sheriff Bascom
and his family for housekeeping. Inside the door sounded
the noise of shouting and wailing children. Abner's repeated knock finally brought a tow-headed boy to open it.
Abner said he wanted to see Mr. Sandage. The youngster
shouted, "Mammy, here's a man wants to see somebody
. . ." and a thin hillwoman presently appeared wiping
her hands on her apron.

"Oh, you want to see Mr. Sandage," said the woman; "he's
upstairs. You can go on up." She pointed to a flight of
dirty stairs in the hallway. They were box stairs without
banisters. At the top Abner found a trap door which let
into the second story. This place was floored with iron
sheeting and was divided into compartments by eight steel
cages, four on a side. An aisle divided these dolorous cages,
and the shadows of their bars lay across the aisle in the light
from the narrow windows. The air smelled of unbathed
persons and unemptied slops.

In one of the forward cells a Negro droned a "blue."
In another cage two moonshiners were rehearsing obscene
catch questions.

In the middle cell on the right side Abner found Mr.
Sandage. The county trustee sat on his iron bunk in the
corner of his cell. When he saw Abner he got up and came

to the bars with both hands outstretched toward his foster-son.

"Thank God, Abner, it's you!" He reached through to grip the youth's hands. "I want you to go to Railroad Jones and tell him to git me out o' here quick. Unless that debt is fixed up right now, I'll shore lose my job, Abner. You tell him how urgent it is. And tell him how I'm fixed. Why, them damn niggers is runnin' me crazy. Have you got any licker with you?"

This was the first time Jim had ever mentioned whisky to Abner. It flattered the youth. He searched his pockets and found his pint bottle with a last swallow in it. Jim drank it, blinked his eyes, then noticed the bandages around Abner's head and around his chewed thumb. He asked what was the matter, and Abner told the story of his fight.

"I declare! The damn skunk! Railroad will shorely have to lissen to you after you nearly got killed helpin' him out. Git Adelaide to go to her daddy. Ever'thing depends on it, Abner. Why, me an' Haly will be right back where we was—tell Railroad to make any sort of sacrifice to git me out."

"I will, I will," nodded Abner, deeply moved.

"I wouldn't say anything against Railroad, but—er—Abner, seems like he's mighty keerless of his frien's when *they're* in trouble."

"I'll shore tell him," repeated Abner earnestly.

"You know it was Railroad who let yore daddy die right in this place of pneumony, Abner."

Abner knew that his father had died of pneumonia in jail. Now the thought of his sick father dying in this cold terrible upper story filled him with horror.

"But I ain't goin' to die here, Abner," nodded Mr. Sandage grimly. "I made up my min' to that. I shore ain't goin' to stay here tull I die. But of course Railroad'll git me out. My job, my good name, my fambly, ever'thing I got in the worl' depen's on his payin' back what I loaned him an' gittin me out honour free."

"I'll shore tell him," trembled Abner, trying to keep back his tears.

They gripped hands again and Abner went back down the trap door.

Beatrice Belle and Mr. Pratt had driven away, so the hill youth walked rather weakly around to the Jones residence. His nerves twitched and his chewed thumb throbbed. He entered the mansion through a wide piazza and knocked at a solemn oaken door. After waiting some minutes he saw a pearl button and pressed it. Presently he heard a woman's skirt rustle and Adelaide opened the door. The girl went pale at his bandaged head.

"Abner!" she cried, putting an arm around him and lifting a hand to his face, "I just heard about your terrible experience—come in, it's cold out here—you look as if you were shivering to death."

Abner kissed the uplifted lips as mechanically as a brother.

"Where's your daddy?"

"Down at the courthouse at the trial, I suppose."

"I must see him right away—you know Jim's in jail?"

Adelaide clenched her hands. "Oh, isn't it awful! Poor Beatrice! Poor Mrs. Sandage! It's all that Perry Northcutt's work!"

"Adelaide, your daddy must get up that money an' git Jim out. Why, it's awful up there in jail. It—it's just—— I kain't tell you, it's so bad!" Abner's face and tone carried his idea of horror more potently than his words.

"Poor Mr. Sandage—and he got in there for accommodating Papa—you know there was nothing wrong about that! Papa simply must get him out!"

"That's what I say—and he's so blue—he's afraid he'll lose his office and be pore again."

"Oh, well, Papa couldn't allow that after Jim's got into this trouble accommodating him."

This whole conversation was a rush of words, of condolements; in the midst of it, the two heard a side door open and there followed the peculiar padded footfalls of Railroad Jones. Both young persons turned at the same time.

"Papa," called Adelaide, "here's Abner to see you."

Came a pause, then the heavy footsteps padded on and the magnate's buzzing voice said, "Tell him to come in the liberry. I'm come after them little vouchers for the trile, Addy."

Adelaide started forward impulsively with Abner, then said, "No, maybe you'd better see him by yourself. I'll wait here," and she squeezed his hand sympathetically and patted his back before she loosed him.

Teeftallow hurried through two rooms into the library with its bookcases, cabinet of minerals, and electric spray. The fat man was stooping over a drawer of the library table stuffing an endless number of papers in a stout meal sack. He lifted his great face as the youth entered.

"Hello, Abner. I hear you got hurt. I shore am sorry. Did it fracture yore skull any?"

"No, I'm all right, Mr. Jones. I've come about Jim. He's over there in jail goin' through hell before he's dead. How much do you owe him?"

The ponderous man paused in his work and reflected with an expressionless face.

"Aroun' thirty thousan', Abner."

"Well, if you paid that off at once, wouldn't that git him out of his trouble?"

"Nachelly, Abner."

"Fuh God's sake, do it, then, Mr. Jones. If you don't he's goin' to lose his office an' his home, an pore Miss Haly is jest heartbroken. Have you ever been in that jail, why it smells like a backhouse and looks like an animal cage."

The fat man twisted up the end of his sack and set it on the thick carpet.

"Abner," he said in his stewing voice, "do you think I don't appreciate you gettin' shot in the head fer me an' my railroad?"

"Why—I don't know—I suppose you do."

"Well, I do, an' it's the same way with Jim. I might be able to git up that thirty thousan' now, if I'd give up my suit an' go to work with nothin' but that in view, but if I hang on an' beat this suit, like I mean to, it'll be worth a quarter of a million to me, an it'll increase my real estate another quarter of a million. Now, you're goin' to marry Addy. You can see how you're goin' to git paid back for all you done. Do you think I'd let Jim Sandage ruin his political career for me an' not put him on easy street? Now, take a business view of it. Which is the most sense, for Jim to stay in jail a few days longer an' all of us get a independent future, or for me to git him out, and all of us, me an' you, an' Addy, an' Jim, be as pore as dust monkeys agin? They ain't no sense to that!

"He's been sendin' for me to come to the jail an' talk to him. What's the use? I know what he wants and I also know that ain't the best for none of us. So why go down to that stinkin' jail an' talk? Now, Abner, if you hadn't struck me as a young man o' brains I never would have picked you up like I done. Jest help me git this sack o' papers over to the courthouse, then you can go back an' tell Jim jest hol' tight an' play shut-mouth, an' he'll come out with thirty thousan' dollars of his own money, 'stid o' the county's."

Under the influence of Mr. Jones's buzz, trouble, financial difficulties, and even life itself had a way of straightening themselves out, of becoming simple, clear, and easily managed. It was on such simple, sensible advice as this that Jim Sandage had ridden triumphantly into office, and eventually into the county jail. However, his emergence from the jail was just as clear and simple as his entrance, and all of Abner's objections to the *status quo* were cut away under his feet.

The youth made one last effort.

"But, Mr. Jones, the dishonour of the thing—and his office will be gone . . ."

"Abner, if Jim ever puts the money back in the courthouse vaults, the people will say he's the honestest man they ever see; an' if he fin'ly gits away with the money, the people will say he's one of the smartest men they ever see—an' they won't know which to admire the most."

"Well," admitted Abner, "they's something to that."

"There you air!" cried Railroad. "No matter what happens he'll be more thought of than he ever was before by the voters. You jest go explain that to him. An' tell him, too, the suit'll be over in a few days, an I'll pay off the county the first thing, an' he'll be out an' in office same as ever. So now, gimme a hand at this sack."

Abner went forward, swung the sack up on his shoulder, and started for a delivery wagon which he could see through the library window standing outside the Jones lawn. As he did so, he recalled that the fat man, with his clear, hard reasoning, had allowed his father, Linsey Teeftallow, to die in the county jail.

However, that personal aura about Railroad Jones, which made all the magnate did and said more arresting and dramatic than the commonplaces of ordinary mortals, drew Abner after the great man on to the delivery cart, and thence to the courthouse with the precious bag of papers. Abner reflected, as they jolted along, that he could tell Railroad's message to Jim later.

Railroad himself rode in the delivery van in deep thought, his body jostling about like a tub of jelly. Abner wondered what he was thinking about; certainly not Jim Sandage; his lawsuit probably. Abner suddenly felt sure the fat man would win the suit. It was impossible to sit near Railroad Jones and not feel that he would win.

As they approached the courthouse square Abner saw crowds of country folk moving about in the cold sunshine, attracted by the million-dollar railroad suit. As the delivery wagon passed the groups, Abner could hear, "There goes Railroad now!" "Well, he's met his match at last!" "He's been a good ol' dawg, but he's about run down . . ."

These gloomy predictions angered Abner, and he mentally

cursed these bad prophets, "Damn fools!" "Bunch o' jackasses!" but they were not sitting near Railroad Jones. . . .

The van drew up at the courthouse gate. Abner took the sack on his shoulder and started patiently working his way among the stream of men up the steps to the second story. The dark stairway, the jammed crowd, recalled to Abner how he had once climbed these same stairs filled with fear lest he had lost Nessie Sutton; and now he had lost her indeed, mother and baby. . . .

The Chancery Court of Lane County seldom has a large attendance, owing to the prevailing practice of conducting its suits with written depositions. However, in the matter of the Irontown Bank versus David M. Jones *et al.*, the courtroom was jammed from door to chancellor's dais.

When the attending constable at last observed Railroad Jones trying to press his bulk through the aisle, he was forced to shout at individuals in the passage to let the defendant into court. He threatened the men at the door to stop crowding or he would shut the doors in their faces.

The chancellor, a thin old man with a long face, a large nose, and a black skullcap, ordered the windows opened somewhat from the top.

Abner, with the bag, followed the course of the fat man and eventually came to a table where the defendant's lawyer was seated with some documentary evidence piled before him. Railroad Jones had only one lawyer, an attorney by the name of Norton, but across on the opposite side of the enclosed space, at the plaintiff's table, were stationed a veritable battery of the bar: Buckingham Sharp, Judge John A. Stone, Turley M. Johnstone, and a swarthy, rather picturesque man with curly black hair, who, somebody eventually whispered to Abner, was a Mr. Swikerd who came from Nashville.

Half of the plaintiff's desk was covered high with leather-backed law books. When Abner saw this array, his heart began to sink again; at his own desk were only himself with the meal bag, Norton with two books, and Railroad Jones empty-handed. An added discouragement was that Norton could never make much of a speech. He stuttered slightly. As a jury lawyer he was impossible, but a counsellor in chancery has little to say, and the chancellor will always wait patiently for that little no matter how retarded may be its utterance. However, the situation was not reassuring.

As Abner came up to the desk, the chancery judge looked down from his elevated seat and said to Norton, "Mr. Norton, does this young man's burden appertain to the cause you represent?"

"Your Honour," returned Norton, rising, "I—I th-think that is my client's b-b-burden of proof."

"It's to be hoped he can shift it to the plaintiff," said the chancellor with a serious smile.

The lawyers smiled, and the crowd followed their lead by tittering emptily at a jest which few comprehended and none would have considered humorous.

Railroad Jones whispered to Abner, "Set it down an' take a cheer," pointing at several unoccupied chairs at his table.

For several minutes Abner's bandaged head and hand drew more attention than the court preparations. His wounds were a sort of materialization of this suit; they were the result of the clash between bank and railroad. The youth sat with the meal sack leaning against his leg, looking about the crowded courthouse. The fact that so many persons were looking at him embarrassed him. He heard an old man saying in the flat voice of the deaf: "They say he flopped from his pap's side over to Railroad because he's gwinter marry his daughter."

Abner flushed. He saw his position might be interpreted thus and he wished he could explain to the audience how unavoidable was his course; but that was impossible.

The chancellor tapped on his desk, and as silence spread over the courtroom, he asked in a deliberate voice, "Is the case of the Irontown Bank versus David Jones ready for a hearing?"

Judge Stone, the leading attorney for the plaintiff, nodded assent.

"The plaintiff is ready, your Honour."

"W-we're ready, t-too," stammered Mr. Norton from the other side of the magnate, and a titter ran through the crowd.

Judge Stone arose at the plaintiff's desk. He moved about on his table several packages of papers bound together with rubber bands.

"I have here, your Honour," he outlined briefly, "itemized accounts of the daily wages paid out by the Irontown Bank on the construction of the Lane County railroad. This bundle contains mortgages given by David Jones to the Irontown Bank covering said railroad holdings and also certain realty belonging to Mr. Jones. This is a simple action of foreclosing a number of mortgages for debt. It was necessary to bring it in chancery because the expenses of the railroad are still current and it would involve a loss to stop all proceedings to await ordinary legal action. The entire indebtedness of the Lane County railroad to the Irontown Bank totals, to date, one hundred and twenty-five thousand seven hundred and eighty-six dollars and forty-two cents. We will deposit the papers and other inventories with the court."

Here Judge Stone made a faint gesture to Buckingham Sharp, who piled the bundles on his arm and transferred them to the judge's desk.

"Is there any denial of these mortgages and accounts?" inquired the chancellor in his deliberate tone.

Mr. Norton arose beside the magnate and tapped nervously on his desk. The whole house watched him intently, with a feeling that some sort of trap was about to be sprung. Norton bent his head over for a last consultation with his client.

"M-Mr. J-Jones, says, y-your Honour, that to the b-best of his r-r-recollection the total is a h-hundred and twenty-five thousand eight h-hundred and eighty-six dollars and s-seventeen cents. H-he says Mr. Northcutt must have left out the s-spur items p-purchased on the seventeenth of last July."

Even the chancellor came out of his mechanical manner at this. He leaned forward.

"Are you suggesting that your client remembers in detail all these accounts and can check off mentally where the bank is in error?"

"I—I don't know, your Honour." He leaned and consulted Railroad Jones, and Abner heard the magnate say impatiently, "Sure, sure, I want them to bring up their whole account. I want this settled here and now."

When Norton reported the result of his conference, the astonishment and admiration of the crowd grew so noisy the chancellor was forced to rap for order.

"Such a slight variation will not affect the substance of the bill, and the plaintiff will amend. So your client admits the bill as it stands?"

"He does," stammered Norton, "b-but he asks to be allowed to introduce a l-little off-s-s-set."

Judge Stone was on his feet at once.

"An off-set, your Honour; on what grounds is an off-set asked?"

"I-illegal interest," stammered Norton.

The little banker leaped to his feet. "That's an untruth, judge . . . " Buckingham Sharp pulled him down.

Judge Stone proceeded deliberately. "The interest charge on funding the railroad, your Honour, has been precisely six percentum per annum, the legal rate in Tennessee, as an inspection of the accounts will convince you."

W-we acknowledge that," stuttered Norton.

"Then I don't understand your plea of off-set," said the chancellor.

"I-it's like this," stammered Norton. "Th-the Irontown B-bank normally charges eight p-per cent. I-it has b-been charging this i-i-illegal rate for y-years, f-for decades, your Honour. M-my client had b-bought up some of the old c-claims against th-the bank, and h-he has them here c-claim-ing off-set, your Honour." Here Mr. Norton motioned to Abner, who heaved the meal sack up on the table.

For a full half minute the peculiar dusty silence of the courtroom was complete. The trap was sprung, but for that length of time nobody understood it. Then the lawyer from Nashville apprehended the sort of pitfall into which his client had stumbled. He jumped to his feet.

"Your Honour!" he cried in a clipped urban voice. "You will not allow any such fantastic claim of off-set against an honest debt owing to the Irontown Bank. Why, this is ingenious, but it's outrageous! It's a tax of two per cent. upon the entire volume of business transacted by the bank throughout its career. It's against public policy!"

Mr. Perry Northcutt understood next, and his face went white to his lips. He leaped up from his chair again.

"Your Honour! Your Honour! These are not Railroad Jones's debts! It's impossible for a bank to do its—its short-time business at six per cent.—the paper work . . ."

"Why, y-y-yes, they are his debts, Mr. Northcutt," stammered Norton genially, "h-he bought 'em."

A realization of Railroad Jones's greatest coup spread slowly and marvellingly over the courthouse, and with it came an outburst of cheers, whoops, stamping of feet, and uproarious laughter. The exquisite delight of seeing the unpopular Northcutt bowled over with all his lawyers by the champion from Lanesburg shook the audience.

The chancellor hammered for order.

"Clear the courtroom, Mr. Sheriff!" he cried with a sweeping gesture.

The officers turned out of the chancel into the aisles and started trying to evict the whole crowd. Order was restored almost as rapidly as it had been lost, save for irrepressible explosions from some of the more convulsed.

At last the judge ceased turning his angry eyes about the room and looked at Mr. Norton.

"How much is the off-set, Mr. Norton?"

"Two-two hundred and eighty-five thousand d-dollars,

your Honour, in r-round numbers. H-here are the s-sworn statements of the ac-accounts and the t-transfer of title to them. It is a v-vengeance, your Honour, you-you might say a d-divine v-vengeance on the b-b-bank's illegal b-business methods."

A burst of applause, quickly silenced by the officers, followed this.

The picturesque Nashville attorney began pleading against the off-set along lines of public policy. He said the admission of such an off-set would jeopardize every financial institution in the country; that eight per cent. was the recognized short-term banking rate, and to allow an off-set against a proper debt for all such claims a client could purchase would rock the finances of the nation.

Here Buckingham Stone drew down the Nashville attorney and whispered in his ear. Mr. Swikerd then continued, "Besides this point, your Honour, the greater part of these claims are out of date, and we plead the statute of limitations against them."

Norton interposed.

"N-no, your Honour, m-my client has a-arranged all th-that. H-he is going to p-pay his d-debt with the out-of-date claims, and c-c-collect the rest."

"Why, that's a damned outrage!" roared the Nashville attorney, quite beside himself.

"It r-redresses the wrongs of the p-people who have been v-victimized by t-that b-blood sucker there!" cried Norton, pointing at the banker.

"Redresses the people! The people!" sneered Swikerd in the height of irony. "This off-set will wipe out the entire capital stock of the Irontown Bank. It will hand it over *in toto* to that crooked trickster there!" He jabbed a finger at Railroad Jones. "Into the maw of that bloated toad of finance will fall the people's money! Redress the people! It will ruin hundreds of stockholders and thousands of depositors! Your Honour, it is impossible for you to allow such an iniquitous off-set!"

Mr. Norton was on his feet again, very cool but still stuttering.

"I admit, your Honour, one m-man must r-redress the wrongs of m-many. It-it seems impossible f-for people to act in concert w-without a l-leader. I—I notice the honourable counsel f-for the p-plaintiff d-does not b-bewail the f-f-fate of the original victims who l-lost their m-money to the b-bank, but only the p-people, who will have to r-refund those losses. N-naturally, your Honour, the p-people finally p-pay everything and, I—I must admit, enjoy very l-little. They p-pay the original wrong. T-they p-pay for its b-being redressed. And it will always b-be like that, your Honour, a-as long as l-laws are m-made p-purely to p-protect p-property and n-never to p-protect the p-people. B-but that is a m-matter completely outside of the p-power of this court either to alter or d-destroy. That f-fault l-lies in the warp and w-woof of our s-social fabric. Our nation is a-aristocratic, n-not democratic. Our s-system of l-law was d-designed to p-protect the rights of the f-financiers, the overlords, the no-nobility, the old b-barons. Y-your Honour can never ch-change that. So the defendant asks a v-verdict of one h-hundred and s-sixty thousand, one h-hundred and thirteen d-dollars and eighty-th-three cents, and a w-writ of execution for the s-same."

The audience, the people who were to pay both for the ancient wrong and its present redress, broke into such wild cheering that the constables became busy again.

Mr. Perry Northcutt seemed to be unaware of his surroundings. He was standing up crying, "O God, spare me this cup! Blessed Redeemer, come to my aid! O Lord, save the Irontown Bank!"

Mr. Norton was pulling at the meal sack.

"I would like to file this evidence with the court, your Honour."

The chancellor considered the bag.

"It is such a bulky file, may I ask you to send it to my home address by express?"

Mr. Norton acquiesced. "Certainly, your Honour."

On a sudden impulse Abner struggled through the crowd, out of the courthouse, and went flying to the county jail to tell Jim Sandage of Railroad Jones's glorious victory and of Jim's coming swift release.

CHAPTER XIII

ADELAIDE JONES brought to the Sandages first news of her father's amazing coup against the Irontown Bank. She flew over in her motor, embraced and kissed her neighbours.

"You see," she cried. "Dad was right—he's always right!"

Mrs. Sandage was so full of joy she could hardly speak. Tears stood in her eyes.

"A-Abner said Mr. Jones w-would fix ever'thing. . . ."

"Imagine," cried Beatrice shrilly, "the bank's his'n, the railroad's his'n, ever'thing's his'n."

"And he just *thought* of a way to do it all!" cried Adelaide with a wriggle of ecstasy, and she embraced her friends rapturously again.

"Jim shore won't lose his office now," blinked Mrs. Sandage.

"Oh, no-o," echoed Adelaide, squeezing her hand. "I drove by the—by the house where Mr. Sandage is staying. I thought I would bring him right over, but Mr. Bascom said there were some forms to go through with yet—it made me so mad!"

"Wouldn't he let him come!" cried Mrs. Sandage, amazed.

"No, he said everything wasn't settled yet," snapped Adelaide with a flirt of her head. "But I know it is. I left Abner to bring Jim right on over as soon as it's settled."

At this point the doorbell rang and the women rushed to welcome the released prisoner, but at the door stood Mr. Pratt, the drug clerk.

"Sim Pratt!" cried Beatrice, who possessed him.

"Have you heard about it?" cried the clerk.

"Oh, yes, isn't it wonderful!" repeated Beatrice.

"I come over to tell you what they're doin' in Irontown," grinned Pratt.

"What?"

"Holding a community prayer meeting asking for their bank back from Railroad Jones!"

The women stared at the drug clerk.

"Imagine! Prayin' for their bank back!" "Ain't that Arntown!"

And suddenly everyone broke into irrepressible laughter.

"Tim Fraley told me about it," went on Pratt. "Bascom had Tim arrested for shootin' Abner. They brought him in the drug store for me to doctor his eye. Abner pretty near put one eye out. Tim was laughing about the prayer meetin'."

"Now, look here," sobered Mrs. Sandage, "it does sound funny, but I'd rather not have them people down there prayin' agin Jim an' Mr. Jones."

"They can't reverse a court decision by prayin'," laughed Mr. Pratt.

"They can't wriggle out of the debts I bought up against the bank," asserted Adelaide. "Goodness, I was running over there in my auto, twice a day sometimes, seeing anybody who ever owed the bank anything. Daddy got the list from one of the clerks there in the bank."

"Did you know what he was going to do with it?" laughed Pratt.

"Of course I did."

"Anyway, I don't like 'em prayin' against Jim and Mr. Jones," repeated Mrs. Sandage, troubled by the superstition of the hills.

After Pratt and the two girls went out in the car again, Mrs. Sandage's fears were redoubled by the news of the Irontown prayer meeting. She went about her housekeeping in Aline's absence with wrought-up nerves. At every sound in the bungalow she started with sharp expectancy that Jim had returned. Now and then she interrupted her own work by breaking into sobs. She had never trusted Railroad Jones, she had told Jim. . . .

A step in the doorway caused Mrs. Sandage to wheel about, but it was only Abner Teeftallow returned from the jail. She wiped her eyes.

"What did they say, Abner?" she asked heavily.

"Well—Railroad says it ain't quite time to make his move yet."

"His move—what kind of a move?" She looked at Abner with red suspicious eyes. "Do you think he's goin' to make a move a-tall, Abner?"

"You know he won't let Jim stay in jail for as little as thirty thou——"

"I don't know nothin'!" cried the woman tremulously. "Sometimes I think he'd let Jim stay in there for thirty cents. Did you ever git him to talk to Jim?"

"No-o, I've ast him till I'm ashamed. He always says, 'What's the use? A jail ain't no place to talk reasonable in!'"

"But it's a place to stay in." Mrs. Sandage suddenly burst into tears again. Presently she controlled herself and adjusted the ghastly teeth in her mouth. "Abner," she began carefully, "you're engaged to Adelaide, ain't you?"

The big fellow coloured and nodded.

"If you wanted to you could make Railroad pay Jim out of jail jest as easy as anything."

"Why, how?" inquired the youth curiously.

"Threaten to sue on your claim against ever' one of his places. That would jest about break him up, I reckon. You air somebody, Abner. You can make Railroad Jones treat Jim right if you want to."

A kind of nervous trickle went through Abner at the plan. He drew a long breath. "I'll tell you, Miss Haly, I'll see Adelaide an' talk this over. I—I'd hate to make Adelaide mad."

"You see her, Ab, an' git her on our side. She can do more with her pappy than anybody else."

Abner agreed to this. Mrs. Sandage flung her arms about his neck, said he was a good boy, and sent him on his mission.

Filled with a kind of uncertain ardour, Abner set out for Adelaide's home when he heard a motor signal. He glanced behind him and saw the girl in her yellow roadster. She said she had been running around town looking for him, intent on a drive. A qualm went through Abner's heart as he climbed in beside his sweetheart. Suppose she should become angry at his interference in her father's affairs.

The girl glanced about at him in her driving.

"How's your head?" she asked gently.

Abner became aware of his bandages.

"It's getting easy." He touched her arm with his good hand. "Adelaide, I wonder if you'd he'p me git your pappy to do something for me?"

The girl looked around from her driving with soft eyes. "Oh, I will. What is it? Doesn't he want to?"

"I don't think he does—much."

"Of course, it's to get Jim out," she understood.

"Yes." Then Abner unfolded the whole of Mrs. Sandage's plan.

Adelaide pondered in silence with the cold wind beating their faces.

"I'll tell you this about Daddy, dear. You and I don't at all understand what he's doing. Neither does Jim nor anybody else. I wish we would all obey, like soldiers do their general. He reminds me of those old barons you read about in the Middle Ages. It seems to me Lanesburg is his city and the jail his donjon—lots of times he has niggers put in there if they try to run away from his places. That's exactly the way the old barons did the peasants. It's funny, isn't it—a nigger can work for Dad year after year, just as hard as he can hit it; then, if he finally gives up and wants to go away, he can't go—he owes Dad too much!"

Adelaide laughed, then became thoughtful. "Of course, lots of men do that. But Daddy does the white folks the same way: banks, wholesale houses, Yankees, anybody. I just admire and love him more than I can ever say. I have loved one or two other men, but I have never really admired anybody but him."

Abner drew a long breath, tinged with jealousy. "Well, let's go to him and see what we can do, Adelaide. You know we want to do right."

"Ye-es—right—Abner, your feeling of what is right gets a little hazy sometimes when you live in the same house with a great man. Is it right to break a horse and ride it somewhere?"

"What do you mean?"

"Oh—nothing," and she manœuvred her motor around in the narrow road and drove back to her father's office on the courthouse square.

When they climbed the high steps and entered the room they found the magnate with a great pile of empty cigar boxes packing his claims against the Irontown Bank.

"I'm doin' this so the mice won't cut 'em," he explained. "Mice don't like t-backer."

Abner offered his assistance, and Railroad Jones was about to accept it when Adelaide interrupted, "No, don't let's get side-tracked. Daddy, Abner has come over to see you about Mr. Sandage."

The magnate looked up in surprise. "Why, he's seen me about him ever' day, Addy, for more'n a week now."

"He wants you to go over and talk to Mr. Sandage."

"No use in that, Addy, I know what Jim'll say."

"It's this use, Mr. Jones," put in Abner. "I kain't make you two fellers understan' each other runnin' back an' forth. I wish you'd git together, talk it over, an' gimme a rest."

"Now that's right, Daddy," seconded Adelaide, taking her father by the arm.

The fat man seemed distressed. "I don't like this," he said with a shake of his head that swung his jowls, "explainin' my plans before I do 'em. Jim Sandage is a good man, but he ain't broad-gauge—no offence, Abner."

"None tuk, Mr. Jones."

"Besides, I know ever'thing he'll say, an' he won't see nothin' like I see it. I don't like it a-tall."

"At least he'll understand somethin'," pressed Abner

"M-somethin'—maybe. I shore don't like this, Addy."

But he closed his boxes, waddled out of his office with the young folks, and heaved himself into the waiting car.

At the prison another of the sheriff's numerous brood admitted the trio. While the child went to call its mother, the railroad builder looked curiously around the bare interior of his "donjon." When Mrs. Bascom appeared in an inner doorway, she cried out, "Law, Miss Addy, you ain't goin' up where the prisoners air, I hope."

The girl insisted. Mrs. Bascom brought in an oil lamp, although it was still quite light in the lower story.

Abner took the lamp and led the way up the plain box stairs, through the trap door, and into the dark, noisome upper story. His light displayed the iron cages on both sides of the aisle. Adelaide held tightly to his arm but said nothing. Behind them toiled her ponderous father, his flat yellow face expressionless in the light. His little burnt-out eyes glanced over the melancholy corridor. As the group moved forward a voice called out, "Abner Teeftaller, thank God, I see you at last. Tell that damn sheriff I didn't shoot ye. You know I was fightin' you a fair fight when somebody come up the dump and shot into us twicet."

"That Tim Fraley?" asked Abner, looking in the direction of the voice.

"Shore God is, Abner, an' yore frien', too. I didn't mean to pick that fight, you jumped on me, Ab, you know you did."

Adelaide said, "Your partner hamstrung two of Papa's mules, Mr. Fraley."

"I didn't have no partner, Miss Addy. Shallburger sent

me out to argue with a guard. I didn't know nobody
followed me."

"How did you leave the strike, Tim?" asked Abner of his
old enemy.

"Oh, it busted up when Perry lost his suit. Mr. Ditmas is
gittin' ever'thing straightened out agin'. She'll go through
with a bang now."

Adelaide pressed Abner's arm at this successful working
of her father's complex plans. The trio walked on through
the corridor to the trustee's cell. When they paused before
the cage, they could faintly discern the prisoner who was
standing beside his foul bunk.

"Jim," began Abner in a somewhat strained voice, "I
never could git no understandin' betwixt you an' Mr. Jones,
so I brung him to talk for hisse'f."

At this all minor noises from the other prisoners came
to silence. The little group, illuminated by the oil lamp,
stood beside the trustee's cell, the fat man peering through
the bars with a frown puckering rolls between his brows. He
cleared his throat.

"I b'lieve you wanted to see me, Jim?"

"Mr. Jones," said the shadow in the cage. "I want you
to pay that money an' let me out of here."

The railroad builder smoothed his jowl.

"How much is it, Jim?"

"How much! You know how much better'n I do!" said
the shadow bitterly.

"Yes, I wanted to call it to yore mind—not mine."

"Well—thirty thousan' then!"

"Thirty-two eight sixty-four," corrected the magnate.
"How much do you git a year fer bein' trustee, Jim?"

"Eight hunderd, but I don't see as that's got anything to
do with it."

"I didn't s'pose you would, Jim," said the magnate simply.
"Eight hunderd a year. It would take you a little over
thirty-eight years, Jim, to save thirty-two thousan' dollars
at that rate, with no fambly expense whatever; but of course

yore fambly eats up more than that. So if we pay this debt accordin' to yore plan, you'll come out at the end of your office holdin' exactly where you started in, with nothin' a-tall, but if you don't pay it, nachelly you'll come out with thirty-two thousan' dollars."

"Come out! I won't come out a-tall!" cried the prisoner. "I'll stay here in jail."

"Oh, no, you won't, you'll come clear at yore trile. You lent the money to me honest—why, this here very talk with all these prisoners an' Addy an' Ab listenin' proves that."

"But what do you want me to do—steal it?"

The fat man went closer to the bars and dropped his voice. "No, Jim," he buzzed earnestly, "but I don't want you to pay it, neither. I kain't bear to see you throw away such a opportunity. It don't come to one man in a thousan'."

The man in the cage came a little closer to the magnate, bringing the odour of his confinement.

"I don't know what you mean," he said.

"It's jest this," buzzed the fat man in a barely audible whisper. "You stay in here a few weeks longer. I'll git out an' buy up enough county bonds and warrants to pay off that thirty-two thousan'—the county will haff to take 'em—they kain't go back on their own paper—an' I can buy it at thirty-five or forty cents on the dollar now. When ever'body hears about you loanin' the county money to me, the bonds'll drap to fifteen or twenty cents on the dollar. In fack, I can set my own price—I'll be the only person who wants 'em."

The magnate explained his plan in a buzz that held a faint excitement. Came a long silence in which Adelaide gave Abner's arm a triumphant squeeze. Abner did not quite follow the explanation, but he gathered it was a scheme to keep the county funds legally. Presently, in the midst of this silence, the railroad builder stewed out almost pettishly, "Well, what's the matter, Jim, ain't you satisfied?"

"What I am wantin'," said the shadow, "is to git out o'

this jail now, Railroad, an' I want to step out jest as good a man as when I stepped in."

"Good as you stepped in!" echoed the magnate incredulously. "You'll be fifteen or twenty thousan' better off than when you stepped in!"

"That ain't what I mean," explained Jim sombrely. "When I loaned you that money, I didn't mean to beat the county out of a nickel. And I didn't mean for you to railroad me into jail either. I thought I was lendin' it to the firmest frien' I had in this worl'."

"You wuz, Jim, you wuz," nodded the magnate.

"An' I made you promise before God," went on the shadow in an aggressive voice, "that you'd pay that money back any time I ast for it."

"But, damn it!" ejaculated the fat man, "kain't you see you're in a position to make money!"

"That don't make a damn bit o' diff'runce to me. I tol' the fellers who voted fer me that I'd take ker o' their int'rusts like they was ny own. I come into this jail clean, Railroad Jones, an I'm goin' out clean if I git out a-tall. They ain't nobody goin' to say, 'Jim Sandage tricked the county out of its money.' So I want you to do what you promised you would any time I ast ye—pay back what I loaned ye."

The magnate drew out his handkerchief and wiped his face in the clammy air of the jail.

"Look here, Jim," he argued desperately. "This is the plan I'd figgered out. Gimme two weeks to git up them bonds. It'll only take five or six thousan'. I'll subtrack that from thirty-two thousan', give you credit for the balance, an' pay you ten per cent. int'rust on it all the rest of your life."

"An' me give up politics fer one grab?"

"It's legal."

"An' cause all my frien's to lose confidence in me?"

The magnate plucked Jim's sleeve through the bars. "That's the point. Folks don't lose confidence in you when you beat 'em out of the public money. They admire you fer it. They'd 'a' done it theirse'ves, only they didn't know how."

"No, 'I God!" cried the shadow in sudden wrath. "You give me that money right now. I've been juberous about it ever sence I put the first check in yore han's. An' as fur as you dividin' with me after this swindle, you never divided with nobody."

"Jim, in two weeks——"

The shadow's voice shook. "I didn't say two weeks, I said now. I know you got it, you jest stole a bank!"

The magnate moistened his lips. "I'll haff to study about this—you're actin' the fool, Jim."

During this colloquy Abner's nerves had been gradually screwed up. The dim figure in the noisome cage moved him with compassion.

"Look here, Mr. Jones," he began uncertainly, glancing at Adelaide, "Jim here is tryin' to pertect his name, and if he don't want to sell it, I don't think you ort to shove the trade on him."

"Neither do I, Daddy," said Adelaide quite unexpectedly.

The magnate made a brusque gesture, "Uh, you two!" he grunted.

"Now, looky here," proceeded Abner more warmly, "I got a claim against nearly all yore farms. I'm fer Jim in this deal. If you don't pay him out to-night, I'll tell Buck Sharp to sue to-morrer."

The fat man glanced at Abner as if worried by a midge; then a half-humorous smile moulded his fat face.

"Yore time of action petered out two months ago, Abner. The statute of limitations begun to run against you an' yore claims the day the county court declared you twenty-one years old—that's why I had 'em do it."

Abner stared at the fat man and a trembling slowly set up in him which became so violent that the jail seemed to quiver and he had to steady himself by holding to the bars of Jim's cell.

"You—you don't mean that all—all my gran'daddy's farms are—gone!" he asked in a dry, shaken whisper.

The magnate spread his hands in indifferent acquiescence.

"Father!" shrilled Adelaide, horrified. "Why didn't you tell him!"

"Tell him! Tell him!" wheezed the magnate disgustedly. "Ever' one of you—my daughter included—talks like a passel of fools. I wish I'd never come down to this fool place! I tol' Abner they wasn't no use me comin'. I knowed what you-all would say. I come aginst my better judgment, an' now I'm goin'!"

Adelaide suddenly flung her arms about her lover.

"You're not going to cheat Abner!" she shrieked. "I love him! I'm going to marry him! And if you try to cut me out of your will, I'll—I'll smash it!" She shook a firm little fist at her father. "You can smash a will—a smart lawyer can smash anybody's will!"

"Addy! Addy!" cried the fat man reproachfully, "how can you say that! Have I ever denied you a thing in the worl' you set yore heart on? They won't be but one name in my will, Addy, an' that'll be yores. But I do hope you'll recolleck that this boy's daddy, Linsey Teeftaller, run through with old man Coltrane's fortune, drove Lydy Coltrane crazy, and brought her to the pore farm to die, an' now it looks like you're fixin' to let Linsey Teeftaller's boy do the same thing with my money—an' my little gal. . . ."

CHAPTER XIV

ABNER returned from the jail with a feeling that he had fallen from some great height. He felt stunned; his legs shook from the blow. His thoughts fell on his mind in sharp fragments as if they, too, had been shattered. His fortune was gone. His claim on the half of Lane County had been dissipated—overslept; and here he was back where he had started, a labourer, a teamster, one of the stew.

A sudden rage seized Abner at his own folly and neglect. He recalled how Railroad Jones had shrugged and smiled at him. In the financier's machinations he had been a straw, a bubble, a nothing at all.

By this time night had fallen and the teamster moved along the dark street muttering imprecations, cursing Railroad Jones for a thief, a swindler, a rascal—unassailable propositions.

A solitary figure was approaching Abner on the dark street, and as it drew near paused to peer at the teamster then ejaculated in a gratified voice, "That you, Abner? Say, I heard Jim Sandage was givin' Railroad Jones hell over at the jail while ago—anything to it?"

"Railroad Jones is a damn swindle!" flung out Abner.

The gossip stared, then clapped a hand over his mouth and presently said, "Oh, you mean he done you!"

Apparently news of Abner's downfall had already circulated over the electric web of village gossip.

"Why, hell!" cried the fellow, beginning to laugh irrepressibly, "didn't you know you wa'n't no match for Railroad Jones! Why, by God, Abner, I'm supprised at ye! You buckin' up agin Railroad Jones!"

And here the fellow gave away completely to his humour and his rachetty laughter rolled down the night wind. "Howsomever," he added with a certain genuine comfort in his voice, "I un'erstan' you're to git the gal. Of course, that ain't holdin' the whip han' like you thought you done— but it's som'pin."

Abner hated this yawping fool who was laughing and philosophizing so easily over a lost fortune. He muttered that he didn't know, and walked on. The villager, with that uncomprehending indifference to mental suffering which marks his ilk, turned a few steps after Abner.

"But d'reckon Jim Sandage is agoin' to *do* anything?" he persevered. "You know Jim's one o' them hell cats when you git him started."

"I don't know what he'll do!" cried Abner in pain.

"Now, you know Railroad Jones ain't goin' to pay him out. He'll shore let Jim go to the pen."

Abner hurried away and the man called after him angrily, "Hell, you needn't be too stuck up to talk to me! You're no better'n I am; yore daddy died in jail." And with this parting shot for Abner's lack of delicacy and consideration the villager fell behind.

As the teamster entered the Sandage home it suddenly smote him that the life which this new bungalow represented was no longer for him; that is, unless he really did marry Adelaide, which, somehow, he did not feel he would. He found that he had based his thought of marrying Adelaide Jones upon the fact that he himself had money. Now a certain hill feeling interdicted a union between Adelaide rich, and him poor. "Ever'body would say I was marryin' her for her money," he brooded, without regard for the logic of events, "an' I'm a man that wears my own boots. . . ."

When Teeftallow opened the door of his home he found Mrs. Sandage sitting white-faced at the desk telephone in the hall. She had the receiver to her ear and was staring at the mouthpiece ejaculating, "What . . . He did . . . Let him go to the pen . . . Oh, I felt all the time

. . . No, I haven't had a easy minute sence I—— What? Oh! Oh! Oh!—Well, thank you for callin' me, Miss Prudie."

Here she seemed to realize that Abner had entered the hall-way, for she jumped up and ran and flung her arms about her foster-son.

"Oh, Abner! Abner! We've lost ever'thing! An' you, too! I knew we couldn't go on like this—that low-down snake-in-the-grass! I wush he was dead! To scheme aroun' an' sen' honest men to the pen!"

"Miss Haly," comforted Abner unsteadily, "I don't believe they'll do anything to Jim—he didn't mean no——"

"Oh, yes, they will, Prudie Rhodes was a-talkin' to Judge Stone's wife, an' Prudie said Jim had to use due diligence and caution—Jim's gone!" And here she fell to weeping out-right.

"But, Miss Haly, you can nearly always beat the law, even if you done somethin'."

"Y-yes, b-but if y-you b-been honest it-it's diff'runt."

Abner stroked the woman's bony shoulders with a sick expression on his own face. "How's B'atrice Belle takin' it?"

"She's in bed—her head's killin' her."

"Well, you better go there, too, Miss Haly. Go to bed an' try to sleep."

The woman clung to the youth a moment longer, then pulled herself away and started up the stairway. "I—I wush Railroad Jones hadn't never been borned! I always thought he was a fine man. . . . D'reckon Adelaide is goin' to marry you, Abner?"

"I don't know, Miss Haly," said Abner.

"She—she's a good-hearted girl . . ." and Mrs. Sandage climbed unsteadily up the stairs with her hard hand leaning on the polished rail.

"I—I don't min' goin' back to the farm myse'f, but—but to think of B-B-B'atrice Belle . . ."

She held her teeth in place, exhaled a long hopeless breath

aspirated to an "O-o-o-o," and entered one of the doors at the head of the stairs. When she was in, Abner turned out the hall light and went up to his own room.

He entered his room, switched on the light, stood for a moment, then sat down on the side of his bed with the hot-and-cold feeling of a person with an ague. The hot-air vent from the furnace had been turned on and presently he was too warm. The dried air pinched his throat and nostrils. Even at the risk of growing ill from the unhealthful night air, Abner opened a window, put his feverish face in the cold draught, and breathed deeply. He had no desire for sleep, but sat on the side of his bed staring into the darkness. Presently he turned off his light, and this changed the outer world to a dull gray and his own room to an unrelieved black except for the counterpane on which he sat; this glimmered faintly in the starlight falling through the window.

In his attempt to console Mrs. Sandage, Abner had to some extent consoled himself. At least, he thought over his downfall more dispassionately. Indeed, his whole surprising elevation and sudden fall repeated itself over and over in his mind. Once he tried to stop it by shutting his eyes and shaking his head, but the drama continued on and on.

In the midst of this annoying reiteration the gasoline engine which controlled the water and lights in the house burst into a quick throbbing. It shocked Abner. It seemed as if the little electric heart of the house had received a sharp fright. It beat at an amazing rate. Abner listened to it intently and presently decided that something was wrong with the engine. He was making up his mind to go down and find out the trouble when the engine stopped as abruptly as it began. It left the silence in the stricken house blanker than ever. It reminded Abner of his own sharp rise to fortune and his abrupt loss; a shoot up, a drop down. . . .

Abner never knew how long he sat by the window, but after some indeterminate time he was aroused to complete wakefulness by a succession of rifle shots. Then he found himself, still fully dressed, lying on his bed with his legs hanging off. He was chilled to the bone. The firing brought him up on his bed shivering and listening intently. Presently came more shots, one-two-three; Abner thrust his head out of the window and counted up to six. So it must have been a pistol. The firing was in the direction of the jail.

Abner listened intently for some other interpretative sound when a door opened in the bungalow and Beatrice's voice called, "Abner! Abner! Did you hear that shootin'?"

The teamster called back that he had heard it.

"Where did it come from, Abner? It's not Pappy, is it? Who is it shootin'?"

"No, 'tain't Jim, of course! He's in—he ain't got no gun." Abner continued staring in the direction of the jail when there came another spacing of six shots. A light appeared in an adjoining house, and then came the sound of a window being raised. Abner saw a head thrust out and a voice called, "What air they shootin' about?" and another voice farther on replied, "I guess it's them bootleggers."

Then other more distant voices with only a phrase or two distinguishable, "From the jail" . . . "Bascom shootin'" . . . "Signallin' for he'p" . . .

The firing started again, hammering the darkness with the hard clipped impacts of smokeless powder.

Abner turned on his own light and hurried stiffly for his door. As he bolted into the passageway he saw Mrs. Sandage and Beatrice Belle starting for the stairs in kimonos.

"Abner!" cried the wife, putting her shaking fingers to her teeth, "didn't somebody say it was Jim? It's from the jail —run down there, Abner!"

"I know it ain't him, Miss Haly—what would Jim be doin' . . ." Abner was striding down the stairs three at a time. He turned out into the cold night, and slammed the door just as Mrs. Sandage from the interior switched on the porch light so he could get to the gate.

Half-a-dozen persons were hurrying through the street with flashlights, and they gave Abner the owl-like impression of having been up all night. Most of them were going to jail, one or two were coming back. One of the returning men explained the firing in a husky one-o'clock voice:

"The prisoners have broke out: Tim Fraley, Jim Sandage, a nigger named Rufus Beans. Bascom come out on 'em as they was jumpin' from his second story, an' Fraley knocked him in the head with a stick."

Abner's heart began to pound; Jim jumping from a second-story window—Bascom knocked in the head with a stick. . . . He ran on and presently met another man who explained it was Bascom's boy signalling for help with his father's gun. That's why the shots came so slowly.

Abner went running down the rocky lane toward the jail with men and flashlights gathering in from every direction. Ahead of him he could see lights in the jail yard and in the jail itself.

When Abner reached the yard, he found the spectators grouped about an uncurtained window through which the crowd could see a Doctor Agnew dressing a scalp wound on Bascom's head. The sheriff sat impatiently in his chair while the surgeon dabbled antiseptic solution on the wound and sewed it up. The doctor appeared to be arguing with the restless jailer.

The men around Abner were saying, "Bascom don't want to wait! He wants to go with the posse. He's mad as a hare, he's got to wait tull mornin'—kain't ketch nobody in the dark."

Other men were flashing their lights up at the broken bars of the window. There were exclamations and oaths at the height from which the prisoners had leaped. "Hell of a jolt!" "Looks like it would uh stove up their laigs!" "Has anybody 'phoned to Florence fer the dawgs?"

Just then a hand touched Abner's shoulder and a voice said, "There are two men in the crowd who don't care if he does get away, eh, Mr. Teeftallow?"

Abner looked around. It was Sim Pratt addressing him.
"Jim didn't hit the sheriff," said Abner.

"No—I'm sorry anybody hit him. He was doin' his duty."

The thought of the bloodhounds after his foster-father re-
visioned for Abner the tragedy of Peck Bradley, and it
filled the youth with terror. The notion of Jim being chased
through hills and swamps in this bitter weather was horrible.

Pratt was at his side again saying angrily, "Sandage was
as innocent as you or I—tricked into it—Jones can talk a
man into believin' white's black. . . ."

At that moment a voice in the crowd called above the
babble, "Look yonder at that light!"

Everyone looked and other voices took up the cry.

"Ain't that the courthouse?"

"God'lmighty, is the courthouse afar?"

Across the night came the clangour of a distant bell. Far-
away voices shouted with urgency in their faintly heard
tones. Above the tops of the intervening trees, Abner could
now see the dull umber of an illuminated smoke column. It
was the only clearly visible thing in the encircling darkness.

By this time the excitement which a fire always creates in
a village seized the crowd. The whole posse rushed pell-
mell out of the jail yard and went streaming up the stony
lane toward the courthouse square. As they neared the
square the tips of the flames underneath the rolling smoke
seemed to be licking straight out of the tops of the water oaks
in the courtyard. The running men panted and cursed as
they stumbled through the boulders in the lane. The whole
thoroughfare winked with flashlights and lanterns. Voices
were crying, "It's the courthouse! Our courthouse is
gone!"

Another man puffed out, "By God, that's no bad trick.
I don't guess any posse'll chase him when they put the fire
out."

"Yes, an' the dawgs kain't trail him amongst so many
tracks!"

Just at this juncture Abner burst out of the lane into the

square. The fire was not at the courthouse at all, but in Railroad Jones's office. The building was burning evenly all around its sides, and the north wind drove the blaze and smoke at a long slant into the live oaks in the courthouse yard.

Under the pressure of the wind and the draught of the fire, the trees surged and strained as if smitten by a hurricane. Streams of sparks and brands whirled through the branches on to the courthouse roof, and Abner could see the illuminated forms of three or four men on the roof with buckets douching the fragments of fire.

No effort whatever was made to save the magnate's office because it was far beyond the strength of the village bucket brigade. However, the fire was just getting under way when the crowd streamed up.

An old man named Lipscomb was telling amid the snap and whip of the flames that he had first seen the fire. It was about forty minutes after he had heard the shooting at the jail. He had got out of bed and later saw a light in the courthouse yard. He ran out and saw the flames spreading around Mr. Jones's office—it burned as if it had been oiled. All village fires appeared oiled.

But "oiled" was the release word which set the whole crowd speculating.

"Oiled!"   "Then, of course it was him!"   "My Lord, burn a man out!"

"But what diff'runce will that make to a millionaire like Railroad Jones!" shouted a voice.

But from another part of the crowd came a pessimistic, "By God, he's ruint. He's teetotally ruint! Ever' damn one o' them claims is in there burnin' up!"

"Hell, that don't make no diff'runce—Railroad'll ricollect ever' one of 'em."

At that moment Abner saw the dazzling light of a big motor enter the crowded square. It came honking, honking to get through. When its rays fell on Abner, Adelaide's voice called the teamster's name excitedly.

Abner could see nothing behind the headlights, but he ran to the car.

"Where's Daddy?" cried the girl. "Is he here?"

Something in her voice plucked at Abner's nerves.

"I—I don't know. I haven't seen him." He began peering over the crowd from where he stood on the running board. He shouted at a man near by: "Milo! Oh, Milo," he called. "Have you seen Railroad Jones?"

Out of the confusion Milo answered back, "No, I ain't see him; ain't he at home?"

"No!" shrilled Adelaide suddenly. "He hasn't been at home to-night; he's bound to be here!"

"He hasn't!" Milo turned and began pushing through the crowd. "I'll help you look for him!"

Abner leaped off the machine and started a search in another direction. The motor moved forward again, honking constantly for a passage. As Abner threaded the throng, he could hear Adelaide's voice calling in increasing terror, "Where's Daddy? Have any of you-all seen Daddy?" Then other voices took up the search, "Railroad! Railroad Jones!" "Is Railroad Jones here?" "Hey, Railroad!" Presently the throng resounded with the hunt.

With a growing and formless fear, Abner hurried through the crowd, peering in every direction. In the dancing light, the faces of the hill folk looked more grotesque than ever. By this time everybody was searching for the magnate. Abner could still hear Adelaide honking her motor.

Suddenly the teamster set off at a trot to make the entire circuit of the burning office. As he trotted a sudden inarticulate shout arose from the north side of the building. A note of horror in it whirled Abner about and sent him flying in this new direction. He heard somebody scream in an extremity of repulsion, "Look! My God, look!" and another, "Jim Sandage must have . . . Keep Addy away! Good Lord, keep her away!" Then everything was lost in shrieks and screams. Abner saw men fling up their hands and turn away as if overpowered by the heat. Women fled backward into the crowd, or stood as if transfixed. Two or three of them fainted in the red light.

With chilled face and twitching nerves Abner pushed to the front of the crowd and stared. The northern window of the office had fallen in; a blast of air had swept the smoke out of the room and set out its interior in fiery brightness. In this shining scene, Abner saw the black, shapeless bulk of a man slumped over on a burning table.

CHAPTER XV

A PAINFUL uncertainty filled Abner Teeftallow as to whether or not he should attend the funeral services of his former employer and of his, perhaps, former friend. The young man was torn between a desire to be with Adelaide in this moment of great shock that had stricken her life, and his fealty to his foster-parents. Mixed pitifully with these emotions was a fear of what the villagers would say about him. In his shaken condition he dreaded the tyranny of the massed spite and unintelligence of the village; the rancour of the spiritual mob.

Mrs. Sandage no doubt divined her foster-son's dilemma, for presently she came to his door and looked in.

"Abner," she said in a colourless voice, "I believe I would go on over to the church if I was you. Adelaide——"

She broke off, pressing her lips together and disarranging her teeth, while her eyes filled with tears. Then she whispered, "You—haven't heard anything from—Florence?"

She meant news concerning the bloodhounds.

Abner shook his head silently and stood looking at her without any words to offer; she turned helplessly back to her own room.

Mrs. Sandage's advice decided the man. He finished putting on the serge suit which he kept for Sundays, and presently went out into the wintry sunshine of the street.

The keenest wound in his heart was for Adelaide. He knew her passion, her idolatry of her father, and now—this terrible end. . . . His chest quivered and the needle of repressed sobs stuck in his throat.

As for his own wrongs at the hands of Railroad Jones, if indeed he had been wronged, they dwindled to nothing at all in the face of the tragedy. The youth held no grievance against the magnate. And, it seemed to Abner, no longer did Miss Haly. The wreck which the financier had made of the Sandages and of Abner's fortunes had been so terribly atoned that nothing was left in Abner's heart except pity and tears. And these were mostly for Adelaide. The tears he stoically repressed, walking along with a strained face and compressed lips, because he was a hillman.

From every direction the villagers were gathering at the Jones home. Some came in motors, some drove horses and buggies ready to ride in the procession. A great many of the poorer folk came to walk in the line.

A feeling of leaderlessness, of being abandoned to their own futilities, filled the whole village. As Abner approached the manor where the dead lay in state, he instinctively framed the thought of the stricken town, "What can we do now?"

A hand took gentle hold of Abner's arm, as men sympathize with each other in the presence of death. The hillman looked around and saw Mr. Ditmas.

"It's a great pity, it's a great tragedy," said the engineer in a hushed voice, and after a few moments he added, "It was inevitable, I suppose."

Abner could not say anything. He bit the corner of his trembling lips and walked on under Mr. Ditmas's hand.

"The work on the railroad has stopped, of course," continued the engineer, "thoroughly disorganized. I doubt if any one goes on with it."

"I—I reckon not," assented Abner unsteadily, thinking of Adelaide.

After some moments, the engineer said, "We had a very bad thing happen down at camp, too, last night."

"What was that?"

"The train hit old man Belshue; the last train in; probably the last train that will ever run."

"Did it kill him?" asked Abner, looking at the Northerner.

"Oh, yes—the way it happened—I doubt if it was ac——"
he broke off his sentence, and Abner did not press the conclusion. Mr. Belshue's death, too, dwindled beside the great
loss of Railroad Jones.

At the house Abner finally did not dare go in and present
himself to Adelaide. He was too nearly in the opposite
camp to do that. He was in the opposite camp. He stood
outside the Jones gate with a great crowd which had filled
the yard and overflowed into the street. He wished from
his soul he could take Adelaide in his arms and tell her how
he grieved for her, but—that was impossible.

He never saw Adelaide until the funeral procession came
out of the manor, through the greak oaken doors. Adelaide
and her mother came immediately behind the huge black-
upholstered coffin. The pallbearers staggered under their
burden. The mother and daughter were supported by other
women of the village.

The undertaker, a tall man of professional solemnity,
walked ahead, making a passage through the crowd to the
black funeral car outside the gate.

Presently more men stepped up to help lift the coffin
into the hearse. Adelaide and her mother got into a car
behind the hearse. The other cars and buggies began
arranging themselves down the street, the drivers directing
one another in low voices and with unaccustomed patience
and charity.

Abner watched Adelaide's car move away, up the rocky
lane toward the cemetery; the head of a long, slow procession
through the cold sunshine.

From across the valley in which the village lay came
the first solitary clang of a tolling bell. A long pause, and
another church bell from another section of the hamlet
struck its note. All of the poor churches in the village tolled
for the passing of the magnate. Somehow, under this
melancholy tolling, Abner's heart broke; the pity, the helplessness, the hopelessness of it all! His sobs squeezed up
past his tight aching throat. He tried desperately to control

himself, but at last walked in the end of the long line, sobbing at intervals, and once he gasped in a whisper to his companion,

"Y-you m-must excuse me, M-Mr. Ditmas. . . ."

The Reverend Blackman conducted the funeral services of the financier. In the silence of the crowd, which was touched here and there by a muffled sob, the evangelist said:

"My brothers and sisters, we stand to-day by this open grave to put away, in the eternal peace of God, a man whose life-long thought has been for the betterment of his country and his countrymen. The hairs of my head could not number the enterprises he has brought into our midst, or the charitable acts he has performed. No poor man ever appealed to him in vain for aid. No beggar was too low for his charity; no cause too remote for his sympathy.

"God, in his wisdom, my brothers, has seen fit to remove David Jones from his earthly labours. A noble, unselfish life here on earth is ended. To this sad dust we must say our last farewells; but, thank God, we Christians know that in Heaven our friend and leader faces the golden sunrise of an eternal day. Dust to dust; ashes to ashes; and the soul back to the God who gave it."

Abner heard the scrape of spades and the soft spreading of the earth over the coffin. Renewed choking sobs burst forth from the family and mourners at the edge of the grave.

At some distance away, in another corner of the cemetery among the melancholy cedars, two Negroes were digging another grave. This next burial was timed to take place an hour after the financier was interred. During the ceremonies for David Jones, the two black men stood in the long rectangular hole they were digging with their poor hats off and pick and shovel at rest.

The grave they dug was not oriented east and west as were the other graves in the cemetery. It was turned at an angle to denote that it was the final resting place of a self-slayer. After the great crowd had flowed slowly back down the rocky lane, a few onlookers, out of a sort of morbid curiosity, remained and drew near this second grave. After a while two horses pulled an old hearse to this place and behind it, in a buggy, a labourer from the railroad camp brought a girl with a baby in her lap. Three other labourers came in a wagon to help with the work of the burial.

There was no ceremony; there was no priest. The girl with her baby got out of the buggy and stood staring, dry-eyed, as the men lowered and covered the box.

Abner went up to the woman with a strange shaken feeling; whether of grief or not he hardly knew.

"Nessie," he said in a low tone.

She looked around at him with solemn, impassive face.

"Yes, Abner."

"I—I heard of yore trouble, Nessie."

"Yes," nodded the girl.

The baby in her arms began to whimper and she soothed it by bending her head down to it.

"Are you going to keep on living at the old Coltrane place, Nessie?" asked Abner after a pause.

"There is nowhere else for me to go."

The teamster stood torn by some vague irresolution which he felt but could not understand. Nessie turned a little away from him and gave her bosom to the whimpering baby.

A profound and entirely unforeseen emotion filled Abner— a feeling of unity with this mother deeper than any he had ever felt even in his most tender moments with her. Without forethought he stammered out, "I—I'll come over in a day or two an' see if I can help you in any way, Nessie."

She made no answer, but stood perfectly still with the baby at her breast, as if she sensed the silent commotion of his heart. The labourers finished filling and mounding the grave.

For some time after the death of Railroad Jones, Abner remained in Lanesburg with the Sandages, waiting to do what he could when some legal action was taken against

Jim. But no indictment was ever brought. The original charge of conspiracy to embezzle the county funds remained on the sheriff's blotter, but the revenge of the hillman on Railroad Jones bespoke his innocence on that count; so by a quirk so characteristic of the hills, public opinion exonerated Sandage of theft because he had committed murder, and excused him of murder because the villagers felt a certain wild justice in his vengeance. Eventually the tragedy would dwindle in the memory of the village until it merely marked a date in county history—the winter Jim Sandage killed Railroad Jones—as many another homicide had done.

During his stay at the Sandages', Abner Teeftallow lived in a state of painful indecision in regard to Nessie Belshue and his little natural daughter. He had told Nessie at the funeral that he would come over and see her in a day or two, but he never had. The condemnation of the village lay over such a course, and Abner was growing chary of opposing it. He began considering his good name; his reputation. . . . He was growing older rapidly these days; being crushed into the village mould; hardening into a villager no matter what generous impulses he may once have had.

On the other hand, after the murder of Railroad Jones, Abner knew that Adelaide was not for him. He had lost both women at a stroke, and an endless emptiness filled his days. He could not contemplate any other girl, so the only real objective in the life of an ordinary hillman, marriage and a family, had been taken from him. Any other career, some constructive work to engage his life with its cold sufficiency, was so remote from him as never to enter his comprehension. Even the simple massing together of property was too abstract an undertaking for the poorhouse boy. Besides, he had had money, and it had brought him boredom. He thought he would go West—to Texas.

One day he heard that Mrs. Jones and Adelaide were going to move away from Lanesburg. The news gave him a kind of shock. It seemed impossible that Lanesburg would no longer contain the Jones family; Railroad had dominated

the village for such a long time, and now for there to be no
Joneses at all . . . and then the thought of never
seeing Adelaide again. It screwed Abner's courage to the
point of sending the girl a note asking to call. She answered
kindly enough, and when he went to the Jones manor he
found all the furniture packed for shipment, the carpets
baled, even the electric fixtures in process of being removed.

Adelaide was in black. She and her mother were going
away, she said. She would find her mother a home, then
she herself meant to go to India. When Abner asked an
amazed question, she explained with that complete frankness
and simplicity which had attracted him from the very first
time he saw her. She said while she was in the seminary at
Nashville she had fallen in love with a man who was going
to India, a theological student. Her position at that time,
her feeling of abhorrence for her lover's work as a mission-
ary, led to their separation, but he had made her promise if
God should ever make her feel the truth she would come
to him.

"And, Abner," she concluded, "if this isn't the work of
God, if—if this terrible sorrow isn't—isn't the work of
God——" She broke off with tears in her eyes, compress-
ing her lips to steady them.

"Do—do you still love him?" asked Abner, aghast.

"I—don't know . . . I did love him . . . Life
twists you about so . . . Anyway, I couldn't endure
just a village existence now, Abner, with you . . . or
Buckingham Sharp . . . or any one at all. I must
have something great somewhere." And her shadowed
eyes took on a momentary burning that reminded Abner of
Railroad Jones.

This last resignation of her was the last and the sharpest
pang Adelaide ever gave the hillman. When he lost her,
even Abner realized that he was losing a high brave soul;
self-centred, no doubt, journeying toward strange and perhaps bitter goals, but courageous and somehow generous.

Before he went away Adelaide suggested that he marry

Nessie Belshue. Abner had no such crystal outlook as the girl. He coloured slightly and mumbled forth the village opinion about "illicit love."

Adelaide stared at him in amazement.

"Illicit love!" she cried. "Why, Abner, what earthly difference does that make? Love is love. Licit may be more convenient than illicit, but the divine thing is love. Why, look at my dear, dear father. What a man, what a glorious man! And he was, as people say, an illegitimate!" And Adelaide's eyes shone like altar lamps lighted to the memory of her great lost idol.

When he left her, filled with Adelaide's warmth and courage, Abner set out walking boldly toward the old Coltrane place. As he hurried toward Nessie his heart beat faster and faster. He remembered with a kind of melting pang the curl of a little rose-leaf baby's palm around his thumb. He strode on with a great rapture dawning in his heart as he set his face against the wintry rock-bound hills.

THE END